Wait Till Summer

Wait Till Summer

Grace Thompson

CANELO

First published in United Kingdom in 2000 by Severn House Publishers Ltd.

This edition published in the United Kingdom in 2018 by

Canelo Digital Publishing Limited
57 Shepherds Lane
Beaconsfield, Bucks HP9 2DU
United Kingdom

A CIP catalogue record for this book is available from the British Library.

Print ISBN 978 1 78863 128 0
Ebook ISBN 978 1 910859 99 5

Look for more great books at www.canelo.co

One

Eirlys Price stood in the crowded school hall looking at the anxious-faced children and wondering how they could possibly find homes for them before nightfall. This first arrival of evacuees from London had been expected, but even so, the bedraggled and clearly unhappy group had been a shock. So many and most of them so young; how could tearing them away from their families be the best solution?

Eirlys was twenty-two and she worked as a clerk in the council offices. Today she had been given the task of helping Mrs Francis to find homes for the evacuees billeted on the town. She didn't mind the duty but would have preferred to have done it with an assistant of her own rather than the tedious Mrs Benjamin Francis.

She tried to stay uninvolved as she had been told, but the plight of the children got to her and she felt her heart squeeze with pity for the youngsters taken from everything and everyone they knew and brought to a strange town with only a luggage label pinned to them to declare their identity.

The school in St David's Well had been closed for the day to allow for the dispersal of the children to be arranged but the pupils hadn't stayed home. They had turned up to watch curiously as the newcomers were walked in a long crocodile from the station along the streets where other, older people stood on doorsteps to gawp at the children, offer sympathy and pat a few heads as they passed.

The forty-five evacuees were given a snack meal which had been organised by the WVS formed sixteen months before, in May 1938. Now, in September 1939, with war declared and the country in a state of turmoil, the new Women's Voluntary Service, local people who could arrange help and comfort wherever needed, was coming into its own.

Eirlys could see that there weren't sufficient chairs, with many taken by the adults who had come to collect them or simply to watch, so she encouraged the children, who were worn out with the travelling and the anxiety, to sit on the floor. Several went instantly to sleep, hugging their gas masks and their small bags of personal possessions in baby hands. She moved some into more comfortable positions, and stepped among them reassuring them, smiling, admiring a small toy here, a smart hat there, hoping that Mrs Francis wouldn't take too long before sending them on the final stage of their journey.

One little girl began to wail, "I 'ates it 'ere and I wanna go 'ome."

"Wait till summer," Eirlys soothed. "You'll love living beside the sea when summer comes round again."

She began to describe the various activities the child might enjoy but had no response. Tears glistened in the child's eyes and she repeated, "I 'ates it 'ere," to every attempt at comfort.

The murmur of conversations and the clatter of plates as the dishes were cleared and washed in the school kitchen was a constant hum that had a drowsing effect and didn't disturb those who were sleeping. The women who had been told to provide homes for the children for the duration of the emergency stood up and approached the bedraggled group.

As the women approached, all searching for the most respectable looking and hoping to avoid the poorest, some of the younger ones began to cry. Eirlys picked up the unhappy little girl she had spoken to earlier, who smelled unpleasantly of urine and unwashed hair, and cuddled her.

She saw three boys scuttle away from the table to stand in a corner, and guessed they were brothers and didn't want to be parted. She stepped closer to read their names. Stanley Love aged ten, Harold Love aged eight and a glum-faced Percival Love, just six. Sympathy for Stanley, who had clearly taken responsibility for his brothers, made her stand protectively near them as the process of rehoming began.

Mrs Francis, who was clearly in charge, stood on a chair and in a loud voice addressed the room. "Welcome to St David's Well, children," she began in an accent that made Stanley and his brothers stifle a laugh.

"Blimey, brovers, she talks like the wireless!" Stanley spluttered.

Mrs Francis didn't speak for long; she simply explained that the women would walk around and choose the child they wanted to take home with them. "And don't forget to say thank you," she reminded the children firmly. "Here in St David's Well we consider manners very important."

Slowly the children dispersed as the women of the town chose and collected their visitors. They gave their name, and the name of the child they had selected, to Mrs Francis and her assistants and walked off, hand in hand, to introduce the newcomer to his or her new family. Some smiled, some began to look uneasy as the numbers dwindled and the selection was reduced to the untidiest and in some cases the dirtiest children. Stanley and his brothers stood unnoticed in the corner, half hidden by a group of curious onlookers.

Eirlys moved around the sad group and reassured one or two who were afraid of being left to fend for themselves if they weren't chosen, embarrassed at some of the comments uttered by the women who were loudly discussing the merits and suitability of each child.

"See, brovers," she heard Stanley whisper, "no one 'ere wants us, so we might as well go back 'ome." They would need an extra vigilant eye, Eirlys thought grimly.

The door of the school hall opened and Eirlys saw her father enter. She waved and he came to stand near her.

"How's it going?" he asked. "Have you chosen our girl yet?"

"No, Dadda. I thought we'd wait till the end and take the one no one wants."

"I'm amazed that we persuaded your mam to take on an evacuee, aren't you?"

"It took a long time and I don't think she would have agreed at all, if I hadn't told her that in my job at the council offices I had to show willing," Eirlys confessed.

"Very proud of you, Mam is for sure," Morgan smiled. "You working in an office when all your friends could only manage shops. Always boasting she is, about how clever you are."

"What are you doing here?" Eirlys asked him. "Aren't you working at ten tonight? You should be asleep."

"I was curious to see the child we're giving a home to. Your mam is busy making piles of food, convinced this lot won't have eaten all day, so I came down for a bit of a walk, like."

The number of children dwindled. Voices became more disapproving as the children were loudly discussed. Seeing the three brothers standing apparently unnoticed, Eirlys wondered vaguely how her mother, Annie, would react if she and her father arrived home with three boys instead of the girl she had agreed to take.

She glanced at her father, nudged him and gestured towards the brothers who were trying not to move in the hope of being forgotten. He stared at the boys with an interested look in his eyes. No! They daren't!

They looked up as Mrs Francis closed her book with a slap and seemed prepared to leave. They heard her say peremptorily, "These last two girls will have to go to the vicarage. The dear vicar and his housekeeper will have to manage until other arrangements can be made. I simply can't wait any longer."

The two frightened little girls were led off. "What's a Vicarage?" one of them asked the other. Then, as she picked up her handbag and moved away from the table she had been occupying, Mrs Francis stopped, suddenly noticing the huddle of children in a corner.

"You over there, come here where I can see you."

"What, us, missis?" Stanley Love didn't move.

"Yes, you," she said impatiently. "Why have you been hiding in the corner?"

"Hidin', missis? We ain't hiding. You can see us plain as plain."

"Just when I thought we were finished," Mrs Francis muttered to her assistants. "Now, who have we left?" There were still a few women edging out of the hall, thankful they hadn't been needed and anxious to get home before someone changed their minds and brought a child back.

"Mrs Casey," she called in a shrill voice. "What about one of these boys for you¿'

"I can't, Mrs Francis. Two bedrooms I got and me with two daughters an' all; it isn't possible."

Two others were asked and had reasons to refuse one of the brothers.

"Just as well," Stanley shouted. "We ain't bein' separated. Me mum said we got to stay together."

"That won't be possible, young man. You'll go where there's a place for you. Now." She turned to a small, thin woman standing patiently near the door. "Mrs Evans, my dear?"

"I couldn't have three." She shook her head determinedly.

"No one is asking you to take three; just one, all right?"

"No it ain't all right!" Stanley's head-shaking was equally determined. "The three musketeers we are, all for one an' one for all. We read that at school," he said proudly.

The hall was practically deserted. Mrs Francis looked impatiently at her watch and sighed. "I have a meeting of the Air Raid Precaution group in an hour."

"Air raids? What air raids?" Stanley demanded. "I thought you wasn't goin' to 'ave any?"

"Tiresome boy," Mrs Francis said loudly. She took a deep breath in preparation for a lecture on how fortunate they were.

"Just stay with me," Stanley whispered to his brothers, "and when we get the chance, we'll 'oppit and clear off back to London. Our ma wouldn't want us standing 'ere like two pennorth of Gawd 'elp us, waiting for someone to like us, now would she?"

Eirlys looked at her father, head tilted in question. They were very close and often read the other's mind. She knew now that he was wavering, discarding common sense in favour of helping these unfortunate children. "Dadda? Could we persuade Mam, d'you think?"

"No, love, we couldn't!" He looked shocked but at the same time his blue eyes — so like her own — shone with excitement. He looked again at the boys standing so defiant and brave. "God 'elp, Eirlys. Persuading your mam to take one girl was a miracle. We'd never talk her into taking on three boys."

"Dad, we have to do something. They'll have to sleep in the school if we don't take them, and imagine how awful that would be. Frightened, away from their mother and everything familiar, unwanted by anyone, abandoned—"

"Go on then, and pity help us when your mother is told. Go on, tell that bossy Francis woman they're coming home with us. It's up to you to talk your mam round, mind."

Stanley continued to whisper to Percival and Harold, ignoring what was being said, when he became aware of someone standing beside them.

"Now what?" Harold asked rudely.

Eirlys smiled and said, "It seems you are all coming home with me."

–

Annie Price was predictably furious when the five of them walked in.

"Who are these boys?" she demanded, placing her hands on her ample hips and glaring at Morgan. "I hope you don't expect me to look after three boys. A girl was what I agreed."

"Don't worry, missis, we'll go back 'ome in the morning," Stanley said jauntily. "We don't want to stay 'ere anyway."

Annie looked at the tired children and her heart softened, as Morgan and Eirlys had thought it would.

"They can stay until we find a place for them, can't they Mam?"

"Our Eirlys was responsible for organising all this, mind. She can't walk away from children, can she? It's her job," Morgan added. "And I'll do what I can to help."

As Annie served a rich stew with mashed potatoes to each of the boys, she said, "How can we manage? You work shifts at the factory, I work every morning in the baker's shop and Eirlys works from nine to five plus all the hours of overtime this damned war is causing."

"We'll manage between us, Mam," Eirlys said. "I don't think Stanley will mind doing his share, will you?"

Stanley didn't reply; he was too busy filling his mouth with the delicious stew. Eirlys was relieved to see her parents share a smile.

As her father left for work that evening, the boys were finishing their meal. Stanley and Harold had consumed second helpings but little Percival ate very little. He sat with his head bowed, chewing with little pleasure on a small amount of food, looking unhappy. When Eirlys tried to coax him, he said solemnly and in a low voice, "These 'taters is boverin' me."

"Percival can't eat no lumps," Stanley explained, scraping the offending potatoes from Percival's plate on to his own.

"I only like chips," the dejected little boy explained. "Chips from the chip shop."

It was late before the children had been bathed and fed and settled for the night and Eirlys knew she would not be able to keep the date she had with Johnny Castle. She had promised to take some magazines and books for his mother, who was unwell, but she knew Johnny would understand once she explained about the plight of the evacuees no one else had wanted. Johnny was kind and never anything but good-natured. He would sympathise with the boys as soon as she explained.

Annie was still angry and Eirlys tried to take the blame from her father. "It wasn't Dadda's idea, Mam, it was mine," she insisted. "How could I walk away and leave them to be pushed into a home where they weren't wanted and separated from each other? If you'd seen those children you'd have taken more than the one you'd agreed, I know you would."

"It isn't their fault, I know that. But your father should have thought it through."

"Mam, it was me, not Dadda."

"I don't suppose he needed much persuading. You two always think alike. You look alike and you think in just the same way, soft you are the pair of you, and I have to deal with the result of it. Remember the rabbits you brought home when someone had moved and left them unattended? And the stray cat you insisted on feeding?" She sounded angry, she usually did, but there was a smile around her dark eyes as she added, "What am I going to be landed with next then, eh?"

"No more waifs and strays, Mam, I promise."

Annie didn't seem to hear. She went on, "Always wanted a big family he did, your father. Never got over his disappointment at not having brothers or sisters for you."

It was a sensitive subject for both of them. Unfading regret for Annie, and unreasonable guilt for Eirlys, who knew that it had been during her birth that her mother had been damaged with the result that she could have no more children.

Eirlys looked at the pile of clothes she had taken from the three boys and wondered where she would find more. The clothes they had brought were not suitable for school unless the Love brothers were able to cope with the teasing they would surely get from the locals. They were crumpled and very worn. There was a small weekly allowance intended to help feed them, but it was not enough to completely clothe them.

When her father Morgan came in from the factory the following morning she was awake and still trying to decide what to do about clothing.

"You'd better start on that washing, hadn't you?" he said as he reached for the kettle to make a pot of tea. "First thing I'll do is fetch the washing bath in and get the boiler lit."

"Yes; I have to be at work at nine so it'll be an early start. Like now this minute," she said.

Together they sorted through the worn clothes, picking out the least worst for the three boys to wear the following day. Today they would have to wear the clothes in which they had travelled. It wasn't ideal but it was the best she could do. None of the clothes were particularly clean and, looking at the threadbare material and frayed ends, at the holes where buttons had once been, Eirlys wondered if any item was worth the effort of mending.

"Your mam's hopeless with a needle, but you could go and ask Hannah Wilcox if she can turn a couple of my things into clothes for them. Good at that, she is."

"She's had to be, with her husband gone and her parents unwilling to help. She keeps those girls of hers beautifully turned out she does, and all by her own efforts. I'm sure she'll make a few things for these three, but we'll have to pay her, mind, she can't afford to do it for nothing."

"It's half seven, she'll be awake. Go and see her now, while the boys are still sleeping. I'll listen for them waking. I won't be going to bed yet. I thought I'd stay up and help your mother with breakfast."

Eirlys hugged her father affectionately. "Thanks, Dadda. I knew you wouldn't mind me taking them on."

"Go on with you. I'll chuck 'em though the window if they don't behave, mind. Oh, and call at the bake house and ask for a loaf of bread, will you? The shop won't open till nine and the lads ate all we had last night. On second thoughts, better get two."

Hannah Wilcox and Eirlys were friends even though their age and their circumstances were different. Hannah was twenty-nine, and had been married to a man who, she had soon realised, was a heavy drinker. While alcohol was in control he had been violent towards her. After a fourth stay in hospital, to her parents' embarrassment and shame she had sued for divorce – something unheard of in most families – and they steadfastly refused to accept it. They were both members of a local chapel where punishment was considered to be ennobling, and the rules of life were rigid. No mitigating circumstances were ever considered.

Hannah knew the religion was one that suited her parents' needs. They hated her but couldn't admit it, so the break-down of her marriage was something of which they could disapprove and for which they could punish her.

Their hatred of her and the need to punish her was because her brother Rupert, whom they had adored, had died of pneumonia after she had passed the flu on to him, and they blamed her for being alive when he was dead. Her refusal to stay with her husband was a gift to them in their unhappiness. They constantly pressurised her to take him back, insisting that he was her husband until death. That solution was something Hannah had thought about often, after a severe beating had left her in pain and she could see no way out of her situation.

It had been Eirlys Price and her parents who had helped her and supported her through the traumatic early months of the divorce procedure. Every move she made had been discouraged both by her parents and their friends, and the solicitor together with his staff also lacked sympathy, believing that a wife had to stay with a husband through everything.

Members of her parents' chapel called on her and talked until she thought her head would burst with the frustration of stating her case to uncaring ears, and listening to their lectures on her wickedness. She was "selfish", "thinking only of herself", "a wicked daughter", she was told repeatedly. She should "spare a thought for the shame her parents were suffering", she was reminded. It was only Eirlys and her parents, Morgan and Annie Price, who saved her sanity.

After the separation and the plans for the divorce had shamed them in front of their Chapel "friends", Hannah's parents, intent on a reconciliation, had twice allowed her husband back into the house and tricked their daughter into being there alone, and twice he had made Hannah pregnant, each time also landing her in hospital with cuts, bruises and broken bones.

Even when her parents visited her in hospital, they still refused to consider Hannah a free woman and insisted that she was married and should take her husband back. They quoted the marriage vows at her whenever she tried to reason with them, chanting them to drown out her reasoning. When they had reluctantly allowed her to return to their house, after she had been forced to give up the flat above the china shop, they had made sure she lived as unobtrusively as possible, confining her and the children to the two small rooms she had been allotted, not even allowing her to take the babies into the garden to play. Her shame was never to be forgotten. The world had to see they did not condone their daughter's behaviour.

When Hannah opened the door to Eirlys on the morning after the evacuees had arrived, she greeted Eirlys with a warning finger on her lips and they tiptoed into the living room where a fire burned low and a gas light flickered and popped in the draught.

"Eirlys, this is a nice surprise." Hannah smiled as she poked some life into the fire and turned the gas light up a notch. "Anything important?"

"I went to collect our evacuee and came back with three," Eirlys laughed. "Dadda was fine about it but our Mam wasn't pleased." The smile slipped a little as she thought about her mother's reaction, wondering if her mother would be persuaded to allow them to stay.

"She'll be as kind as your dad, don't worry," Hannah assured her. "Her bark is always worse than her bite." She waited for her friend to say something more but recognising the hesitancy, guessing there was a favour to be asked, said, "Can I help? Mam and Dad can't take one, not with us being here – at least that's a point in my favour," she laughed. "But if I can do something to help you?"

"The fact is, they don't have many clothes and the ones they do have are very worn. I wondered if you could make them some trousers and shirts out of some of Dad's old ones? It will be expensive to buy new for all three of them. We'll pay of course."

"Bring around what you've got and I'll look in my odds-and-ends cupboard and I'm sure we'll sort out something. Good practise maybe. There was a piece on the paper last

13

week about us having to manage without new clothes if the war lasts more than a year or so."

"But it won't, will it? This time next year we'll be laughing at all the scaremongering, won't we?"

"The last war went on for four years," Hannah said doubtfully.

"Yes, but we've learned something since then, haven't we?"

Hannah didn't think so but she said nothing. Talk of war was frightening and rumours varied from a brief skirmish, over by Christmas, to years of deprivation and horror. Hannah didn't want to think about it. Like many other women she preferred pretending the battles would happen far away and to people she didn't know.

"How is Johnny?" she asked, hoping to change the subject. "What does he think of Stanley, Harold and Percival Love?"

"Oh, I didn't see him last night. Sorting out the evacuees took most of the evening. Luckily we were meeting at his mam's house so I wasn't letting him down. Besides, he knew the evacuees were coming; he'd have guessed what happened and understood."

"What is he doing now the beach is closing for the winter? Has he got a job yet?"

Because Johnny Castle's family ran Piper's Café and their stalls on St David's Well Bay during the summer months, when the town was filled with day-trippers and holiday-makers attracted to the small town and its lovely sandy beaches, they all had to seek other employment during the winter.

"He's decorating old Mrs Piper's house at the moment, and hating it. Johnny loves working on the sands, and likes to be out of doors, working with people. He dreads the end of the beach season. He never minds painting the stalls and swingboats and the like, smartening them up for the season, that's a part of the work on the beach, but painting Granny Molly Piper's house is not a favourite pastime."

"Poor Johnny. Mrs 'Granny Moll' Piper isn't even his real gran, is she?" Hannah smiled.

"No, but she acts as though he is. He and Taff have to do as she says the same as their cousins."

The friends said goodbye, with the decision made to use the newly washed clothes as a guide to making new outfits for the boys in time for the following week when they would all be starting at the local school.

Eirlys was thinking about Johnny Castle as she closed the gate behind her. She knew something of the protest about the name of the cafés and stalls owned by Molly Piper.

It was the Castle family who ran the businesses belonging to Moll Piper, which had been started by her grandparents, Joseph and Harriet Piper, with a small wooden café close to the sands. Moll Piper's daughter Marged and her husband Huw Castle had worked on the sands since they were children and Huw's brother Bleddyn had worked beside them. As soon as they were old enough, their own children had become involved, the cousins working happily as a team. Although most members of the workforce were called Castle, the name of Piper was still used and would be, Moll told them, until the last Piper was dead.

As she and her unmarried daughter, Marged's sister Audrey, were the last two, Huw and Bleddyn constantly tried to persuade her to change her mind and rename the business – but to no avail. Bleddyn and Huw felt it was an injustice, as they had managed the business since Moll's husband had died and Moll had practically nothing to do with the day-to-day organisation. Huw's wife Marged avoided discussing it; agreeing with her husband, agreeing with Moll, using lots of words but saying nothing.

It was past eight o'clock that morning as Eirlys walked thoughtfully back to her parents' house in Conroy Street. She hastily prepared breakfast for them all, offering toast and eggs to the subdued boys. Then, leaving her father to look after them until her mother returned from work at one o'clock, when he would at last be able to get some sleep, she made her way to the council offices and the continuing work of arranging schools and checking on the accommodation for the children.

Every placement had to be investigated, the schools prepared for the extra pupils, meetings arranged for the families to sort out any difficulties before they developed into problems. There were endless reports and forms to deal with, people to send out with questionnaires regarding the evacuees and their welfare. She ate a snack lunch at her desk, stopping only briefly to look out at the bustling town. As all the shops and offices closed between one and two o'clock, the shoppers gradually disappeared and only a few people walked the pavements.

She saw Johnny riding past on his bicycle and guessed he had been sent to buy more paint to finish his decorating for Granny Moll Piper. She didn't wave. He wouldn't expect to see her there at her window high above the street.

He was whistling and wobbling his way through a group of workmen standing examining a delivery of buckets and stirrup pumps that had been unloaded on to the road. How everything was changing. Even though not a single bomb had been dropped, the town was being turned inside out in preparation for war.

She shivered as she thought of the dangers to come in the pretty little town, and the young men who were leaving in droves to fight an invisible enemy far away across the sea.

She thought of Ken Ward from whom she had parted recently. He had wanted so badly to join the army and fight, but asthma had meant he received Grade Four at his medical, too low for any kind of enemy action. His family had moved to London and Ken had accepted a job with a small theatre group there and had asked her to go with him, but she had refused to leave St David's Well. She had often wondered if the decision had been the right one and each time decided it had been.

She wouldn't have stood on the railway platform without regret and watched him leave if she had really loved him. An unwillingness to leave her parents and a job she enjoyed wouldn't have entered her mind. She missed him, though; they had been friends for several years.

At five thirty, when she began to tidy her desk and prepare to leave, she was handed another pile of papers and asked to try to get them filed before she went home. With a sigh, she agreed. She was anxious about the evacuees, and wondered how they had fared during their first day, but the work at the council offices had to be kept up to date. With so many men already gone to join the forces she couldn't refuse to work longer hours.

She stretched her arms, yawned widely, walked around her desk a few times to refresh herself. A cup of tea, then back to the paperwork. She gathered the papers and began to sort them out. Judging by the size of the pile, it looked like being two more hours before she could go home.

As she walked up the back path towards the kitchen door later that evening, she almost fell over a bike. With the blackout already in force the nights were dark with only the occasionally ground-facing light of a bicycle passing, or the partially covered car lights that only made the night seem darker.

"Who left their bike where I could fall over it?" she demanded as she closed the door and switched on the kitchen light to examine her shin.

"Me, and I'm sorry," Johnny Castle grinned.

Her spirits lifted at the sight of him, her tiredness was forgotten. He was small, as most of the Castle family were, only five feet seven, dark and strong and bursting with an energy that seemed to have laughter as its main ingredient. Johnny, more than the others, seemed to be filled with the joy of life. No one, Eirlys thought as she leaned forward for a brief kiss, no one could be miserable with Johnny Castle near.

"Sorry about last night, Johnny. I'll take the magazines to your mam later. Did you hear about the three boys? Stanley Love, aged ten, Harold aged eight and little Percival who is six."

"Yes, the news has spread, so I thought I'd call to see how you're managing. Granny Moll said she has some bedding if you need it, and some boys' clothes left from my cousins. Heaven alone knows why she kept them but perhaps we'll be glad she did, eh?"

"Thanks. I'll go and see what she's found at the weekend."

"Who looked after them while your mam was at the shop?"

"Our Dadda. He's so good about taking them in." She turned and smiled at Morgan, who was reading the paper.

"He should have been sleeping after working the night shift, but until we get them into school and properly settled we have to muddle through."

"I took them to the park," Morgan told them, "then Mam made them some chips. Harold said they weren't bad, but little Percival told her they weren't as good as the chip shop," he laughed.

"He's going to be hard to please, that one," Johnny smiled. They crept upstairs and looked at the three sleeping children. Stanley and Harold looked peaceful, but there was a scowl on Percival's face that made them smile.

"He's a cheerful-looking chap, I don't think!" Johnny said as they went down again.

"He's only six and I don't think he can possibly understand what's happening to them."

"I'll bring them a stick of seaside rock tomorrow, and at the weekend perhaps we can introduce them to the joys of the beach, eh? The swingboats and the helter-skelter and the stalls have all gone but Auntie Audrey is still opening the rock and sweet shop this month."

"Do you know, Johnny," Eirlys said in wonder, "Mrs Francis told us they might never have seen the sea. Isn't that amazing?"

When Eirlys's mother came into the kitchen and saw the pile of old clothes on the kitchen table, sorted for Hannah to use as patterns for newer ones, she put her hands on her hips, a well-known gesture meaning she was not pleased.

"When am I going to get this table cleared so I can set it for supper?" she demanded.

Seeing them together it was clear that Eirlys had inherited little from her mother. Annie was not tall, but she was plump, with dark eyes, and her long straight hair was always falling out of the bun with which she tried to control it. Eirlys was so like her father with their fair curly hair and blue eyes, and the wonderful milk-and-roses complexion to match. Johnny thought Eirlys would be ever young and Morgan would look as youthful when he was fifty as he did today. They were both slimly built and with an elegance in the way they walked, and a neatness that was always apparent, whatever task they undertook.

After greeting Johnny, Annie turned to her husband and daughter. "What were you thinking of, girl?" she demanded. "I was told we had to have *one*." She waved a solitary finger in front of Eirlys's face. "One girl. Now you and your father tell me we have three and you expect me to have them permanently? And boys at that. I never could cope with boys!"

"I'm off," Johnny laughed. "Remember the Queensbury Rules, mind, Mrs Price!" He could hear the shrill voice complaining as he jumped on his bike and wobbled his way down the path and on to the road. Thank goodness Eirlys followed her father in temperament as well as looks, and not her quick-tempered mother.

—

Johnny Castle lived in Brook Lane with his father Bleddyn, his mother Irene and his brother Taff. Apart from his rather sickly mother, Irene, who refused, they all worked on the sands during the summer months, sharing responsibility for the various entertainments as well as Piper's Café on the cliff above the beach and Piper's fish-and-chip shop and café in the town. Bleddyn's brother Huw and his family were the owners of the businesses together with Granny Moll, whose parents had begun it all, but Bleddyn had helped since he and Huw were children and he was very much involved, although, to his occasional irritation, Granny Moll, Huw's mother-in-law and owner of the business, always had the final word on any decision.

Running the fish-and-chip shop in town was Bleddyn's main duty, and as Johnny parked his bicycle in the shed and went into the house, he was closely followed by his father, who had just closed the café for the night.

"Been somewhere nice?" Bleddyn asked. "Pictures?"

"No, Eirlys couldn't come. She's been helping find homes for the evacuees who arrived yesterday and guess what?"

"Don't tell me we've got to have one?" He frowned. "Your mother couldn't cope, could you Irene?"

"No, not us, but Eirlys only came home with three boys!"

"What did Mrs Price have to say to that?" Bleddyn laughed. "I bet she let everyone know she wasn't pleased. Annie Price doesn't whisper at the best of times and they probably heard her reaction in Grange Road!"

"Mr Price seemed all right about it. He's a good-natured man, isn't he?"

"Yes," Bleddyn agreed. "I get on well with Morgan Price. He's all right, isn't he, Irene?" He looked across the room, trying to encourage his wife to take part in the conversation.

"What are they like, these kids from London, then?" Irene asked, ignoring his comment about Morgan Price.

"Most of them were tidy enough but a few of them looked real poor. Eirlys said theirs were clean and well nourished but they need clothes and a few possessions to make them feel at home. I was wondering, Mam, would you mind if I took my old train set over? And perhaps a few of our games and books?"

"Good idea, love. I'll sort through and see what I can find."

"I'm working for Granny Moll tomorrow so could you take them over?" Johnny asked.

"No I can't." His mother's voice was sharp. "You go tomorrow evening – you'll be seeing Eirlys, won't you?"

"Go on, Mam, they're so unhappy, a few toys would brighten their day."

"No. You go when you can. A few more hours won't hurt them."

Johnny frowned. Since he and Eirlys had begun going out together Eirlys's mother had invited his mother over several times but Irene had always refused. He shrugged. Perhaps the two women didn't get on, although it was disappointing for his mam to refuse an evening out. She was always complaining of being bored, and blaming his dad for never taking her out.

His brother Taff came in and they all sat down for supper. Twice a week Bleddyn brought fish and chips home; on other evenings they had something on toast, or a bowl of soup. It was Bleddyn's conviction that they should eat a meal together and talk about their day so they kept in touch with each other and didn't allow the family to drift apart. Lately, though, Irene had frequently set out the meal and wandered off to bed without joining them.

"Nice bit of hake for you tonight, Irene," Bleddyn said, hoping to persuade her to stay. "Saved it special, I did."

"I had a slice of cake earlier and I don't feel hungry. I think I'll go on up."

With Johnny and Taff arguing over possession of the fillet of hake, they didn't see the hurt disappointment on their father's face.

"Why don't you go and meet the evacuees, Mam?" Johnny asked as Irene went through the door. "Fancy that daft Eirlys taking home three boys! What her mam said when they all walked in I daren't think. She had plenty to say about it tonight. I hopped out as soon as she started on." Then he turned to share a smile with his mother and realised he was talking to himself. He began to tell his brother and Bleddyn instead.

Bleddyn knew Irene would be feigning sleep when he went up. She had no time for him lately, couldn't even spend a few minutes to share the family supper, something they had once both enjoyed and considered important.

He forced a cheerful tone as he began telling Taff and Johnny about some of the customers he had served, encouraging their laughter to cocoon him from his worries. He and Irene were more like strangers these days.

When he went upstairs after dropping the plates into a bowl of water to soak, Irene wasn't in bed. But when she saw him enter the room she hurriedly covered her semi-naked body with a dressing gown.

"It's all right, Irene, it's only me and you haven't got anything I haven't seen before," he joked.

"Don't be coarse," she said.

"What? Since when have you lost your sense of humour? That remark wouldn't have upset you a few months ago. What's happened? Do you find me so repulsive?"

"Of course not, Bleddyn. I'm tired, that's all."

"You aren't ill, are you? You don't seem to be with us these days."

"I'm all right, I'm just tired and it's late, so let's go to sleep, shall we?"

Bleddyn heard her breathing fast as though angry or upset. He didn't move when it slowed and became even as she dropped off to sleep. He slept fitfully, worrying about the way Irene was distancing herself from them all. He was awake when the hooter sounded to tell the factory workers it was time for the morning shift.

He was the first to rise that morning, knowing that Irene would probably stay in bed until he and their sons had left for work. With her present attitude he did more of the house chores than usual, hoping that his willingness would help her get over whatever was troubling her.

Irene had never been robust, or even truly happy. There were periods when she drifted through the days, half sleeping, reading magazines and novels, and then went out when she should have been cooking their meals. But between these spells, she had managed the house and cared for him and the boys reasonably well, until the mood came on her and she began hiding away from him again, into this shell she built around her; a situation that usually eased once more after a few weeks. He never learned the reason for the strange periodic indifference and aloofness. When he tried to talk to her she ignored him until he went away or changed the subject to one she was willing to discuss.

This time was more worrying. She had never been so indifferent to them for so long. Bleddyn had always been afraid that a more serious mental state would develop, which was why he was careful to help her and reassure her whenever these moods, euphemistically referred to as "nerves", occurred.

–

Johnny called on Eirlys the following evening when he had finished work painting the outside of Granny Moll's house in Sidney Street. He had gone home first to change out of his working clothes and gather up the toys he had chosen to give to Stanley and Harold and Percival.

Eirlys was just in from work too and she whooped with delight when he staggered in carrying a large cardboard box filled with his abandoned treasures.

Stanley, with assistance from Harold, set up the clockwork train set while a solemn Percival looked on.

Eirlys asked them what they had done that day but they were either too shy or too wrapped up in their new toys to answer her. "It's as though we're invisible," Eirlys whispered to Johnny with a laugh.

"What say we take them to the pictures tonight?" Johnny whispered back and was rewarded with the three boys' full attention.

"What have you done today?" Johnny then asked but Stanley shook his head.

"Nothing. That woman with the posh voice sent someone to collect us and we went to the school hall and listened to the headmaster chatting on about how we have to behave. What do they think we are, strange animals from a zoo?"

"What happened after the meeting?" Johnny asked, stifling a grin.

"Nothing. We just sat here and waited for you to come home. Your ma" – he addressed Eirlys – "said she was too busy and your pa was out."

"We'll make up for it at the weekend," Eirlys promised, disappointed that her mother couldn't spare an hour or two for the lonely and confused children.

"Too soft you are," Johnny smiled when she commented on this later. "I was telling our Mam about you coming home with three when you were supposed to have one."

"What did she say?" Eirlys grinned, expecting a humorous comment.

Johnny's smile faded. He couldn't tell her his mother had shown no reaction at all. "I told her you were daft. But, really, Eirlys, you're such a sweetheart."

He kissed her, startling her with his intensity. Until then his kisses had been nothing more than a peck, a greeting such as her father and mother gave. She felt the pleasure of it warming her and the embarrassment of it colouring her cheeks. Perhaps they were becoming more than friends. Shyly she looked at him and he kissed her again.

–

Eirlys was an only child without cousins or aunts and uncles. If envy could be said to be part of her character, she was envious of Johnny's large family. A growing fondness for Johnny was tinged with a longing to become a part of the Castle family's closeness. A lively throng of relatives all involved with each other's lives, caring and sharing, had long been yearned for. Johnny's kiss had given flight to that dream.

A few days after the evacuees had arrived she went to call on Johnny, but found his father, Bleddyn, there with Taff. She was invited in but immediately sensed a tension, as though an argument had taken place. Both men were standing. Bleddyn walked around the room as she entered and words hung in the air, waiting to be said.

At home in the place she visited often, she offered to make tea and went out into the small kitchen to do so. She hummed to herself, aware that things were being said that Bleddyn did not want her to hear. Rattling the china unnecessarily to make sure they knew she was re-entering the room, she was surprised to see Taff's girlfriend Evelyn there.

"Hello Evelyn, I'll get another cup, shall I?"

"Thanks," Evelyn said, in a low voice. Something was seriously wrong, Eirlys could see that and she wondered whether she should pour the tea and make an excuse to leave. This was clearly not her concern.

When she had filled the cups she reached for the jacket she had abandoned with her handbag and said, "Best I go. You're obviously in the middle of a discussion. Tell Johnny I'll be home all evening if he wants to call."

"No, don't go," Evelyn said. "You can be the first to congratulate us."

She looked at Taff, who forced a smile and went to stand beside her before saying, "Evelyn and I are getting married."

Throwing down her coat again, Eirlys hugged them both and wished them every happiness. "This is sudden, isn't it? I didn't know you were even engaged!"

"We are now, from today, and the wedding will be very soon."

"Wonderful," Eirlys said. But she was curious to know the reason for the rush. Surely Evelyn wasn't – Her eyes dropped front Evelyn's face to the region of her waist and quickly back again.

"No, I'm not expecting," Evelyn said. "We've just decided, that's all."

Making her excuses to get away from the strange atmosphere which should have been joyous but was not, Eirlys hurried home. She was at her back gate when she heard Evelyn calling and she waited for her, wondering what to

27

say. More congratulations? Or should she wait for Evelyn to speak first?

"I'm sorry you walked into that scene," Evelyn said.

"I thought it best to leave." Eirlys hesitated. "I had the impression that I interrupted something. I'm the one to be sorry."

"I don't want this talked about, mind," Evelyn told her, "but I want you to know what happened."

"Only if you want to tell me. Will you come in? We can go to my bedroom."

"No. It isn't a long story. Taff and I were kissing and, well, it was getting a bit out of control, and well, my mam walked in and thought we'd been – you know. She and our Dad insist that after debasing me – what a way to talk about love, eh? – after 'debasing' me in that way, we had to get married before it went too far and I was 'ruined'."

"Taff's mother seemed relieved somehow, glad to be getting one of her sons married and off her hands. She was in one of her strange moods, you know, as though she was there in body but not in her head. I wouldn't be surprised if she's forgotten all about it before tomorrow."

Eirlys could see that Evelyn was upset. It was a sad way to begin planning a wedding. "I am sorry, Evelyn, but you do love Taff, don't you? You and he have been together for years. It isn't such a dreadful thing, is it?"

"I love Taff, yes, of course I do, I think I always have, but I don't know whether he loves me and now I'll never know, will I?"

There didn't seem to be anything to say to comfort her and Eirlys watched as she walked away, head down, dejected. It was not a good way to begin a marriage. She hoped Taff would be kind and loving and convince her that he would have proposed anyway. Evelyn needed to be reassured of his love or her life would be incomplete.

Excited by the story in spite of her concern for her friend, her thoughts flew to the kiss she and Johnny had shared and she wondered if, one day, she and Evelyn would be sisters-in-law and be able to share all their confidences.

To her surprise and pleasure, Evelyn was waiting for her at lunchtime the following day and they went to a café for a snack, for which Evelyn insisted on paying.

"I need to talk to someone or I'll burst," she explained. "You know that Taff and Johnny and their father all work for Granny Molly Piper over on the beach and in the cafés, don't you?"

"Yes, of course. They all help during the holiday season." Eirlys nodded. "It's a family concern."

"That's the problem. Granny Moll came to see me this morning to welcome me to the family as though she was Taffs grandmother, which she isn't. She's related to Bleddyn's brother Huw, she's his mother-in-law in fact, but although she acts as though she's the head of the whole family, she's no relation to Bleddyn. But as Bleddyn and his brother Huw have worked for Pipers all their lives she has taken it upon herself to become matriarch. And her control includes Bleddyn and Irene, Johnny and Taff."

The family-hungry Eirlys could see no problem with this.

"What's wrong with being accepted into the whole family? They work together, don't they? I think it's wonderful that Mrs Piper welcomed you."

"Mrs Piper, or Granny Moll as she likes to be called, welcomes me as an extra pair of hands during the summer months. I'll be expected to give up my job and work on the sands or in the café."

"They all give up their winter jobs and work on the beach. They've done so for years. You wouldn't like that?"

"No, I'd hate it and I've no intention of giving up a job I enjoy because Granny Moll Piper tells me I should."

"Is that what you were discussing with Taff and Johnny's father?"

"They all do what Granny Moll says. I don't understand it. Taft's and Johnny's father, and his brother Huw, started on the sands when they were still at school and Huw married Granny Moll's daughter. Fine. But that doesn't give her the right to tell Bleddyn and Irene and their sons what to do, does it?"

"Bleddyn and Taff and Johnny work on the sands because they love it. Johnny's mother hates it so she doesn't, so why do you worry about it? Surely you can choose? I wouldn't give up my job if I were in your position. I enjoy it too much. But I'd love to help when I could. And if I found it more enjoyable than what I do now, I might be pleased to be involved and be a part of a big family like the Pipers. Why don't you talk it over and tell them how you feel?"

"You don't know Granny Moll! It's a family business and new members are expected to automatically give up their job and help."

"I'd love it," Eirlys breathed happily, seeing the dream and not the reality.

"Then you'd better tell Granny Moll and she'll make sure Johnny proposes to you!"

Eirlys was startled at how much that thought excited her.

She went inside and told her parents that Johnny's brother, Taff, was marrying Evelyn.

"Not before time if what I've heard is true. Carrying on they were and in her mam's house too."

"Kissing they were, Mam," Eirlys protested. "Her parents have made too much of it and now they're shaming her."

"If that's what's called kissing in this day and age, then you'd better watch out or you'll be in a worse position than her, my girl," her mother warned.

"Mam!" Eirlys ran upstairs in embarrassment.

"I don't want no hasty marriage for you," her mother called up the stairs. Eirlys covered her ears. She didn't want to hear any more. Loving someone was being reduced to something sordid, and the love she felt for Johnny was nothing like that. It was calm, and tenderly affectionate. Then she relived his kisses and thought of what Evelyn had said about the way she and Taff had been kissing and she was overcome with the reminder that perhaps love was more exciting than she had yet experienced.

Two

Eirlys and Evelyn did not know each other well, but once the engagement of Evelyn and Johnny's brother Taff was announced they began to meet more frequently. Neither had a sister or a brother and Evelyn needed someone with whom to discuss the arrangements for her special day. She didn't want to approach Beth or Lilly, Taff's cousins. The Castles would take charge of things soon enough.

Eirlys and she went together to look at wedding dress, "Although," Evelyn explained, "my mother will want to be with me when I make the final choice."

They talked about the Castle family at first, Evelyn having some doubts about belonging to such a possessive group, Eirlys, in her euphoric mood of burgeoning love, convinced it would be heaven. "I love Taff," Evelyn said, "but I'm uneasy about taking on the Castle family with Granny Molly Piper at its head. She's kind at first but you soon realise how manipulative she is, persuading you something is your idea when she wants you to do something."

"Come on, she isn't that bad, surely?"

"Did you know Taff wanted to train as a carpenter? But Granny Moll insisted he was needed on the sands and his father agreed with her."

"Taff loves it though, like Johnny does."

"Yes," Evelyn said cynically, "it's childhood for ever, Moll running their lives."

"He'll stay in the family firm though, won't he?"

"Unless something crops up to give him the strength to leave," she said thoughtfully.

"And Johnny?"

"Oh, Johnny has never wanted anything else… You know, Granny Molly Piper has all but taken over the arrangements for the wedding," Evelyn complained as they watched the assistant removing a dress from its layers of tissue paper.

Eirlys sympathised but, surrounded by the magical displays of wedding gowns and all the extras, she imagined that if it were her marrying Johnny Castle, she'd be thrilled to be made so welcome.

As time went on and dress after dress was slipped carefully over and then off Evelyn's head, the two girls laughed and oohed and aahed and frowned and considered their way through the gown department of the largest shops in the town, and eventually selected two from which Evelyn would finally make her choice.

Saturday afternoon was the only time when they were were free to meet and shop, as both worked office hours five and a half days a week; Eirlys at the council offices and Evelyn in a factory making cables for army vehicles. When they finally settled for two, Evelyn whispered, "The truth is, Eirlys, I'm not really thrilled with either. D'you think Hannah Wilcox would be able to make one for me?"

"I don't think there's time, unless you delay the wedding for a few weeks."

"Come with me to see Taff. Johnny will probably be there and we can scrounge a cup of tea and a sandwich."

"Do you mind if I call for the boys first?" Eirlys asked. "I try to give Mam and Dadda a break from them when I can."

After collecting Stanley, Harold and Percival they went to Bleddyn and Irene's house but it was empty.

"Of course, they'll be at the chip shop, won't they?" Eirlys said.

"I thought today was his father's Saturday off." Evelyn frowned.

"Never mind, we'll go for a walk instead."

"A walk to the chip shop?" Stanley said hopefully.

"I 'ates walking," Percival complained.

—

Bleddyn Castle had gone to see his brother to discuss the wedding of his son to Evelyn. As usual the house was full, with Huw and his wife Marged entertaining Marged's mother, Granny Moll, her sister Audrey and Audrey's fiancé of many years, Wilf Thomas.

"Where are the kids?" Bleddyn asked as he flopped into a chair near the fire.

"Our four are all out, thank goodness," Huw sighed.

"Our three now Ronnie's married," Marged corrected. "Our Lilly's got a date but we don't know who with."

"Secret meetings with a bloke she won't talk about," Huw grumbled. "Twenty-six she is, mind, and going out with someone she won't even put a name to."

"Our Beth is at a dance with Freddy," Marged went on, glaring at Huw to remind him they didn't want to discuss Lilly and her secret boyfriend, "and young Eynon is at the pictures."

"Beth at a dance? I didn't think Beth liked dancing."

"She doesn't, but that Freddy Clements does, so she goes with him and sits while he dances with other girls." Huw shrugged. "Daft, but there you are. They've been friends for so long they don't seem like a couple about to get engaged, do they?"

"Where are your lot, Bleddyn?" Granny Moll Piper asked. "We haven't seen your Irene for ages."

"I don't see much of her myself," Bleddyn admitted. "Irene isn't very well. You know how tired and depressed she gets sometimes. As for Taff and Johnny, they're probably out courting and it's Taff I came to talk to you about. He and Evelyn are going to get married as you know."

"D'you think that's wise, with the war and everything? There's the conscription that will soon take the eighteen-year-olds away, and the future isn't that cheerful," Moll warned. "I think they should wait."

Bleddyn shook his head. "All the more reason to get settled. It'll give the boys some comfort, knowing there's someone at home waiting for them."

"Just so long as it's what Taff really wants," Marged said pointedly.

"When are they planning to tie the knot?" Huw asked. "If it's soon, then it's best we get some food hidden away before the food rationing threatened for next year, eh, Marged? We'll want to give them a good spread."

"Don't be so hasty, Huw," Marged laughed. "They've only got engaged now this minute! Give it a bit of time."

"Fact is," Bleddyn said slowly, "they plan to marry very soon and we wondered, me and Irene, whether you'd make the cake and do the food, Marged."

"When exactly?" Moll asked, suspicion quirking an eyebrow.

"Three weeks' time and no, before you ask, she hasn't got a bun in the oven!"

"We weren't—" Marged protested.

"Yes we were," Huw grinned. "At least I was! So, Bleddyn, boy, what's the rush then?"

"Her mother and father want it sooner than later because they think they're getting a bit too passionate on the way they say goodnight," Bleddyn grinned.

Within an hour the plans had been discussed and finalised. The wedding would take place on Saturday October seventh at St Cenyth's church. The wedding breakfast for family and close friends would be held in Piper's Café over on the beach, specially opened for the occasion, and the bride would wear white as she walked down the aisle of the church, as befitted an innocent young girl and to stop tongues wagging.

Bleddyn wondered when Evelyn's family would be brought into the discussions but didn't ask. He knew it was best left to the women, although, he thought sadly, it was doubtful whether Irene would contribute much.

Bleddyn's brother Huw and his wife Marged had four children: Ronnie, now married to Olive; Lilly, with her mysterious lover; Beth, about to become engaged to Freddy Clements who worked in the local gent's outfitters and Eynon, who at sixteen was the "baby" of the family and hated it.

When seventeen-year-old Beth came in from the dance, her dark eyes were glowing and her smooth black hair cut in a bob with a straight fringe was a shining cap around her smiling face. Everything about her revealed a woman in love.

She was delighted to hear that her cousin Taff was to marry. Having just left the arms of the man she loved, her reaction was more enthusiastic than the others. She decided to go and see Evelyn the following evening after finishing work in the greengrocer where she was working throughout the winter. Like the rest of the family she worked on the beach during the summer season and found other work for the colder months.

"Pity they didn't wait a while longer, though," she said. "Me and Freddy are getting engaged on my eighteenth birthday and we could have had a double wedding next year."

Huw and Bleddyn went out into the small garden and stood looking around at the dark night. "Everything's all right, is it, Bleddyn?" Huw asked. "There's no pressure from Evelyn's parents that Taff doesn't want, is there?"

"No, nothing like that. He says he wants to marry Evelyn, but they didn't intend to marry in a rush like this. Engaged for a couple of years first is the usual carry-on, isn't it? To give themselves time to gather the things they need, fill their 'bottom drawer' and get to really know each other."

"What happened to change that?"

"Evelyn's mother got home earlier than planned and found them in a passionate embrace and insists that if she hadn't, her Evelyn would be in the pudding club."

The brothers smiled in the darkness, remembering their own courting days and the haste with which Huw married Marged before tongues wagged.

"Runs in the family, eh?" Bleddyn laughed. "You and Marged facing the wrath of Moll, and me and Irene not far behind, so your Lilly and our Taff were as good as twins, eh?"

"Irene bad again then, is she?" Huw asked after a while. "What's the trouble this time?"

"The usual depression. I've tried to work out what starts her off but there's no accounting for it. She walks around the streets and the beaches and I never know where she is or where she's been. Stays out for hours she does. When she is

37

at home she's morose and won't talk. I don't understand it, but I do what I can to help keep the house running for the boys' sake. We just wait till she crawls out of the pit that she creates for herself, and gets back to normal. Then I just hope, every morning, that the black mood hasn't returned."

"Can't the doctor do anything?"

"Tells her to pull herself together and insists that she's fit and well and maybe doing it to avoid the work she hates."

"Rubbish. She never has done anything she doesn't want to." Huw coughed, embarrassed that his irritation with his sister-in-law was allowed to show. "Sorry, Bleddyn, I shouldn't comment when I don't know the full story."

"You know as much as I do, and that's practically nothing at all. It's as though she shuts herself off from her life with me and the boys, for weeks and sometimes months, then she comes back. But where she goes in her mind during those times, I don't know."

"Where does she go bodily, that's what I'd want to know. She can't just walk around. There has to be a place where she goes. Nobody sees her wandering about, do they?"

"Sometimes, yes. She's seen in the fields sometimes. But she's never been seen in a café or the pictures or anywhere like that."

"Strange," Huw frowned. "Now if she'd only help us on the beach in the summer months, keep herself busy, like, it might take her mind off herself and maybe it would help her."

"You know how many times I've asked her to come on the sands."

"I know, but if you told her how much we need her help?'

Bleddyn shuffled his feet, a sign that he was getting tense and didn't want to discuss it further, and Huw dealt with the blackout curtain as he opened the door to return to the others.

Irene was Bleddyn's wife and he couldn't interfere, although he believed that the basis of Irene's "illness" was idleness rather than medical.

–

Eirlys knew that her mother was being kept busy with her part-time work and looking after the boys as well as dealing with the housewifely chores. Annie hadn't wanted the extra work involved in caring for Stanley, Harold and Percival, and she still threatened occasionally that they would have to go somewhere else to live. Eirlys spent as much time with them as she could. On the following day, a Sunday, it rained, but she was determined that they should see the sea.

In borrowed clothes, and wellingtons that were either tight or too loose, they made their way through the dreary streets towards the beach. Stanley asked a stream of questions, Harold was rude about everything and Percival walked head down, his rare comments making it clear that nothing interested him except getting back to his mother.

As they reached the promenade at St David's Well Bay, a light rain still fell, but across the water the sun showed its face and provided a rainbow – specially for them, she insisted, as she showed it off. With the low, dark clouds, the brightness across the sea on the distant shore and the magical appearance of the rainbow, Eirlys thought that considering the time of year, their first sight of the sea could have been a lot worse. Even Percival seemed impressed.

Then the rain stopped and everything sparkled like new, the sun giving the horizon a band of gold. Gradually they emerged from their outerwear and walked along the almost deserted, off-season beach while she tried to explain to the young Londoners what it would look like in the summer, when the entertainments were going full tilt and the beach was crammed with noisy families having fun.

She had walked a few yards before she realised that she only had two. Looking back, she saw Harold staring over the sea wall, where she had stopped for their first sight of the sea, amazement opening his mouth wide.

"Come on, Harold, you look like a dead fish standing there," she teased.

"I never thought it would be so big. What's that on the other side?"

"That's Somerset. Wait till we get home and I'll show you on the map," she promised.

With wellingtons coming into their own, they were able to run in and out of the water, pretending to run in fear from the white edged waves, laughing, sharing the joy of it with each other by occasional glances. Even the solemn Percival managed a glimmer of a smile.

A few entrepreneurial stall-holders had arrived and opened for the few hours of daylight left and soon the sands were full of people. It was as though summer had returned. Only the Pipers' helter-skelter and roundabouts and swingboats were missing. They had been stored away at the end of August.

The three boys watched in amazement at the sight of children running about, laughing, chased by assorted dogs, at dads formally dressed in suits trying to walk on the soft sand without getting any in their shoes, or sitting to make sandcastles. The women were neatly dressed and some carried baskets from which they took a few biscuits and a bottle of lemonade.

Eirlys smiled at a little girl carrying two cones which dripped, were licked and which finally fell into the sand. The child's mouth opened in a silent cry, easily recognised as such from a distance.

Crying could soon become commonplace, Eirlys thought sadly, as more and more fathers and brothers and sons were taken away to fight against Hitler.

They were returning to the promenade when she saw a figure she knew coming towards them waving and calling.

"Johnny!" she shouted, thankful for the release from her morbid thoughts.

"I called for you and your Dad said you'd be here," he said. "Have you shown them Piper's Café yet?"

She shared a hug and an affectionate kiss with him, then bent down to Percival's level and pointed to where, high above the beach, Piper's Café stood precariously on the cliff path, jutting out over the beach. It could be reached from the path and also from the beach, when the tide was low, by means of metal steps.

"I've got the key, what say we take a look?" Johnny suggested, waving the bunch of keys in front of her face.

Walking up the open-work metal steps that echoed each footstep, clanking in an alarming way, was an excuse for laughter and a few yells of fright which resulted in Johnny carrying Percival, who travelled upward with his eyes tightly closed.

The café was larger than it appeared from below and consisted of a dining area and a kitchen which was fitted with a frying range and an enormous sink as well as a cooker on which sat two large kettles.

"This is my family's business," Johnny explained as the boys prowled around examining everything. "We feed the hundreds of summer visitors that come to St David's Well Bay for their holidays every year."

"Got anything to eat then?" Stanley asked.

Johnny regretfully shook his head. "We closed at the end of August and we won't be open again until next summer."

"Not much of a caff then," Harold complained. "Some places are open, why not you?"

"Partly because we need to get jobs and wanted to take our pick, but mostly because of the blackout. We didn't fancy working here with the windows blacked out, or packing up in the dark, so rather than closing early, we finished altogether."

"What did you bring us here for if we can't get nothin' to eat?" Harold asked rudely.

"I ain't 'ungry," Percival said. He was a poor eater and even in the short time he had been staying with Eirlys's family had become anxious at the thought of mealtimes and the persuasions to eat.

"Sit at the table," Johnny instructed, pointing to the table close to a barred and partially boarded-up window. Little Percival sat disconsolately with elbows on the table, his hands supporting his chin, the epitome of misery. Then Johnny produced three sticks of seaside rock and his face changed. Now *this* looked more like food.

Leaving the boys chomping happily and discussing the sea and the sand, Johnny put an arm around Eirlys and asked, "They're great kids and I admire the way you're helping them settle in, but are we going to find a few hours for ourselves? Or will I have to wait till Hitler's been beaten and they go back home?" he teased.

"Sorry Johnny, but I thought I'd spend the weekend with them, get them out from under Mam's feet and show them around the neighbourhood."

"Of course, love."

The word "love" hung in the air. He had never called her that before, or greeted her with a real kiss when they met. She realised he was speaking, and pulled herself together and asked him to repeat it.

"It might be an idea to introduce them to some of the boys they'll meet at school so they won't feel so strange when they start there on Monday."

"You don't mind?"

"I can spare you for a while. I realise how important it is to help them." He turned his head and looked at the three brothers whispering, sharing opinions and most likely making fun of some of the things they had learnt.

Eirlys tilted her head to one side, smiling as she watched them. "It makes you realise how lucky we are to be here and not in one of the cities where they are threatened with bombs, and have to send their children away to live with strangers. I don't suppose we'll get off scot-free, though."

"No. For one thing, the call-up hasn't missed out St David's Well. Even the smallest village has been touched by that. I'll have to go next year unless they allow that the work on the beach justifies an exemption on the grounds that it's war work. That's not likely, is it? Taff will probably be going before me, so Evelyn won't be enjoying life as a married woman for very long. Living on her own she'll be, in the rooms they've rented in Curtis Street."

"Got a drink of pop to wash that sticky stuff down?" the cheeky Harold called hopefully.

Once again Eirlys was glad that he had broken the sober reminders that St David's Well was at war, and she replied cheerfully, "All right; as Johnny supplied the sticks of seaside rock, I'll treat you to a drink of pop in Piper's fish-and-chip shop."

"That's ours too," Johnny explained to the boys as they left the café perched high above the sands and walked back towards town. "My father runs it, but it belongs to the Piper family, same as the café. He takes a boat out for pleasure trips in the summer. You'll enjoy that next summer," he promised. "Right out across the bay he goes."

"Why isn't it called Castle's, then?" Harold asked.

"That's a long story, for another time, Harold."

"Rich, are yer?" Stanley wanted to know.

"Not rich enough to be idle; we have to work long hours for what we get. We earn our money by working in the café and the chip shop and, in the summer, we have swingboats and helter-skelters, stalls and hoopla and the like, right there on the sand."

"I do want to go home," Stanley explained, "I do want to see our Ma, but I'd like to be here in the summer and have a go on the helter-skelter and land on the sand. It sounds like fun."

"Softer on your arse than concrete," Harold said, looking wide-eyed at Eirlys, who chose to ignore the swear word.

"Swingboats make me sick," Percival said, with a brief demonstration.

–

Plans for the wedding of Taff Castle and Evelyn Power were set in motion, most of the arrangements being made by Evelyn's parents and swiftly changed by Granny Moll. Irene seemed happy about her son's wedding plans but did little to help. It was Bleddyn and Taff who liaised with the bride's family and dealt with ordering cars and other tasks allotted them by Evelyn's parents. The catering was firmly in the hands of Granny Moll Piper.

"D'you know what Granny Moll did?" Evelyn confided in Eirlys when they met one day to go and see how the wedding dress, being made by Hannah after all, was progressing. "Only went straight to the paper she did, and told them it would be the wedding of the year and for them to be sure to have photographers there. This was before Taff and I had decided on the church! And Mam wanted the reception in the church hall but no, that wasn't good enough for Granny Molly Piper. It had to be a wedding in Piper's Café. My wedding, mind!" She frowned. "I wish it was all over, and I think Taff does as well."

"You still want to marry him?" Eirlys asked anxiously.

"Of course I do, but not with this circus arranged by Granny Molly Piper!"

--

Marged and Huw made arrangements to cater for thirty people, which was all Piper's Café could comfortably hold, for the official wedding breakfast. The rest would wait for the real party at Sidney Street in the evening.

"Pity it isn't a summer wedding, we could have spread out across the clifftop and had a wonderful buffet meal-cum-picnic," Marged said, smiling as she envisaged the scene.

"Oh no," Mrs Power said in alarm. Whatever would the woman think of next? "That wouldn't do at all. It has to be a proper sit-down, three-course meal."

"And it will be," Marged assured her. "If there's one thing we Pipers do well, it's providing food in the right quantities and with the appropriate choices. Piper's Café was started by my great-grandparents and has maintained a reputation for excellence ever since," she reminded them firmly.

Eirlys wanted to be involved, she wanted to be considered a member of the family, but there didn't appear to be anything needed that she could do. She could hardly offer. She wasn't sure she would even be invited. Weddings were for family and close friends and she hadn't known Johnny very long. They had met at the beach a few days after she and Ken Ward had parted. That day she had been glad of the lively crowds to conceal her loneliness and the fear that she had made a mistake by not going to London with Ken. The beach atmosphere and Johnny's gentle teasing had soothed her and convinced her that her heart and her future was here, in the warm, friendly seaside town of St David's Well.

Watching Johnny flirting with the customers as he helped them on and off the swingboats, and comforting a child who wailed that he didn't want to go home, with the promise that it would all be there for him next year, she had felt her unhappiness fade away.

Later, when they had met by accident in the town, and talked and made a date for a visit to the pictures, she had become more convinced that her decision had been the right one. But they hadn't known each other long enough for her to expect an invitation to his brother's wedding.

When she received an invitation to the wedding a few days later, she was so excited she ran out and accepted it within minutes of the postman delivering it. She brushed aside the thought that it might have been Evelyn's idea rather than Johnny's. She would be attending a Castle wedding with Johnny. It was all going to happen; she and Johnny would be accepted as a courting couple before the year was out.

On the night before the wedding, Johnny and Taff went out for a drink. They had invited a few friends to join them but Taff didn't want the traditional pre-wedding booze-up.

Taff was not an enthusiastic drinker and he didn't want to face his bride with a hangover.

His cousin Ronnie was there – as Taff's best man he had arranged it. The choice of Ronnie for best man rather than his brother Johnny had been Moll's. "It's a chance to show everyone what a united family we are," she had said.

To begin with it was a friendly chat around the table they had chosen near the bar-room fire, but, as the evening progressed, they were joined by more and more as news of the occasion spread. Other tables were joined to their own and the talk and singing grew more and more bawdy. The room became full and very warm and noisy and the party was no longer Taff's as the crowd increased to include people he hardly knew. Slipping away unnoticed, Taff went out into the street to cool off, wishing he'd never agreed to a stag night and wondering how soon he could leave.

Johnny saw him go through the double passageway with its heavy curtains hung to prevent the light spilling out during the hours of darkness, and followed him.

"You are happy about tomorrow, aren't you, Taff?"

"I wish it was over, that's all. I want to be married to Evelyn but I don't want to go through all this fuss. Why couldn't we have just gone and got married and forgotten all this nonsense?"

"Because the family would kill you, that's why," Johnny said mildly.

"Evelyn and I wanted a quiet affair."

"What, miss the chance of a party? An opportunity for Auntie Marged and Uncle Huw to show off their expertise at catering for a wedding? And Granny Moll to get a piece in the paper? You wouldn't deprive them of that, would you?"

"I suppose not."

Taff didn't want to discuss it. His wedding was not turning out to be the day he had imagined. Some of Evelyn's resentment had wriggled into his mind and had grown into discontent.

"What about you, Johnny?" he asked, to switch the conversation from himself. "Are you and Eirlys thinking of tying the knot? She seems very keen on you."

"Me and Eirlys? No fear! I'm too young. I want to have a bit of fun first; I'm only twenty-one."

"I just wondered, you know, whether Eirlys is hoping for something more permanent. The way she looks at you, you know, admiring glances and the like."

"Never. Just friends we are."

"You've invited her to the wedding and she'll be coming as your guest, sitting next to you for all to see and comment on. Serious stuff that. Is it wise, brother mine?"

"You don't think that she'll think – that I think—? No. We're just friends, that's all, she won't see anything more in an invitation shared by three dozen others to come to your wedding and the other three dozen who'll join us for the party later on."

"And you haven't kissed her or – anything else?"

"We've kissed, yes, but there's no 'anything else', you cheeky sod, and there won't be. I want to stay free for a few years yet. No, Taff, Eirlys is great, but she isn't my one love for life, like your Evelyn is yours."

It was almost ten o'clock and everyone had reached the maudlin stage when Johnny suddenly sobered up fast. "Damn Hitler!" he said to everyone's surprise. "I forgot to fix the blackout on Piper's Café!"

Amid shouts of "The wedding's off!" and "Lucky escape!" Johnny left the pub and hurried to see Eirlys. Inexplicably he had a sudden desire to see her, to find out perhaps whether what he felt for her was the beginnings of love. Talk about weddings often had this effect, he'd read that in a magazine somewhere. He'd better be careful!

–

In the boys' bedroom, Eirlys was reading *Swallows and Amazons* to them as a bedtime story. It was very late, but she had promised them and didn't want to let them down by refusing them even the smallest thing.

So far, apart from Stanley, they weren't impressed and Harold had explained, reasonably politely, that he and Percival preferred comics. She promised to order one for them to be delivered each week. "Something to look forward to," she explained. "In the mean time, we'll go on with this, right?"

The promise of the weekly comic persuaded them and they settled down to listen. On Stanley's pillow were the three letters they had so far received from their mother, Teresa Love. Scrappy notes written in pencil, the writing large and ill formed. The boys treasured them, reading them again and again. Eirlys knew she would be asked to read them aloud once more as soon as she closed the book.

When they were asleep, the precious letters tucked under Stanley's pillow, Eirlys stood for a while looking down at them and imagining herself in a few years' time, her and Johnny happily married and with children of their own.

Working on the beach in her spare time and being a part of the Castles' large family was a wonderful prospect. The recent kisses which had been more than the traditional peck, the hugging when they met and hearing him call her "love" had changed her expectations in the most exciting way, and she was convinced that they would stay together for always.

Tomorrow she would be going to his brother's wedding, that was a big step forward in their relationship. It was Johnny's way of telling everyone they were together. Everyone would see them as a couple after that.

She went to her wardrobe and stared at the suit she had bought specially for the occasion, a light blue-grey two-piece with tan accessories. She was having her naturally curly hair specially set in the morning. She wanted to impress his family, and the suit and the hair-do and the Californian Poppy perfume would be just perfect.

There was a knock at the door and her mother opened it to Johnny.

"Eirlys, can you and your dad spare an hour or two to help? We've just realised the café will need blackout curtains as the wedding isn't till four and it's bound to go on a bit. There'll be no time in the morning."

"Where will you get material at this time of night?"

"Granny Moll bought it ages ago in case something like this happened. It's in the café ready to be fitted."

"Dad's working but I can help if you like?" Eirlys offered.

Johnny turned to Annie as Eirlys reached for her coat. "I'll see her safe home, Mrs Price, don't worry."

They went on bicycles, Johnny borrowing Morgan's, packing the saddlebag with a few simple tools and necessary oddments. The roads were quiet, but with their poor lights they were extra careful when vehicles overtook them. Since the blackout began, there had been a large number of accidents.

The blackout "curtains" were in fact paper, forty inches wide and costing ninepence a yard. With a generous supply of drawing pins it took them two hours to complete the job.

Walking up the path to put the bicycles in the shed at one o'clock in the morning, Johnny put an arm around her and kissed her lightly on the cheek. "Thank you, Eirlys. I'd never have managed it on my own."

She turned her face as she smiled at him, hoping that the next kiss would touch her lips, but he hugged her then released her and increased his pace, hurrying off through the silent streets and leaving her with a feeling of dejection.

–

Hannah had made the wedding dress, after long discussions, using the skirt of one pattern and the bodice of another, embroidering it with pearls to a design of her own. She had worked long into the nights to get it finished in time as much of it was hand sewn. Her own two girls, Josie who was three and nine months and Marie aged two and a half were to be flower girls in white dresses matching, in a much-simplified style, the bridal gown.

On the day of the wedding, Johnny was up early, waiting on his brother and determined that the day would go smoothly in spite of his mother's inability to help.

He was the first to arrive at the church after making sure Taff was ready to leave. He stood back as the ushers welcomed the families and directed them to their seats. When Taff came, he would wait with him until their cousin Ronnie, who was best man, arrived to stand with him.

He guessed from the excitement engendered by the crowd that the bridesmaids had arrived and he couldn't resist going out to look at them. He knew their mother, Hannah, would be with them. He saw Hannah first. Dressed in a simple two-piece in a soft blue he thought she looked lovely. Her face was always rosy, as though she had just stepped away from attending to the fire. Her eyes, dark like his own, and large enough to lose himself in, glanced his way and she smiled shyly, turning his heart in a surprising way.

He went across to help the little girls in their long skirts, holding tightly clutched posies of flowers, out of the car, while Eirlys looked on, smiling happily at the pretty scene. Then Evelyn's mother came running up and elbowed Johnny out of the way, but he stared at the shy but proud mother and her two small girls for a long time before going with Eirlys into the church.

Ronnie was late. He was cleaning Taff's old shoes because Taff had insisted the new ones were too tight. He was battling with Taff's stiff collar, searching for a collar stud that refused to slip into place and repeatedly fell on the floor. He was assuring the over-anxious groom that the borrowed suit was an excellent fit. And that the ring was safely in his pocket.

Johnny returned to sit beside his brother, anxiously glancing from time to time towards the door, until his cousin Ronnie Castle running in late, arrived in the role of best man and took his place, leaving him free to join Eirlys.

Eirlys was smart in her new outfit but she felt uneasy, convinced that Johnny didn't like it. He had barely looked at her and they had exchanged very few words. She must be embarrassing him in her ill-chosen clothes. She felt the heat of humiliation and longed to run away.

He seemed indifferent to her presence, sitting well away from her and looking around at all the guests, smiling, waving, and ignoring her. She must look a sight, she thought and shrank down in her seat wishing the whole affair was over.

Johnny was uneasy. He knew he should have complimented her on her appearance; she did look rather lovely. But uneasy about how she would behave, not wanting to give the gossips any further fuel, he treated her like a casual acquaintance, and felt mean and unkind. He really would have to make up his mind or slip out of her life completely. Somehow he didn't want to do that.

"Where are the boys?" he asked, more for something to say to break the iciness of their situation than because he wanted to know.

Eirlys gestured with her head to the back corner of the church where three solemn boys sat in silence beside her parents Annie and Morgan, over-awed by the spectacle of so many smartly-dressed people and the whispering silence of the church. Johnny chuckled. "I never thought them capable of sitting so still. Or looking so well scrubbed!"

"I made them bathe at the very last minute. They've developed a knack of finding mud and water or anything else that's smelly or dirty. Thanks to Hannah's help, we managed to dress them in something that fitted them for a change. None of their own clothes would have been suitable."

"Have you known her long?" Johnny asked.

"Hannah? We got to know her when she was having trouble with her husband. Her parents refused to support her even though he used to beat her," she whispered. "Mam and Dadda helped her a lot and we've kept in touch with her."

"She's very kind, isn't she, Hannah?" Johnny said after a brief pause. "I wonder that she had enough time to help so willingly. Dad says she cleans for some shops every morning while the children are at school or being looked after by her friends, and again in the evening after the children are asleep. It must be exhausting to do all that, then settle down to work at her sewing machine for hours."

"Shush, the bride is coming!"

Every head turned to catch a first glimpse of Evelyn as she entered the church on her father's arm. She looked very beautiful, the dress was stunning, and there were many gasps of admiration as the organ music swelled and she came to stand beside her groom, who looked justifiably proud. In the silence that followed, as the congregation waited for the vicar to speak, Harold was heard to say, "Is that what we've been waiting for? Can we go back with you, now, Uncle Morgan?"

"Hush up, boy, you're in church!" Morgan whispered back.

Eirlys frowned. "They did promise to behave," she said ruefully.

There was a brief moment of amusement when Taff was called by his real name of Arthur Brian Castle, and the vicar interrupted the service to remind them of the seriousness of the occasion.

Eirlys glanced at the three boys from time to time and saw her father stride out of the door before the service was half-way through. She gestured to her mother with a philosophical shrug of her shoulders. Morgan Price wasn't one to sit dressed up in church for long. Always neatly dressed, even in his work clothes, Morgan preferred casual wear and had always hated wearing a suit and stiff collar.

He'd clearly been there on sufferance, tugging at his viciously starched collar and fidgeting worse than the boys. But when the boys stood to go with him he had shaken his head and they settled disconsolately to wait till Annie took them home.

The photography session seemed to go on for ever. Unable to decide whether to go or stay, Eirlys took the three boys for a walk around the beach where most of the photographs were taken, and answered questions about the people they had met.

There was no professional photographer engaged; Huw and Bleddyn took turns at snapping the various groups. Granny Moll insisted on taking one of the whole family, which consisted of her daughter Marged and Huw, their children and daughter-in-law and also Bleddyn, Johnny, Taff and his new bride. Irene wasn't to be found. With her usual authority, Moll waved for Eirlys to join them and, feeling rather self-conscious, aware it had not been Johnny's idea, she did.

This was what Evelyn had been trying to explain, she realised. Granny Moll was making it clear that this was a Piper wedding even though the couple getting married were Castles. But she smiled anyway. Today she was Johnny's guest at a family affair. That was a good sign. His strange mood during the ceremony had faded. It had clearly been nothing more than worries about Ronnie being late.

Arranging everyone so nobody blocked anyone else took some time and there were laughs about the evenness of their height. Apart from Bleddyn who towered above the rest, all the Castle family were average height or below. Eventually some sat on chairs, some formed a line behind the rest by standing on more chairs, so a formal arrangement was achieved.

Huw shouted insults at his brother, telling everyone jocularly that Bleddyn must have been a by-blow or had been changed at birth because he was taller and heavier than the rest.

"Or better fed!" Moll added.

Johnny was slightly uneasy at the happy expression on Eirlys's face and as soon as the camera gave its loud click, he hurried away.

The party was held in the home of Granny Moll in Sidney Street as her house was the largest. Irene didn't seem to mind that her son's wedding party was held in someone else's house rather than her own. "It's less work for me," she said honestly, "and if everyone else wanted it, why should I complain?" She disappeared a short while after the crowd arrived and apart from Bleddyn, who searched for her to drink a toast to the young couple as they set off for their honeymoon in Weston-Super-Mare, and Johnny, who wanted her to talk to Eirlys while he looked for Hannah, no one missed her.

Stanley, Harold and Percival had sat in a row at the wedding breakfast and were plied with food. Percival hid his under the chair but the others enjoyed the fancy food, the like of which they had never before seen.

When Bleddyn came and talked to them, he asked them about their home.

"It ain't nothing like this," Stanley said. "We got two rooms for the four of us and the lavvy's in the yard."

"What about your father? Doesn't he make five?"

"Nah. He 'opped it years ago," Harold told him flippantly. "Good riddance too, Mum says, don't she Stanley?"

"I want to go home," Percival muttered.

"Go on with yer, it's all right with Auntie Annie and Uncle Morgan. And Johnny's going to show us how to make a treehouse next Saturday."

In a convoy of cars they had moved to Granny Moll's house and continued the party there, with the numbers increasing as friends and neighbours came to join in. Marged's sister Audrey had left the wedding breakfast early with her friend Wilf Thomas, and they had already prepared trays of glasses and set out food ready for the second half of the celebration.

Taff and Evelyn didn't stay long. They had arranged to take a train at seven.

Seeing the couple off by taxi to the station meant everyone was out on the pavement. Up and down Sidney Street, doors opened and neighbours crowded out on to doorsteps, adding to the cheers and good wishes. Bleddyn looked for his wife but Irene was not among the crowd of well-wishers. Her son was going on honeymoon and she wasn't there to see him off. Irritation flared and died. She was ill, he told himself, and couldn't be blamed. He just hoped that Taff hadn't noticed or would understand if he had.

Finding Eirlys with Annie and the three boys sitting in a corner, while Johnny began to play records on the gramophone, Moll sat near them. "I just hope Taff will be able to make that young girl understand that she's now part of the Piper family," she said. "She can't refuse to help on the beach next summer, not with the boys having to register for the armed forces. The family will have to stick together more than ever now. Piper's will need every pair of hands."

So filled with the happiness of the day, Eirlys was on the point of offering to help on her days off, but she stopped herself in time. How embarrassing to be so forward. She would have to wait to be invited. She wondered if Moll was leading up to do just that, when Marged and Huw and their son Ronnie heard what had been said and came nearer.

"Oh, Granny Moll," sighed Ronnie. "Give the girl a chance. Married five minutes and here you are, complaining about how she'll be next summer. Besides, we don't want to think about the war, not today."

"Why not? It won't go away because we pretend it isn't happening. The boys will have to go, but the business carries on as usual. Evelyn must realise that."

"Olive doesn't help, Granny Moll, we manage without her; perhaps Evelyn feels the same."

"I know she likes what she does," Eirlys dared to say. "She's an inspector on a factory bench, isn't she?"

"I know full well what she does, and I also know that checking up on someone else's work isn't more important than working on the sands."

For a moment Eirlys felt sympathy for Evelyn. Marrying Taff meant belonging to the family. And the head of the family, Granny Moll, was unlikely to allow her to forget it. Yet she was so anxious to impress, to make Moll look at her as a useful member of the family if she and Johnny became close, she swallowed her brief compassion, smiled at Mrs Moll Piper and said sweetly, "I agree, Mrs Piper. Piper's is more than a business, isn't it? It'll be helping to win the war by keeping up morale. I've read about how important entertainment was in the last war in keeping up morale. I'm sure Evelyn will see it too, as soon as she calms down from the excitement of her wedding day."

"Yes, I must give her time, mustn't I?" She looked thoughtfully at Eirlys's bright face and smiled. "You understand about Piper's, don't you Eirlys?"

"Oh yes, I understand fully the importance of Piper's," she replied as enthusiasm and the need to please blotted out common sense. She could give up her job and – She looked for Johnny, wanting, needing to tell him that she would accept what belonging to the Pipers really meant, and that she would willingly give up her job at the council offices to become a part of it. Then she felt colour suffuse her cheeks. What was she thinking of? Apart from a few kisses, Johnny hadn't given the slightest hint that he thought about her in that way. Acting as though he had already proposed? She must be crazy! She had let today's celebration, the romantic occasion, go to her head. But the dream warmed her for the rest of the day. At least she had Granny Moll on her side and that was a start.

–

Johnny found Hannah raising the fronts of the skirts of Josie and Marie's dresses a little, with the aid of a couple of kilt pins attached to ribbon bows, to allow the little girls to run around more freely.

"Is there anything they need?" he asked. "They've been so good today. If there's anything they want they only have to ask." He was bending from the waist and looking at the girls as he spoke. A shyness prevented him looking at their mother, a shyness which confused him.

"Go and smack that boy over there," Josie said haughtily. "He's been calling me names."

Without looking, Johnny guessed that Harold was the culprit.

Hannah laughed, a pleasant musical sound, and Johnny was caught by the humour and joined in. "I think we'll forgive him today, as he's new, shall we?" he said.

He walked Eirlys home with a sensation of doing a duty instead of it being a pleasure.

Eirlys lay on her bed for a long time without sleeping, wondering what had gone wrong. She went over all the conversations of the day. It was only during the one with Granny Molly Piper that she had presumed too much. Perhaps Granny Moll had repeated it and passed that presumption on to Johnny. Dismay filled her and she knew embarrassment would spoil her next meeting with Johnny.

–

On the morning after the wedding, Johnny's first thought was of Hannah and her merry laugh. He lay there in the bedroom he had shared with Taff all his life, and wondered why.

-

Eirlys waited for Johnny to call the following morning, a Sunday. She had promised the boys a walk through the fields to search for a likely place to build a treehouse and she had hoped that Johnny would go with them. When eleven o'clock came and he hadn't appeared she dressed the three musketeers, as they liked to be called, and set off.

Their route led them through the allotments where her father had once grown a few vegetables, though since the call to grow more food, urged on by leaflets issued by the Ministry of Food, more enthusiastic gardeners had clearly taken it over. Its neat, evenly dug surface was broken only where sprouts and a few leeks survived, all that remained of her father's half-hearted efforts.

On through the lanes until they came to the field where more vegetation had been cleared. The field belonged to Mr Gregory, the owner of a small holding of a few acres, who was increasing the crops he grew. As well as vegetables and a few flowers, he had ducks on the pond and chickens in the large hen-coops and wire runs. He was a well known figure, as he ran donkeys on the beach during the summer with his son, Peter, who was now away from home in the army.

Eirlys was strolling along enjoying the pleasant walk when she was startled by a yell of fright from Harold.

"What the 'ell's that!" he shouted, and after the initial shock, Eirlys saw to her amusement that the boys had been frightened by the sight of a cow walking along the lane, followed by the rest of the herd, returning from the fields to the milking parlour for milking.

"Surely you know what a cow looks like," she teased.

"No one told us they was that big!" Harold said in awe.

Eirlys explained their usefulness in providing milk, butter and cheese and, after studying the creature with disapproval on his face, Percival announced that he wouldn't touch another drop of milk till he was home where it came in bottles.

The oak tree at the furthest end of a sloping field was the site Eirlys had chosen but she knew that without Johnny or her father helping, she would be unable to do what she had promised.

There was a stone building in one corner of the field and as they approached, the boys running about and shouting in delight at the wide spaces where they were allowed to roam, she saw someone leaving the place and, for a moment, thought it was her father. But it couldn't have been him. Why would he be out here when he should be at home?

Curiously she began to head for the place to investigate but once the boys realised which tree would be "theirs" there was no holding them back. As though they had been climbing trees all their lives they clambered up into the ancient branches and for a while played happily as the tree became a house, then a mountain, then a ship.

When they had decided on the position of their house, Eirlys led them back to the corner where the stone barn stood. She was just about to enter when a voice called and she turned to see her father waving to her.

"Didn't I see you coming out of this old stone barn?" she asked. He shook his head.

"No fear, love. Mud, rubbish and rats is all you'll find in there." He waved an arm to encompass the whole field and went on, "There used to be a rubbish dump in this field. Crawling with rats it is. Best you keep right away."

"I will," she said with a shudder.

"What's this about a treehouse then?" he asked the boys. He listened to their plans and instructions and told them that he had found just the thing. "But a lot closer to home than this," he said, frowning at his daughter. "We need to be able to get hold of you quick if the air raid siren goes, don't we?"

"Sorry, Dad, I didn't think. I remember there was one here years ago and thought we might use the same spot."

By evening Morgan had the base of the treehouse made. When darkness came the work continued as he used his skill of splicing thick rope to make the all-important ladder. The boys went to bed contented, but Eirlys was disappointed that Johnny hadn't called. Everything had been so wonderful until the day of the wedding, so what had happened overnight to change it?

–

Johnny didn't go out that day. Several people had referred to Eirlys as his girlfriend and his denials were treated as a joke. Then Granny Moll cornered him and told him how pleased she was that Eirlys realised the importance of Piper's and would be more than willing to take her place if she married into the family.

"But Granny Moll, I'm not marrying her. Friends we are."

The knowledgable look that appeared on Moll's face as she said slowly, "We'll see," terrified him.

How easily things could get out of hand. Taff had been right, it had been a mistake to invite Eirlys to the wedding.

He needed to be very careful if he wanted to go on seeing her, and he did. There was no one he enjoyed being with more. But he wasn't ready to commit himself to a permanent partnership with her. Her kisses pleased him but had so far failed to engender that special excitement he knew they should.

Just how much of his reticence was due to the sight of Hannah as she tended her little girls he wasn't sure. But that was silly. Hannah was far too old for him, getting on for thirty. Yet in his imagination, when he felt his lips touch her soft, generous mouth it was a joy and a happiness, and he longed to make the dream a reality.

He decided that if he stayed away from Eirlys for a while, then casually invited her and the boys to go out for a walk, and avoided even the most casual of kisses, then things might return to how they had been. It was nice having a pretty girl on your arm. He enjoyed her company, but didn't want things to develop an impetus of their own and take him along a way he didn't want to go.

Three

Later that month, Morgan joined the local Air Raid Precaution group. Working shifts at the factory he was able to spend some time on most days helping to organise the rotas and deal with finding a place in which to meet and get the unit under way.

Because he had once owned his own business, the others presumed it was something he would do well, and it was. He wrote letters, persuaded the council to allow them to use a room in the school for their meetings, he acquired equipment and gathered information and set it out in leaflet form to distribute among the members of the organisation.

On being congratulated, he sighed and wished he had found it as easy to cope with running his own business. He had lacked the enthusiasm for the complicated store his father had left him; it had been too big and he felt he had failed because its success had been so essential for Annie and Eirlys. If he had been able to treat it as a hobby rather than a necessary full-time commitment, he might have managed better. It had been its importance that had made him fail, he was sure of that.

Annie didn't mind his involvement in the air raid precaution group although she did doubt its usefulness. The war showed no sign of ever coming to St David's Well; it was centred on France and how could that make their little seaside town vulnerable? She understood that the war effort needed everyone to do their bit, though, and she decided that looking after three evacuees between them was not enough.

"Perhaps I'll join too," she said to Morgan one day. "I can't do any evening work with the boys to look after, but I could help with the training classes, once I have been trained myself."

Morgan discouraged her. "Plenty of people at the moment," he told her. "It's later, when the novelty wears off and the enthusiasm wavers, that people will probably stop bothering. That's when we'll need new recruits."

Annie shrugged. She wasn't very keen to give up more of her time; there was plenty to do now she had evacuees as well as the part-time work in the bakery.

She didn't enjoy working in the shop. It was hard to forget that they had once owned a business and employed four people besides having help in the house. Reminded of it, she showed her irritability with Morgan and asked why he didn't do more to help her instead of spending so much time with the ARP.

"You let the allotment go and you never do the decorating that the house needs. I work all the hours the day holds and you just disappear and meet your friends."

"More than that, Annie," Morgan protested.

"It isn't even needed at the moment," she went on. "I think you men just use the meetings as an excuse to get out of the house and idle away a few hours."

Aware that she was steamed up and ready to argue, Morgan said nothing, just waited for her to continue.

"Years I've had to work at the bakery. Years of people talking to me as though I were their inferior. Ever since you lost the business your father left you. Comfortable we'd be now if you'd looked after it properly."

"I wasn't made to run a business. I tried to tell Dad, you know I tried to persuade him to sell. But he was convinced that given the chance I'd do all right."

"Wrong he was then, wasn't he?"

Morgan's father, Reginald Price, had owned a successful business fulfilling the various requirements of farmers and smallholders. Fencing, barbed wire, chicken wire and the like. Creosote and special paints. Sheep dip, harness soap and polishes, cart-grease, buckets. Everything he was asked for he somehow found room to stock.

Morgan had allowed the business to run down and down until it was sold as a property only, a property on which he had borrowed until there was nothing left. He had taken a year to pay off the remaining debts. He didn't think Annie would ever forgive him.

He waited until Annie had finished listing her complaints, then told her he was going to work. It was early, but sitting chatting to the men was kinder on his ego than listening to her telling him how he had failed everyone, including his poor dead father.

–

On Sunday morning, leaving the three musketeers helping Annie to make a cake, Eirlys went to take a closer look at the barn where she thought she had seen her father. There was no real reason, it was simply an excuse for a walk, a destination to head for. On an autumn day when the sun shone weakly with a pretence of warmth, it was a pleasure to be out of doors.

Around the entrance, deeply rutted mud revealed the regular visit of cows and she almost turned back but she forced herself to ignore the mess creeping up the sides of her shoes and delicately made her way across to where she could look inside, although by this time with little hope of seeing anything of interest.

The door was partially open and she squeezed inside and stood a while waiting for her eyes to become accustomed to the poor light. There was nothing there but old, abandoned farm machinery. A broken-down tractor that looked as though it had been cannibalised to repair others stood drunkenly against the far wall and other, less easily recognisable pieces of metal were strewn carelessly around amid empty sacks, coils of baling twine, oddments of barbed wire rusted and decorated with dead leaves and rotting hay.

Everything was covered in mud and there was an air of abandonment that suggested that little had changed over past years. She must have been mistaken. Her father couldn't have been coming out of here.

She smiled as she thought that the man must have been a tramp who had just been given some new clothes. Shirt, Fair Isle pullover, grey trousers and a sports jacket were almost a uniform for the working man on his day off these days.

She stared around looking for clues to suggest the barn's use as an occasional night shelter but found none. She had been wrong about the tramp. No one could live here. The man she saw had obviously been just passing by and had chosen not to talk to them – or, she thought with a grimace of distaste, he had been using the place as a urinal!

She noticed an area just inside the door that had been spread with paving stones and was clean of mud. On the wall above her head there was a nail on which hung a key. She smiled to herself. It must be a long time since anyone had bothered to lock this place against thieves.

Standing outside, thankful for the mild clean air away from the dankness within, she still didn't feel like going home. The air was fresh, the sky an unbelievable blue and although there wasn't any wind, leaves fell from branches as a reminder that summer was gone. She ran and tried to catch a falling leaf. Catching one as it left the tree and before it touched the ground meant a day of good luck in the year to come. Like a child, she ran about idiotically until she had caught three.

Thinking of Johnny Castle, she whispered to herself, "One for a proposal, one for our engagement, and one for our wedding day."

Through a hedge she spotted a caravan parked near the corner of the next field. Not a healthy place to choose if Dadda had been right about rubbish and rats. She climbed over the gate and walked around to examine it. The curtains were clean, as were the windows. Beside the steps a pair of wellingtons stood, thick with mud. These gave her the feeling that the place was occupied, even though the curtains were drawn and no smoke climbed out through the chimney. Afraid of being seen and accused of nosiness, she crept quietly away.

She didn't see the curtains move and a pair of eyes watch her until she regained the hedge and disappeared.

There was a stream at the bottom of the field in which the barn stood, and she made her way down and stood for a while looking at the water glistening as it made its way towards the distant sea. A movement to her right caught her eye and she turned to see Johnny's mother walking, head down, along the other side of the field. She was not wearing a coat and, even though the sun was bright, there was an autumnal nip in the air. The green cardigan and thin brown dress Irene Castle was wearing did not seem suitable for a country walk.

Eirlys was about to call out and go to meet her but held back. Johnny's mother was known to be ill and she didn't feel confident enough to engage her in conversation. She spoke strangely at times and Eirlys felt guilty, but not sufficiently so to walk across and say hello. Besides, the woman probably wanted to be on her own and wouldn't appreciate her intruding into her thoughts. She would tell Johnny and make the excuse that she was too far away.

She was pleased to have an excuse to call on Johnny. Home was suddenly a more enticing idea. Turning uphill away from the stream she cleaned her shoes as well as she could with the aid of a stick and handfuls of grass, and headed for Brook Lane.

Invited in, Eirlys removed her muddy shoes and explained that she had been for a walk and had seen Irene, Johnny's mother, inadequately dressed for the crisp autumn weather.

"Mam often gets upset and goes off for a walk on her own," Johnny said, signalling for her to lower her voice. "Dad worries about her but can't stop her. She'll be back when she's calmed down."

"But she was wearing a thin brown dress and no coat," Eirlys whispered. "Frozen solid she'll be when the sun goes in, in nothing but a skimpy green cardigan."

"She'll be back long before then."

Bleddyn had heard Eirlys arrive and he appeared from the kitchen bearing a tray filled with steaming cups. Gratefully she took one and settled near the roaring fire to drink it. Johnny didn't seem at ease and he hadn't sat down, just wandered around the room restlessly. It was as though he was expecting her to leave. He took the tea offered by his father and eventually sat down, not near her but at the table some distance away. Perhaps her visit had been ill timed and there was something he had planned to do.

"It's all right if you're going out, Johnny. I just called to tell you that I saw your mam, you don't have to change your plans for me, mind," she said cheerfully.

"Oh, I wasn't planning much. In fact, if you're free this afternoon we could go for a walk. I want to see Taff and Evelyn but you could come with me."

"Thanks, I'd like that. I'd like to see their rooms. Done them out nice, have they?"

Johnny shrugged. "They look fine to me."

As she was leaving, Irene came in and to Eirlys's surprise the woman was wearing a thick brown coat with a fur collar. Johnny looked at his mother then turned to Eirlys with a frown.

"I thought you said – Hello, Mam, had a nice walk?"

"Lovely, Johnny. And I'm starved. I hope your father has kept an eye on the meat and roast potatoes."

"Yes, I have," Bleddyn said, emerging from the kitchen. "And the vegetables are simmering nicely."

Eirlys looked at Irene and saw not a sick woman, but a woman with a face glowing with health, her dark eyes shining as though she had just been happily surprised. Surely she hadn't been mistaken again in the area where she thought she had seen her father? Had the sad woman she had watched walking along with her head dropping low, and without a coat, not been Irene Castle? The place must be haunted by ghosts of the living!

"I thought you said she wasn't wearing a coat?" Johnny demanded in a whisper.

"But, I saw her, and she had a green cardigan and a thin brown dress on," Eirlys said, confused.

At that moment Irene took off her coat and hung it on a peg. Eirlys stared when she saw that Irene was wearing the clothes she had described. Stumbling her way out of the door, unable to think what, if anything, to say, she shouted back, "Call for me later, Johnny."

"No, meet me at fifteen Curtis Street at three," Johnny replied. "Where have you been, Mam?" he asked his mother as she washed her hands and began to make the gravy.

"Oh, just looking at the shops. I want to choose something for Evelyn's birthday next month. D'you think she'd like a new purse?"

"Not across the fields?"

"Fields? At this time of year?" she smiled.

Johnny looked at his mother's shoes. They were clean and well polished. Eirlys must have been mistaken, or had made up the story about his mother. He wondered why.

He arrived at the rooms occupied by his brother Taff and his sister-in-law Evelyn long before Eirlys was expected. He told them Eirlys's story about seeing their mother.

"Johnny, that's an old trick, making an excuse to call on the boy you fancy. I remember finding a button and knocking on your door to ask if it belonged to Taff," Evelyn laughed. "She likes you and—"

"She couldn't find a button?" Taff finished with a grin.

"Mam said she hadn't been near the fields. She walked around the shops looking for a birthday present for you, Evelyn."

"Eirlys said she saw your mother in the fields?" Evelyn said.

"That's what she said. Why would she make up a story like that?"

71

"Evelyn's right, she likes you and wanted an excuse to call," Taff said.

"Trouble is, Taff, I don't think I like Eirlys as much as she likes me," Johnny said seriously.

"Then keep out of her way, make arrangements so you're never free when she calls; she'll soon realise you don't feel the same," Taff advised.

Evelyn looked thoughtful, staring into space with a frown crinkling her eyes.

"I have a feeling that she'll be a bit clingy," Johnny went on. "I like her, but how do I tell her it's no more than friendship, without hurting her feelings?"

"Perhaps Evelyn could have a word," Taff suggested.

Evelyn shrugged and agreed.

Eirlys arrived just before three and Evelyn invited her in. The rooms, which consisted of a bedroom, living room, a kitchen into which a small table and two chairs had been squeezed, and – rather grand – a shared bathroom, were examined and admired. Then, while the brothers sat in the small, neat living room, Evelyn took Eirlys into the kitchen to prepare tea.

Evelyn had made a cake, a few sandwiches and fruit and custard. As they were setting it out on the table, she said quietly, "You don't want to crowd Johnny too much, you know, or you'll frighten him away."

"What d'you mean?" Eirlys asked.

"Don't always be available when he wants to go out, make him see that you have a life of your own without depending on him for the social side."

"But I do sort of depend on him," Eirlys explained. "I like doing things with Johnny and I want him to know that."

"Men respect you more if you have other interests. It gives you something fresh to talk about when you're together."

"I work from nine till five thirty. I don't have a lot of time for hobbies. If I did, I'd want to share them with Johnny."

Evelyn placed the sandwiches on the centre of the freshly-ironed blue-edged white tablecloth and said firmly, "Don't drift through the days waiting for marriage, Eirlys, get out and do things while you have the chance."

"My job—" she began to explain.

"Come on, Eirlys, like so many young girls you dreamily sit in a safe job waiting for a safe marriage."

Stung by the harsh truth, hurt by hearing it from Evelyn, whom she had begun to consider to be a friend, Eirlys was relieved when Johnny stood up and offered to walk her home.

She said little on the short stroll to Conroy Street, said goodnight at the gate without giving Johnny the opportunity for a kiss. Going inside, she announced, "Dadda, I want to learn to drive, so I am joining the ARP."

"What? Never, my girl. I don't want you to even think of it. I don't know what's got into you and your mam to want to deal with the things we might have to face. So it's no! Right?"

Surprised at her father's vehemence, Eirlys insisted rudely, and on the verge of tears, that it was none of his business and she would go to the headquarters the following lunchtime and sign up.

Seeing the distress on her daughter's face, Annie Price urged her husband to be quiet.

"No, I won't hush up. I don't want our daughter having to face fires and injured people and risking death by driving around while bombs are falling." Morgan was adamant.

"What bombs?" Eirlys demanded. "If there was a chance of us being bombed we wouldn't have been chosen as a safe place for evacuees, would we? I am going to join and I am going to learn to drive."

Trying a different tack, Annie asked, "What if Johnny wants you to go to the pictures or somewhere? It will take a lot of your time, love."

"Johnny will have to go on his own. We all have to do something to help the war effort and if he doesn't understand that, well, it's too bad!"

"They've had a row," Annie mouthed to Morgan, who nodded and wisely said nothing more. But he was worried. He didn't want Eirlys knowing his movements. Spending a few evenings with the Air Raid Precaution group gave him some welcome freedom and his daughter or, worse still, Annie belonging to the same organisation would interfere with that.

"Perhaps we can persuade her to run the Girl Guides pack instead," he said to Annie.

"That doesn't have the same ring as fighting Hitler, now does it!" she retorted. "Let her go if she wants to. What harm could it do?"

Morgan didn't reply. He coped with his marriage and with Annie's disappointment by escaping sometimes. He needed time away from the home. The instigation of the ARP had been a lifesaver.

–

Eirlys began to think about the things her father had promised to make for the boys, among them a treehouse. She decided to go back to the area near the barn where she had seen the sturdy oak tree that would be perfect for a hideaway house for them.

As she approached the field she saw two dogs and recognised them as belonging to Evelyn's parents. She looked around and, seeing Evelyn some distance away, called out and began to make her way towards her. This was nice; someone with whom to discuss her ideas.

She called out again as she saw Evelyn stop, then turn away from her and hurry off. Surely she had seen her or heard her shout? Why hadn't she at least waved? On her way home she knocked at the house in Curtis Street but there was no reply.

-

Stanley, Harold and Percival had settled down in school surprisingly well. Stanley amused the others in his class with his spurious adulthood, understanding things of which they were unaware. His different background and upbringing added a freshness to the class that even the teacher – after a few misunderstandings – began to encourage.

Stanley's love of books led him to the library too, and he was reading *A Christmas Carol* to his brothers, reading ahead then changing the wording to make it easier for his brothers to understand. There weren't many books in the Price household but Morgan's copies of *The Three Musketeers* and *Twenty Years After* found their way into Stanley's bedroom, where he was allowed to read for an inch of a candle after the others were asleep. Eirlys knew he also sneaked a torch under his pillow and used that to read a while longer when the candle had burned down to its mark.

Stanley looked through the daily paper too and it was he who read out the tragic news of the *Royal Oak* being sunk at her base, Scapa Flow. That disaster was a shock to everyone and was on the lips of customers in every shop and bus passengers as they travelled to and from work. For many, it was the realisation that the enemy could strike them in their homes too. Sobered by the ship being struck with the loss of so many men when it was supposed to be safe, with that incident people were made more aware of being at war than by anything that had happened previously.

They were at the library one Saturday morning, when Eirlys had a rare few hours off, and they met Evelyn there. Smiling a welcome and walking over to talk to her, Eirlys was struck by the angry look on her friend's face.

"Evelyn? What's happened? Is anything wrong?"

"You should know that, Eirlys Price! I don't know how you can look Johnny in the face and smile your sweet innocent smile, knowing what you do. Shamed you should be."

Puzzled, Eirlys watched Evelyn walk out of the library, pausing only to turn and give one more devastatingly furious glare. She had no idea what had happened. Since they had last met she had been at work. She hadn't seen Johnny for several days. What on earth was wrong? First the incident near the barn when Evelyn had run away without speaking, and now this.

She had defied her father and gone along one lunchtime to make enquiries about joining the ARP. She had arranged to attend a lecture explaining the various ways she could help. Her enquiry about driving lessons was noted and she had thought at the time it might justify a visit to Johnny to ask for a few lessons from him in Piper's van. Now, after Evelyn's strange anger, she wondered how she would be received, and also whether a visit might result in an explanation. It was this thought that made up her mind. She would call on Johnny Castle and demand to be told what was wrong.

She knocked on Bleddyn and Irene's door that evening but there was no reply. A walk around to the back lane showed the house to be in darkness, but whether that was due to the blackout or because it was empty she had no way of telling. Disconsolately she walked back home.

"Johnny called," her mother told her as she went in through the back door. "Said he was going to meet Taff and Evelyn and would you like to go with him."

Remembering the attitude of Evelyn to her and Johnny's friendship, she decided she would be better staying away. Evelyn's home was not the place to go for explanations. She needed more neutral ground than Evelyn and Taff's home. Settling near the roaring fire she looked idly through some magazines, not taking much in, just using them as an excuse to allow her thoughts to wander.

There were several articles about handiwork. Mostly knitting but other crafts as well. One attracted her attention. It showed attractive rugs made from strips of material and the idea looked simple.

"Mam, have we any old coats I could cut up to make a rug for my room?"

"Rug-making? You? You'll never finish it. There's me having to complete the gloves you started last winter, and the angora jumper is still on its needles from months ago."

"This is different, it uses a sewing machine."

"You want me to let you loose on my precious sewing machine? You've got a hope, my girl!"

"Mam, you only use it to mend sheets and the like and you never let me use it."

"No, and ask yourself why. You muddle it up and it takes hours to sort it out. Bad-tempered you are when you get a needle in your hand. You lack the patience to learn and I lack the patience to teach."

"I thought I'd ask Hannah to show me how; I can't learn from you. We end up arguing every time."

The method was simple, and used as a base a piece of sacking. It entailed winding lengths of cloth or thick wool around a length of thick wire which had been bent into the shape of a large hairpin. By machining a line up through the centre, then removing the wire, a double row of loops was left. Then the wire was covered again and sewn as close to the first as possible. This was repeated until the piece of sacking was covered in loops of coloured wool or material.

Eirlys found Hannah working at her machine and when she explained about the rug-making Hannah was intrigued enough to experiment with the instructions. Two days later, Eirlys took delivery of a second-hand treadle sewing machine and a corner of her bedroom was transformed into a workshop.

Over several days, friends supplied material. The colours were mostly drab, with the occasional camel coat the only cheerful addition to the dark navy, browns and black. Sacking was easy to obtain; flour sacks from the bakery where Annie worked and any amount of potato sacks collected from the greengrocer where Johnny's cousin Beth worked. To Annie's surprise, Eirlys's interest began to grow. Instead of simply covering the sacking with strips of material, she developed ideas for designs, usually after a discussion with the talented Hannah, who helped work out some simple patterns on the sacking for Eirlys to follow. The whole family, including Stanley. Harold and even Percival were intrigued. They helped with the cutting of strips and Percival asked her to make one to take home to his mother.

"What about one for this treehouse then? When we get it," Harold demanded in his abrupt manner.

"No, but I will make you one for beside your bed," Eirlys promised.

The new hobby helped to take her mind off the mystery of Evelyn's sudden dislike and Johnny's absence. Johnny did call one evening. She was alone, her parents having taken the three boys to the pictures, and she jumped up, guessing it was he. Then she stopped and, in the darkness of the front bedroom, looked through the blackout curtain and watched as he picked up his bicycle and walked away.

–

Johnny was restless. Twice he had called on Eirlys and twice she had been out. Now he began to wonder just what Evelyn had said to her. He didn't want to display feelings stronger than he felt, but he did miss her. Wherever he went, whatever he did, it was more fun with Eirlys. Most of his friends were either courting seriously or flirting with several girls. He was the only one without female company and he was beginning to feel regret for worrying about Eirlys taking their friendship too seriously. He had obviously been mistaken and now he was on his own, a situation he found displeasing.

One evening, unable to wait any longer, he met her from work, standing outside the council offices and watching the door through which the staff left. She was the last to leave, emerging in deep conversation with a colleague. She smiled when he called to her and ran to greet him.

"Johnny, this is a surprise. Don't say you've come to walk me home?"

"Well, yes. I was in town and I thought as it was almost half five, I'd wait. D'you fancy a walk later?"

"I'd love it, but I've promised to go to a friend's house to collect some old coats."

"Old coats?" he laughed. "Don't tell me you're going into the second hand business?"

She was reluctant to tell him about the rug-making. He might misconstrue and think she was making it for her bottom drawer in preparation for their marriage – which it was; but that was a private thought, not for anyone else to know, especially not Evelyn!

"I could help you carry them?" he offered.

"Thanks, but perhaps we could meet tomorrow instead?"

This was agreed and a curious Johnny left her at her gate and walked slowly home.

An hour later Eirlys and the three boys set off, Stanley pulling a bogie cart borrowed from a neighbour, in which Percival was given a ride. They called at three houses where friends had promised Eirlys some unwanted coats and another where huge parcels of wool were handed to her, remnants of a sewing circle long since disbanded.

Although it was dark, a sliver of a moon gave a little light and near Curtis Street Eirlys saw Irene, Johnny's mother. She knew she wouldn't tell him; he wouldn't believe her. Besides, the woman was wearing a coat and there was nothing strange about her walking along the street properly dressed against the cold evening.

Irene stopped near a shop on the corner and as Eirlys passed they exchanged polite "good evenings" as though both were uneasy about the meeting.

"Nice bit of stuff in that coat," Harold said loudly. "Bit of old tom cat would trim the edges of our rug a treat, eh?"

A cowardly Eirlys pretended not to have heard.

Percival couldn't manage to sit on the top on the way back but Eirlys carried him piggyback while his brothers struggled with the assorted load. Annie grumbled about the chaos of collecting so much material, but was pacified when she realised how excited her daughter was with her new interest.

Morgan made shelves and Annie found a pine box which held the wool. A washing bath that had sprouted a leak and had never been thrown away was used to hold the cut-up strips of material. Eirlys was grateful for her parents' support, especially when they went on helping with the boring job of unpicking the coats and cutting the material into strips. Twice Johnny called but each time she was too busy to go out.

She was grateful to Evelyn for saying what she had, even though she had been very hurt by her strange antipathy since. She had never discovered what had changed Evelyn from a friend into someone so critical and unkind. Yet she might not have started on this fascinating hobby without her harsh words.

The first rug was a bit lumpy and uneven, but it found a place of honour beside the bed Stanley shared with Harold, with another promised for Percival's corner. Hannah came once to see how the work was progressing and declared herself impressed.

"You could earn yourself some money with these," she suggested. "Hand-made rugs are prized and you could use shades to suit the customer's colour scheme."

Eirlys laughed disparagingly but the idea didn't quite go away. The main difficulty was finding material in sufficient quantities and in suitable colours.

–

In despair, Johnny began working on the treehouse. Rain had prevented it being completed during the first weekend, but with a dry cold snap coinciding with a day off for both Morgan and himself, he arranged with Eirlys's father to carry the ready-made platform to the tree Morgan had chosen, and begin to fix it securely into place.

Working all morning and returning in the afternoon to stain the wooden structure an unobtrusive brown, they walked back to the house tired but satisfied.

"Tomorrow we'll have a grand opening," Morgan announced to the three boys who were eating their evening meal.

Eirlys smiled and blew her father a kiss. "Thanks, Dad."

"All except Percival," Annie said sternly, "unless he eats that egg on toast."

"I'm havin' a bit of bover with me crusts," Percival complained solemnly. Stanley reached out and helped himself to the crusts pushed to the side of his youngest brother's plate then Percival began to cry. "I wanted that bit! There was some egg on that bit!"

Annie ignored him and removed the plates to where Eirlys was washing up in the kitchen. Percival ate very little. The appetites of his brothers had increased and their improved weight had shown it clearly, but Percival's hadn't. He chewed for ages on a mouthful, lips open, dismay clouding his eyes, insisting that he only liked "proper" chips, by which he meant those from a chip shop.

"And sweets and chocolate," Annie said with a frown. "You never have any 'bover' with chocolate, do you?"

"Everyone can eat chocolate," he replied disparagingly.

"Cup of tea, Johnny?" Annie asked, hiding a smile. Percival really was a character. "There's egg on toast for you too, if you're hungry."

While her father and Johnny washed their hands, Eirlys and Annie cooked fresh meals and the two men settled down companionably to eat.

"Do you fancy going to see the treehouse?" Johnny asked Eirlys, but she shook her head.

"Tomorrow I'll come with you for the grand opening. Tonight I have something to finish."

"Tell him what you're doing for goodness' sake, Eirlys; he'll think you're making illegal whisky or something!" Annie said in exasperation.

So Johnny was taken up to her bedroom where cloth strips and hanks of wool covered the floor and a half-made rug hung over the single bed.

The most recently completed one was wrapped in brown paper and she unfolded it to show him. She had improved her technique and also her choice of colours, no longer taking randomly from the box of strips but choosing with greater care. The result was a simple pattern with each shape filled with a blend of hues making the overall rug an attractive and well-made item. This one had a diagonally striped pattern, with assorted blues filling some and assorted greens others, with a border of rust and browns.

"It's really smart. Is it for anyone special, or for your bedroom?" Johnny asked.

"This one is for Hannah to thank her for helping when I started. D'you think she'll like it?"

"She'll love it for the kind thought as well as for the quality."

They went together to give it to Hannah, who, as usual, was sewing, busily finishing off a child's dress she was making for a client. Johnny sat and watched as Eirlys and Hannah examined the rug and admired its colours. He watched Hannah and marvelled again at the aura of peace and calm surrounding her, when life for her must be so hard.

Disturbed by his attraction for Hannah, he kissed Eirlys with more enthusiasm than was wise. Remembering Evelyn's warnings, he said goodnight without suggesting anything about the following day. Although, he thought as he walked back to Brook Lane, the arrangement to meet and show Stanley, Harold and Percival their playhouse in the oak tree had already been planned.

He couldn't sleep for a long time, even though the work on the treehouse had pulled at a few rarely used muscles and he had been pleasantly tired when he and Morgan had finished it. It was thoughts of Hannah, not Eirlys, that drove away sleep. There was something very appealing about Hannah; a tranquillity overcame him in her presence. He told himself he was being foolish to even think about her in that way. She was too old for him, and Eirlys was a good friend in the way that would eventually lead to love. Why was he agonising about Eirlys? He knew deep down that when he had reached the stage when marriage was what he wanted, she was the one for him. But he couldn't put Hannah out of his mind.

–

When Annie Price went to the newsagent to pay the weekly paper bill, she thought she would give the three boys a treat and buy them some sweets. They didn't receive pocket money, except the occasional two-shilling postal order their mother sent for them to share. She chose smarties and handed the money to Mrs Downs, the manager of the shop.

"There's a face for sweets young Percival's got," Hetty Downs smiled. "He eats them as fast as his brother buys them, hardly waiting till he gets out of the shop. I tease him that I put them in a bag for fear of him biting my fingers off."

"Percival? Our Percival you mean? I don't think so. He doesn't get money for sweets that often. Poor his mother is and she can't send money very often. There's no father, see," she explained confidentially. "Morgan and I buy for them occasionally and I know Eirlys does, but they don't have money to spend of their own."

"Someone is being generous then," Mrs Downs insisted. "Come in here two or three times a week for sweets, they do."

"No wonder he'll never eat his dinners!" Annie frowned. "But who is giving them money?"

Annie asked the boys whether they had received any money from their mother without telling her and the answer was a firm "No."

"Then who is giving you the money to buy sweets several times a week?" she demanded.

Harold and Percival looked at the oldest brother, utterly confident that he could explain.

"All right, I'll tell you," he said. "We was in the park and I found a ten-shilling note. I went to the post office and got it changed into shillings and I've been spending it on sweets because that's what Percival likes to eat. Never no dinners, just chocolate and cakes and stuff like that."

"Chocolate an' cakes," affirmed Percival with a knowl-edgeable nod or two.

Annie looked thoughtful. Ten shillings was a lot of money and they should have handed it in to the police station, although she could understand the temptation to keep it. But how long would ten shillings last if what Mrs Downs had told her was true? Three or six bars of chocolate each time would soon see the end of a ten-shilling note. She wondered uneasily whether the boys were stealing. She couldn't accuse them, but decided that in future she would keep an extra careful check on the amount of money in her purse.

Stanley was thoughtful too. His decision was to use different shops for his purchases. Going to the same place where Mrs Price bought her newspapers had been a stupid mistake. That Mrs Downs would know them too well. He made a mental list of the sweet shops and cake shops he could use, determined that Percival wouldn't be deprived of his sweets and cakes, whatever he had to do to keep him supplied.

–

Johnny called on Eirlys on Friday evening and found her clearing the dishes from their meal. He felt ill at ease, still unsure what his sister-in-law had said to Eirlys to discourage her from thinking of him too seriously.

"Evelyn and Taff are going into Cardiff tomorrow. Fancy coming?" he asked her. "They want to do some shopping and we could eat out and perhaps go to the theatre for a change."

Eirlys's heart began to thump unpleasantly. This was a chance to persuade Evelyn to tell her what was going on in her mind.

"Please?" he added as the silence lengthened.

She turned and smiled at him in a way that made his heart behave oddly. "I'd love to, Johnny. What time are we leaving?"

"About two. Taff fancies going to Roath Park to feed the ducks, would you believe? I think he's trying to build a few memories before he goes into the army."

"Don't talk about it," Eirlys shivered.

"I'll be off soon, sure to be. I only hope Dad can cope all right without us. Mam isn't much company for him these days."

"I did see her without a coat that day, you know. I didn't imagine it."

"What could she be doing?" Johnny said, as though believing her, although he still wasn't convinced that Eirlys hadn't mistaken another woman for his mother.

Sensing his doubts, she added, "I described her clothes before she took her coat off, didn't I?"

"Mam is behaving oddly," he admitted. "I think Dad is afraid she'll get worse and he won't be able to cope."

"Has she always gone off like this?"

"I think she might have done, but Dad has always protected us from knowing."

"It isn't – it isn't other men?"

"I think Dad would know if she went off with other men," he said disparagingly. "No, it's nerves. A lot of women suffer with nerves and it shows itself in different ways." He was quoting his father's explanation. "Thank goodness it isn't drink or fighting," he added, quoting Bleddyn again.

–

Eirlys felt uneasy as she waited for Evelyn and Taff to join them. Why had she agreed to this day out? She began searching her mind for an excuse to go back home.

When they arrived at the station, it was swiftly obvious that Evelyn didn't want to show Taff or Johnny how she felt because she greeted her with every impression of pleasure. It was only when they were on their own that she allowed her dislike to show.

When Johnny and Taff went to check on the times of the return trains, Eirlys turned to Evelyn and demanded angrily, "What is the matter with you? What am I supposed to have done?"

"You know very well what's happened." Evelyn began to walk away and Eirlys pulled on her arm roughly to make her face her.

"If you won't tell me, then will you at least stop creating this atmosphere and ruining my day out? I work long hours and an afternoon out with Johnny is a rare treat. I don't think you should spoil it. If you can't bear my company, please go home now, for Johnny's sake if not mine!"

"You Prices think you can do anything and get away with it!"

"Get away with what?" Eirlys said in exasperation.

"You two look serious," Johnny said as he and Taff returned unnoticed by the two girls.

"Yes," Eirlys said lugubriously, to cover their argument, "I've brought the wrong colour lipstick." It raised a smile and the atmosphere cleared.

The four of them did manage to enjoy their day out. The uneasiness remained hidden from the two brothers and Evelyn made no reference to the affectionate way Johnny and Eirlys behaved, to Eirlys's relief. When she stepped on to the train to travel home, and sat close to Johnny, arm in his, head on his shoulder, she was light-hearted and convinced that her reticence toward Johnny over the past days had cleared the air and allowed Johnny to decide whether or not they should continue to see each other. Surely nothing would spoil their courtship now? Evelyn had said nothing more. She was happier than she had been for a long time.

Johnny was contented too. The four of them had enjoyed their day and there hadn't been a moment of dissension. Plans were suggested and carried out amicably. Laughter had been plentiful and he didn't think there was a cloud in his particular sky.

He left Eirlys after a loving kiss and walked home, passing the house of Hannah's parents, where Hannah lived with her two little girls. Suddenly it was as though a cloud had burst and brought rain and storm and misery.

–

Eirlys was too excited to go straight into the house. She stopped at the door, the key in her hand. She could hear the radio playing dance music and the buzz of conversation, rising and falling, punctuated occasionally by thumps as her mother banged to emphasise a point. They were arguing again, her father's voice low, reasonable, her mother's more shrill and obviously angry. She was glowing with the joy of Johnny's kiss, dreamily reliving it and allowing her thoughts to travel with it to other, as yet unlearned delights. Walking in to a quarrel would be a cruel awakening.

She had hoped that after all these years the quarrelling would have ceased. Dadda losing the business left to him by his father had been a devastating blow. But it was years ago and life had moved on. Mam had been forced to find work and she, Eirlys, had given up hope of further education. Her father had worked cheerfully enough in the factory now making munitions and she had found a good position in the council offices, thanks to their determination. Paying for her to learn shorthand and typing had been a struggle and she was grateful to her parents for depriving themselves of other things to do so.

She looked up, forgetting for a moment the blackout which enclosed the house and gave no clue to what was happening within. The boys would be in bed and fast asleep by this time. The euphoric mood expanded to remind her of how grateful she was for the way her parents had accepted Stanley, Harold and little Percival. Fortunately they had been very little trouble, apart from Percival's refusal to eat proper meals, handing much of what he disliked to his brothers below the level of the table, in the hope of not being seen. Like Annie, she sometimes wondered how he managed to survive on the little he ate.

A number of the evacuees in the town had already gone back home. There were others who had been giving problems to the families who had taken them in. Their three musketeers had settled well and for that she knew her parents could take most of the praise.

Moving away from the house and its warring occupants, she walked back on to the pavement and stood for a while on the corner of Conroy Street allowing the quiet of the night to settle her before she went inside. She still savoured the happiness of the day out with Johnny and the resumption of their friendship, and was not yet ready for it to end.

There was no moon, yet she gradually made out shapes and began to recognise buildings and even the lamp post into which several people had walked when the blackout had begun. A sound across the street disturbed her and a cat skidaddled across the road before disappearing into a hedge.

A light shone brightly out of the side of a house opposite. She put a hand to her mouth in alarm, imagining a lone German plane with a beady-eyed pilot, circling around waiting for such an opportunity, then laughed at her stupidity. On tiptoe she crossed the road to investigate and saw, coming backwards out of a side window, a figure. A thief? Had she disturbed a thief? If so, what should she do?

Fear of confronting a dangerous and angry burglar ran through her mind but she hurried towards him, still making hardly a sound. He was smaller than she expected, only a boy. Grabbing him around the shoulders as he touched the ground, she turned him and gasped in horror.

"Stanley!"

Four

Stanley stood at the kitchen table red-faced and defiant, while Morgan and Annie threw question after question at him. He refused to answer, except to say, "Got plenty they have. They won't even know they've gone!"

"That's not the point," Annie said in exasperation. "It isn't yours. And breaking into someone's house and taking things belonging to them is a criminal act."

Threats of calling the police didn't move him. Jaw tight, eyes defiant, he stared into space and told them he didn't care. Threats of every kind of punishment had no visible effect. Sending him away from his brothers did.

"If we call the police they will probably take you away from us and who will look after Harold and Percival if you aren't here to look after them?" Eirlys asked softly.

Stanley's head rose and he looked at her with questioning eyes.

"Don't let them take me away," he said, and Eirlys saw not a defiant thief but a very frightened young boy. She opened her arms and he clung to her while sobs racked his body.

Annie turned away, affected more than she would have imagined by the little boy's fear. She had tried to remain aloof from the evacuees, knowing their sojourn would be brief, but they were only children and had been taken away from everything familiar without fully understanding why. "I'll make you some cocoa," she said, glad of the excuse to leave them and hide her own distress.

Stanley eventually told them that the money they had found in his pockets had been in a rent book on a shelf and there were several shilling pieces he had taken from a pile stacked near the gas meter ready to feed it when needed.

"We'll sort it out," Eirlys murmured. "No one will take you anywhere. Dadda will find a way of getting the things back to their owner, won't you, Dadda?"

Morgan looked at the things taken from Stanley's pocket and wondered. Beside the one pound seven and sixpence, there was a small ashtray, a cut-glass posy jar and a wooden musical box, plus a bag containing some biscuits. "Were you going to sell them, Stanley?" he asked. "Why? Is there something you want that we don't give you? And why the biscuits? I mean, why take food?"

"The biscuits were for the birds in the park," he explained. "Percival likes to feed the birds."

"And the rest?"

"They was for our mum. She ain't got nothin' like this. They got so much nice stuff they have it packed away in the back of a cupboard where no one can see 'em. Waste, that's what that is!"

"You still can't take things that don't belong to you," Eirlys admonished.

Tired out with the shock of discovery and the questioning, Stanley yawned and Annie reappeared and told them she was putting him back to bed.

"Now what?" Morgan asked, rubbing his face with his hands in a kind of despair. "If they were mine I'd give them a wallop they wouldn't forget, but how can I deal with someone

93

else's kids over something like this? Out of my depth here I am, Eirlys."

Eirlys was thinking and after a while she suggested a solution. "If we hide the stuff somewhere far away from this house, then tell the police we'd found it, they might find the owners and return it all."

"Where do you suggest?" her father asked.

"Well, there's a barn on the field leading down to the stream. Cows gather there so there wouldn't be any footprints to find. If we covered some of them with mud?"

"Why that smelly old place?"

"Because it's a place people are unlikely to go."

"It might work," Morgan agreed.

"I'll take them on Saturday. Johnny will help."

The plans to hide the stolen items were delayed, however. Eirlys's boss, Mr Johnston, called her into his office on Monday morning and told her he needed her to work on the following Saturday. They were expecting a visit of important dignitaries who would arrive on Friday evening and would attend a special meeting that would go on through lunch on Saturday. It was Eirlys's responsibility to arrange hotel accommodation, organise drivers to ferry them about over the weekend, as they wished to travel around the area, and also to prepare luncheon for sixteen people at the office on Saturday. It was something she had never been asked to do before and was at once daunted by the importance of it. Mr Johnston hinted at promotion and she knew she couldn't refuse.

She felt guilty at letting Stanley down; they had hoped to have the whole unpleasant situation dealt with before Sunday. Yet she felt excitement too. She enjoyed her work and had ambitions to make progress, even though marriage to Johnny was her strongest desire. Or was it? Johnny, yes, but giving up her job was beginning to be a less attractive prospect. She realised then how difficult it could be to have Granny Moll insisting on making Piper's the number one priority.

She felt guilty at this new attitude to work as she remembered her declaration to Granny Moll of the importance of the family business. She might not have that commitment after all. Allowing her imagination to soar, she thought that she could even become manager of a whole section one day. Although those positions were usually held by men, with the outbreak of war and men being conscripted, she knew she had a better chance than ever before. That thought brought on more feelings of guilt. Perhaps being selfish was an essential part of success?

In the office that morning she spent a lot of time on the telephone making bookings, then writing confirmations, besides running across the town to speak to people who had no telephone. She was exhausted when half past five came.

The catering was in the hands of a firm who supplied cafés and hotels and, although costly, they were reliable and that, she had decided at the outset, was her number one priority for this special weekend.

The culmination of a frantic week was a smooth-running weekend in which she acted as minutes secretary taking notes at the Saturday meeting. The main subjects under discussion were the delivery and erection of air raid shelters and other needs, beside ordering some of the many leaflets being distributed giving information and advice to the local people. It was the ARP and the WVS who figured large as these things were discussed, and Eirlys went home at three o'clock to tell her father all she had learned.

Although she was very tired she went to the barn with Johnny as promised, late in the afternoon, as darkness was falling. To add to the gloom it was raining when they set off, Johnny carrying Stanley's stolen treasures: heavy relentless rain that seemed set to continue for hours, with gusts of wind to add to the torrent. They felt the cold immediately, carrying boxes in their arms and being unable to swing them to keep warm. Wearing wellingtons and heavy raincoats they walked with heads bent against the driven rain and were relieved to see that a dozen Hereford cows were standing near the entrance to the barn.

"Good. They'll mess up our footprints within minutes," Eirlys said and they went into the barn, their boots squelching in the deeply churned mud and sometimes becoming lodged so that Johnny needed to pull her free. They messed up the objects a little then left them and made their way back to the slightly less soggy grass.

As they were about to turn for home, Eirlys hesitated. "I wonder if that was the first time Stanley had broken into houses and stolen things?" she mused. "It might be worth a look in the treehouse in case he's hidden other stuff there."

Johnny agreed and after wiping the worst of the smelly mud and manure from their boots they headed for the oak tree not far from Mr Gregory's smallholding.

The walk through the dark countryside was neither pleasant nor romantic. They talked a little, mostly about Stanley who, at ten, had taken responsibility for his brothers and even tried to help his mother with beautiful gifts.

"He's such a mixture of adult and child," Eirlys said. "He's lost the chance of a normal happy childhood, hasn't he, having to grow up so fast?"

"Perhaps, but people aren't all the same. Living in a flat in London, he wouldn't have had the same values or expectations as the children around here. He probably thinks we're deprived."

He waited to help her climb the gate into Sally Gough's field where Mr Gregory sometimes kept his donkeys. Taking her arm as she clambered down, he didn't let go when they were both safely over. "It's very dark," he explained. "A torch is useless and I don't want you to fall over this hummocky grass."

"I can't see a thing," she laughed, holding him tightly. He guided her to where the branches of the oak tree were just visible in the dark night.

"I'll go up," Johnny offered and, feeling rather than seeing, he took the rope-ladder from its hiding place, shinnied up and went inside and carefully used his torch. "Eirlys! Come and look at this lot!"

With difficulty, holding the rope and occasionally a branch, she managed to reach the four-by-three-foot building set in a wide fork of the old tree. The floor was made from wooden planking and the sides had three narrow windows and a doorway through which to enter. As she crawled in there was very little light from Johnny's torch and it took a while for her eyes to accustom themselves to the darkness and the thin beam. Johnny was standing bending over on the far side and between them was a piece of old carpet. Moving it he revealed an assortment of household objects: a teapot and silver-and-glass sugar bowl and matching jug, a few plates and a picture of some children playing on the sands. There also were two books, one of which was about Orlando the Marmalade Cat and had a small stick as a bookmark showing the reader was half-way through.

"Stanley is probably reading it to Harold and Percival," Eirlys whispered. "He tries to make a life for the boys that's separate from us. He knows this life is a temporary one and constantly reminds his young brothers that their home is not with us, not to forget the life they left behind when there were only the three of them and their mother."

A cardboard box was underneath the rest and while Johnny shone a torch, Eirlys opened it. Wrapped carefully in layer after layer of newspaper was a delicate porcelain cup and saucer. In lustre, with a wide top and an ornate handle, it was a very pretty object.

"The boy has an eye, I'll give him that," Johnny whispered. "He doesn't steal rubbish."

"Why hasn't it been missed?"

"Because they're someone's treasures, stacked away for safety and probably only used on very special occasions. My mam has stuff like that, hasn't yours?"

"Oh yes," Eirlys agreed wryly. "In fact, I recognise the teapot!"

The rain continued to fall around them like a curtain and although there was no warmth and hardly room to move, they settled themselves as comfortably as they could to discuss what they should do.

"Funny that your father chose this tree," Johnny mused. "I wonder why?"

"He said the other was too far from the house in case of air raids."

"Yet this one isn't any closer, is it?"

"Rats," she said.

"What?"

"The area near the old barn is infested with rats, or so he said. Although perhaps this tree was an easier one in which to build."

"Fond of the boys, isn't he? Wants to do what he can to make them feel wanted. Everyone needs to be wanted."

His voice was low and intimate, their bodies were touching in the most exciting way and he seemed hesitant to move.

Eirlys began to feel tense, wondering whether Johnny felt as aware of her closeness as she did of his. Then a mundane remark made her realise she had been alone in her thinking.

"We ought to take this and put it with the rest of the stuff, in the barn," Johnny said.

"Except the teapot," she laughed. "Little devil. He told us he wanted to take all his loot back for his mother."

"Strange that he stole from you."

"He thought anything hidden away had no value." She chuckled. "He'd have had a job getting all this into the little case he brought with him!"

Eirlys wondered when Johnny would suggest leaving their uncomfortable perch. She didn't want to. In spite of the discomfort of soggy clothes and mud-covered hands and boots that felt as though they were encased in lead, she could have stayed close to him all night without complaint.

Struggling in the confined place, Johnny put an arm around Eirlys's shoulders and she was glad of the warmth of him. She snuggled closer and they stared unseeing out of the entrance, their wet cheeks touching, listening to the gentle hissing of the rain through the leaves above them. It was a cosy sound and if only they had been dry it would have been heaven. Now and then a gust of wind stronger than the others seemed to move the weaker branches of the sturdy tree and they clung closer.

The kiss when it came was sweet and gentle and Eirlys thought she had never felt greater happiness than this reunion with Johnny in the peculiar hideaway in the oak tree surrounded by the spoils of a child's robbery.

They were both reluctant to leave but knew that if they were to transport the items from the tree and put them in the barn, they had to get it done soon, in case another lone walker took shelter and discovered the items already left there.

Carefully rewrapping the teapot, the cup and saucer and the rest, they carried them down and set off to retrace their steps to the barn where the patient cows stood exactly where they had left them.

"I hope they shiggle about a bit after we've gone," Johnny said. "We don't want our footmarks to be seen."

"Hardly a problem; we're going to tell the police we found them while sheltering, aren't we?"

Johnny went back with her and they explained to her parents about the extra items. Harold and Percival were listening while Stanley read to them out of the most recent Beano comic, which had been first issued a few months before. Harold laughed at Stanley's ad libs and his interpretation of the drawings but Percival was stony-faced, as usual refusing to be amused.

When Johnny and Eirlys explained to Annie and Morgan about removing the treasures to the barn, their explanations reached Stanley's ears and he handed the comic to his brothers. "Now, I've started you off, and you got to see how much you can work out for yerselves."

On being confronted with the teapot he looked, shamefaced, at Annie and explained, "I took it ages ago, when we first came, and I thought we was going 'ome the next day.

I've been tryin' to get it back without you knowin'." He was shouting and Eirlys knew he was close to tears.

As Annie turned to place the teapot on a shelf, he suddenly grabbed a mac from the back of the kitchen door and ran from the house.

It was Johnny who ran after him, talked him into calming down and brought him back to the house. Johnny said nothing but secretly admired the boy for doing what he could to take care of his family in a situation for which nothing could have prepared him. Stanley was only a child himself, although to hear him talk you'd imagine he was an old man, he thought with a chuckle.

–

The police called and listened to Eirlys's explanations about finding the stolen goods when she and Johnny were sheltering from the rain.

"Sheltering from the rain? Wasn't it raining when you set off, then?" the constable teased. "I don't know, what it is to be young, eh, Mr Price?"

Eirlys's father grinned and winked at Johnny. "I reckon that's why half of us get married, because there's nowhere to go for a bit of a kiss and cuddle, don't you, constable?"

Eirlys blushed and Johnny looked uncomfortable.

A few enquiries were made around the area and most of the items were returned to puzzled owners. They hadn't been missed.

"Nor would they be, not till Christmas, and then we'd have been searching the house trying to remember where we'd put them," one old lady laughed as she claimed two pretty blue lustre fruit bowls.

"I wonder who owns the caravan in the field next to the barn?" Eirlys asked anxiously. "Someone there might have seen Stanley there and will tell the police."

"Oh, it's a mess of a place, used now and then by a couple from Brecon when they want to do a bit of walking," Morgan explained. "Certainly never in winter. I met them once. Better than a tent, I suppose, but only just."

The excitement and fears faded. Nothing more was heard about the robberies and the Price family were convinced that the Love boys, especially Stanley, had learned a powerful lesson.

Eirlys eventually went to a training session organised by the ARP but she was disappointed. The request regarding her driving lessons had been noted, but, it was explained, "We have to use the skills you can bring to us and yours, Miss Price, is the important skill of typing, making rotas, that sort of thing." She guessed her father was responsible. When Mr Johnston gave her a ten-shilling increase in her wages and told her she would be kept extra busy, she happily accepted and told the ARP officer that she no longer had the time to help.

Her next task at work was changing the offices around so a room could be cleared to hold the fire-watchers, who would be on duty every night once the air bombardments, which were already expected, had begun.

Moving furniture, placating staff who had to accept smaller accommodation or even share with a colleague wasn't easy but the job was completed in a week. To be given a job to do and told to use her own initiative to do it was frightening at first, but immensely satisfying. She was hardly at home in the days following the "discovery" of the stolen items. It was cold and misty and she wondered how Stanley and Harold and Percival were amusing themselves.

Morgan had made them a sled in readiness for the snow that would come after Christmas and possibly before. He had also promised them a bogie cart using a set of pram wheels and some planks of planed wood when the better weather returned.

Annie still complained about the amount of work they caused, rarely missing a chance to remind Morgan of the big house they had lost and the servant they had employed to enable her to work for various charities. Morgan seemed unaffected by her tirades and having Stanley, Harold and Percival clearly added joy to his life. He told Eirlys several times that he dreaded the day when they would go home.

—

Annie didn't spend a lot of time talking to the evacuees. It had been Eirlys's choice to take them in and it was her responsibility to look after them, she reminded her daughter when her help was requested at an inconvenient moment. But the distress on Stanley's face when he had been threatened with separation from his brothers had upset her.

"What do you think of my taking the boys up to London for the day to see their mother?" she suggested one evening when the boys were settled in bed. "They have to stay with us, but if they think they can visit now and then, it might be easier for them."

"Or they might refuse to come back, or Mrs Love won't let them! And where would that get them? Blown up and out of it. Is that what you want? Hitler might not have sent any bombs yet, but he will. And the IRA have planted a few, haven't they? Some of them have been sent down, but there'll be more. Take them back to London for a visit? Damn stupid idea, Annie!" Morgan spoke with unusual anger. "If those boys go back home they'll never come back and settle."

"You'd miss them, wouldn't you, Dadda?" Eirlys said.

"Well, yes, I definitely would."

"What if I use it as a promise, then, for good behaviour?" Annie said. "A bit cruel maybe, but I will take them, one day soon. There hasn't been any bombing yet, or I wouldn't suggest it. We should be safe enough. I don't want to have my head blown off any more than theirs."

Next morning she put the idea to the three boys. "Would you like me to take you back to your mam, just for a visit? You could all write her a letter asking her to find somewhere for me to stay. Then you can come back knowing she's all right. Or if you prefer, she could come and stay with us for a night or two. How would that be, eh?"

"I want to go home to see Mum," Percival said. "I eat when it's chips from the chip shop, don't I, our Stanley?"

"Not yet," Annie warned, "but soon. Only as long as you behave yourselves, mind. Any stealing, either sweets or anything else and you won't go, do you understand me, Stanley Love?"

"Yes, Annie Price," he replied cheekily.

–

The postman was becoming increasingly important in the town of St David's Well as elsewhere. Families waited for news of their sons and husbands and the Love brothers were no different. Teresa Love was not a great letter writer, but she managed to scribble a short message for her sons every other week. Eirlys made sure they wrote to her, Percival laboriously writing a brief message as a PS on the end of Stanley's letter, with Stanley's patient help.

One morning the postman brought two letters for the boys, the usual scribble and a reply to Annie's suggestion that she take the boys to visit her.

This excited the boys and they whooped and cheered as they danced around the small kitchen until everyone was laughing. Plans were discussed, but Annie made sure they understood that no date had been fixed.

By the same post Eirlys heard from Ken Ward, who she learned had been turned down by the army but had found a job with the NAAFI, met someone called Max Moon and hoped to join a concert party travelling around entertaining the forces. Ken had a pleasant voice, she remembered, and also played the mandolin well.

She wrote straight back, friendly, affectionate, giving him impersonal news about the people he had known. She ended by wishing him luck.

She had no regrets about telling Ken goodbye, but hoped they would always be friends, wherever they ended up. His letter did unsettle her though. Everyone was doing something to support the war effort; there must be something she could do!

Annie was late leaving the bakery. She had been serving Hannah and had spent a while talking to her after locking the shop for lunchtime closing. She dashed into the house, handed Morgan his packed lunch, which she had bought in the shop, and saw him hurry off to work for the two o'clock shift. When he had left for work she settled to the sewing basket which was overflowing with the boys' clothes, needing darning, replacement buttons and other repairs.

"I would never believe how boys rip and dirty their clothes," she complained to Eirlys who was home for lunch that day. "I've heard people tell me how lucky we were to have a girl when you were born, and I didn't know what they meant until now." She held up a pullover that had once been a carefully knitted Fair Isle design but which was now a tangle of pulled woollen threads with no recognisable pattern at all. "Climbing trees on the way home from school they were. This was given to me by Mrs Daniels last week. Almost new it was. I daren't let her see it now!"

"I was given a pile of wool yesterday, to knit things for the Christmas Bazaar in aid of soldiers' comforts. There might be something suitable to repair it," Eirlys said without much hope.

"I doubt it! We've been told to keep all our rags for some savings scheme or other – well, they can have this for a start-off," Annie said, throwing the offending article in the corner of the couch.

"Why didn't Dadda want me to go with him to the ARP meetings, d'you think?" Eirlys asked.

"Tell the truth, I think he and his cronies like a bit of an evening out without the women, and you'd cramp his style. They go for a drink after and he wouldn't take you, would he?"

"I'd still like to help, Mam, once things at work have calmed down a bit. Everyone is doing something."

"Heavens, girl, you do plenty! All those extra hours of work and no overtime pay? What's that if it isn't helping the war effort?"

"Will you have a word?"

"I'll try, but I don't think he'll be persuaded. You know what men are like, wanting to get together 'off the leash' as they call it. Talk a lot of old nonsense and act the fool like a bunch of schoolboys they do. They're all the same."

Morgan didn't go to the factory at two o'clock the next day. He drove a van on an errand for a friend, missing a shift, hoping Annie wouldn't query the difference in his pay packet. When the van spluttered to a stop seven miles from St David's Well he gave a groan. Now what could he do? He turned to the woman sitting beside him and after a brief conference and an affectionate kiss she left him and caught a bus back home.

Fortunately there was a phone box not far away and he telephoned his daughter at her office in greatly exaggerated panic.

"Don't tell your mam, she'll kill me for missing a shift," he said. "Can you find your Johnny and ask him to help? Keep his tongue in check he will, for sure."

Eirlys gave him Moll's number as very few people had a telephone and Piper's didn't run to the expense of providing Bleddyn with one.

Eventually, after a second even more frantic call from Morgan, Eirlys used her lunch hour to go and find Johnny. He took the firm's van and went to Morgan's rescue, and, on seeing the ladies' scarf fallen down between the seats, promised to say nothing about the incident.

He told Eirlys though. "Seems he was giving a lift to a lady waiting for a bus that had failed to arrive and he knows how suspicious your mam would be," he laughed. "Left her scarf she did or I'd never have known."

"You're sure it was innocent?" Eirlys asked. "It's odd him losing a whole shift to do a favour for someone and then giving a lift to a mysterious woman."

"Some people seem to court trouble and it's often good-natured people like your father," Johnny told her.

Thinking of Ken and his recent letter, Eirlys was reminded about how important it had been for her to stay at home where she could keep the peace between her parents.

–

Johnny went home and under promise of secrecy, told Bleddyn and a disinterested Irene something of Morgan's problem.

"What was he doing?" Bleddyn asked.

"Collecting some leaflets from Cardiff on how to deal with incendiary bombs was what he told me," Johnny replied, "I didn't see any, mind!"

Irene walked away from the table and put on her coat with the fur collar.

"You aren't going out again?" Bleddyn complained. "Only now this minute you've come in!'

"If I don't get some fresh air I can't sleep," Irene replied.

"Shall I come with you?" "No, I'll be all right."

–

Irene kept well away from the field in which the barn stood. The police had hinted that they would be watching it in case the thief returned with more of his stolen goods. Instead, she went along the lane towards the next village, turned in through a farm gate and walked around the field, feeling her way in the darkness, wary of unseen branches, guessing how far she had come before crossing to come up against the caravan. Three knocks and the door was open and she slipped inside.

"Hello love, it's perishing cold. Isn't there anywhere else we can meet?"

"I've got the fire ready to light."

"Well done, love. Well done." Slipping off the wellingtons she kept hidden in the barn, she stepped inside.

–

Eirlys was walking out of the office a few days later when a tall, thin young man approached her.

"Miss Price?" he asked hesitantly. "Eirlys Price?"

"That's me," she replied pleasantly, amused at the height and the thinness of him and the sparseness of the red hair on his head. "You are… ?"

"My name is Max. Max Moon and I've been sent to ask for your help. I am starting to arrange for children's entertainment in the locality next summer and although it's looking a long way ahead, we want to get a few programmes in place."

The name rang bells but she couldn't place it. Frowning, she said, "I'm sorry, there must be a mistake. I don't know anything about children's entertainment. I think you want to talk to the Pipers who work on the beach. They'll know all about what's available."

Max Moon took a pad from a pocket and ran a pencil down a list of names. "Would that be Mrs Molly Piper and her family?" he asked.

"If you wait while I go and tell Mam I'll be late, I can take you there," she offered. "I know them quite well."

He thanked her and, bending slightly to talk to her and referring to his neatly written list, explained a little more of his plans.

"With the war creating shortages of fuel, we are already starting to think about encouraging people to stay at home instead of going away for a holiday," he explained.

"Going away for a holiday? Who does that? I've never been further than Cardiff!" she laughed.

"Well, you live in a town where people come for a break, so you know what I'm talking about and you can imagine the saving in travel costs if they all stayed home."

"I know a few families here who would go hungry too! We depend on holiday-makers and day-trippers," she said. "What d'you think will happen to this town if we discouraged visitors?"

"It has been worked out that the local people would make up for the lack of visitors and there would be very little difference in the income of the town. Everyone would cater for their own local people, that's all."

"Rubbish! We cater for our own people already."

"We need to keep the railways and roads free for the troops," he patiently explained.

Unconvinced, Eirlys led her new acquaintance, who insisted she called him Max, to have a brief word with her mother before they set off for Johnny's house in Brook Lane.

"What did you want from me?" Eirlys asked curiously, as they reached the door of Johnny's house. "The only time I've been involved with children is when I helped Mrs Francis with the evacuees."

The door opened then and she left Max to explain the reason for his visit to Bleddyn.

Bleddyn invited them in but shook his head when asked for help. "Trouble is, we're very busy in the season. Working from early morning to eleven at night sometimes, with the sands then the chip shop. I don't think I'll have time to help with extra entertainments. Now Eirlys knows a lot of people at the council offices and I'm sure she'll put you in touch with a few willing and able people with a few hours to spare, eh, Eirlys?"

Max turned once again to Eirlys. "Seems I'll need your help after all," he smiled.

Johnny was out so Eirlys didn't stay. "I think you'd better come back to the house with me and see if I can think of a few likely names for you," she said to Max.

Talking about entertainers brought Ken Ward to her mind and the name Max Moon found its slot in Eirlys's memory.

"You're a friend of Ken!" she said in delight. "He wrote to me about you!"

After exchanging news and giving Max messages to pass on to Ken, they continued the walk back to Conroy Street like old friends.

Johnny was visiting Hannah. He had a box of apples which he planned to offer to Hannah for the girls. Carrying the box of fruit he manoeuvred his way around a new, shuttered porch, lifted a heavy curtain hanging outside the door and knocked.

She opened it, and seeing him, said, "Johnny? How nice. D'you have some sewing for me? How can I help?"

"Not work this time, Hannah. I've brought a few apples for the girls. Some are cookers and some are eaters," he explained. "I know they like to take an apple to school. Given to me they were, a friend at the wholesaler had a lot left and as Piper's is such a good customer, what with the potatoes for the chip shop all the year and the beach café in the summer, he asked if I could find them a good home."

"Thank you." Hannah smiled her delight. "Will you come in?"

The door to the front room stood open and he could see into the over-crowded room. A sewing machine stood against the window with material spilling out of it across the couch beside it. Hannah was making curtains. He wondered how many of the night hours she spent earning a living for herself and her daughters.

He stepped backwards and pushed the front door shut behind him, but to his surprise Hannah moved around him, reopened it and propped it open. It was a chilly night, dank with unshed rain, mist wreathing the trees and hedges. Curious, he asked her why she didn't close it and keep the warmth in.

"One of Mam's latest rules," she said, clearly embarrassed. "That's why she had the porch and the double curtains fitted, to keep the light from showing. The door isn't to be closed when I have a man caller. A lot of fuss, eh?"

"Why? Do you have many callers?" Johnny asked, disbelievingly amused.

"Oh, the man delivering groceries. The man come to read the meter, a husband collecting some sewing for his wife, a friend bringing apples." She tried to smile but there was deep sadness in her lustrous eyes.

He put the box on the table and asked, "Are we all suspect, then?"

"No, not the men, it's me my mother doesn't trust. Wicked and wanton I am, didn't you know? I divorced my husband and that is something my parents will never forgive."

Impulsively Johnny gave her a quick hug and said, "Never think you're without a friend, Hannah. If there's ever anything I can do you only have to ask."

After he left, Hannah stood watching the movement of the curtain until it was still, separating her from him. She heard his footsteps crossing the road and daydreamed, imagining how sweet life could be.

Johnny stood across the road and heard the door close and the house became anonymous, just one of a row, but with such sadness locked inside he imagined it stood out from the rest. He felt moved by Hannah's plight and wondered what he could do to ease her misery.

There were no lights either from the street lamps or from shop windows. Usually during the dark months, the window displays would light the way down the main road, enticing passers-by to stop and look and then come back to buy. Now, with the lighting restrictions so diligently kept, there wasn't a glimmer.

Another month and the windows would be showing Christmas delights. This brought his mind back to Hannah and her children. What sort of Christmas would they have, with a disapproving mother and nowhere to have fun? He wondered whether he could persuade his mam to invite her to share their day. They usually joined Uncle Huw and Auntie Marged and his cousins on Christmas afternoon; there would be plenty of company and plenty of food. An escape from the sad little overcrowded room.

Irene reached home at the same time as he did and when Bleddyn opened the door to them he stared at his wife but said nothing.

"Was Hannah pleased with the apples?" he asked his son.

"Yes, but Dad, she has such an awful time of it, no husband and a miserable mother."

"Don't interfere, Johnny. She's better off than some. Being alone isn't the only way of being miserable." The words were harsh, the words pointed.

Johnny watched his mother take a glass of water and make her way up to bed without a word for his father, and understood what was being said. But it was Hannah for whom he felt concern. Mam and Dad had to sort out their own problems, he daren't interfere in that quarter. Hannah was different. She needed a friend to stand up for her and persuade her that there was more than one way of dealing with a problem, and it wasn't necessary to deal with it alone.

Eirlys came into his mind as he was making a hot drink for himself and his father, and he wondered why he found Hannah filling his thoughts more than she. Hannah was too old and she was a divorcee with children. Why couldn't he accept that and put her from his mind? Tomorrow he would call on Eirlys and ask about the boys.

"Eirlys called while you were out," Bleddyn said, breaking into his thoughts. "There was a tall, skinny bloke with her, wanting help to set up some extra entertainments next summer. Max Moon he called himself – what sort of a name is that? Know him, do you?"

Johnny shook his head. "What did he want with Eirlys?"

"She thought we could help, but I explained we were always too busy during the season. This Max Moon chap said there'll be more people staying home next summer. That's what he thinks!"

Johnny glanced at his watch. It was a bit too late to call on Eirlys now, and besides, he admitted to himself, he wanted to sit and think about Hannah.

–

At the Prices' house in Conroy Street, there was something of a party atmosphere. Max had produced an accordion and he played a few chords. This brought the three musketeers out of bed and running down the stairs.

"We 'aving a party, Auntie Annie?" Harold asked, eyes shining. "Always having parties when we was 'ome, wasn't we, Stanley?"

To everyone's delight, Max sat and played several popular tunes, party songs in which the boys lustily joined. Even little Percival seemed touched by memories of other days and mouthed a few words of "Knees Up Mother Brown", which brought tears of laughter to Annie's eyes.

It was eleven o'clock before the boys settled back into bed. As Max prepared to leave he made a suggestion.

"I've been thinking," he said. "Wouldn't it be fun to give the evacuees and some of the local children a Christmas party? We could hire the hall and, if we could persuade the council to pay for it, we could ask various families to help with the food and give them a good time."

"What about entertainers?" Annie asked. "Are you volunteering to play the piano for pass the parcel and things like that?"

"Better than that. I am an entertainer, it's my job. Ken and I are getting together a concert party and we hope to travel around giving concerts as soon as everything is sorted. For the children I'll do a puppet show and if we can arrange a small gift each, I'll be Father Christmas, with the aid of a few cushions. Or, if you prefer, I'll be Maxie the Clown."

Eirlys stared at him. "You do that as a job? Entertain children?"

"And adults." He smiled. "I was turned down for the army as I have a weak chest, but I have arranged to reapply and I think they'll take me for ENSA, the organisation for entertaining the forces. I'm going to London in a week or so to be interviewed. Ken too."

"Max knows Ken Ward," Eirlys explained to her parents.

Max stayed another hour and talked about his work with children in which he was helped by Ken. It was as though they had found a long-lost friend.

Eirlys was filled with excitement at the thought of being involved in arranging the party for the children. Several families had already returned to London, as no bombs had yet fallen, but there were still a large number of them staying in the town.

Mr Johnston agreed to fund the hire of the hall as it was good publicity for the forthcoming arrangements for local holiday entertainment. It was no surprise that he put Eirlys in charge of arrangements and allowed her to take two members of staff to assist her.

–

"I think I'll take the boys to see their mother next week," Annie announced one day in late November. "If you'll go and buy some fresh eggs from Mr Gregory, Eirlys, I'll take a dozen or so with me. I don't expect they get fresh eggs up there. Not still warm from the hens like we do, eh?"

Eirlys was apprehensive about the proposed visit. Not because of the danger, should German bombers begin to attack, but because she was afraid that once they were back on home territory the boys would refuse to return.

"Don't worry," Morgan said when she expressed her fear. "I doubt their mother would want to risk their lives when they can be safe down here. Stands to reason." He was trying to reassure himself, Eirlys and Annie both knew that.

"There haven't been any air raids and people are starting to think there never will be," Annie said doubtfully. "They might stay with their mother."

"There's always Plan B," Morgan smiled. "I'm getting bikes for them for Christmas. Old ones, mind, but I'll paint them up all smart and Johnny has promised to help me replace the old brakes with new ones and check everything is sound. With fancy new handlebar grips and a shiny new bell each, they'll look a treat. If we accidentally let them see the bikes, well, that'll bring them back for sure."

–

Johnny and Eirlys were ill at ease when they met and even when they went to the pictures there was no hand-holding, no real togetherness when the film was romantic or scary or funny. Neither could explain what was wrong. Johnny suspected it was thoughts of Hannah getting in the way of his growing attraction for Eirlys. Eirlys wondered whether Evelyn had passed on her unexplained animosity. They were both relieved when the boys went with them and they didn't have to pretend that everything was all right.

When she mentioned going to see Annie and the boys off at the station, she was pleased when Johnny offered to take them in Piper's van. He carried their luggage on to the platform and paid for the platform tickets they needed.

The boys were very excited and insisted on Annie repeating their travel plans again and again. She told them they would change in Cardiff, then they were being met at Paddington by Teresa Love, the boys' mother.

The journey was an exciting one for Annie as well as the boys. She had never travelled so far away from home before. They had a picnic on the train, which they shared with a young soldier who was returning to camp after a week's leave. He amused the boys, showing them card tricks and a few simple sleight-of-hand mysteries to confuse their friends.

She was grateful to him. He wasn't much more than a child himself, she thought sadly.

He talked bravely about what lay ahead of him, and the new friends he had made to replace the ones left behind. Annie felt sorry for him. He looked so young and was obviously unprepared for the dangers he would certainly face in the next months. He lived only a few miles from Conroy Street and she promised to call on his parents one day and tell them that she had travelled with their son.

Mrs Love, the boys' mother, was a surprise. She looked hardly any older than Eirlys and was dressed so smartly that she stood out like an exotic bird among the navy-blue, black and khaki surrounding them. She was dressed in a rather smart white coat and a hat with a cheerful feather, stockings that looked like pure silk and high-heeled red shoes to match the feather. Annie was still looking around her trying to recognise a woman in her thirties who looked poor and downtrodden and when she saw the boys running towards this smart young girl she tried to call them back. "Wait for me, come here, I don't want to lose you!" When they stopped and hugged the girl she decided it must be a sister they hadn't told her about.

A hand covered in a good-quality calf-leather glove was offered for her to take and the girl said jauntily, "How-di-do! I'm Teresa, the boys' mother. Mrs Price, I'm pleased to meet yer."

"You aren't what I expected and that's a fact," Annie smiled. She turned to the trio and added, "Why didn't you tell me you had such a beautiful young mother?"

With Stanley and Harold either side of her and Percival clinging to her skirt, they made their way off the platform and down to the Underground trains. Annie had never been so nervous in her life but hid her panic well. She picked

Percival up and held him as a shield when the train came rushing out of the tunnel and pulled up like an impatient and bad-tempered animal at the platform.

"I feel as startled by this as you lot did when you first saw one of the fanner's cows," she laughed, as they pushed their way into the already crowded carriage.

Mrs Love lived in a single room and had managed to make bed-space for her three sons by pushing chairs together to make a bed for herself and putting the boys to sleep widthways along her double bed.

Although Teresa Love was smartly dressed in good-quality clothes, Annie thought the room was not very clean. The bed was covered in satin sheets that slithered as the boys sat on them, and there were several pillows, but it looked, to Annie's fussy eyes, very impractical and it all needed a thorough washing. But then, she excused, it must be difficult keeping such an inconvenient and cluttered space clean. And with dust floating in from the road outside, from where there came the continuous noise of traffic.

"Well, now I know where to find you, I'll make my way to my hotel," Annie said when she had been plied with tea and biscuits. "I'll come to collect you for the four o'clock train tomorrow, shall I?"

"Oh, don't go yet," Teresa said.

"But I thought you would want to talk to each other, catch up with family news and all that."

"Look, stay and have a bite to eat; we could go to the chip shop. Our Percival loves chips, don't yer Percival?" She looked around and frowned. "It'll have to be chips in paper. I don't think I can find enough plates for us all. They get broken, don't they? I'll put the kettle on and Stanley will show you where the chip shop is. Go on, Stanley, while I find the forks. Although, we don't need forks do we? Fingers is fine, eh, Percival?"

Annie bought the fish and chips, Stanley insisting that his Mam only liked the best bit of hake. When they had finished the food, Teresa put on her coat. "There's no need to take me, I can find the way if you'll give directions," Annie protested.

"Well, I wondered if you'd hang on a bit longer, Annie dear. I have to go out and I'd be much happier if you stayed with the boys."

It was three thirty a.m. when Teresa returned, smelling of drink and hardly aware of her being there. Dozing lightly on the chair, with Teresa opposite her, the night passed.

The next day Teresa didn't feel well, so it was Annie who found a shop selling bread and made them some sandwiches for their breakfast, and Stanley who led the way and took them to see the sights. He showed them the Thames and boasted about the bridges, found a place for them to eat, then took them to Buckingham Palace, guiding them through the intricacies of the Underground train system like an expert, while the tickets were paid for from Annie's dwindling purse.

"There's just time to feed the sparrers," Stanley announced and he dodged through the traffic and took them into the park, from where they made their way, via the Underground, back to Paddington station.

"There isn't time to go and say goodbye to your mother," Annie said, having repeatedly tried and failed to persuade them to return to the bedsit and Teresa.

"It's all right, Mrs Price. She'll be sleepin' it off," Harold said. "Won't she, our Stanley?"

Annie had a lot to think about on the journey home, with Percival snuggled against her and the other two fast asleep on the opposite seat. Morgan met her in Cardiff and during the last leg of their journey she whispered some of her observations to him, trying not to let the boys hear her disapproval.

"Mum is only twenty-six and she says she wants a bit of fun," Stanley said in a spuriously adult tone. "Had me when she was only a kid."

"Sixteen," Harold supplied sleepily. "Lovely, ain't she, our mum?"

"Absolutely beautiful," Annie agreed, hugging them. "You're such lucky boys to have a lovely young mam like Teresa."

"Ain't we just," Stanley said sleepily. "Now, how long do we have to wait for them bikes, Uncle Morgan?"

Five

Plans for the Christmas concert for the evacuees went ahead with few problems. The entertainments committee refused at first to pay for more than the use of the hall but changed their minds when Max pleaded for some compassion for the poor children taken from home and everything familiar, on account of Hitler. Then they agreed to pay for the hall plus his expenses and something towards buying a gift for each child. Everything else needed for the concert, including stage and curtains, had to be found by Max and his supporters, who at that moment seemed to include no one except Eirlys.

For Eirlys, the organisation of the concert seemed to be an extension of her work at the council offices and she began to enjoy the challenge more and more. Marriage to Johnny was still enticing, but she beginning to like the idea of giving up her job less and less.

Johnny, Taff and a still suspicious Evelyn were persuaded to help, a carpenter was found to knock up a rostrum or two and Max was encouraged sufficiently to arrange auditions for a number of local people prepared to take part. Ken Ward wrote to tell Eirlys that although he was unable to help beforehand, he would definitely be there in time to support Max on the day of the concert.

Eirlys found it all very exciting and involved herself enthusiastically. It was easy to forget everything else. She would hurry home from work and start at once carrying out the instructions Max had left for her.

Johnny called twice and found she was out. He made his way to the hall, lent free for auditions and rehearsals, where she would be running around sorting out lists of names and skills, a pile of jugglers' equipment in one corner, ventriloquists' dolls and puppets in another.

Annie had to remind her that Johnny was feeling neglected. Ashamed that her enthusiasm had left him out, and to make sure he felt really involved, Eirlys put him down for various tasks, mainly searching for the hundred and one things they needed to get the hall ready. She also included him in the team of scene painters, using paint scrounged from a local shop and many garden sheds.

Hannah too offered her help and, after being given the material, made a pair of curtains for the makeshift staging Max had managed to acquire.

"It's all good practice for ENSA," Max told Eirlys. "I expect to be faced with worse than this if I have to entertain forces in strange places. There won't be doors to knock on and kind neighbours to ask, if I'm up where the fighting is taking place. Scavenging and making do will be a way of life for me if this war continues to run."

"You sound as though you want it to," Eirlys commented.

"No," he protested. "Like every other thinking person, I'd be relieved if it ended now, this minute. Many are going to be killed before it's over – how can you think I want that?"

"Sorry, Max. I didn't really mean it."

"I hope you didn't. I want you to think better of me than that, Eirlys." He looked at her and when she met his gaze, he smiled and she saw an interest in his bright blue eyes that made her turn away. She didn't want to see that look on anyone except Johnny Castle. But it was flattering just the same.

Between work, meeting Johnny, helping Max and amusing the evacuees, Eirlys still managed to work on her rugs most evenings. With the wireless for company, she worked until past eleven o'clock and had soon used up all the material she had gathered. If she were to continue, she had to find more unwanted coats and skirts. She was toying with the idea of making more attractive rugs using good quality wool, better colours as well as texture, but, it would have to be cheap if she were going to make a profit.

She saw an advertisement for Readicut rug-making kits which included a pattern set out in squares to represent each tuft, the canvas marked into sections to make the pattern easy to follow. The wool needed to complete the design was also included. Impulsively she sent for one. Heaven knew when she would find time to work on it with so many calls on her time, but an idea was growing in her mind about one day running a business of her own. Her father hadn't managed it but there was no reason why his failure should discourage her from trying.

That brought her thoughts back to Johnny. She didn't want any ambition to come between them: whatever the future held, she hoped Johnny would be a part of it. She smiled inwardly. Evelyn could hardly accuse her of sitting waiting for marriage; she had filled her life with so many things since that rather unkind remark. Life was full and it made her feel more confident. She was important and needed by her boss Mr Johnston, by the three musketeers, and hopefully by Johnny too. When things had settled down and she had more free time she would concentrate on a business of her own, earn lots of money and make Johnny proud of her.

Money was on her father's mind that night. He had missed a couple of shifts that week and he knew Annie would demand her usual housekeeping. He had nothing in his pocket, not a penny. When Eirlys had gone to bed, he asked Annie for the loan of ten shillings.

"Where do you think I can find a spare ten shillings?" she asked. "If you didn't get to work too late to start your shift you wouldn't be broke all the time. I have to work and I manage to get there on time, so why can't you?"

"I hate the job, that's why," he muttered.

"Pity you let the business fail then, isn't it!" she snapped.

"But I can't go a week without any cash at all," he pleaded.

Annie went on in her usual way, reminding him about how he had failed her and Eirlys by not looking after the successful business his father had left him.

Upstairs, Eirlys covered her ears with her hands. When the argument went on and Annie's voice grew louder she ran downstairs and begged them to be quiet before they woke the boys.

Annie eventually gave Morgan a half-a-crown coin – two shillings and sixpence. He stared at it in the palm of his hand until she went upstairs, then he took another one from her purse.

He needed money. How was he going to get some without working extra shifts in that damned factory?

–

Johnny worked well beside Max most evenings when he wasn't needed to help out at Bleddyn's fish-and-chip shop. They soon had their stage sets worked out and, with Max drawing the scenes in outline, and Johnny and several others filling them in with paint, they had all the scene changes they needed, and stored them in a garage behind one of the shops. Lighting was the province of Johnny's cousin, Ronnie, helped by Morgan.

With a week to go and only final rehearsals of the acts to worry about, Max felt content.

"Will the invitations be for the evacuees only?" Johnny asked him one evening when they had closed the door of the local hall on another evening's work.

"I think we'll have room for a few more. In fact, I was intending to go to the school to ask the teachers if there are any children who would benefit from a night out."

"There's Hannah, who made the curtains," Johnny suggested. "She has two girls, Josie, four, and little Marie who's three. There's no father and I don't think they get many treats."

"I think that's an excellent choice. Thank you for telling me, Johnny. Will you invite the girls when you next see them?"

Johnny excused himself from walking Eirlys back to Conroy Street and called on Hannah on the way home.

As usual, the sewing machine was in use, with pretty pink-and-white material under the foot, the needle poised for Hannah to continue.

"Don't you ever rest?" he asked as she propped the door open and invited him in.

"I'm lucky to have this much work," she smiled. "This dress is one of five I've promised for the end of the week. They're for children who are to sing at Max's concert. Aren't they pretty?" She held one up for him to admire.

Josie and Marie were still up, looking at a book, sitting beside the fire in their nightdresses.

"I'm good at reading stories," he offered and Josie handed him the book. Trying to ignore the open door, he settled beside them and began to read, accompanied by the sound of the treadle machine as Hannah continued with her work. He gradually ignored the words in the book and instead invented a story using the characters in the pictures. Josie frowned and looked at the page as though searching for the part of the story he had found, but soon they were both sitting enthralled as he wove tales about beautiful princesses and magical animals and tables that only needed a tap to produce the most wonderful food.

Reluctantly, he stood to go when Hannah said it was time for bed. He waited while Hannah attended to the nightly routine and settled the girls in their bed in the next room.

"It's about the concert I've called," he explained when she returned and settled once more into her seat. "Max would like you to take Josie and Marie."

"Oh, they'd love it. But isn't it for the evacuees?"

"More a practice run for Max," he grinned. "There are some spare places. A dozen or so of the London children have gone home and we don't want the entertainers to perform to a half-empty room, do we?"

"Thank you," she smiled.

"Don't thank me, thank Maxie Moon."

"I think the invitation comes from you, and I appreciate it," she insisted.

Johnny ran home with her voice ringing in his head and a happy feeling around his heart.

–

When Eirlys had completed a small woollen pink and blue rug of which she felt reasonably proud, she went to see Hannah and gave it to her for putting beside the girls' bed. "It's a practice piece to see how well the wool works," she explained. "I made a smaller hairpin shape of wire, of course. The tufts are smaller and the pattern easier to plan."

"But I can't accept this!" Hannah held up the neatly patterned rug, which was pink squares on a mid-blue background. "You've already given me one."

"Why ever not? If it wasn't for you I'd never have tried."

"Nonsense. You and Johnny are more than generous to my girls."

"Johnny?"

"He called yesterday and told me that Josie and Marie are going to the concert. There are a few spare seats, he said, but I know he arranged it as a treat for them."

"Oh, the concert. Yes, he knew you'd be pleased," Eirlys said, although it was the first she had heard about the idea.

"He loves children, doesn't he? He plays so well with my two, and he reads to them like a professional actor. I can see he'll make a wonderful father one day."

A twist of jealousy went through Eirlys and she didn't stay for the proffered cup of tea. Johnny seemed to be seeing rather a lot of Hannah, and, she decided, it was her own fault. She had begun to take him for granted.

She stood for a moment outside the door to allow her eyes to become accustomed to the darkness, and to allow her painful thoughts to settle.

Morgan was walking past when she moved away from Hannah's door. He recognised his daughter's voice as she and Hannah called their goodnights, and darted into an alleyway between two houses, before crossing a garden into the next road. One good thing about this blackout, it meant you could take short-cuts over gardens without being seen.

He stopped when he came to the house of Bleddyn and Irene and melted into the shadows.

Eirlys set off home, but for some reason she was edgy. It was only half past nine, and on that Friday evening there was a slight remnant of a moon and the night was crisp and clear. Yet there was an eeriness about the streets lit only by moonlight, and with no lights to mark the pavements. Deep shadows in doorways, beside trees and in the entrances to lanes and alleyways gave a sensation of emptiness that was unnerving. Her footsteps echoed in the silence and it sounded as though someone was following her. She hurried, anxious to get inside and warm herself at the fire. She wished she had asked Johnny to go with her. Voices and laughter would have driven away her foolish imaginings.

Her anxieties were not all that foolish, she reminded herself. The blackout had caused numerous accidents and she didn't want to be a victim of a fall from unmarked kerbstones or a knock from a bicycle gliding almost soundlessly past, or trip over an unseen cat, as someone had done the previous week, resulting in a broken leg.

She remembered that it was one of the nights for the ARP meetings and decided, impulsively, to go and wait for her father. The place where they met, a small stockroom in the school, wasn't far and it was better than allowing her fears to build up and make her afraid of the familiar streets. If she allowed that to happen she would be a virtual prisoner, as many already were, afraid to go out once darkness fell.

Like every other building in the town, the room in the school building was in darkness. Blackout restrictions were strongly upheld and no chink of light was allowed to be seen. She felt her way through the school gates and walked warily across the yard. In the wan moonlight she could make out the walls of the building and made her way to the main door. She pushed but it was locked.

She called but there was no reply. Perhaps they used another entrance.

She made her way back along the wall and screamed when a voice close to her said, "What are you doing here, miss?"

Even in the weird light she recognised the unmistakable outline of the warden with his blinkered torch and his helmet.

"It's me, Eirlys Price. I was hoping to catch my father and walk home with him," she explained.

"No one here, miss. There isn't anything here on Fridays."

"I thought the ARP—"

"Not Fridays," he said firmly, and she began to smile. Mam was right, he used the ARP as an excuse to meet his friends. He was probably in the pub!

"I'll walk you to the end of the road, miss. Conroy Street won't be far then."

She thanked him and was grateful for the chatter that drove away the emptiness of the dark night.

In Brook Lane, Irene stepped out of the empty house. Bleddyn was working at Piper's fish-and-chip shop, and Taff no longer lived at home since he and Evelyn were now married. Johnny hadn't been home since morning.

A shadow separated as Morgan stepped away from the fence and reformed as she melted into his arms.

–

Teresa Love, the boys' mother, wrote more frequently for a while after their visit. She wrote separate letters to Annie too, and in these she usually asked for money. Once it was the gas bill. Being unable to settle it would mean she had no heating and no way of cooking food.

As Annie had seen no sign of anything to suggest she ever cooked, she wasn't too concerned. Percival's famous chip shop was only a few houses away, she thought wryly. She had sent five shillings on an earlier occasion and two shillings on another, but this time Teresa had asked for ten shillings to pay the rent, stating that unless the money was found she would be out on the street in less than a week.

Annie put the letter away in her drawer, wondering whether Teresa was telling the truth. She had told Annie she worked in a shop where the wage was likely to be low, but from what she had surmised during her short visit, Teresa depended on men friends to feed her and the expenses of that tiny, drab room could hardly be crippling. She didn't dress like a struggling mother either. And those fancy sheets told her plenty!

She said nothing to the boys but discussed it with Morgan and Eirlys when the boys were in bed.

"I don't think she can be that desperate," Annie said. "She hasn't got the boys to feed and there's only the rent and heat for that one little room."

"You've seen it, we haven't," Morgan said. "You know better than us if she's telling the truth."

"I don't think for a moment that she can't find the rent. So I think I'll write back and tell her I haven't any money to spare. What with us feeding her sons an' all, she's got a real cheek, hasn't she, to ask for money as well? Besides," she couldn't help adding, "we aren't rich. You hardly earn enough to keep us in plenty, do you?"

Morgan looked away. Annie never missed an opportunity to remind him.

Eirlys looked thoughtful. "What if it is true? What if she's got herself into debt and she really is threatened with eviction?

How would we feel if we were told she had been thrown out on to the streets because she hasn't enough to pay the rent?"

Upstairs, clinging to the banisters and leaning as low as he could to catch every word, Stanley's heart was racing. He was shivering from his chilly eavesdropping as he got back into bed, but it was nothing to the chill in his heart. His sleep was disturbed by frightening dreams, seeing his mother lying ill and neglected on a pavement, while Annie walked past her uncaring, and the snow slowly covered her lovely face. He had to do something. He was eleven now, and head of the family. There was no one else to help her. It was up to him. The promise to Auntie Annie didn't count any more, not with Ma in need of help. He needed money and he needed it fast, and there was only one way to get it.

Harold and Percival picked up on his concerns and when he explained about the lack of rent money, they began to feel afraid.

"If she sleeps on the pavement, will she end up stiff like that dead cat we found once?" Percival asked in a trembling voice.

"Don't be daft, our Percival! I look after you, don't I? Ma sleep on the pavement? Course not! Got friends up there, ain't she? One of them'll 'elp until I can get her some cash. An' I will, I promise yer.

Not a word to Auntie Annie or Uncle Morgan, though. They mightn't understand."

—

Morgan and Irene spent many moments together in the various places they had discovered during the past months. As the increasingly cold weather made spending time out of doors less and less appealing, they began to use the caravan for most of their illicit meetings.

Irene still used her depression, from which she genuinely suffered, as an excuse for her wanderings. Since very early in their married life Bleddyn had been aware that his wife suffered from "nerves" and twice she had threatened to take her own life. Because of this he didn't interfere when she spent days living apart from them in a world of her own. He looked after the house as well as he could and made sure their sons didn't suffer neglect. He had no way of knowing that several of these periods of "depression" coincided with a brief love affair, although that special glow in her eyes when she came home straight from a lover should have told him.

For Irene the affairs had never before been important, just a way of adding a little spice to her boring days. This one, with Morgan Price, was different. She wanted him to leave Annie and take her away from St David's Well so they could start a new life together. So far she had failed to persuade him. He treated her suggestions as part of a game they played, a "let's pretend" game of which they were very fond.

If only something would happen to change the game into reality, to make him understand that a fresh start was possible.

Then her prayers were answered.

They met one day when Morgan came off the morning shift and walked deep into the bleak countryside to meet her at "their" caravan. Morgan lit a fire in the tiny grate and they lay on the bed and pretended.

"This is a beautifully furnished room, isn't it darling? So spacious and with such wonderful views of the garden."

"I love the smooth bedspread, such a rich green satin, and the eiderdown is so warm."

They played the foolish game for a while, pretending they couldn't smell the damp rising from the cushions or hear the wind on the windows, or the tin-kettle sound of rain on the roof.

"Why don't we make it all come true, Morgan?" Irene whispered. "We've only one life and why should we spend it in misery? Annie expects too much of you; Eirlys is grown up, earning a good wage and doesn't need you to stay. I'm stuck in that house all alone, while Bleddyn is so tied up in routine I know what he's doing every moment of every day. I feel I'll go mad with the boredom of it all."

"We'd be so happy, wouldn't we, Irene darling. Just you and me with no one else to think about."

"Just us, and maybe later our children."

"If only we could. We'd be so happy."

"Then why not do it? Take ourselves off and start a new life?"

"We'd need money. I'd have to make sure we had enough to see us through until I found a job. A job I enjoyed, not that damned factory."

"I'd work too, Morgan. I'd work if it meant being with you, even though I wouldn't help Bleddyn and that Molly Piper. She expected me to work on the sands every summer once we married. Who did she think I was, to expect me to do what I was told by the likes of her! Bleddyn, Huw, Marged and Moll, they all tried to persuade me it was my duty to help the family business. I soon put them right on that. But I'd get a job if you were with me, Morgan, love."

"First we need some money, a lot of money," Morgan said, but to him it was still fantasy, still the unattainable vision of sitting in a beautifully furnished room in a beautiful house in dream country. Irene was extending the game they often played; she didn't really mean they would abandon their families and walk off together into the sunset. He wouldn't know where to start.

Irene put a hand against her stomach and imagined the tiny speck of a thing that was hers and Morgan's child, and smiled contentedly. "One day soon everything will be perfect, Morgan, love."

"Just perfect," he agreed.

–

Johnny found himself searching for excuses to call on Hannah. With the decorating in Granny Moll's house completed, he now worked as general dogsbody in a shop selling linoleum, hardware, kitchenware and tools. Boring jobs: tidying up, cutting customer's requirements and delivering goods in the firm's van.

There were no leftovers in this business to offer her. No more apples. The invitation to take the girls to the concert seemed to be the last excuse. Then he thought, Why do I need an excuse? Eirlys is busy at the hall, I could just stop by and ask if I can read to the children, take a few sweets. A friend would do that, surely?

Hannah answered the door to him and invited him in, making sure as always to prop open the front door with its protecting porch and heavy curtains.

"No one can see in," he whispered, "so what's the point of letting the icy cold wind into the room?"

"I find it easier not to argue," she whispered back.

"Who is it?" A voice from the back of the house asked.

"Johnny, Johnny Castle," he shouted back.

"Don't be long then. It's blowing a gale through this kitchen."

"Sorry. I only brought some sweets for Josie and Marie, and I thought I might read to them again."

"Sorry Johnny, but they're in bed. Only on Fridays are they allowed a late bedtime as a sort of treat."

"Oh, well, I really came to see you, to ask if there's anything you need. I might be able to get a bit of firewood from where I work, if you need it. You know, boxes the goods are delivered in that are only thrown to the rubbish or burned in the yard."

"Thank you; I'm often a bit short of sticks to start the fire."

"Is there anything else? I mean, if you have a problem you only have to ask and I'll sort it."

He stood close to her, feeling the warmth of her filling his body in a way he had never experienced before. "I didn't really call to ask about firewood," he whispered, staring at her, willing her to feel the same as he did, wanting to gather her in his arms, make everything right for her, smoothing the tiredness from her gentle face.

"Johnny, I like you a great deal and I love the way you are with the children, but don't make the mistake of thinking there could be anything more." She touched his face and then stepped away, backwards towards the door, and stood there waiting for him to leave.

"I think I'm falling in love with you, Hannah."

"How old are you, twenty-one? I'm almost thirty. I'm divorced – disgraced according to some. I have two children. You need someone younger so you can start at the beginning and write your own story."

"Why do I feel this way if it's wrong?"

"It isn't wrong. It's never wrong to love someone, but I'm not the right one to accept that honour. Thank you for being such a wonderful friend to the three of us. We will stay friends, won't we? I haven't driven you away by my frankness?"

"You haven't driven me away," he said as he left.

He walked swiftly from her door and headed away from the town and out into the dark anonymity of the lanes. He felt a little foolish but that passed and he thought seriously about how he felt. The moon was almost done and he could hardly see where he was going. Once or twice he stopped to get his bearings and eventually found himself at the edge of the field in which the barn stood, just visible, a bulky black shadow looming out of the darkness.

He smelled smoke and wandered, feeling his way with care across the hummocky grass and the unevenness caused by cattle, hard now in the grip of frost. He was led by curiosity. He hadn't seen any gypsies, but it must be them, back for their winter stay, choosing a different field by choice or necessity. He moved closer, expecting every moment that one of their dogs would bark. The caravan was close and he went to stand in its shadow, then realised that the smoke was coming from its chimney. Not the gypsies then.

He heard someone approaching, walking fast, confidently, a thin torchbeam pointing at the ground, and he stood back not wanting to be seen. He didn't want to talk to anyone, he needed to memorise every word Hannah had said to him; relive it, gather comfort by altering, in his mind, the tone of her replies.

—

Irene Castle was waiting for Morgan. The evening was raw, with frost already glistening on branches as she had made her way to and from the woodpile and fed the fire she had lit in the caravan. Once it was burning satisfactorily she went outside. She didn't bother to put on her coat but walked a little way to see if she could hear Morgan coming. She got as far as the lane and turned back, hugging herself to contain her shivers, anticipating the warm fire waiting for her. She didn't see her son hiding in the shadows but he saw and recognised her.

"Mam? What on earth are you doing out here, and without a coat?"

"Johnny!" The name came out as a scream as she came upon him.

"Have you been following me?" she asked as she quickly recovered.

She continued to shout loudly, her voice high and shrill. Morgan had to be warned if he was in the vicinity.

"I came out for a walk and my feet just led me here. But what are you doing and where's your coat?" He took off his overcoat and wrapped it around her shoulders.

Her shoulders drooped and she said, "I don't know why I'm here. I just had to get out of the house. Your father's working at the chip shop and won't be back till eleven, Taff has moved out and you're never there. What am I supposed to do with my time?" She still shouted and he tried to soothe her, leading her carefully away from the caravan across the field and on to the level surface of the lane.

"Come home, Mam, and we'll sort something out. Evelyn and Taff will come and stay with you sometimes and I don't have to be out every night, do I? Once this concert is over, Eirlys and I will enjoy a night in with you, listening to the wireless, playing cards."

He went on talking to her, telling her about the concert preparations and relating stories about the three evacuees. She walked beside him, saying nothing and from the hedge

Morgan watched them disappear into the dark November night. He had made an excuse to change his shift from eight hours to four, something, the foreman warned him, that very soon wouldn't be allowed. He had finished at six instead of ten for nothing.

–

Stanley found it a simple business to push open the door of the greengrocer where Johnny's cousin Beth Castle worked. The door was old and the lock poorly fitted. One good shove and the weakened wood offered no resistance.

He had heard people talk about float and understood it meant that some money was left in the till ready to start the following day. He didn't think it would be much, but a pound was all he needed to keep his mother safe for a week or two. He found fifteen shillings and pocketed it happily before going to try somewhere else.

He even managed to close the door after him. The damaged wood was pushed into place and he heard the lock click as he pulled on the door knob. "Knackered," he muttered succinctly.

–

Morgan was walking back from the caravan after sitting there for a while wrapped in Irene's discarded coat and staring into the fire. So long as they weren't suspected, they could start using the place again in a week or so. Until it was safe, he wondered whether the school caretaker was still careless about locking the door to his room. He had the keys because of his occasional attendance at the ARP meetings. There was an electric fire they could use as long as they were careful to shield its glare, and a comfortable chair.

He was in no real hurry to get home; Annie wouldn't expect him until after ten and he had told her he might be late, using the excuse that he might join others on ARP business looking for possible sites to station fire-watchers in the event of air raids. He wandered disconsolately through the lanes and back streets of the town.

He was filled with self-pity. He was broke, doing a job he hated, Annie did nothing but remind him of his failures and his daughter was too busy to speak to him.

A shadow separated itself from the dark and he leaned into a hedge and watched as a body emerged from a ground floor window. He ran on tiptoe to intercept the thief, for that was what he must be, leaving a property in such a suspicious manner. A pretty stupid one at that, climbing out where he was in full view from the street.

He was grinning at the story he'd be able to tell as he grabbed the surprisingly small figure and whisked him around to see his face.

"Stanley! What the hell are you thinking of, boy? Why aren't you in bed?" he demanded stupidly. Then, "You've been thieving again! Do you want to be sent to prison, boy? Is that what you want?"

Stanley tried to run but Morgan held him firmly. "What have you been doing, boy?" he hissed. "I thought you'd promised us—"

"I had to get money so our mum won't get pushed out and have to sleep on the pavement, that's what – and don't expect me to say sorry, 'cos I ain't!"

"You won't find much money in a shop. They take the money home or put it into the night safe."

"The float. I took the float." Stanley was still defiant.

"Pubs, now they're the places where you'd find money," Morgan said with bleak humour.

"Pubs is where wardens hang about. And they lock and bar them places," the expert told him. "Shops is easier."

"You've done this before!"

"Course I 'ave. Mum's often broke and I look after her and my brothers."

"Pubs might lock up downstairs," Morgan said thought-fully as though to himself. "But they don't worry about upstairs windows, do they? And pubs aren't the only place worth a visit. We could go to the pictures for the late showing and on the way back—"

"You mean you'd help me get Mum's rent?"

"Let's say we'll help each other, is it?"

"Blimey!"

Since preparations for war had begun in 1938, several stores of food for feeding the army had been set up in the vicinity, and Morgan knew just how to get inside the Nissen hut built close to the perimeter fence. Stanley, long and slim, was just the right person for the job.

The following day Morgan's shift changed to afternoons and he offered to put the boys to bed so Annie and Eirlys could go to the pictures. When Harold and Percival were asleep, he and Stanley left the house.

Prising up the slightly damaged window was easy. Sammy Richards had unwittingly told him which was the faulty one. Sammy had helped supply the glass for the windows and had noticed the poor fit of several of them. Made of metal, they had warped and no longer fastened properly.

"Don't forget, boy," Morgan said, repeating his instruc-tions. "If there's any sign of trouble, you run for it and leave the explanations to me, right? Get out of it fast and make sure you're not seen till you get safely home."

In less than half an hour, Stanley had handed out half a dozen six-pound tins of corned beef and some tins of ham. Tinned fruit was found in a far corner and after helping the boy out through the window and fixing it as well as they could, they carried the loot in sacks across their shoulders and hid it in an elderly neighbour's yard until it could be retrieved later.

"Not a bad night's work, Stanley my boy," Morgan said and promised the boy four half-crowns. "Maybe more once I've got rid of it. We'll have no trouble selling this little lot."

He was dozing when Annie and Eirlys returned. The wireless was playing dance music, the fire blazed cheerfully.

"Enjoyed a quiet evening then?" Annie said.

"Fell asleep I did," he said, getting up to make the night-time cups of cocoa.

–

Ken Ward arrived on the day of the concert and found accommodation in the same boarding house as Max. He and Max were experienced at producing shows in small halls and the minor problems that developed as curtain-up approached were quickly dealt with. The hall was very overcrowded. Intended to seat forty, Max counted at least fifty-two before the doors were closed for the performance to begin, and he saw them open several more times before the introductory music began.

The excited chatter from the audience was counterbalanced by the hushed nervousness behind the curtains, where Ken confidently organised the adults and children into the order in which they would appear. With a chord on Sammy the carpenter's accordion, it began.

Five little girls in the dresses made by Hannah sang a few favourites and the audience was encouraged to join in with the chorus. A clown appeared next: Maxie Moon juggling and falling about in the casual way perfected by clowns over hundreds of years. Then a comedy duo with their humour aimed firmly at children so everyone had fun; the children laughing at the entertainment and the adults enjoying the children's laughter.

As the interval approached, three men came on dressed as rats and sang:

"Nobody loves a rat, boo hoo, Nobody loves a rat. They'll cuddle the cat and admire the bat, But nobody loves a rat. Three cheers for the rat!"

"Boo!" went the audience.

"Three cheers for the cat!"

"Hooray!" the kids shouted.

"It's true what we say, Do what we may, Nobody loves a rat. Boo hoo!"

At that moment there was a commotion at the entrance and the air raid warden came running down the aisle, blowing his whistle and shouting, "Put that light out!"

The rats squeaked and began to chase the man around the hall, through the seats and out of the door.

"Three cheers for the rat!"

"Hooray," the laughing audience shouted.

–

Stanley was not in the audience. He had made his excuses to his brothers, promising them a Cadbury's chocolate bar if they didn't give him away, and made his way to the corner of Sidney Street where Morgan was waiting for him.

After repeating his instructions to run for it if there was any sign of trouble, Morgan led him to a small window at the back of the newsagent run by Mrs Hetty Downs and her daughter Shirley. Both women were out as, having given a contribution to the concert fund, they had decided they were entitled to see it and had gone to the hall determined to bluff their way inside with several others.

As the "rats" were giving an encore, Morgan was entering through the door opened by the lithe Stanley after he had slipped in through the window.

It wasn't difficult to find the day's takings and it was a sizeable sum. With cigarettes and sweets as well as newspapers being sold, they guessed the leather bag used at weekends to put the money in the bank would be full.

Morgan cut the bag open, intending to put it under some rubbish in the allotments as they went home, and Stanley excitedly watched, imagining his mum's face when she saw the money he was going to present to her one day soon.

The sound, when it came, was slight and for a moment neither of them reacted. Then they realised that someone was pushing against the front door of the shop.

"They've come home early!" Morgan gasped. "They didn't get in after all."

He didn't have to tell Stanley to run. The boy pushed the door shut, locked it and pocketed the key before he wriggled out through the window with Morgan close on his heels. The original plan was for Morgan to use the door and Stanley to lock it after him and escape by the window. Stanley didn't stop to think, he ran.

Morgan listened and the sound seemed to have stopped. Someone sheltering, that was all. Where was the boy? Dammit. Now he'd have to leave the door open and their theft would be discovered straight away, when the police did their usual check of shop doors. No breathing space until the morning as he had hoped.

It was then he realised that the door was locked. He was trapped unless he could break the door down. Panic began to rise and he looked around him, wondering if there was another way out. Perhaps the shop door? But he couldn't get out of the store room.

He looked at the window and wondered if he could get through. Pushing it closed after him would mean no one would notice before Mrs Downs and her daughter Shirley opened up in the morning. He wasn't all that big; it was worth a try, especially when he thought of the alternative.

He stretched up and began to climb on to a cupboard. But overcome by curiosity he looked inside. It was full of cigarettes packs of 200 Player's Weights, Park Drive, Kensitas with "four for your friends", Woodbines, Du Maurier, Player's Navy Cut and Wills' Capstan. And, utterly irresistible, pink, elegant packets of Passing Cloud. He grabbed three cartons, stuffed one into his inside pocket and held the others under his arms and tried to slide out of the window.

He managed to get half-way out by throwing the cartons on to the yard below the window but when he greedily went back for more cigarettes he fell. His foot went under him and all his weight pressed on it. He tried to stand but the pain was frightening. There was no escape. He would be here when Mrs Downs opened up in the morning. His deepest fear was having to explain to Annie.

Stanley, meanwhile, hurried back to his seat and at once joined in with the rest, singing loudly, "It's a long way to Tipperary."

Morgan was writhing on the floor behind the shop, holding his ankle, cursing his stupidity, and Stanley laughed louder than the rest, making sure people remembered he had been there, blissfully ignorant of what had happened.

In the aisle the audience stood to dance to "Knees Up Mother Brown" and sat again while Max the clown played and sang a silly song about a lazy hen, standing up at one point to reveal an egg on the piano stool, to the delight of the children.

The applause was rowdy and it took a while to empty the hall. Max and Eirlys and Johnny and the others stood exhausted and declared themselves satisfied. Outside, Stanley looked for Morgan.

When they reached home, having been met by Annie, there was no sign of him.

Stanley said he had left his new cap at the hall and before Annie could tell him not to, he was out, running down the dark streets to the newsagent. If Morgan hadn't got out, he'd be trapped. Mrs Downs and her daughter Shirley were on their way home for certain now.

Racing past the hall he was relieved to see that groups of chattering people still stood around, reluctant for the evening to end. Jumping over fences and skirting through gardens to save time he reached the shop, clambered up and called through the window.

"I can't get out, boy, my ankle's busted I think."

"I'll go for help."

"NO!" Morgan shouted. "Get me out of here, and fast!"

Taking the key from his pocket, thankful he hadn't thrown it away as they had intended, Stanley unlocked the back door and, with Morgan grimacing at every move, managed to help him out of the building and into a nearby lane.

"Now you can go for help," Morgan groaned. "Fetch young Johnny Castle, he's sure to be with our Eirlys."

His chest was tight with all the running he had done, but Stanley ran back and to his relief found Johnny talking to Eirlys and Max as they dismantled the stage.

"It's Mr Price," he whispered to Johnny, his chest heaving with the effort. "He's hurt himself and he doesn't want Mrs Price to know."

"I won't be long," Johnny excused himself. "I have to take Stanley back home. I'll be back for you, Eirlys." It must be a woman, Johnny thought, half with disgust and half with admiration. How did he get away with it with Annie? How dare he even try!

"Don't worry," Max called after him. "I'll make sure Eirlys is safe."

"'E's got a nerve, muscling in on your girl," Stanley puffed as he led Johnny back through gardens and across the corner of the allotments.

"Where are we? Where are you taking me?" Johnny asked.

"Short-cut this is. Blimey, mate. Don't you know your own back yard?"

They found Morgan with his coat covering his spoils, from which he refused to be parted. "I can't suffer all this for nothing," he argued when Johnny tried to persuade him to leave them behind. "What, leave them for someone else to pinch?"

"Not ruddy likely, eh, Uncle Morgan," Stanley encouraged.

The sharp-eyed Stanley had noticed an abandoned pram not far from the allotment gate and he and Johnny went to fetch it. On this contraption, with two wobbly wheels and no handlebar, Morgan made his undignified way home.

"I'll make you a good bogie cart with this at the weekend, young Stanley."

"Big enough for the three of us I 'ope, Uncle Morgan."

"Stop it you two!" Johnny was angry, just realising the seriousness of his involvement. He had been so caught up in the haste, he hadn't been thinking clearly. "I can't help you with a robbery! You casually make plans as I rescue you after you've committed burglary and chat as though nothing has happened? I haven't decided yet whether or not to inform the police! I can't just ignore it!"

"You can't inform on your girl's dad, now can yer?" Stanley said reasonably. "She wouldn't never forgive yer."

"At least promise you won't ever do anything like this again." Johnny was confused, he didn't know what he was supposed to be thinking. This was a completely new experience.

"I can promise that, hand on me heart," Stanley said seriously as they stopped to catch their breath. "I only did it to get the rent paid for our mum. I'll never touch another thing that ain't mine. Never. Not even a pencil from the boy sitting next to me at school and that's a God's promise."

Johnny accepted the boy's word but he was embarrassingly aware that no such promise came from the wounded warrior in the broken pram.

Six

Johnny felt like a thief himself as he walked through the streets pushing the injured Morgan on the old pram. The man was obviously in pain although he tried to hide it. He was concerned about Morgan but anxious about the cigarettes young Stanley had hidden in spite of his entreaties to hand them over to the police.

"I hope you haven't put them where the police will find them, Stanley," Morgan said as though Johnny wasn't listening.

"Give them up," Johnny pleaded. "It'll go better for you if you do."

"Give over," Morgan said with a weak laugh. "If they find them I'll be stuck in prison and I'll have to face Annie at her worst." He winced as the pram lurched over a kerb. "And you want me to do all this for nothing?"

"I don't want my ma sleeping in no gutter," Stanley said. "I did it for my ma and I ain't doin' it for nothin' either!"

Johnny gave up. He was bemused by the bizarre situation and felt as though he had been caught up and driven along with them without a mind of his own.

Eirlys and her mother were waiting at the door when the peculiar procession appeared out of the darkness accompanied by Morgan's moans to generate sympathy. Once they were inside, a glance at Morgan's swollen leg made it clear that a doctor was needed and the rest of the night was spent dealing with hospital admissions, waiting for news and all the other alarms and confusions and irritations that go with an accident.

Johnny stayed with Eirlys, wondering how much of the night's adventure he should tell her. It was two o'clock the following morning before he told her the full story. They were in the hospital waiting for news, having asked a neighbour to sit with the boys. He felt uneasy and ashamed at the casual way he had accepted the situation and helped Morgan and Stanley to hide stolen goods and outwit the police. Dammit, he'd even carried some of the spoils!

He tried at first to avoid her learning the truth and at first said, "He fell in the lane."

She only had to look at his stricken face to know that wasn't true. "Come on, Johnny, you don't just fall and do that much damage."

"He climbed a wall or something, chasing a burglar he told us."

"Burglar," she muttered. "A woman more like."

"What? Your father doesn't chase other women does he?" He widened his eyes, feigning ignorance.

"Forget I said that. Dadda needs flattery sometimes. Mam reminds him constantly of his failures. He needs someone to tell him he's wonderful. There's nothing more to it than that – and don't try to change the subject!"

"I wasn't. I just don't know any more than he told me. Why is it so hard to believe?"

She hesitated to reply as they heard someone approaching. They smiled encouragingly at a young soldier, bandaged and using crutches, who was being helped and gently teased by a pretty young woman.

"It doesn't make sense, that's why," Eirlys said when they had passed. "For one thing, how did Stanley know exactly where to find him?" She sighed. "Please, Johnny. Before Mam comes back I need to know the truth. I need to if I'm to protect him."

"You always protect your dad, don't you? Why do you think he needs your help?"

"I love him, but I know he's foolish sometimes. Remember when we had to rescue him when that van broke down? Mam thought he was at work. He hates working. He never had to work hard when his parents were alive. They indulged him and did everything for him. When they died he couldn't cope. The business failed, then he lost job after job. I've always been afraid that one day Mam will have had enough and tell him to go."

"You're very loyal," Johnny said. The vision of the soldier had remained with him – the soldier and his loving girl. He imagined himself in uniform, coming home on leave like the soldier. How fortunate he was to have a girl waiting for him, helping him, loving him. He knew he needed someone if he were to go away and that was very likely. He looked at her and knew she would be loyal and loving and very good to come home to.

"Loyalty can be misplaced," Eirlys then said. "I didn't go to London when Ken Ward asked me and my decision was partly because of loyalty to my parents."

"Do you have any regrets?" he asked, his dark eyes staring into her slightly troubled blue ones. Her response was important to him. He felt a flood of relief when she shook her head.

"No, Johnny. No regrets. I couldn't have loved him or I wouldn't have been able to refuse, would I?"

"I'm glad you stayed," he said, drawing her into his arms, holding her close.

She broke away and stared at him as though deciding whether it was right, before moving close to kiss him again.

The hospital seemed deserted at that late hour. Just occasionally a nurse would walk briskly through the tiled corridor, stiffly starched clothes swishing, shoes squeaking on the highly polished floor.

"Does this mean you feel the same way as me, that we're more than friends?" Johnny whispered.

"I feel more for you than I've felt for anyone."

"If I asked you to move to London, would you come?"

"Whatever you want to do, Johnny, I'll support you." She smiled as she added softly, "I think we'd have to come home to separate my waning parents quite often, though, don't you?"

"I love you, Eirlys. I know this isn't the best time to say it. I'll be leaving next year to join the army, unless I manage a deferment which is doubtful. We'll be getting to know each other through letters, mind, not meetings like this. If you don't want to stay with me, I'll understand."

"Johnny, it's never the wrong time to fall in love. We'll deal with whatever happens, together."

He felt relief as he held her tightly and succumbed to the pleasures of a deep and emotional kiss. A huge decision had been made. No more dreaming about the quiet and gentle Hannah, who was eight years older and had two lovely daughters. He was committed to Eirlys, he was the luckiest of men and they would be very happy.

"Mam will be back any minute." She stood up and brushed her hair back and glanced in the mirror, knowing that whatever she did she wouldn't be able to remove the shining excitement in her eyes, a tell-tale sign of love. Then she returned to the subject of her father.

"Johnny, please, quick – before Mam comes in, tell me what really happened." When he told her, coldly and briefly, she stared at him – but not with love in her eyes; that look had been wiped away by horror.

"Dadda was breaking into a shop?" She stared at him, a half-smile on her face, waiting to be told it was a joke.

"He used young Stanley to get in through a window, then when they thought someone was coming in through the front door, he told Stanley to run, which he did, but your father tried to get out through the window Stanley had used and, well, he slipped and couldn't get away."

"What was he stealing – money?"

Johnny hesitated and she insisted on knowing the full story, so he said, "Cartons of cigarettes, and some money."

She was silent while horror and disbelief filled her thoughts, then she said, "Mam mustn't know."

"Young Stanley hid the cigarettes. I don't know what happened to the cash."

"We'll have to find it all and send it back."

"That's too risky. There's more chance of being caught than when they stole it."

"Dadda a thief? I can't believe it, Johnny. He's always been lazy, he hates his job, but stealing? Entering someone's house and robbing them? Why did he need money so desperately? Is he in trouble, d'you think?"

She was white with shock, trembling so much that her arms shook uncontrollably. Johnny felt a strong sympathy extending the love he had declared, and he took her in his arms and held her, talking soothingly to her as the tremors slowly left her.

A nurse appeared with a pale-faced Annie and they were told that her father was all right but would stay in hospital until the ankle had been set.

"I'll stay with him, you two go home and get some sleep," Annie said.

Johnny hardly heard what was being said until Eirlys told her mother that Johnny would walk her home.

Walking through the silent streets his thoughts were confused again. In a corner of his mind was a picture of Hannah, but a part of him wanted to hold Eirlys again, repeat that exciting kiss that had been full of promise. It was a powerful sensation, the arm-aching need to hold her again, to experience once more that almost overwhelming love and protection. She made him strong, with a newly born ability to deal with someone else's problems, take them on to his own shoulders.

Words of love teetered on his lips but this time he held them back, afraid to say them while the image of Hannah was still there in his heart in case they sounded as insincere as he felt. Hannah had been right to discourage him, common sense told him that. She was eight years older and at times it seemed she was a generation away from him in experience. But did common sense matter when love had spread its web?

Going back into the house, Eirlys revived the fire while he made tea. He watched as Eirlys poured, such a homely everyday act, yet with his newly declared love, a sensual one. He wondered if she knew how confused he felt? She had been strange lately, avoiding him, seeing rather a lot of Max Moon too. Perhaps that was why he had declared himself, afraid that if he didn't, then he might lose the chance. Perhaps if Max had spoken first, Eirlys might have already turned away from him. He couldn't really love Eirlys, he was simply playing safe, afraid of ending up alone, stuck in his father's house with no life of his own. His thoughts were like a tangled ball of string, not making any sense.

"Are you going to tell your mam?" he asked as they sipped their tea. When she shook her head he added, "She might find out from the boys. Kids of that age aren't reliable about keeping secrets, are they?"

"Why did Dadda involve Stanley? That's what I find hardest to accept. He's only just eleven. It was a wicked thing to do."

"I think Stanley wanted money to send back to his mother."

"He should have told us, not try and steal it. We'd have done something if only we'd known about his worries."

Johnny stood up, reached for his coat and was preparing to leave when a weary Annie returned from the hospital.

"Keeping him in, they are," Annie told them. "They have to set the ankle and put him in plaster." She frowned as she took off her coat and hat. "I still don't understand what he was doing in that lane. Thought he saw a burglar and climbed a wall for a better look, he said, and he fell awkwardly with his weight on the ankle."

"That's what he told me," Johnny told her.

"The police seemed to think he was right about the burglars," Annie went on with a yawn. "They had a call to tell them that Mrs Downs has reported a break-in at the newsagent."

"So he was telling the truth, then," Eirlys said, glancing at Johnny to support her lie.

"Seems that he was, but I still don't know why he was there in the first place."

"Dadda often goes for a walk, Mam. Nothing strange about that."

"Working in a factory like he does makes him a bit stale," Johnny added. "He says he needs fresh air and some exercise."

"Did they find what had been stolen?" Eirlys dared to ask.

"They wouldn't say. Now, I'm off to bed. Thank you, Johnny, for staying with Eirlys. What an end to the night of the concert, eh?"

"Great, wasn't it, Mrs Price?" Johnny enthused. He looked at Eirlys. "Max Moon did a marvellous job, didn't he?"

"I hadn't realised how talented he was," Eirlys said. "When I first met him he looked so – so—"

"Ordinary?" Johnny offered.

"What's ordinary? Everyone is capable of surprising us!"

Annie was surprised at the vehement way her daughter responded to Johnny's comment. Hastily, Eirlys smiled and added a few complimentary remarks about Max, with which her mother concurred.

Jealousy surged and for a moment Johnny forgot Hannah and feared to lose Eirlys to the man who had suddenly entered their lives and taken such a large role in Eirlys's.

"Pity he has to go. We'll miss him," he said.

"Oh, he won't be going back just yet," Eirlys said airily. "He's staying on to discuss next summer's plans with the council."

Johnny kissed her as he left, almost fiercely, reinstating his claim.

–

Stanley was frightened, wondering what the outcome of the robbery would be. Every time he saw a policeman he edged away as though his guilt were written on his face. He didn't talk to Percival, who was too young to understand, about the seriousness of not paying rent, but he and Harold discussed the problem whenever they were alone.

"If Mum doesn't get the money, she won't have a home and neither will we when we go back," Stanley explained. "She'll be thrown out into the streets."

"You mean we could go back and she wouldn't be there?" Harold began to cry and Stanley punched him affectionately on the shoulder.

"Come on, I ain't going let that 'appen, am I? Look after you, don't I?"

"What are you going to do, Stanley?" Harold looked hopefully up through tears.

"I'm going to ask Auntie Annie to take us to see Mam again, then I can hand her the rent money and everything'll be all right."

They asked her that evening as she was leaving to visit Morgan in hospital.

Annie refused. "I can't afford to take you all to London again so soon. But," she added quickly as faces fell, "I will take you after Christmas, how's that?"

"I'm bovered about Christmas," Percival said solemnly, in his low, defeated voice. "If we don't go back 'ome and leave a note, how's Father Christmas going to know where we are?"

"I've sorted that," Eirlys said at once. "There's a special address and I got it from the Christmas Fairy at the council offices. If you all write a note I'll see they get sent off."

When Johnny called to enquire after her father, Eirlys was advising and helping the three boys to perfect their letters, Harold optimistically asking him to kill Hitler so they could all go home.

Annie came in a little while after him and they all admired and more or less approved of the boys' efforts.

"I got to see Mam," Stanley said. "Can't you just take me, Auntie Annie?"

"Sorry, Stanley, but you'll have to make do with letters for a while. I can't afford it. Besides, I can't take the time off work," she explained. "In fact I'm working longer hours than usual with all the Christmas orders to see to."

"What if I pay for the tickets; will you come then?"

Annie laughed. "How can you pay for the tickets? Giving you too much pocket money, are we?"

Eirlys stood up, dropped the letters, talked about her hectic day's work, offered to cook, trying to distract her mother from continuing the conversation. Johnny stood up too and asked if he could have a cup of tea. Annie laughed, ignored the distractions and asked again, "How much d'you think it costs to go to London, Stanley? Tuppence ha'penny?"

Stanley drew from his pocket several pound notes and ten shilling notes and a handful of silver coins.

"Where did you get that?" Annie demanded. Johnny reached out and put an arm around a shocked Eirlys.

"It was what me an' Uncle Morgan got when we went into the shop, when he hurt his leg," he said, as though surprised they had to ask.

Eirlys's mind closed down. She was aware of the shouting that went on as Annie demanded a full explanation, but couldn't remember a word that was said. She clung to Johnny, who tried to calm Annie down, begging her to think before she did anything, as her actions would have long-lasting effects.

Eventually Annie's storm of anger was reduced to tears and Eirlys went into the kitchen to make the inevitable tea.

"I can't face him. You mustn't go and see him either," Annie said to her daughter. "All these years of marriage and I don't know him. How could he do such a thing? And involve a little boy too. I'll never forgive him. Never."

"She will," Johnny comforted Eirlys. "People who are married usually do."

"Mam's had so much to forgive him for, now this," she sobbed. "Can you see why I stayed when Ken asked me to marry him and move to London?"

"Things will be rough for a while but I bet in a few months they'll have put all this behind them. Look at my mam and dad. Mam's been ill with her funny moods for years and Dad doesn't give up on her, does he?"

"Better or worse, richer or poorer?" Eirlys said sadly. "I sometimes think it's a lot to ask of someone, don't you? Think of Hannah. I don't think she was wrong to leave her husband, do you?"

"Hannah is a brave woman," Johnny said. "I admire her a lot."

–

The decision to give back the money was not easy to put into action. Morgan came out of hospital to a storm of abuse. He didn't get the chance to ask why he'd had no visitors during his last few days in hospital; Annie gave the explanation the minute he set foot in the door.

In the first tirade she told him the money had to go back. When she had calmed down from the first onslaught, he asked mildly, "How?"

No one could think of a way.

Morgan was soon out and about, with a plaster on his leg that he wore like a medal for bravery except at home. His friends wrote silly messages on it and asked for the story of his chase to catch the burglar time and again. He was a hero outside the home, a villain inside. Neither Eirlys nor Annie spoke to him. It was only the "three musketeers" who gave him any comfort.

He was careful not to mention it when Annie or Eirlys were around but he learned from Stanley where the cigarettes were hidden. Together they moved them to a safer place, in the shed of a stranger's garden. The man who lived there was elderly and rarely left the house. There was little likelihood of the goods being found during the days it would take for Morgan to find buyers.

Morgan was not unhappy. Besides the cigarettes and the money, there were the tins of food to sell. It was more fun than working. Pity Annie had to find out.

–

Eirlys saw a lot of Max Moon and Ken Ward in the short time they were staying in St David's Well. They arranged concerts around Cardiff, entertaining in the army barracks and also giving impromptu sing-alongs in a few factories. They also did some fundraising to buy comforts for the forces. They didn't organise the events themselves but were paid a small fee for taking part; a few of the concerts took place in theatres, but most were small affairs in village halls.

They called one evening to take Eirlys and Johnny out. Johnny felt like an outsider as Ken and Eirlys shared so many memories, but with his own calling into the armed forces imminent, he listened with interest as they talked about the NAAFI, the Navy Army Air Force Institute, which would supply food and shopping facilities to the men at the front line.

Both Ken and Max were unable to serve for medical reasons but both had decided to serve in the capacity of entertainers and would soon be using their talents to help the men in France to take a break from the stresses of battle. Johnny admired them and congratulated them on their bravery, but at the same time wished them gone. He didn't want Eirlys to admire them too much.

Their newly revealed feelings for each other and the events at the newsagent had brought Eirlys and himself closer together. Most evenings she worked on her rug-making for an hour or two, then went with him to spend the evening with Bleddyn and Irene – who seemed to spend more time at home these days. They listened to the wireless and to records, played cards and talked. Johnny explained that his mother seemed to be coming out of her latest depression, but Eirlys cynically wondered if it was simply the weather that made it less attractive to wander the streets without a coat and alone. Irene certainly appeared to be more cheerful, smiling to herself as though harbouring a secret.

One evening, Johnny invited her to go with him to see his Auntie Marged and Uncle Huw. "I think Granny Moll has found you some coats you might be able to use," he told her. She had sold all the rugs she had made and the shortage of material was slowing her production, so she was delighted.

Bleddyn encouraged them to go, assuring them that Irene would be perfectly all right on her own for a few hours.

"Don't talk around me as though I'm the family dog." Irene said mildly. Bleddyn laughed affectionately, pleased at her light-hearted mood.

–

Bleddyn had said nothing to his wife, for fear of worrying her back into the dark depression that plagued her, but had told his brother Huw that he was relieved to see Johnny spending time with Eirlys. "Better than him getting too fond of Hannah Wilcox," he explained. "There's trouble brewing there if that affair gets out of hand. She's been married before and with children too; it would be a burden for him to take on. Plus there's disapproving parents and an irate husband on the prowl. I feel sorry for the girl, she doesn't deserve such a rotten hand, but I want better for our Johnny than that."

It was due to that conversation that Bleddyn and Huw's mother-in-law, Moll, heard about Eirlys's hobby and had gathered a few unwanted coats. Eirlys was welcomed warmly when she went with Johnny to collect them and she felt an excitement, a feeling that perhaps it was going to happen, and she would one day be a part of this large, close family. With her father disgraced, her mother not speaking to him except to shout accusations, a place within this family had an even greater attraction.

When two more rugs had been completed, using coats given by Granny Moll, Eirlys sold them and posted the money to Teresa in London, unaware that Morgan had defied Annie and, as soon as he could walk on crutches as far as the post office, had bought postal orders for Stanley to do the same.

–

Teresa stared at the postal orders, which had arrived by the same post. Now she would be able to move to a better place.

Packing didn't take long. She put her tidiest clothes in a suitcase borrowed for the occasion, threw away all that needed washing, packed a few boxes with the odd pieces of china she possessed and was ready to leave when her friend came to take her to a larger flat in a street near Paddington Station.

Moving into the new place was even quicker. She simply threw open her suitcase and, using it as a drawer, she spread skirts and dresses across the table and left the rest of her clothes inside it. She draped her satin cover over the rather lumpy bed. The ancient cooker didn't work but the gas fire did. She'd manage just fine.

She checked to make sure she had the address of Annie and Morgan Price and promised herself she would write back and thank them for the money the very next day. She threw the piece of paper casually on to the bed; it fell to the floor and was picked up and discarded with rubbish and yesterday's newspapers, left by a previous tenant. When she couldn't find the address she put it out of her mind. When she had time she would easily get the address from the WVS who had organised the evacuation. Or she could even go to the town of St David's Well. After all, it wasn't like London. Tiddly little place like that, she'd find them easily.

Putting on her new high-heeled shoes and her last pair of silk stockings, she went to join her friends for a celebration drink.

–

The boys still wrote regularly to their mother, Eirlys and her mother made certain of that. They knew how important it was for the family to keep in touch so there wouldn't be any strangeness when they were eventually reunited. They didn't hear for a while, but Teresa had never been the most reliable correspondent and Eirlys made them keep writing.

There had been two bombing incidents in London in the month of November although these were not from German

163

aircraft, but caused by the IRA. Nevertheless it was still worrying for Stanley, who listened to the news avidly, and he watched for the post every day, anxious to be reassured that his mother was safe.

"Perhaps she didn't get the money," he whispered to the still-ostracised Morgan.

"Can't you take me to London to see her if Auntie Annie won't?"

When Morgan refused, and Eirlys had explained that with Christmas in a few weeks she couldn't take time off work to go with him, Stanley called a family conference. In bed one night after the lights were out, he woke Harold and Percival and told them he was going on his own.

"I'll set off for school at the usual time, but I'll head for the train."

"I want to come," Percival said. "I'm bovered about bombs, but I want to see Mum."

"You can't come and that's that. I'm going to persuade her to come here and see us," Stanley promised. "I've got enough money to pay for my fare and she's bound to have lots of money now we've paid her rent. Didn't she tell us in her last letter that she was working in a big dress shop and selling posh clothes to the nobs? No doubt about it, she'll be coming back with me for a little holiday."

He found his way to London, assuring the guard that he was being met at Paddington by his mother. The Underground created no difficulties; he had been using the trains since he was five, ducking under the barriers and out-running the porter on occasions. As a precaution, he had written down what Annie had told him through careful questioning, in case things had changed. He stepped off on to the platform where they had alighted on their earlier visit. He found the flat, his heart racing as he knocked on the familiar door.

Back home, Morgan had hobbled to the school to hand in Stanley's lunch, which in his anxiety he had forgotten. Learning that Stanley hadn't arrived at school, he questioned the other two until they told him where Stanley had gone.

He went to the police and explained the problem. A boy of eleven on his own in London was a serious situation. The phone calls exchanged between St David's Well and the Paddington police failed to result in Stanley being met off the train, but at the moment Stanley learned, to his disbelief, that his mother no longer lived at the same address, he turned to be met by a smiling and friendly policeman, who promised to make enquiries for him and let him know where his mother had gone.

"Don't you worry, son, we'll find her. Now, I bet you're starving after all that travelling. Clever boy you are, ain't you, to have come all this way and found the right door? She'll be right proud of you."

Settled in an office with a tray of sandwiches and tea to restore him, Stanley answered the constable's questions. "If you could describe her, that would be a help," he was asked.

"She's beautiful," Stanley muttered, as he fumbled in his pocket. He handed the constable a crumpled photograph.

"Got a picture, have you? Marvellous. My, what a pretty mum you've got."

They were unable to find Teresa, but the police promised to search for her and let him know where she was living. "Only an oversight. She's a bit forgetful, what with the upheaval of the move an' everything. She'll be in touch before we even start looking, you can bet your life, young Stanley," the policeman said cheerily. "There might even be a letter when you get back home."

Stanley was tired and dejected, aching with disappointment at failing to find his mother. He felt in his heart that they would never see her again. He sat on the train with the guard keeping a special eye on him, and even sharing the man's sandwiches, thinking of the best story to tell Harold and Percival. In his pocket were two bars of chocolate to give them, but he and the guard finished them off before they reached Swindon.

—

Hannah called on Eirlys to ask about Stanley, whose story was the talk of the small town. Johnny was there and when Eirlys saw a shared look of intimacy between them, she was startled by her jealousy and somewhat ashamed of it too. As if Johnny and Hannah could be anything more than friends, she chided herself. She couldn't ignore it, though, and she moved closer to slip her hand into Johnny's, a proprietorial gesture which he seemed to resent. She must make sure not to be too demonstrative when they were together, some men found it embarrassing, she reminded herself.

Annie and Morgan were still not speaking and it was Johnny and Eirlys who met Stanley at the station. He emerged from the carriage accompanied by the guard, who had kept an eye on him throughout the long journey.

Stanley was full of his adventure, telling it with many dramatic moments to entertain his brothers. He told them a completely fictional account of seeing the policeman running up as the passengers emerged from the train and how he had darted around to avoid being spotted, "Just in case he was after me." He went on to describe how he had gone into the café at Paddington station and had sat eating crisps and drinking pop, looking around him at the other passengers, many in uniform. "I've never seen such a crowd, not since we got on the train to come here."

"What else did you do?" Harold encouraged.

"Did you buy chips from our chip shop?" Percival wanted to know.

"Nah. I bought Mum a leather handbag from a barrer boy," Stanley said proudly. "I brought it back so we can give it to her when she comes to see us. Lucky I had the money from the shop, eh? It was a real bargain, the man told me."

Eirlys and Johnny exchanged a look of horror. Johnny gestured with a tilt of his head for her to go into the kitchen where they could talk.

"If Stanley carries on boasting about the money he's spent, word could reach the ears of the police and we'll all be in trouble. Knowing who broke into the shop and not reporting it is an offence in its own right; besides your father being arrested, we'll all be found guilty."

Johnny looked serious and Eirlys said, "What can we do? I can't tell the police my father is a burglar. I'm sure he'll never do anything like that again."

"What makes you so sure?"

"It was a dare, a bit of fun, a childish prank, showing off to Stanley, that's all."

"A one and only time?" Johnny looked so serious that Eirlys clung to him, prepared for worse news.

"You said he went out every Friday and told your mother he was going to the ARP meeting, and there isn't one held on Fridays. Where does he go?"

"You don't think… That's too frightening to believe."

"I'll look back through the local paper and see if there is a pattern of break-ins on Fridays, shall I? If there isn't, we'll be able to put our minds at ease."

"Johnny, I don't know what I'd have done without you being here," she said. "Talk about a nightmare. I still can't see an end to it."

"At least he won't try any fancy footwork with that great lump of plaster on his leg," he chuckled, and succeeded in making her smile.

The voice of Stanley droned on, repeating his stories over and again until Percival fell asleep and Harold and even Stanley were yawning fit to split their faces. Annie herded them up to bed while Morgan sat listening to the late news. Bumps and shouts came from upstairs as the boys tried to prove they weren't tired at all, but could stay up all night, and in the privacy of the kitchen Eirlys and Johnny stood wrapped in each other's arms and kissed.

–

Morgan hadn't managed to walk far on his crutches. Living in an aura of misery, hearing nothing but criticism that he knew he deserved, he didn't think he could be more miserable. He wanted to see Irene. But how? He couldn't call at the house in Brook Lane and the caravan was too great a distance to walk to leave a note in the hope she would call there. Anyway, he was too noticeable to do either. Everywhere he went people stopped to speak to him. A face exposed on the local front page was disaster to someone having a secret affair, he thought miserably. Having a great lump of plaster on his leg didn't make him invisible either.

Then the problem was solved by Irene herself.

He was sitting morosely reading the *Daily Chronicle* and debating with himself whether or not to go out to walk to the park and freeze, when there was a knock at the door.

"Hang on, I'm coming," he called and struggled through the kitchen to the back door. "Irene!" he gasped. "What a sight for sore eyes! Come in. Annie won't be back for hours yet. Am I glad to see you. Bored half to death I am."

Irene slipped off her coat and they fell into each other's arms. They clung to each other and whispered endearments, then Irene explained the reason for her visit.

"I know you can't get to the caravan for a while," she said. "But our house is empty for most of the day; why can't we meet there?"

"Damned risky." Morgan frowned.

"The chance of us being seen is slight. Come though the back lane.

You can always say you called with a message from your Eirlys for our Johnny."

"What if we're caught in the house? Annie would never forgive me for that."

"So what? You'll always have me," she said.

The expression on her face as she made the remark gave him a jolt. Was that what she really wanted? For him to leave Annie and Eirlys and live with her? Did she think he had enough money for a fresh start?

As though aware of his thinking, she said, "Isn't that what we both want, now your Eirlys is grown up and no longer in need of you?"

"Of course, love," he said, pressing his face against hers to hide the consternation in his eyes. This was no longer play-acting, this was real. "Wouldn't that be wrong, though, with our Eirlys and your Johnny becoming so close?"

"How can that affect us? We aren't related, even if they marry, silly boy."

"No, but it does seem wrong somehow. They'd be upset to say the least and would certainly separate because of ill feeling."

"You don't want to finish with me just in case your daughter marries my son, do you?" she murmured, wrapping herself around him in a loving embrace.

"Come into the front room and you can convince me it will be all right," he murmured, guiding her, hopping about with her arm for support until they both fell on to the big, generously cushioned couch.

Bleddyn was busy with the fish-and-chip shop and restaurant for much of the day, opening at twelve until two thirty for lunches, and again at five until ten thirty most evenings. With Johnny working at the linoleum and hardware shop from nine until six p.m., the house in Brook Lane was empty for several hours during the day. It was such a relief to be able to talk to someone who didn't accuse him of stupidity and worse, Morgan decided the opportunity, when the chip shop was open for business, was far too good to waste.

It quickly became a regular event. Morgan walked through the lanes at the back of the houses and rarely saw a soul. It was so easy. He would take a bottle of beer, he and Irene would spend a happy few hours together and Morgan would stomp home on his plastered leg, discarding the empty flagon at a convenient place and carrying library books or a magazine.

It was a pattern that pleased them both. "A damned sight warmer than that caravan, too," Irene agreed.

For Morgan, the evenings at home were spent in an angry silence. Annie was still refusing to talk to him, and Eirlys either out with Johnny or working on her rugs. He fielded

Annie's scornful looks with wide smiles and if she wondered why he was so happy, she never thought deeper than to presume it was bravado, or pretence.

—

Johnny didn't call on Hannah again, but when he passed the house he always looked up at the window, hoping to see her smiling at him. He dreamed of her beckoning him in, propping open the door and sitting with him to talk for a while. Her pale, gentle face often came between himself and Eirlys although he told himself it did not.

When they did meet it was not in such romantic circumstances. Hannah cleaned offices most mornings, leaving the children with a friend until it was almost time for school by which time she was always back home. On a cold crisp morning in December, Johnny was standing out on the lane behind the hardware shop loading goods on to the van for delivery. Hannah came running towards him and she looked upset.

"Hannah? What's wrong?" he asked as he intercepted her. "Can I help?"

"Marie is not well and my friend left her with my parents because I was late, and they'll be furious. Of all the mornings to be held up it had to be this one!"

"Wait a minute," he said, holding her still. "I can take you home in the van; I can always find an excuse to change my route. But why will your parents be angry because they have to look after Marie for a few minutes?"

Pink from her exertions, Hannah explained between deep breaths. "They allow us to live there but refuse to help me in any way with the children. 'You made your bed', and all that."

"But that's inhuman! I can't imagine any woman not wanting to help her grandchildren." He hurriedly pushed the last of the packages into the van, locked it and opened the passenger door for her.

"You'd better let me out on the corner or you bringing me home will be another excuse for criticism," Hannah said sadly.

"Why do you put up with it? Why can't you get a place far away from them? Is it because of the rent you'd have to pay?"

"I pay rent now. Only five shillings, but I have to earn that and enough to pay towards the gas before I start paying for food and coal – Sorry, Johnny, I shouldn't be talking to you like this. It's my problem, I made this situation and I have to deal with it."

"And take their punishment for the rest of your life? Why are they so uncooperative?" he asked as he slipped into neutral and applied the handbrake at the corner of her road.

"They want to keep on the right side of God I suppose. Their church strongly disapproves of any wrongdoing."

He watched her run down the road and enter the house, and wished he could have gone inside with her and protected her from the unreasonable anger of her parents. But he didn't have the right. He had to forget ideas of protecting her. If he could.

When he met Eirlys later that day he was confused, twisted up inside, not knowing what was wrong with him. Here was Eirlys, a beautiful, capable, uncomplicated young woman who was obviously in love with him. And there was Hannah, who had told him to go away and forget her, who had escaped from a deeply unhappy marriage and was struggling to bring up two girls. Two daughters who would be reluctant to see their mother bring another man into their lives. They would find it hard to share the mother who, because of the circumstances, was such an enormous part of their lives.

There were posters going up on every billboard. He didn't need to read them, he knew them by heart: they were asking people to join up, urging mothers and wives to let their men go. Women were required for the land army and munitions. It was clear that before very many weeks had passed, he would be going away to fight. A wife at home, someone to build a place for when he came back, someone loving him, caring about him. It was suddenly becoming more and more important to him.

The confusion of his thoughts, first about Hannah and Eirlys, then about being called to fight, led him to think far into the future. Marriage was for life and when he was being sensible, he knew that he would be fortunate to have Eirlys as his bride. She would manage his home, care for his children and never cause him any worries. Eirlys was the sensible choice and, with Ken Ward writing to her, keeping in touch, and with Max Moon still hanging about, this was no time to be undecided. He had told Eirlys he loved her and he had to stay with that decision. It was the best and most sensible thing to do.

He went out that evening telling himself how fortunate he was, and how others would envy him his future wife. He called for Eirlys that evening and suggested a walk. On the headland, high above the empty, silent sands, he asked her to marry him and she said yes. Her happiness showed in her shining eyes and her glowing face and in the passion of her kisses. For Johnny, however, there was a feeling of anti-climax that didn't leave him, even when they went to tell Annie and Morgan, and his father and his vague and indifferent mother.

It was Eirlys who went to tell Hannah. She took a few patterns for rugs she planned to make, and after handing them to Hannah for her approval or comments, she burst out with it.

"Oh, Hannah, I'm so happy. Johnny and I are going to announce our engagement in the spring and we'll probably marry before next year is out."

Hannah congratulated her and said all the right things. It wasn't until Eirlys had gone happily on her way that she collapsed into tears for herself and her stupid dreams.

Seven

The best Christmas present of all for the three musketeers was a letter from their mother. They painstakingly made highly decorated Christmas cards for her and Eirlys posted them off, ignoring the fact they had already sent others. The need to keep in touch, convey their love for her, was something with which she could sympathise. The approach of Christmas made absences far worse.

The boys followed her to the pillar box, watched as the envelopes slipped through the slot and listened while she told them of the journey by van and then train and by bicycle until they were popped through their mother's front door all those miles away.

"I'm going to be a postman when I'm grown up," Harold said. "Everyone's pleased to see you, aren't they?"

"I'll be pleased to see my mum," Percival muttered. Eirlys hugged him and promised him that it wouldn't be much longer.

–

The policeman had found Teresa Love and explained about her son travelling all the way to London to see her. He didn't quite understand about the money Stanley carried but when he said that he thought the boy had brought her money to pay her rent, Teresa cried.

She had paid a month's rent on her new place, but had been arrested soon after for prostitution, charged and fined, so she had no more money until she could get back the job she had lost in the gown shop, or go on the street and earn more. If only she had written to tell them her address before she lost theirs.

Standing on corners was not her way – she usually met clients in pubs – but she hadn't been lucky and one or two of the regular girls had aggressively warned her off the area. She was wondering how she would survive Christmas, and berated herself for not being there when her son had come to the rescue. She bought a newspaper and under its shelter stole a packet of greetings cards. She had nothing else to give them.

She had runs in her stockings and she stopped them with nail varnish. Then, after repairing her make-up, straightening the seams in her silk stockings and pulling down her skirt so the holes didn't show, she smiled and went out into the street.

–

Ken and Max had left St David's Well to audition in London at the Drury Lane theatre, for ENSA. They had realised that song-and-dance men who played an instrument moderately well were very thick on the ground so before they attended they wrote and perfected a comedy act. Max was tall and very thin and with a wig to hide his meagre red hair he made a passable "female" performer. His voice was deep and he sang well and they were accepted on a trial basis for a short tour in France. Ken wrote to tell Eirlys, adding that they hoped to spend at least part of the Christmas holiday at St David's Well.

There was an urgency about Christmas in St David's Well in 1939 that was difficult to explain. Since the warnings about possible food rationing had begun and before they had become a reality, people had built up stores against the shortages to come. Now, only three months into the war, they opened their hoarded tins of ham and salmon, and used the dried fruit and sugar to make one last splendid cake. Tins of fruit and Nestle's cream were taken from their hiding places too and were included on the menu over the holiday period.

It was bravado. People told themselves there was no need to hoard, that if they were bold and confident, by next Christmas everything would be back to normal. All the fears would have become a memory. Warnings about future shortages and statements about the reduction in the manufacture of everyday objects were treated with scorn. The war was on the continent, not at home, and anyway, it would soon be won.

The shops were emptied of food and gifts and even household items ran out as people bought a new mat or a fresh pair of curtains or some new china for Christmas. Even the wallpaper shops had a hectic few weeks as women cajoled their husbands and sons into redecorating a room or two – for Christmas. As savings clubs paid out, the money was spent. Economy was a word to make you smile. This wasn't the time to consider tomorrow. or next week or next year.

Temporary stalls appeared on street corners, moved on by the police only to open up again a few yards away. Many sold holly and mistletoe and Christmas trees of all sizes. There were also those selling paper trimmings for living rooms, and cards and calendars which the vendors waved enthusiastically, shouting that the calendars were special souvenir issues on which to mark the end of Hitler and his war.

Butchers' windows were filled with geese and chickens and a few turkeys for those who could afford them. Rabbits were displayed less noticeably for those who could not.

Bernard Gregory delivered his annual supply of birds to the butchers who had ordered them, stripped of their feathers and ready to put on display. He had worked through the night, two nights in a row, taking a nap occasionally to keep himself going so the job would be finished on time.

He wished his son Peter were there to help, but Peter had volunteered for the forces long before war had been declared and Bernard didn't even know where he was. Scotland maybe? Holland? Or even France? He hadn't heard for eighteen days and didn't even know if he still had a son, he thought sorrowfully, as he handed the last of his turkeys to Keys the butcher.

He accepted payment and went home and slept for twelve hours. Christmas was not worth thinking about, or planning for. This year it would be just another day. Feeding the donkeys and the remaining livestock, cooking a bit of bacon and a couple of eggs and listening to the wireless or reading the copy of *The Hobbit* that Peter had given him last time he came home.

–

In the house at Brook Lane, Bleddyn cooked Christmas dinner assisted by Johnny, Taff and Evelyn. Irene was there but vague, as though unaware of the importance of the day. She opened presents, smiled and put them aside, handed Taff, Evelyn and Johnny their presents – which had been chosen, bought and packed by Bleddyn – and picked at her dinner, all with hardly a word spoken.

The rest of the family wore paper hats, laughed and cracked jokes and pretended to be having a good time, but the ghostlike presence of Irene made it all a farce, Bleddyn thought, temper simmering as Irene made no effort to make the day a good one for them all. As soon as was polite, Evelyn and Taff left to spend the rest of the day with Huw, Marged, and their family in Sidney Street, where the atmosphere was sure to be more cheerful.

Johnny went to call for Eirlys and her family, who were also invited to spend the rest of the day in Sidney Street with his Auntie Marged, Uncle Huw and the rest.

"I'll follow on later," Bleddyn said, and, when the young people had left, he tried to get a reaction from Irene by showing an anger he didn't really feel. Anger was spent long ago, and even concern had faded to become nothing more than mild contempt.

"Couldn't you make a bit of an effort for Johnny and Taff and Evelyn?" he demanded, raising his voice in frustration. "What will Evelyn think of you, acting like this on Christmas Day?"

"I don't like Evelyn. She doesn't look after Taff as she should; working all day in some factory, how can she?" Irene spoke softly, looking towards a cushion, as if talking to someone he couldn't see.

"You're a fine one to talk. When did you ever look after Taff? Or Johnny, or me?"

"I'll make a cup of tea," she said and went into the kitchen. When the sound of clattering cups stopped, Bleddyn went to investigate. Irene had made a pot of tea, poured herself a cup and gone back to bed.

Irene sat against the pillows, rocking slightly. Her life would be so different once Morgan and she told the world about their love. He wouldn't bully her or expect her to do things she hated. Her eyes were sharp and intelligent as she went over in her mind the plan to make Bleddyn accept her leaving. Non-communication was so easy. All she had to do was walk off as they were talking to her and sit in her room. They would be relieved to see her go.

Persuading Morgan to leave Annie might be more difficult. She shivered slightly as she thought about how she would deal with rejection if Morgan refused to leave his wife. That was something she wouldn't be able to face. She'd rather be dead than cope with the humiliation of being spurned by Morgan.

It wouldn't happen. Not now. He would never leave her now.

–

Bleddyn sat staring into the fire for a while, then decided that he was wasting his time here with a woman who refused to speak to him. Ill or not, Irene was driving him away and from where he was looking, it was deliberate. He left the remainder of the dishes, reached for his overcoat and trilby and went to join the other members of his family.

In his brother's house the atmosphere was completely different. Dinner had been cleared away and dishes of sweets and displays of party crackers decorated the table. Besides Huw and Marged, their four children were there. Ronnie with his wife Olive; young Eynon; Bethan with her soon-to-be fiancé, Freddy Clements. And Lilly, who was putting on a coat and preparing to go out.

"Where are you off to, Lilly?" Bleddyn asked as she fastened a scarf over her long dark hair. "Meeting some friends?"

"Don't ask," Marged moaned. "Not a word will she say. Got some secret boyfriend but he must have a face like a codfish, because she won't let us see him or even tell us who he is."

"I'm going to follow you one of these days," Huw said jokingly. "I want to know who my daughter is seeing that she can't bring home to meet the family. Ugly is he?" Then, "You aren't ashamed of *us*, are you?"

"You do that, our Dad, and I'll walk out of this house and never come back."

"Promises, promises," Huw sighed, winking at Bleddyn.

–

Johnny hadn't gone straight to Sidney Street. He had some chocolate money in his pocket for Josie and Marie and he went to see Hannah. He felt slightly embarrassed, knowing his excuse was a feeble one, but took out the gold foil-covered sweets and handed them to the little girls. Avoiding looking at their mother, he began to squeak, pretending the sound came from somewhere else. He fooled about searching for the cause of the squeaking, making the girls laugh, then produced a couple of sugar mice, each in its own sugar bed.

If he was surprised when they didn't go at once to show their grandparents in the next room, he didn't comment. Instead, he said, "I'm off to visit my Auntie Marged and Uncle Huw and all my cousins. Then we'll all be going for a walk to get some exercise before tea. How would you like to come with me, you two and your mam?"

"Thank you, Johnny," Hannah replied softly as Josie and Marie turned to look at her questioningly, "but I don't think this is a time for strangers to turn up uninvited."

"Extra friends calling is what Christmas is all about. You *are* invited; *I'm* inviting you," he laughed.

Hannah shook her head. "Your Christmas is with Eirlys, with her family meeting yours. And that's how it should be."

The children complained a little but she promised them they would go with Johnny and Eirlys another day, when it was warmer.

She didn't emphasize the fact he and Eirlys were a couple, but it hung in the air, making him inexplicably angry – not with Hannah for quite reasonably refusing what she saw as an unofficial invitation, but with Eirlys, even though she would surely not have complained.

He forced himself out of the mood of melancholy that was settling over him and called for Eirlys. They arrived soon after Bleddyn, with Annie, Morgan and the three evacuees, who were carrying their new game of Ludo, hoping to find someone to play with them, and boasting about the bikes Morgan had bought for them.

There were already four empty flagons on the kitchen table and the gramophone was playing music to which Huw and Marged were trying to dance, and, in the impossibly overcrowded room, causing much laughter. There were gifts to exchange and Eirlys was delighted to receive several items for her "bottom drawer".

"I suppose you have got one?" Moll asked. "Most girls start one as they approach twenty."

"Oh yes," Eirlys assured her. "There's quite a lot of linen that Mam has given me which I've embroidered. Some china too. It's surprising how much you need to start off, isn't it?"

"I'll look in my cupboards and see what I can find," Moll promised.

Johnny smiled his thanks but there was little joy in it for him. Shouldn't he be more excited about collecting things for their future home? Or was it more the responsibility for women to make sure they had the necessities? He decided he would talk about it with a few friends and with his brother Taff.

Every seat that could be squeezed into the room had been taken, with neighbours calling, finding it impossible to leave, and adding to the numbers. When they had pushed a few children out of the way and found seats in the very crowded room, Morgan announced that he needed a walk and everyone had to move again.

"For heaven's sake, Morgan, sit down and stop disturbing people," Annie sighed.

"It's as hot as Old Nick's kitchen in here," he grumbled, loosening his tie and collar.

"Always like this, he is, never can sit still," Annie said as she glared at him.

"Likes to be out and about, doesn't he, Mrs Price?" Evelyn smiled, glancing at Eirlys as she spoke as though the exchange should mean something to her. Eirlys frowned then looked away.

–

With crutches supporting him, Morgan made his way to Brook Lane, swinging himself along at a fair old pace with the ease of practice. The streets were deserted. Everyone was either sleeping off their dinner or listening to the entertainment offered by the BBC. No one wanted to move; even the children had given up parading with their new toys and were indoors where it was warm and the food was plentiful.

He went along the back of Brook Lane and through the garden and Irene opened the door as soon as he touched the knocker.

—

Morgan wasn't the only one to need a walk. Eating more than usual and sitting in the overheated room put several of the others in danger of falling asleep. As the day was dry, if a little chilly, Eirlys and Johnny decided to take the three musketeers and walk down to see Mr Gregory's donkeys in Sally Gough's field.

Mr Gregory seemed pleased to see them. He found a bottle of pop for the boys and made tea for Eirlys and Johnny. Eirlys asked about his son and was told that he was on secret service for the government, and he knew nothing more than that.

"I'll see Peter when I see him." Mr Gregory shrugged sadly, then he forced a smile and put aside his concern. It was Christmas Day and no one wanted to listen to his worries about Peter out of touch in a foreign country, with the war beginning to threaten them all.

As they approached Sidney Street again they heard music.

"That doesn't sound like the wireless," Johnny frowned. As he opened the door he saw that the party had got its second wind and several others had arrived. Among them, as promised, were Ken Ward and Max Moon, on a brief visit to Ken's grandparents. Ken had brought a set of tubular bells made for him by the local blacksmith out of tubes of varying length, and Max had brought a piano accordion on which he began to play songs for the children to sing.

"Hang on," Johnny said, waving a hand to stop him. "There are two little girls who would love to join the party. Eirlys, why don't you and Beth go and fetch Hannah and Josie and Marie? They won't have had a party this year."

The others readily agreed and after Eirlys had greeted Ken affectionately and promised to talk later and exchange news not covered in their letters, Johnny saw her off on her errand.

The party seemed to slow into a neutral mood as he waited impatiently for them to return. The music was soft and sentimental and the food was prepared but not served. Crackers were temptingly on display but were held back until Josie and Marie could share the fun.

Johnny had difficulty hiding the delight on his face when Hannah came in, rosy-faced from the cold evening, with her two cosily dressed, very excited daughters. Moll found them a place near Ken and Max while Hannah sat between Granny Moll and Marged, both of whom made her feel very welcome.

Ken gave his seat to Johnny and went to talk to Eirlys, greeting her with an affectionate kiss.

"I've heard all about your war efforts and your promotion at work. You're doing a great job from what I've been told," Ken said, staring at her, admiring her, his eyes glowing and revealing his pleasure at seeing her again.

She left him as he and Max were asked to play and sing, and she hugged Johnny and told him he was the most thoughtful of men to have invited Hannah and her girls. When she looked up to see others agreeing, she saw that Evelyn was glaring at her in her usual belligerent manner. Eirlys hugged Johnny tighter and decided to avoid looking at her for the rest of the evening.

For a while it had seemed that Evelyn's dislike of her had faded. They had been out together, the two of them with Johnny and his brother Taff, and the atmosphere had been tolerably pleasant. Not as relaxed as when they had first became friends, but there had been signs of a thaw in Evelyn's previous frostiness. Eirlys wondered what she had done this time to upset the girl, and decided that Evelyn was one of the unfortunate people who had inexplicable moods. She fervently hoped Taff hadn't married someone like his mother!

It was as they both went out to wash a few dishes that Eirlys asked Evelyn why she was so unfriendly. "You seem to dislike me, but I don't know why. Have I said something or done something to hurt you? I certainly haven't intended to. I want us to be friends when we are sisters-in-law."

"I don't dislike you. I just don't think you are the right person for Johnny."

"But who Johnny marries isn't anything to do with you." Eirlys frowned. "Why are you so concerned?"

"Look to your own family. See what standards they set and you should understand only too well why I'm concerned!" Evelyn threw down the tea towel and left the room.

A chill swept through Eirlys's body. Did Evelyn know about her father and the robbery? Had she learned the truth about how Dadda had broken his ankle? Johnny knew so it wouldn't be too much of a surprise to know he had told Taff. Yet, she thought, the dislike goes back further than the robbery at the newsagent. Could there have been others?

Puzzled, more than a little frightened, but unwilling to follow Evelyn and question her further, Eirlys went on dealing with the dishes. When she picked up a tray of sandwiches Marged had made and went back to rejoin the party, Johnny was dancing with Hannah, with Marie in his arms. They were all laughing and she felt a pang of alarm. He looked so happy.

Hardly surprising, she chided herself, it was Christmas and everyone else looked just as merry. Drink, the occasion and having the family crammed in together plus a few friends could hardly have resulted in sad faces. Nevertheless, she was relieved when he put the little girl down and came to dance with her.

She looked at Evelyn, sitting close to her husband Taff. Was she simply trying to place doubt in her mind? Surely she didn't consider Hannah a better choice for Johnny to marry? That would be too ridiculous.

To try and ease her mind she asked Johnny if he had checked on whether many of the burglaries had taken place on Fridays, when her father pretended to go to the ARP meetings.

"There wasn't a regular pattern," he said, reassuring her. "Besides, your father has been seen once or twice drinking with some friends, and on many Friday evenings he works, because of the shifts the factory uses. Forget it," he said, squeezing her hand as he led her to what Marged laughingly called the dance floor.

The dancing was a comfort to her. There wasn't much room and it was little more than being in Johnny's arms and luxuriating in the sensuous delight of having him near. Soon everyone slowed down and sat where they could find a seat, until the music stopped and people succumbed to the lethargy of too much heat and too much food.

She was reluctant to let Johnny go, needing his nearness, but he left her and went into the kitchen to get cold drinks for Hannah's girls, leaving her standing, conscious of Evelyn's stony stare.

Ken came over and when Johnny rejoined them said, "Congratulations to you both. Eirlys is a special person and you're a lucky man, Johnny Castle." He thumped Johnny on the back, winked at Eirlys and went to take a drink to Max, who was teaching Johnny's cousin Beth to play "Silent Night, Holy Night" on the tubular bells.

Hannah had never been so happy. In the stuffy, overheated room, the fire was kept as large as possible, with chestnuts piled and slit ready for roasting. A washing bench had been brought in to provide extra seats and the youngest lolled against its legs with cushions to add to their comfort. Faces were red and damp with sweat, but no one wanted to move, although, Hannah thought with fascination, no one could if they wanted to! This family gathering was something she had never experienced before and she knew she would remember it all her life.

While they recovered from the effort of dancing, a few party games and tricks entertained them all, everyone contributing, even serious little Percival who sang "Daisy Daisy", da–di–da–ing when he couldn't remember the words.

Max put down the accordion and began to play carols on the tubular bells and they sounded magical. Ken sang once or twice and the others listened in silence, wallowing in the atmosphere of peace and contentment, the war a million miles from their thoughts.

Most of the children were asleep before he finished and the silence that followed was more telling than applause. It had been a perfect end to the day.

"Will you be all right going home with your mam and dad?" Johnny asked Eirlys as they all began to move and gather coats and hats. "I'd better make sure Hannah and the children get home safely – in fact, I think I'll have to carry little Marie, don't you?" He pointed to where Marie was sleeping, rosy-faced, in the arms of Granny Moll.

"Would you like me to come with you?" Eirlys asked.

"No, I'll be able to go straight home if I'm on my own." The truth was, he admitted to himself, he didn't want her to. He had spent very little time with her that day; even walking to Mr Gregory's had been more a walk for the evacuees than a romantic stroll with the girl he was planning to marry. What was the matter with him? He should be glad of the opportunity to extend the day and walk her home at the end of it.

"Thanks for a lovely day, Johnny," she said, offering her face for a kiss. In his strange mood, he thought the "thank you" was too casually said: polite, a necessity, but without any real feeling.

Walking back through the silent streets with their breath showing in balloons of steam on the cold air, he felt a greater happiness than he'd felt all day. First the mood Mam had been in had ruined the atmosphere at dinnertime, then, in some way he couldn't fathom, Eirlys hadn't behaved as he had expected either. Now, with the sleepy Marie in his arms, and Hannah beside him trailing a weary Josie, he felt as though this was what he had been waiting for all day.

At the door they went in quietly without turning up the gas light which she had left burning low. "For fear of waking Mam," Hannah explained. So, as she guided the children toward the bedroom behind their living room, Johnny took the opportunity offered, and held her in his arms and kissed her. He hurried away before anything could be said, and ran home feeling like a schoolboy after a first date.

–

Ken and Max left soon after Christmas. Eirlys was sorry to see them go. She didn't wish them luck as she normally would; with the job they were going to do it was too much like tempting fate. They had added a great deal to the celebrations and she knew that Christmas 1939 was one she would never forget.

—

A few days after the festivities had ended, Morgan called at Irene's house in Brook Lane after seeing Johnny in the hardware store and Bleddyn opening up the fish-and-chip shop ready for the lunchtime session.

She opened the door to him and fell into his arms with the usual enthusiasm, but then she stepped back and said softly, "Morgan, there's something I have to tell you."

"That sounds serious. You aren't going to tell me goodbye, are you? Irene, love, I couldn't bear that."

"No, it's more the opposite."

"We meet or we don't meet," he laughed. "How can there be another opposite?"

"I think I might be expecting. We're going to have a baby, Morgan love. A baby. Isn't that wonderful?"

"What?" The shock distorted his face as the horror of what she was telling him hit him. He stared at her, then shook her gently, forced a laugh. "Don't make jokes like that, love. Don't try and scare me."

"Don't say things like that! How can you be scared? It's wonderful."

"Irene, you can't be."

"It's true. I've been telling myself it's a mistake, but I've checked and checked and there's no other explanation."

"Will Bleddyn believe it's his?" She didn't reply and when he forced himself to look at her, let her see the dismay written on his face, she had tears in her eyes.

"No, Morgan, this is ours, yours and mine, and I think it's wonderful. I thought you'd be as happy as I am."

"But if we could persuade him, just for the present, while we made plans?"

Tears drizzled down her cheeks and she shook her head. "I can't convince him of that. We've lived like strangers for more than a year.'

"I don't know what to do." He sat on a chair and hid his face in his hands.

"Leave Annie. There's nothing else we can do. We have to leave Bleddyn and Annie and the children and go away and start again. Preferably where no one knows us."

"I can't do that. Sorry, Irene, but I can't leave Annie and Eirlys. What would they do? How would they manage?"

"Let them try. We need you more than they do, me and our baby. They're always telling you how useless you are, well, let them see how they manage without you. They don't deserve you, Morgan, love, you know they don't."

They sat discussing it for a long time, each becoming more and more depressed as an alternative solution evaded them. Irene was insistent that Morgan leave Annie and look after her, and Morgan was equally sure that he wouldn't. After the first subdued exchanges, the comforting words, the declarations of everlasting love, they became more heated and within ten minutes they were quarrelling. Irene was crying, her voice reaching higher and higher until she was almost screaming. Morgan stomped out, for once uncaring about whether or not he was seen. Irene shouted after him, "If you don't tell Annie, then I will!" He sat in the park where the grasses and trees were white with frost. A wonderland of wintery beauty, of which he was unaware. He'd been in trouble before but nothing like this. He couldn't expect Annie to forgive him this. He couldn't tell them. He couldn't face losing Annie and Eirlys. His daughter wouldn't take his side over this. Pacifist she might be but she wouldn't support him now. The decision to stop seeing Irene was easily made but he knew that the solution to the wider situation was not. How could he just walk away and pretend the past few months hadn't happened? She was going to have his child. Whatever he decided, Irene wasn't going to allow him to walk away and face it alone. Scared as he was, he knew he couldn't ask her to do that. The best decision was to wait, do nothing at all in case it was a ghastly mistake. Then, when – or if – it became a certainty, he would have to tell Annie.

–

Eirlys had called at a wool shop which was closing down and ordered a large quantity of knitting wool at a bargain price. Some was for knitting but much of it, best quality but boring colours, she planned to use for her rug-making. As background to her designs, grey, navy, dark green and maroon were ideal. She was passing the end of Brook Lane when she thought she saw her father. Unlikely, she thought, as he was at work during the afternoons this week. She went to call out to him, but hesitated. Surely it couldn't be him, and wouldn't she look a fool if she chased after a complete stranger? He couldn't have been the only man with a leg in plaster.

A woman was watching her from her front garden: hair in curlers, wearing a cross-over apron, wellingtons on her feet, she was carrying logs she had collected from the pile at the side of the house.

"Looking for someone, are you?" the woman called.

"No, it's all right. I thought I knew that man, but I'm probably mistaken."

"Oh, him. He's always around here, going in through the back gate and thinking no one will see. Furtive he looks to me. That tells you something, eh?" The woman nodded knowingly.

Eirlys was embarrassed, understanding the insinuations. "Then it couldn't have been my father. He has no business around here."

"You can hardly make a mistake with that great lump of plaster on his leg, can you? Your father you say?"

"No, no. It wasn't him. Too tall," she said, inventing any reason to convince the woman she was wrong. She was probably making it all up, Eirlys decided; she looked the sort to enjoy spreading gossip. True or untrue, it probably didn't make any difference.

She hurried away, working hard to convince herself she had been wrong. Then she sighed with relief; if it had been her father he must have been calling on Johnny. Probably returning the scarf Johnny left a few days ago.

–

Morgan went to work on the bus and got off at the factory. They were pretty lenient about his timekeeping since his accident. He only had to tell them he had a hospital appointment and they didn't ask for proof.

He worked the last hours of his shift and left the factory with the rest. Going straight home he was relieved when

Annie was there. After the shock of Irene's announcement he needed the ordinariness of home.

Throughout the late evening, after he had eaten the snack she had prepared for him, he was solicitous, making tea for them and bringing in the tin of biscuits, offering the last of the chocolate ones to her, raking out the fire before being asked, and even going out and, in the thin beam of a torch, bringing in firewood for the next morning in case there wasn't enough already dry. All the time Irene's words echoed around in his head. "Our baby, Morgan. Our baby."

How could he tell Annie he had been carrying on with another woman? She didn't deserve it, she hadn't done anything wrong. In fact, compared with wives of friends, he had been very fortunate, apart from not having a second child. He felt a leap of guilt. That would be another devastating blow for her, another woman bearing the child she couldn't have. His child.

Irene was right about one thing, if they decided to stay together they would have to leave St David's Well. The humiliation and embarrassment would be more than he could cope with. He looked at his wife, hard-working and strong, fierce-looking at times, gentle at others, with a full, generous figure, still very attractive. She was working away at the sock she was knitting, concentrating on turning the heel, counting stitches, frowning slightly. Such an ordinary task, such an ordinary scene, but one to which he might have to say goodbye.

A letter came for him the next morning and, seeing the scrawled writing, he took it from a curious Eirlys and stuffed it into his pocket. It wasn't until Annie had gone to the baker's shop and Eirlys had left for the office that he looked at it, staring at it for a long time before daring to open it. He had never seen Irene's writing, but knew in his heart that she had written it.

Surely it was good news. It had to be. She had been mistaken, she had miscounted the days, it was a false alarm. Several of his friends had told him about those.

In trepidation he tore off the top of the envelope and unfolded the single page. The writing, large and untidy, swam before his eyes.

"If you don't help me I will kill myself," it said.

–

Irene sat in the doctor's surgery. She was smiling slightly, her eyes glowing with an inner happiness. This was a wonderful thing to have happened. Now she and Morgan would be together. She could leave the boring Bleddyn with his fastidious routines and organised life. She could relax and enjoy herself with the easy-going Morgan. When she considered how they would live she promised herself that she would find work and help pay the bills. That was something she would never do for Bleddyn. He insisted that the only way to help was to work on the sands in the family business and the family made it clear they disapproved of her because she had always refused. She would show them how wrong they had been about her all these years. She wasn't sick or helpless, just bored.

The doctor reached for his pad when he saw her. "More tablets, Mrs Castle?" he asked.

"Not this time, Doctor. I think it's something far more interesting." She bowed her head shyly and said, "I think I am going to have another child."

To her consternation the doctor didn't gasp and tell her it was wonderful and exciting, or jump up and shake her hand

and congratulate her. Instead he asked, "How old are you now, Mrs Castle?"

"Old enough not to expect such a wonderful gift."

"I make it forty-four. A little old for babies."

After asking a lot of questions, he examined her, then sat down again behind his desk. "Sorry to disappoint you, but there's no sign of a pregnancy. I think you might be starting the menopause. The change," he added when she looked puzzled. "A little early I agree, but we're all made differently, and there have been other patients of mine who have had a similar experience."

Irene was stunned. All the excitement, the hope of a fresh new life, the thrill of being a mother again, the attention, the pride, it was all gone in those few casually spoken words.

The doctor could see she was upset and added comfortingly, "Mrs Castle, you must realise that nature is kind not to allow us to have babies when we lack the energy to look after them properly. Of course, it might not be the change; what you are experiencing could be due to some other cause, and we will investigate further. Either way, you can relax and know you won't have to face motherhood again. What a relief that must be."

He wrote on his pad, giving her a prescription for her usual pills, and stood as a signal that her time was up. She said nothing, and seemed unable to rouse herself and leave his office. With a hand under her arm he coaxed her out of her chair. "You can sit in the waiting room for a while if you feel tired. Having surprising news sometimes has that effect. It will wear off soon and you will be relieved. Much the best result after your worries, Mrs Castle."

He emphasised that there being no baby was good news, but Irene hardly heard. She had taken in nothing since being told she was experiencing the change of life. She sat in the waiting room and stared at the dull walls. She was old, past child-bearing age, past the age when she could look ahead with hope. She was old, old, old. Her dreams were no longer possible. Her best years were behind her.

Mrs Grainer sat in a chair waiting her turn to see the doctor and she spoke to Irene, but received no response.

–

Morgan didn't start work that day until two p.m., and he went in search of Irene. He had hardly slept the previous night, worrying about what had happened. Since their talk, every knock at the door threw him into a panic, convinced she had come to tell Annie about their affair. Somehow he had to persuade her to wait, do nothing until they were sure. When she had spoken to him, she had not seen a doctor and it was on this that he based his prayers.

She wasn't at the house on Brook Lane and, finding Bleddyn there on his day off, he made some excuse about wanting Irene to help with the tea-making at the fire-watching station. Bleddyn didn't think it was worth the trouble of asking her. "She won't be keen to help, but I don't know where she is anyway." He was shaking a large mat out in the garden and seemed a bit impatient at being interrupted. "She walks around on her own for hours and I never know where she's been. Ill she is, you know that, don't you? I've given up trying to find out how she fills her time."

"Must be awful for her," Morgan said sympathetically.

"Awful for all of us," Bleddyn replied shortly. "You might try the shops, although shopping is something she rarely does, leaves it to me she does. Like everything else."

Morgan's leg was aching but he stomped along the main street looking for her in the shops without much hope of finding her. At one o'clock he gave up and went home to join Annie and Eirlys for eggs on toast before going to the factory.

–

Bleddyn didn't see Irene before leaving for the evening shift at the chip shop. He had spent his time off from the lunchtime session doing work that Irene could reasonably be expected to do and he was tired and irritable.

As the time came for him to leave the house, he was also concerned. He didn't like her going out after dark, although as he worked most evenings he could never be sure she was in as she promised to be. He left a note telling her that there was stew in the saucepan for her to heat, called at the hardware shop and told Johnny to make sure she ate it, and went to open up. Something was worrying him and he couldn't understand what it was.

Irene often stayed out until he was at the shop, and he didn't normally worry, but not having seen her all day and being told by Mrs Grainer that she had been to see the doctor set alarm bells ringing. At nine o'clock, unable to wait any longer, he left the assistant in charge and ran home. The house was empty.

He searched through the rooms looking for something – he knew not what – to give him a clue. Then he realised what had been worrying him. Her coat with the fur collar, her only winter coat, was on the back of the door. She was out in the harshness of the January night insufficiently dressed.

He ran to Annie and Morgan's hoping to find Johnny there. Gathering up several of the neighbours, Bleddyn and

Johnny began to plan their route to search the streets. "She's done this before," Bleddyn told them as they each collected a blanket and some torches.

Eirlys looked at Johnny and said accusingly, "You didn't believe me when I told you I saw her in the fields without a coat."

"Sorry; I knew you weren't imagining it. I saw her myself a while later and brought her home wrapped in my overcoat. I should have told you, but I try to pretend it isn't true sometimes. She's ill and I can't cope with it."

"You should have told me, Johnny."

"Forget that now, let's just find her."

"I'll go to your house and wait, in case she turns up," she offered.

-

Morgan came in from work at ten, and was sent around to the ARP centre to ask the wardens to look out for Irene. Everything possible had been done, apart from telling the police, and Bleddyn didn't want to do that until they had tried to find her themselves. "The less fuss for her to deal with the better," he explained. He didn't admit to his fear that another result of police involvement might be her being taken away for treatment in the mental hospital, his greatest dread.

-

Irene had been given a lift to the outskirts of the town and had walked through the fields towards the caravan. She had left her coat at home and was shivering, dressed only in a black dress and a black cardigan.

She had stood perfectly still against the hedge when Bleddyn and Morgan passed her, stabbing the darkness with their torches and calling her name. The icy cold air had made her shake uncontrollably, but she had smiled as their voices faded away from her.

She sat in the caravan for a while, wrapped in the blankets smelling of mildew, seeking warmth and comfort from the memories it revived. With one of the blankets around her she walked over the now hard and brittle grass to the road and, throwing the blanket away, stopped a van and begged a lift.

The young couple inside were on a visit to the girl's parents and they chatted amiably but without getting much response from Irene. Thanking them for the lift, she got out of the van and went to a lorry park where there was a café, which she had visited several times in the past. It was closed.

A group of lorry drivers were huddled in a corner sharing hot drinks from their flasks and she drank gratefully from one and accepted a lift into the next town. She moved from one town to another and finally, at two a.m., she was standing near the entrance to the docks of a town some thirty miles away from St David's Well.

She knew that the access to the dock area would be heavily guarded, but dressed in dark clothes and being small she thought she might succeed in getting past the soldiers who stood, shuffling their feet, changing position, clearly bored and impatient for their shift to end.

Her chance came when the guard changed and at the same time challenged a workman going to deal with a consignment of food just arriving at the dockside. She slipped easily under the wire and slid out on the other side. She felt a chuckle swell and fill her throat. It was a daring game she was playing, outwitting the soldiers who were armed with guns.

Slowly she made her way to the very edge of the dock. It took her almost an hour but instead of becoming tired, she felt more awake with every minute that passed. She was clever, level-headed, resourceful, talented, all the attributes Bleddyn accused her of lacking. She would succeed without anyone even trying to stop her.

-

The search continued in St David's Well, hampered by the intense darkness. Once they thought they had found Irene, and the call that went around the countryside and the subsequent relief was felt by everyone.

It turned out to be a female tramp who, when woken, issued a stream of abuse that startled Johnny and Taff, then reduced them to laughter as they imagined their quiet mother knowing such words.

-

Irene sat near a bollard for a while thinking about the cheerful decorations still covering shop windows and showing at the windows of houses. Tawdry they were, she thought. A pathetic attempt to make Christmas a special time when it was nothing more than an excuse to drink and eat more than you needed. She tried to remember Christmases when the boys were small, but then, as now, she had backed away from any fun. She blamed Bleddyn. The Castle family tried too hard and made it artificial. Yes, Bleddyn was to blame. And now Morgan was letting her down too. No baby, but he didn't know that. He had refused to help her. There was no one anywhere who cared for her.

There was little light but she could see the water, moving sluggishly, greasy and looking very cold. The surface was several feet below where she was sitting. If she went in there, she would not be able to get back out. She vaguely wondered whether the soldiers would be punished for allowing her to reach the dockside. She was curious but not concerned.

–

At two o'clock, as Irene was crawling through the wire towards the dockside, Huw called his brother and insisted on informing the police. "Damn it all, Bleddyn, we might be talking about her life here!" he said in exasperation.

Bleddyn agreed and then, as was often the case, their reaction made him wish he had spoken to them earlier.

At once teams were sent out and a series of signals arranged to report if Irene was found or any clues or ideas needed to be shared. The streets of the town and the fields surrounding became unusually busy and activity increased as the night wore on.

"She might have been wandering and now the cold might have made her try and find a place to sleep. We have to find her before her body temperature falls too low," one of the officers told them. Ignoring the fields, they concentrated their searches on the streets near her home. Frustrated by the lack of light, thin torch beams pricked the darkness in alleyways and lanes and on waste ground again and again. People who now worked in close proximity called to each other as the intensive search gathered momentum.

Bleddyn and Huw searched together and they knocked on the door of anyone who might know Irene to ask for news, but no one had seen her. Morgan sneaked off to see if she had gone to their caravan, but the air of neglect and the stale smell that greeted him made him doubt whether the place had been used that day. In the darkness and his melancholy mood he didn't notice the absence of one of the blankets. He told the police about the caravan and explained that it was a place where Irene liked to spend time. He told them he had searched it and thought it had not been recently opened.

–

Irene became aware of how cold she was. Her whole body was stiff, there was no feeling in her feet and her hands just wouldn't move. She rubbed her arms with her hands once or twice, to try to bring life back. She soon gave up and accepted the lethargic sensation of non-feeling like a friend. A deep sadness overwhelmed her and she slipped gently into the water, momentarily imagining that it was warmer than the air.

Eight

In the mortuary chapel, Bleddyn sat and stared at the body of his wife and wondered what had caused her to be so unhappy that she couldn't face another day.

"I failed her," he said, "but I don't know what else I could have done."

Johnny and Taff were with him, and Taff's wife Evelyn was waiting outside the room.

Taff said, "She was ill, Dad, you can't blame yourself for this."

"But I do. I should have cared for her more. I worked long hours, specially in the summer, and she was left on her own day after day."

"I can't remember a time when she was not ill," Taff said. "We were always making excuses for her. How can this be your fault?"

Johnny asked, "Did you know how ill she was?"

"I learned recently that she was a difficult and confused child and was suicidal when she was a very young woman, besides the attempts I knew about."

"I mean, when you married her, did you know about the depression? Her strange moods? The family must have known. Did they tell you?"

Bleddyn shook his head. "No, I had no idea. They kept it from me."

"If you had known, would you still have married her?" Taff asked.

Bleddyn stared into space but did not reply.

Johnny wasn't a man to show his emotions easily, certainly not within his family, but he had a strong impulse to hug his father.

–

Unaware that Irene's body had been found, Morgan walked up and down the living room. It was four in the morning and he hadn't slept. The air was painfully cold and most of the searchers had given up at three a.m. planning to begin again at dawn. Even the places they looked for her would have to be examined again, as, with the limited light from weakening torches, no one could be sure she hadn't been there, tucked up small, hiding from them in her confusion.

Where was Irene? He dreaded her being found. This time she would have a reason to explain her black mood: his refusal to accept her child and go away with her. He had avoided her since her announcement. She was bound to tell Bleddyn, and Annie was certain to find out. Or, worse still, she would come here and tell Annie to her face about their affair. He had to save Annie from that humiliation. He had to tell Annie himself. At least then she would be able to prepare her response, salvage a little dignity. He owed her that.

He imagined Annie opening the door to Irene, inviting her in, smiling and welcoming, then listening as Irene told her about her affair with Annie's husband, told her she was carrying his child. That would be cruel, and, coward as he undoubtedly was, he had to save Annie from that.

His thoughts drifted and returned to the shock of the note Irene had sent him. He had to see beyond the words. It had been a wanting that Irene would tell Annie and Eirlys if he didn't agree to take her away. She wouldn't kill herself as the note threatened, that was just a touch of drama, to frighten him into agreeing to go away with her.

He had kept the fire burning and the room was stifling. He opened the back door and to his surprise it was snowing. He imagined Irene lying somewhere, slowly, silently being covered by the beautiful but insidious and deadly flakes. Shivering more from the image than the temperature, he closed the door and leaned against it trying to blot out the fearful pictures his mind was creating. He had to find her, but where could he look? He searched his mind for clues but thought only of the caravan, their secret love nest. How pathetic that sounded now.

He went into the living room and lifted some ashes to liven the fire. It burned brightly in the frosty air. He still shivered. Would he ever feel warm again? Sticks snapped and blazed but he didn't add coal; he needed the flames to take away the darkness in his heart. But he knew the brightness was a sham, just as his pretence of loving Irene had been. The fire burned itself out, became a heap of grey ash, and looked dead.

At five thirty a.m. he could wait no longer. He made a tray of tea and went up. He shook Annie, pulling her reluctantly from a deep sleep. "Annie, love. There's something I have to tell you."

He would never forget the way his words altered her sleep-rosy face. The way her eyes – reluctant to open – suddenly widened in disbelief. Her scream of anguish woke Eirlys who came running, presuming her mother had had a nightmare.

"Nightmare? No, Eirlys, not a nightmare, this is real. Your father—"

Morgan stopped her by putting a hand across her mouth. "Think, woman. We don't want our daughter to hear all this."

He released his hand and Annie stared at him in silence.

"Go back to your room, Eirlys, love. Your mam and I have something serious and very private to discuss."

Puzzled and not a little worried, Eirlys did what she was told, getting back into bed and covering her ears with a pillow. It was yet another row and she didn't want to hear, to try to take sides.

Ashen-faced, Annie stared at her husband. "I want to hear the full story," she said, her voice distorted by grief.

"Irene Castle and I have been meeting secretly for months."

"Where?" Annie demanded.

"Sometimes at her house in Brook Lane, and we had a caravan where we used to spend some time."

"Go on."

"Now she says she's going to have a baby and she wants me to leave you and I can't. I don't expect you to understand this, but I love you, Annie, and I haven't the slightest excuse for the stupid way I've behaved."

"A baby? Irene was going to have a baby? Your baby? But she's past forty. I was told it was too late for us when I was much younger than that."

Both were momentarily distracted from the present, thinking back to the large family they had both wanted. Irene's baby was the greatest agony of all. Neither of them knew what to say.

Then Annie pushed the tray angrily from the chair beside her bed and stared at it as it clattered to the floor. Morgan bent to pick up the shattered china but stopped. Picking up broken cups, clearing up the mess was too ordinary. They stared at each other in confusion. Both were stunned. This was something for which neither of them was prepared. If only he hadn't had to tell her about the baby.

Annie's mind flittered over all her friends and their families, aware than none of them had ever been involved in anything as sordid as this.

"I'll go and see Johnny and ask if there's any news," he said, backing out of the room.

"No you don't! I'll go!" Annie announced, bouncing out from under the covers. "I want to see this Irene when they find her; I want to tell her she can have you as from now this minute. I never want to set eyes on you again. Ever!" Turning to her husband she stared at him as though he were repulsive and said harshly, "Get out! I want you and your things out of this house before I get back."

"Don't try to see her, Annie. You'll be better off hanging on to your dignity and saying nothing."

"Give me the pleasure of telling her to her face what I think of her and her nonsense about depression! Depression indeed. Just an excuse to hang around waiting to meet her fancy man. Or men! It's unlikely you're the only one, so don't kid yourself you're so special! Or that you're the father," she added bitterly.

"I told her I wouldn't leave you, that's why she went off like she did," Morgan said.

"Well, you were wrong! As always, I have to make the decisions in this house. You *are* leaving and you're never coming back." She held back a sob as she added, "You and that tart and her child – who might or might not be yours – gone from this house you'll be before I get back. Right?"

Morgan followed her downstairs, where Annie reached for a long mackintosh and wellington boots. "Annie, love, you can't go out like that!" he protested. "You have to get dressed."

"Why? The mood I'm in, how I dress isn't important. Scragging that woman's neck is!"

"You're in the position of strength here, you haven't done anything wrong. Dress and put your make-up on, look smart and in control. That's the way to best someone."

Annie sagged as though all the strength had flowed out of her. "You're right. For once in your miserable life! I'll have a cup of tea, calm myself down, then I'll dress and go and face her. She's bound to be home by now. Stupid woman. Forty-five if she's a day and having half the town chasing after her as though she was a runaway child!"

There was a knock at the door as she was filling the kettle and she opened it to Johnny. At once she felt a twisting pain. How could she face him, knowing her husband had been having an affair with his mother? She stepped back and invited him inside.

"Mam's dead," he whispered.

She gestured for him to go into the living room where fire glowed meanly amid grey wood ash. Behind her she heard Morgan gasp. She turned and he pleaded with his eyes for her not to stay what was on her lips. He pulled her aside and whispered, "Wait, Annie, please. Not for me, for others. If we don't want to ruin everything for Eirlys and Johnny, we have to keep this from her. Don't say anything yet. Think of how this would wreck her and Johnny's life if she finds out. Let him tell us what happened, shall we?"

Somehow the plea worked and Annie remained silent and continued to make the tea with hands that shook uncontrollably.

They went into the living room where Johnny was sitting upright and uncomfortable on a hard chair. His voice shock as he told them how his mother's body had been taken from the dock after being found in the water by soldiers. She had been seen as the dawn light exposed her body, caught in some lengths of wood, her dress tangled and holding her from the depths.

Morgan heard him out then ran upstairs and locked himself in the bathroom. Imagining the scene as Irene had been pulled from her watery grave, he was crying like a child. He kept pulling the chain of the lavatory to drown the sound of his despair. He needn't have told Annie; that was the cruellest part. She need not have been made to suffer the pain of his betrayal. He could have avoided her ever finding out. If he had only waited another hour, he would have been safe. What an irony to have ruined his life and Annie's, for the sake of an hour's silence. To think he had woken her at that unearthly hour instead of waiting till morning.

Johnny waited while Annie woke Eirlys so she could be told. Morgan left the house then, and went across the picturesque fields, white with the brightness of the rising sun, to sit in the cold caravan, wrapped in misery, shame and the remaining mildewed blanket.

–

Eirlys went at once to see Bleddyn when Johnny told her the news.

She expected to help, but Bleddyn told her firmly, "I've managed more or less on my own all these years, I don't think I'll suddenly become useless."

"I just thought, with the funeral, and all the running around you'll have to do, I might help Evelyn prepare the food or something."

"It's all in hand." Bleddyn spoke abruptly and Eirlys shrugged and looked at Johnny as though to say, Well, I tried.

For days the snow stayed on the ground and frost had the streets in such a grip that people had difficulty getting around. The pavements were cleared and immediately covered again with treacherous ice and a covering of snow, and several people fell and broke bones.

Morgan stayed indoors and grieved for Irene and for his ruined marriage. Annie went about her usual routine: the bakery each morning, household tasks and shopping during the afternoon. She and Morgan didn't exchange a word. The pain of his betrayal ruined every moment of every day for Annie, remorse and bitterness affecting his.

Eirlys knew something was wrong but had no idea what it could be. She did tell her mother once that with Johnny's mother dead they should be thankful they had each other and manage to agree at least until the funeral. Annie shouted at Eirlys in such anger that she burst into tears without, for once, Annie's comfort there for her.

–

The post mortem revealed no pregnancy. No rumours had reached Bleddyn's ears about Irene having a secret lover. He believed that her insistence that there was both had been pure fantasy. Irene had lived in a fantasy world, cut off from reality; the imagined baby and lover were just symptoms of her sickness.

The newspaper reports were kind. They said that she suffered from depression and had become confused, and added that her devoted family were in shock.

Having read the reports, Morgan was convinced he was safe from discovery, and on the day before the funeral he dared to visit Bleddyn. In a bag, hidden under a few apples, he had a large tin of corned beef.

"Don't ask where it came from because I don't know and I daren't ask," he said, lifting the heavy tin from the bag. "I thought it might be useful for you to make sandwiches when the mourners come back. Hide the tin, mind. It has Ministry of Food stamped on the side!"

"I want to get rid of her clothes as soon as possible," Bleddyn said accepting the tin and putting it on the table.

"Hide it, man, unless you want us both arrested!"

"It'll upset Johnny and Taff to see her clothes hanging there, and they wouldn't like to help me to clear them out." He seemed not to have heard Morgan's warning. "I don't suppose you'd help, would you? Perhaps your Eirlys would like some of the stuff for her rug-making. I hear she's sold a few. Clever girl she is, mind. A clever girl. Johnny's a lucky man."

Morgan felt sick. If Bleddyn only knew what he was asking him to do. Yet he couldn't refuse. He looked at Bleddyn's face, strong and without a sign of suspicion. If only he hadn't told Annie, the secret of their meetings would never have come to light. Confession good for the soul? That's a laugh!

Bleddyn handed him a clean sack and beckoned for him to follow. He began to sweat as he walked up the stairs and couldn't believe how casually Bleddyn was talking. It was more like a discussion on the possessions of a stranger than his wife, and the mother of his sons.

"You seem very calm," he said, as Bleddyn led him upstairs and into the room where, so recently, he and Irene had spent passionate moments.

"Outwardly perhaps. I show control and strength for the sake of Johnny and Taff. Inside it's different. I think anger is my greatest emotion at the moment. How could she have cared so little for the boys and me that she could kill herself?"

"Best you believe it was an accident," Morgan advised. "That would be easier to cope with, and she was wandering around the docks in pitch blackness, wasn't she? How are we to know she didn't slip?"

"Because she left a note, telling me she was sick of her boring life and sick of me."

Morgan's heart leapt painfully. "Did she say anything else?" He looked at the powerfully built Bleddyn. Had he found out about him and Irene? Had he led Morgan up to this room so he could thump the life out of him? But the man seemed in control.

"She said she had a lover, but I don't believe that."

"Trying to hurt you, was she?"

"Succeeded too, for a while, until I realised she was living a fantasy. She also said she was carrying this man's child. She was going on forty-five, for God's sake! Anyway, the post mortem found no sign of it. The doctor told me she was very upset at being told it was probably the change of life and not a baby. She had a fear of getting old." He pulled open a drawer and began throwing clothes angrily onto the bed, his control slipping for a moment. "Fantasy, that was how she lived, by pretending that some wonderful life was just around the corner. A life that didn't include me," he finished quietly, and for the first time Morgan saw a hint of sadness and grief in the big man's dark eyes.

-

The funeral was sombre and made worse by the messy snow that still lingered. Morgan attended and stood beside the family, shaking with fear lest something about his involvement should come to light. He began to work out an escape route, but with this damned plaster he couldn't even run away. What was he doing here? Annie had insisted, telling him he owed the woman this final show of regret and reminding him he must look at the coffin and take at least some of the blame.

He had the face of a grieving man, but the grief was for himself and his ruined marriage.

-

Annie wondered how she would manage on her own. With Eirlys and Johnny getting married soon and her insistence – so far ignored – that Morgan should leave, she would be on her own for the first time in her life. It was tempting to forgive him sufficiently to allow him to stay, but her pride was strong. She dug her nails into her hands, trying to make the tears come. If only she could have a damned good cry and release the awful agony, she might start to feel stronger. Thank goodness she had Stanley, Harold and Percival. It was partly for their sake she hadn't thrown Morgan out on that first day. They needed him and didn't deserve to be deprived of an important person in their lives because of her pride and unhappiness.

Stanley and Harold and Percival had integrated well at school and with the neighbourhood's children. Most of the other evacuees had left and they were separated from their school friends only by their spurious maturity and their accents, although Percival was already beginning to copy his friends, coming out with pronunciation different from his brothers' accent, and Welsh word patterns.

Sledging and snowball fights were not new experiences for them but walks in the woods and fields were, and they came home at night cold, soaked right through to their skins and starving. Their appetites were enormous apart from Percival, who still had trouble with anything that needed chewing.

The snow returned, and, much to the boys' delight, Morgan had to dig his way around to the coal house and cut a path to the street. As it was a weekend they were introduced to the delights of sledging.

Dragging the home-made sled through the field, with Percival sitting on it like a disapproving master pulled by servants, dressed in so many layers he could barely move, their progress was a noisy, colourful sight. Led by Eirlys and Morgan, with Stanley and Harold pulling their small brother, they were not the only ones heading for the steep field beyond those owned by Mr Gregory. They were soon at the head of an ever-growing procession with others appearing from different directions. Some had sleds and gathering around them hoping for a ride or two were several of their friends.

Once the snow had been flattened and the ice had done its bit, the rides became faster and faster, the shouts louder and the faces redder. Scarves and even coats were discarded as they toiled up the slope dragging the sleds ready for another ride down the steeply sloping field, to come to a juddering stop on the hard furrows of the ploughed field below.

There were moans of regret when Eirlys and her father insisted that it was time to go. Even Percival ate without complaint when Annie served up some warm stew and freshly baked bread and they all declared it was their best day ever. Annie wondered whether they would be able to resist the temptation of running away from school if the snow was still there on Monday, and decided to ask Eirlys to walk them there and make sure they went in!

–

On the following Saturday, with the snow "still hanging around for more", as her mother insisted, Johnny called, and Eirlys apologised for not being ready to go out with him as planned. "The boys are due back from the fields any minute and Mam has had to go out. Sorry Johnny, but I have to be here to dry them off and get them a hot meal."

"Something smells good," Johnny sniffed appreciatively.

"They're up in Sally Gough's field next to where Mr Gregory's donkeys spend the winter. Spending the morning sledging down the sloping grass on a sled Dad made them," Eirlys explained. "Not much snow left, but they insisted on trying to find a place. Why don't you stay and eat with us? I'm cooking one of their favourites, sausages and mash."

"Thanks, I will. Is your dad eating with us?"

"How do I know? If Mam is in, Dadda is out and vice versa. I don't know what's wrong, but they've had a serious quarrel about something."

"They'll soon forget it. This isn't the first time, is it?"

"Not by a long way." She smiled ruefully. "Always arguing about something or other, and Mam usually wins. Even if she's in the wrong it's Dadda who does the apologising. Daft isn't it?"

"Anything for peace. I know a few blokes like that." He looked at her quizzically. "Will I have to say sorry when it's you who burns my dinner?" He nodded towards the grill, where the sausages were beginning to spit angrily.

She took them away from the heat and on to a rack to drain the fat into a basin. "Can't waste good dripping. Not now fats are rationed."

Johnny helped set the table then the boys came in, soaking wet, freezing cold and starving, and excited by a letter from their mother telling them that a few weeks ago, "their" River Thames had frozen over. He waited contentedly while Eirlys took the boys upstairs to rub them dry and dress them in clean, warm clothes.

Stanley and Harold cleared their plates fast, but as usual, Percival pulled a face and chewed the same mouthful for a long time, reluctantly, with his lips apart.

"These sausages is boverin' me," he whined in a low voice. Before the words were out, two forks were winging through the air and the sausages were whipped off his plate.

"You could at least ask!" Eirlys scolded, glaring at the two elder boys happily chewing their extra treat. Then she saw Johnny trying in vain to hide his laughter and they relaxed and enjoyed the joke. Pudding was chocolate cake heated and served with custard, and this Percival ate with relish.

"I'm concerned about Percival's poor diet," Eirlys said as she washed the dishes.

"'These sausages is boverin' me'." Johnny mocked Percival's complaint, laughing. "I don't see why you worry. He eats what he wants and he's the best judge of what's good for him. You worry too much," he said, standing close, nuzzling her neck affectionately, his arms around her trim waist. "If you're like this with strangers, what will you be like with your own?"

The prospect made her blush. "I can't imagine letting my child go away from me to live with strangers. I'd want to be with him every minute. As he grows up, and wants to go out on his own, I'll delay the day for as long as possible, then I'll march up and down until he comes back to me." She smiled. "That's how I feel now but I expect mothers gradually learn to let them go. We have to or we'd be a nation of madwomen."

"You'll be a wonderful mother," he assured her.

"Talking about mothers, I saw Hannah on my way home from work. She was dressing a small snowman for Josie and Marie. I watched as Josie and Marie threw snowballs at it, laughing, even throwing one at their mother. They were so excited. I think she's wonderful the way she copes without any help. Don't you think so?"

"I do. Those little girls are so content and well behaved, she must be doing a remarkable job. We were right to invite them to share our Christmas, weren't we?"

"Perhaps we can invite them to tea when the weather is better and they can play in the garden with the boys."

"Or sooner, so the boys can introduce them to Snap, Old Maid and dominoes."

"All right then, what about tomorrow?"

Having given up on the walk they had planned, Johnny left by mid-afternoon. It was Saturday and he had promised to help his father in the chip shop that evening to give him an evening off.

"He's still very shocked and I know he isn't sleeping very much," he explained. "I hear him wandering downstairs at odd times, and I sometimes find him sitting looking through photograph albums as though trying to find a clue to her unhappiness. It was the way she died that makes it worse," he went on. "Dad can't accept that Mam chose to leave us. We hoped the verdict would be accidental death, but the note, and the deliberate way she went to a place where she was unlikely to be seen, all suggested suicide."

"Was she always ill? I mean, when you were small, did she play games and have fun?"

"It was Dad who played games and provided our fun. I asked him if he knew before he married her that she suffered with her nerves, and he said her family kept it from him. That was wrong, I think."

"I wish I could help, but your father is a solitary man, isn't he? He'll deal with it in his own way and in his own time."

When Johnny left Eirlys, he didn't go straight home. There were a couple of hours yet before he needed to get ready for the chip shop. Unplanned, his feet led him to Hannah's door.

With the brief discussion about his mother still in his mind, when Hannah invited him inside, leaving the door open and letting in the cold wind, he continued his thoughts with her.

"Why can someone hate life so much they want to die?" he asked. They were in the kitchen leaving the girls in the living room where they were too far away to hear him.

"I know that kind of despair," Hannah told him sadly. "I wanted to die when I could see no way out of my situation. But with your mother it couldn't have been anything like that," she added hastily. "She seemed to me to have everything she could possibly want."

"I should have seen her desperation and been able to help her."

"You have to accept that she was sick, Johnny, seriously sick, and no one could help her get well. There are many kinds of terminal illnesses, remember. She suffered from one that is less easy to accept."

Her words soothed him as no others had. He felt the strain of the past weeks leaving him. Her suffering had not made her bitter but more sympathetic; she had a greater understanding because of it.

"Your marriage was deeply unhappy. Can I ask you whether he was violent before you married, and whether you were warned?"

"He had beaten up a young boy once, when he was sixteen. His parents and he convinced me it had been an experience he would never repeat. When you're in love, Johnny, you hear what you want to hear, believe what it's comfortable to believe."

"Dad and Mam didn't have a real marriage. Eirlys's parents are rowing all the time. You suffered real distress. I wonder if there is such a thing as a happy marriage."

"Don't become cynical. Some couples argue but still love each other. Don't mistake that for an unhappy marriage. Like terminal illnesses, there are many different kinds of marriage, except most kinds of marriage are good." She went in to see that the girls were warm enough then returned to the kitchen where, for the moment, with her mother out shopping, they were able to talk in private.

"I married at twenty-two, to escape from my parents' criticism and disapproval, and went from one set of problems into another. They disliked me for being alive when my brother was dead. He died of pneumonia you see. I had the flu first, just after the last war, when I was eight. I recovered, I passed it to him and he died, so his death was my fault and there was never a day when they didn't remind me of that."

"That's so cruel," Johnny gasped.

"Yes, I found it hard to bear. So when Laurie came along and offered freedom, I took it. We had two rooms over a china shop in Barry, and I thought I was in heaven. I worked in a shop not far from where we lived and he worked on the docks. The first few months were good ones. Then he was injured. He suffered a broken leg, crushed ribs and head injuries as he was unloading a cargo of pig-iron, and he changed from a loving husband into a foul-tempered bully.

"He accused me of neglecting him if I was late back from the shop. Then I discovered that he was using our money for drink. We couldn't pay the bills and were thrown out of the flat. I found us a room and he went on blaming me for everything. He hit me if the meal wasn't to his liking, or for some other imagined slight." Her lovely eyes clouded. "I lost the baby I was carrying, and he and my parents blamed me for not taking proper care of it. My parents told me it was God's punishment. As if a caring God would kill an innocent baby to punish me! I was never that important, was I? No God of Love for them. Their God was just an excuse for disapproval and punishments."

"So you left him," Johnny coaxed as she paused.

"So I left him. My parents disapproved of my leaving him and wouldn't help. I stayed with a friend, and James, but my mother told Laurie where I was and he came and—" She couldn't go on.

Johnny guessed she was thinking about rape and he hugged her until her sobs subsided. "Don't tell me any more, love. It's upsetting you too much."

"If you can bear it, Johnny, I want to tell you the whole story. I can't talk about it to anyone else."

Johnny continued to hold her as she went on, "One day he attacked my friend Iolo thinking it was me and the police caught up with him."

Iolo and her husband took me to a doctor then to a solicitor, and they supported me through the divorce. Then, unfortunately, they moved away to look for work. It was Eirlys and her parents who were my only friends at that time. Using their quasi-religion against them they persuaded my parents it was their Christian duty to give us a home. My parents reluctantly agreed to my sharing their house. I'm here under sufferance, but I stay so Josie and Marie can have some stability in their lives."

"I think your parents should be immensely proud of you," Johnny said, pressing her against him as her sobs began again. For a long time they didn't move. The kiss when it came seemed the most natural thing in the world, and when they walked back into the living room to sit with the girls, who were playing with a doll's house Hannah had made from shoe-boxes, they sat close together, hand in hand, silently digesting what had just happened between them.

–

Annie didn't think she would have coped with Morgan's revelation without Stanley, Harold and little Percival. Although she had been unwilling to accept them at first, she dreaded every letter they received from their mother, expecting that, like the rest of the evacuees, she wanted her boys to go home. So far the feared bombing of London had not happened, with the Germans fighting on land, pushing their way through France, and using the might of the Luftwaffe to destroy shipping.

Teresa's letters were full of cheerful little anecdotes about the building of air raid shelters and the boring lectures given to householders about the way to deal with incendiary bombs. She wrote about the queues and the meanness of the grocers when they doled out the ration of butter; no pleading would persuade them to allow the knife to slip back beyond the weekly allowance of four ounces, she reported. Annie sent her a cake, made with butter, for which she had exchanged some sugar of which she had plenty.

She wrote assurances that the boys were missing her but were well and happy, reminding Teresa of the importance of their staying in St David's Well where they were safe. With the estrangement between her and Morgan continuing into the foreseeable future, she needed the boys as much – if not more – than they needed her.

-

Johnny couldn't get Hannah out of his mind. They had parted that afternoon without anything being discussed. Memories of the kiss had shone in Hannah's eyes as they said their good-byes, and he knew she could recognise the desire lingering in his. He had to talk to someone, but who?

He was in love with Hannah. He had to admit it and face the consequences. She refused to marry him but how could he marry Eirlys feeling this way about another woman? Could he persuade Hannah to change her mind? Every strand of common sense told him he was being stupid, giving up someone like Eirlys for a woman who was older, divorced and with two little girls. He was very fond of Eirlys and she was a perfect choice for a wife – clever, ambitious and quite lovely – so what was wrong with him? Perhaps he should wait until the army took him away from St David's Well and marry neither.

The thought of going to war loomed and momentarily obliterated his confusion. He could walk away. He had to forget Hannah and marry Eirlys. Once they were married the dreams of another life would fade. Wouldn't they?

He went to the chip shop and worked there until eleven o'clock, staying behind to drain the fat, clean out the cooking range and wash the last utensil. His actions and responses had been automatic and he remembered hardly a thing about the hours he had spent cooking and serving the food.

He walked home past the houses of Granny Moll Piper and his Uncle Huw and Auntie Marged. No light was visible in either house, but on impulse he knocked on the window of Granny Moll's and waited to see if she answered.

The door opened and Moll's sharp voice asked who was there.

"It's Johnny, Granny Moll. I know it's late, but can I come in?"

Juggling with the blackout curtain, Moll led him into the living room, where a low fire still burned, grey ash at the front with only a faint glow of red at the back. "The fire's gone next door," Moll said, with a smile, adding a couple of logs to rouse it.

"I wanted to talk to someone and I thought you might still be awake," Johnny began. "Not the call-up, is it?" Moll asked at once. "I don't know how they expect us to run the business if they take all our able-bodied men."

"No, nothing yet, although I don't think they'll hang about much longer. Millions gone and it still isn't enough. No, it's about how I feel about Eirlys; that's what's worrying me."

"Don't tell me you've changed your mind about marrying her? I was depending on Eirlys joining the family to help us next summer! People will still want to come to St David's

Well Bay for some fun, Hitler or no Hitler. We'll need her on the sands or in Piper's Café."

"I don't know how I feel about her any more."

"What went wrong?" Moll asked, pushing the kettle over on to the fire and stirring the coals with a poker.

"I have strong feelings for someone else."

"Who is she? Someone who'd fit in with the family business?"

"Granny Moll! It's my life I'm thinking about, not Piper's cafés and stalls!"

"We have to be practical." Moll grinned. She got up and began to mix cocoa, sugar and milk in the bottom of two cups, then added water from the gently simmering kettle. "Drink this and tell me all about it."

When Johnny mentioned Hannah she frowned. "She's too old and she's got a ready-made family. That's not what your father would want for you, Johnny."

They talked over the situation until two a.m., by which time Johnny was far more confused than when he came. Moll's advice was for him to arrange to marry Eirlys as soon as possible. He was assured that once he was married and settled down in a home of his own with a loving wife, all thoughts of other women would magically vanish from his mind.

Walking home through the dark, silent streets, Johnny wondered wryly whether Moll's solution was the best one for him or for herself and Piper's Café. She might be right about that early wedding, though. Several of his friends had married sooner than intended, wanting to be sure there was someone waiting for them when the war ended and they came home. They told him that it would make them strong to have someone to survive for and now he was beginning to understand what they meant.

When Johnny discussed Moll's idea of an early wedding, he put it to Eirlys as his own, explaining that his application to defer call-up on account of the family business might not be successful.

"I want to know you'll be here, waiting for me while I'm away. Helping on the sands, keeping everything safe until I come home. Lovely word that, 'home', it's what you'll be making for us while I'm away."

There were the usual misgivings in Eirlys's heart, so she didn't answer him immediately. She loved Johnny, she longed to be his wife, but she didn't want to give up on her dreams and become a housewife until she had created a life of her own. So far the idea of how that would be achieved had not materialised.

"I love my job," she told him, trying to explain how she felt. "Now, with fewer men available, I'm being given more and more responsibility and I love it. The stalls in the summer would be fun but it wouldn't be enough for me, specially if you go away. I want a career or a business of my own, not sharing your family's."

"And is that the only reason you're refusing me?"

"I'm not refusing you. I love you, Johnny and I want to be your wife more than anything in the world. I want us to have a home of our own. I could build it ready for when you come home, but I don't want to give up my job and ambitions and work for Piper's."

"You don't have to. Although," he added with a grin, "I'll be surprised if Granny Moll doesn't persuade you to spend some spare time helping out, mind."

"I'd like that very much."

"So if we can find somewhere to live, a place where we can build a home, you'll say yes?"

She loved him. Why was she hesitating? Unromantically she knew too that at twenty-two she might not have another chance to do all the things women wanted to do, marry and have children, create a home. If she let Johnny go because of some vague idea of a business of her own she would be a fool. There would never be anyone else she could love as much as she loved Johnny. There was also the pull of belonging to the Castles' large and lively family. Apart from Taff's wife Evelyn, they had all been very welcoming.

"All right, Johnny, let's get married soon."

A little later, when they had celebrated their decision with a kiss, Johnny laughed and said, "I'm so happy, Eirlys." For a while, he meant it.

"Who knows," Eirlys laughed, "it might even bring Mam and Dadda together."

—

Predictably, Bleddyn and Taff were pleased but Evelyn was not.

They met as they were each calling separately on Bleddyn's house in Brook Lane. Evelyn proudly placed a cake on the kitchen table and told Bleddyn she had made it for him. Rather self-consciously Eirlys put her offering beside it. Annie had made him an apple tart with apple rings dried the previous summer. They eyed each other, the gifts a challenge.

Bleddyn smiled at them and said, "I'm beginning to see the advantage of having a couple of daughters-in-law."

"Rushing it, aren't you," Evelyn hissed when Bleddyn left the two girls alone, "getting married before you're even engaged?"

"It's Johnny who didn't want to wait," Eirlys explained. "Why don't you ask him?"

–

The wedding was fixed for the end of March, Saturday the thirtieth, and they both hoped that the army didn't claim Johnny beforehand.

At once Annie started talking to Morgan.

"You can forget that suit you wanted to buy, and your shoes will have to do for a while longer. I'm not having those Castles showing us up. You can hire a suit and I'll get a good dress and we'll show them how it should be done. Right?"

They had hardly exchanged a word since Annie had learned of his "carrying on" with Irene Castle, and Morgan had only been allowed to stay on condition that he slept in the boxroom with the suitcases and the artificial Christmas tree, the discarded picture frames and boxes of children's books and abandoned toys. She reminded him, when he complained, that a two-foot-six camp bed was better than he deserved.

Now that they had something to discuss, barriers fell, although the conversation was extremely one-sided. After Annie had reeled off lists of things to be done, she would glare at Morgan, who had been more or less silent throughout, and demand that he took a greater interest in his daughter's big day.

"I don't think our Eirlys is really sure about this," Morgan said, doubtfully.

"Nonsense. Of course she wants to marry Johnny Castle. They've been discussing it for weeks. It's only this war that's making them change their minds about waiting till next year."

"Will there be a party?" Stanley wanted to know.

"A boring one for grown-ups, I expect," moaned Harold.

"Food?"

"Plenty of it," Annie promised. "A really splendid meal."

"I just want the pudding," Percival told them firmly, "or I ain't going."

–

On the subject of where they would live, Johnny suggested asking his father if they could live there with Eirlys running the house for them.

"I'll be keeping my job," she told him, "but I can easily manage both."

When they put the idea to Bleddyn he rudely refused.

"I've run the house most of my married life," he said. "I don't see the need to change that. You two can find a couple of rooms somewhere, can't you, without me having to disrupt my life?"

Eirlys began looking at the "To Let" columns of the local paper and asking all her friends to make enquiries. "We'll find something soon," she said to Johnny, "and your father is right, we need to start off with a place of our own." She was hurt by the abrupt refusal but hid her feelings from him, supporting Bleddyn in his decision. She did not want to start married life by upsetting Johnny's father.

–

Two days later, Bleddyn called on her. When Morgan saw the big man walking up the front path, an aggressive expression on his face, his heart began to race and he was filled with the desire to run. His injured ankle throbbed in sympathy with the rest of him and he felt the strength leak out of him. He wanted to hide but knew his legs wouldn't support him.

Bleddyn had found out about him and Irene! Why else would he call? He never called.

"Annie? Eirlys?" he called. "We've got a visitor." He waited for his wife or daughter to open the door. Like a coward he remained in his chair and succumbed to panic.

Bleddyn took off his hat and sat with it resting on his knee when Annie showed him into the living room. Morgan stuck out his injured leg as a shield to prevent attack, but Bleddyn smiled and shook his hand.

"Good news about your Eirlys and my Johnny, eh?" he said shaking the nervous Morgan's hand. "It's Eirlys I came to see. In, is she?"

Eirlys entered the room and he said at once, "I'm sorry, Eirlys. I was very rude to you when you suggested moving in with me. It was a generous thought and I shouldn't have been so unkind."

"It's all right, Mr Castle. It was Johnny thinking you needed looking after. I knew you were perfectly capable of running your life without any assistance from us," Eirlys replied.

She tried to smile but her lips were stiff with tension. From his demeanour it was clear he had something more to say, and she waited, dreading to hear his opinion that they were wrong to plan the wedding so soon. It had to be that. Why else would he have called? Like her father she thought, he never calls.

Bleddyn took a piece of paper out of his pocket and slowly unfolded it. Morgan, guilt making him imagine the worst, peered over to try and read it, envisaging a newly discovered letter from Irene, telling of his guilt. The man was tormenting him, playing him like a cat with a mouse, hoping he would relax before he dealt the first blow. Then he realised it looked like an address.

For a moment he felt relieved, then he remembered. The caravan! Bleddyn had found out about their meeting at the caravan! He sank deeper into his chair, wishing he could disappear.

"What's the matter with you?" Annie asked coldly.

"Bellyache. Too many pickled onions last night!"

"This shop is closing down," Bleddyn explained, handing the paper to Eirlys. "It was a wool shop and there are boxes and boxes of wool to be sold. Skeins of every colour so far as I could see. I thought, with your rug-making, you might take a look, and if you can use it, I'll help you to buy it if you wish. Some of it is in a right old muddle; looks as though a cat's had fun with it, so it's bound to be cheap."

Morgan was shaking when Bleddyn and Eirlys left to investigate the possibilities and Annie told him that if he was getting a cold he could sleep downstairs as she wasn't going to risk catching it. He wondered if anyone except Eirlys knew he and Annie weren't sharing a bed. It would only need a slight suspicion and something like that could start Bleddyn thinking.

Two and two weren't difficult to add up, he thought anxiously. He was still in danger of something being said. Someone could easily have seen them together and it would only take a word to Bleddyn for him to guess the rest. He shuddered.

"I've made a decision," he said to Annie firmly, although afraid to look her in the eyes. "I'm not sleeping on that damned camp bed any more. If you don't let me come back to a proper bed so I can have a good night's sleep, I'm going to find lodgings. And," he went on, as courage grew out of desperation, "and I won't go to our daughter's wedding either. It'll be a farce with me pretending to be your husband, and, well, I'm not doing it. So?" he asked, daring to look at her.

For a moment he thought his gamble had failed then she nodded and said, "All right, but—"

"No buts," he interrupted. To his relief she turned away, nodded and said nothing more.

He went upstairs and folded the camp bed and threw it at the bottom of the garden. The sooner it rotted the better.

-

Eirlys was smiling. Keeping her job and her interests wouldn't be a problem after all. With the strong-minded Moll as head of the family she had been so afraid it would be impossible to marry Johnny on her own, not unreasonable, terms. But Bleddyn was helping her with the rug-making so he must understand about her unwillingness to give up everything for the Pipers.

Marriage to Johnny; belonging to that large, affectionate family and keeping what she wanted from the old life to take to the new – everything was perfect. Nothing could happen to spoil it.

Nine

When Eirlys saw the amount of wool waiting for a buyer, she was daunted at first, but as she examined the variety of the stock, some very old and uselessly tangled, some perfect, she admired the colours and the varying thicknesses and began to imagine the swirls and concentric circles and diamonds within diamonds that she could create with them, and her interest grew.

"I don't think I can afford all this," she whispered to Bleddyn, who had come with her to introduce her to the owner, Mrs Hibbert.

"I could help if you think you can use it," Bleddyn offered. "I don't want you to take it if you aren't sure, mind. The amount could be frightening. Although you could sell most of it easily enough, I would think."

She stared around her at the dark and rather gloomy shop. The shelves were tumbling with piles of knitting patterns and needles were strewn about carelessly in their assorted sizes and colours. The wools were no longer set out in an orderly arrangement, but mixed up, higgledy-piggledy, revealing the lack of interest on the part of the owner.

"I know it's a mess," Mrs Hibbert smiled. "I've just lost interest and I want someone else to take it all off my hands." She shrugged and added, "I thought of having a closing-down sale, but the stock is in need of sorting and I can't be bothered."

The shop was far from full and the stocks hadn't been replenished for a long time. There were large quantities of some colours, small amounts of most. Customers would want enough of one colour and shade number to knit a jumper or something similar, and Eirlys surmised that there were few colours with sufficient amounts in the same shade. The yarns that remained in larger quantities were rather dull. Perfect for background for her rugs, but not exciting enough to tempt someone to tackle the work involved in knitting a complicated pattern.

An idea for using the smaller amounts and oddments began to grow and Eirlys searched through the piles of knitting patterns that littered the shelves and slithered to the floor.

After stepping outside and discussing it with Bleddyn, who seemed very willing to help, she made an offer, which Mrs Hibbert accepted with relief.

"I can change this back into a room where I can sit and watch people walking past," the old lady said happily. "Hate living at the back, I do. Nothing to look at and no one to talk to once the shop closes. I might rent the back of the house. It's too big for me to look after."

"That's a good idea," Bleddyn told her. "Better than being on your own in a big old place like this."

They made their excuses and left, after arranging for the goods to be collected on the following Sunday morning.

"Now," Eirlys laughed, "now, all I have to do is find somewhere to keep it all!" The van belonging to Piper's Café was filled twice with boxes of wool, which Eirlys would have to sort out at a later date. The priority was to empty the shop so Mrs Hibbert could arrange for it to revert to its previous use as a living room, or "best parlour" as she had called it.

The wool was taken to Brook Lane after further discussions, and housed temporarily in the stable in Bleddyn's yard. It couldn't stay there long as mice would quickly ruin it. Once there Eirlys and Johnny began sorting through it. The immediate fears over the large quantity had fled and for Eirlys, this was what she had been looking for: the beginning of a business of her own, a way of being independent. She wondered why she felt the need, now she and Johnny were planning their wedding. For most of her friends, marriage was an end of something, for her it was a continuation.

It was still very cold but on several evenings, sometimes with Beth's help and sometimes with Johnny and even Bleddyn, the wool was separated into colours and type and in quantities suitable for the various items Eirlys had in mind. Running through her fertile mind were ideas for soft toys, children's garments and simple novelties beside the rugs with which she had begun.

She became so absorbed in her plans she neglected the arrangements for her wedding. It was Annie who dealt with the immediate preparations which consisted mainly of making a great many lists.

One lunchtime, when Eirlys would have preferred to stay in the warmth of the office, she had to do some shopping in her lunch hour and had promised to go home. The weather was harsh and the town looked grey and gloomy from the effect of the lowered clouds. Even the slates on the roofs of houses looked a different colour, Eirlys thought, a dullness she associated with the approach of snow. The air was still and painfully cold and the streets were empty, the threat of more snow keeping most people indoors. Eirlys was curled up and tense with the effort of keeping warm as she ran from the bakery to the greengrocer where Johnny's cousin Beth worked.

She felt cold but Beth looked seriously chilled. "Can't you get an hour off and come home with me for a warm meal?" Eirlys coaxed. "I have lots to tell you, and Mam will be there with something hot ready for us."

A pleading look at her boss and Beth was given permission to take one hour. She pulled on a fur-trimmed coat and covered her black, neatly bobbed hair with a woollen scarf and the two girls ran through the streets to Eirlys's home where the fire burned brightly and Annie was warming up some potato and leek soup.

Annie finished work at one p.m. and Morgan was on a morning shift, but she had managed to get home to have food hot and the fire lit for when her daughter arrived.

"I'm looking for people to work for me," Eirlys explained to her mother and Beth. "I have design ideas for rugs which I will pay people to make for me, then once a month on my Saturday off I'll take a market stall and sell them."

"How many rugs d'you think you'll sell?" Annie asked pessimistically. "It's not like a packet of sweets. You'll be wasting your time."

"I'll have a shop one day," Eirlys said firmly.

"Selling only rugs? How often do people buy a rug?"

"If they only buy one every five years, I'll want them to buy it from me."

"Looking a long way ahead that is, Eirlys. In a small place like St David's Well you won't get rich on a few rugs. Best you marry Johnny and forget it."

"The wool from Mrs Hibbert's shop has started me thinking," Eirlys said, ignoring her mother's discouragement.

"Most people knit and I could get people to knit toys from the small oddments of wool I've bought. I would make them up – that's where the skill lies, stuffing them and sewing them professionally – and I'll pay the knitters for their work." She looked at Annie, hoping for a show of interest or even an offer of help, but Annie shook her head.

"Toys? That's even dafter than selling rugs!"

"I'll ask a few people I know who might be interested," Beth offered, as they walked back to work, restored by Annie's soup and chunks of fresh bread. She listened for a while longer as Eirlys explained her plans more fully, then asked, "What does Johnny think of all this? Won't you be expected to work on the beach in the summer? I'd hoped you'd be working with me in Piper's Café, or with Johnny and Taff and my brothers Ronnie and Eynon on the sands below."

"Your Granny Moll has already decided where and what I'll be doing, but she'll be disappointed. I don't intend to give up my job for a summer session on the beach followed by a winter looking for anything that I can find… Oh, Beth, I don't mean to belittle what you do. In fact, when Johnny and I first started going out together, it was my dream, to work with the Piper family."

"Castle family," Beth corrected. "We're all Castles except Granny Moll and Auntie Audrey who hasn't married."

"Sorry. The truth is, I'd have wanted nothing more than to work with Johnny and the rest of you. But things have changed and I'm no longer so willing."

"What changed it? You still love Johnny, don't you?"

"I love Johnny, of course I do. I think my attitude changed when I was given more responsibility at work. I might have stayed an unimportant clerk, not believing I was capable of more, if it weren't for the war and men being called up. Now

I have a big, big dream of owning my own business, and the trouble with having a really wonderful dream is that it throws all your other dreams into turmoil."

"I never wanted anything other than working on the beach and becoming Mrs Freddy Clements. Oh Eirlys, can't you do both? You'd have a perfect winter occupation and that's something most of us don't have."

"I've thought of it, but every time I think of doing something else, the big, big dream comes back and gives me a nudge and I know I can't do anything else but make a seriously concentrated attempt to succeed."

"Poor Johnny," Beth laughed.

"Why poor Johnny?"

"He's got a successful businesswoman on his hands and you know how men hate to be bested."

"He won't be bested," Eirlys said seriously. "He'll have as much from me as he needs, more probably, as I'll be happy doing something I enjoy."

"Good luck, Eirlys. I think Johnny's a lucky man."

Walking back through streets, taking care on the icy pavements, Eirlys was engulfed by feelings of guilt. Was Johnny lucky? She no longer felt able to offer him the commitment she had previously felt. The excitement of planning a future, of owning a business in which she was her own boss, had filled her mind to the exclusion of everything else. Plans for a wedding to take place in just over two months seemed trivial by comparison. She should be boring people by talking about nothing else, planning every last detail, dreaming romantic dreams. Nevertheless, rugs were what she dreamed about, and every spare moment she could find was used to build a stock of hand-made rugs.

Some would be thick and practical for kitchen use, made from strips of strong material given by various friends and sometimes found in second-hand shops. Others were less robust and delicately coloured, intended for a bedroom or a nursery.

She worked late into the night and sometimes woke bleary-eyed and had to force herself to get up and cook breakfast for Stanley and Harold and try to coax Percival to swallow a few mouthfuls of porridge. She even sat and cut strips of material ready for the evening as they ate their breakfast.

The disappearance of the camp bed gave Eirlys hope that the latest, and by far the fiercest row between her mother and father was fading away, although they were still not speaking to each other. Her parents sometimes sat and cut material for her during the evenings, and she tried to tease them out of their ill humour by laughing at them working together, looking in opposite directions and pretending not to know the other was there. On one occasion, Annie's response was to pick up a pile of material and throw it at Morgan.

Her father was working regularly, first having a lift to the factory on the back of a friend's motorbike and later, under his own steam, walking to the bus stop and being dropped at the factory gates by kindly bus drivers. The plaster was off and apart from a walking stick – to give him confidence rather than support – he was recovering satisfactorily from his accident.

He was gradually relaxing from the fear of Bleddyn learning about his "carrying on" with Irene, and growing more and more convinced that neither Bleddyn nor Eirlys would ever find out. Surely if they had been seen, if something had been noticed, it would have come to light before this?

The postman's visit was always one highlight of the boys' day as they waited for letters from Teresa. Her notes were short but filled with loving messages for each of her sons, and the pile under Stanley's pillow was taken out regularly and re-read when they went to bed.

Eirlys received letters from Ken describing his progress in becoming involved in the forces' entertainments plans. His letters were full of affection and he always asked about her interests. "Have you learnt to drive yet?" he asked in one letter. "How many rugs have you sold?" in another. It was enjoyable to write back and tell him of her progress and her ideas for the future. Ken was a loving friend and she valued him greatly as such, but she always made sure she saved his letters for Johnny to read so they wouldn't give rise to misunderstanding. Sometimes Johnny even added a note of his own when she wrote to Ken, reassuring her he understood.

Johnny was a little worried, though. He sensed that something was worrying Eirlys and hoped it was not belated regret at letting Ken leave without her. His own recurring doubts made him aware that she too might be less than certain about their marrying. One evening when they were sorting through one of the boxes bought from Mrs Hibbert, he sat untangling a skein of soft blue baby wool and asked, "Are you going to tell me what's wrong, love?"

"Wrong? There's nothing wrong. I'm frowning because I'm concentrating, that's all."

"You haven't changed your mind about marrying me so soon?"

"I love you, Johnny Castle, and I want to be your wife. In fact, I think I might have found us a couple of rooms."

"Really? That's marvellous. Where?"

"Mrs Hibbert told your father and me that she's changing the shop back into a room where she can sit and look out at the street. She said she has always hated living at the back with nothing to look at except the garden. She has two other rooms downstairs and said she might be renting them. Shall we go and take a look?"

They examined the two rooms and, seeing them overfilled with Mrs Hibbert's treasured possessions, Eirlys had to force herself to show interest. The rooms were shabby and would need a lot of work before they could move in. It would involve a lot of time and, for her at that moment, time was precious. Finding a place to live was beginning to become an upheaval and the thought of it had the opposite effect than it would have had a few months previously. Why couldn't they simply move in with her parents and wait until something really suitable turned up?

Right now, all she wanted was to find people to work for her and get her business under way. Home-hunting was an unwelcome chore. She was ashamed of her reaction and knew she was cheating on Johnny by not explaining how she felt.

Every day she was told of young men going away to join the army or the navy or the air force, and every week there were reports of injuries, imprisonment and deaths. She understood the urgency felt by Johnny and thousands of others, to marry and get their lives in order, but it was an urgency she didn't feel able to share.

Johnny too continued to have doubts but they were hidden in a flurry of enthusiasm for his marriage to Eirlys. He had to face a life without Hannah, and he constantly reminded himself how fortunate he would be to have a wife like Eirlys: talented, intelligent, very lovely, and someone who would build up a business of her own.

On that subject Granny Moll didn't agree with him and she asked him to try again to persuade Eirlys to help in the summer season on the sands. She promised help with the rug-making during the winter months as compensation. He had called to collect clean white overalls for the chip shop that evening and as Moll handed him the carefully ironed clothes, she asked him to talk to Eirlys.

"Don't count on it," he warned, then speaking proudly he added, "She wants to start a business of her own, Granny Moll. Isn't she marvellous having such a grand ambition? She'll succeed too for sure."

"She'll soon forget all that," Moll said confidently. "When she's a part of the Piper family, she'll be happy working with us all."

Johnny shook his head. "I want to help her get the business under way. I don't want to pressure her about Piper's in any way. Then, when she's ready I think she'll come and work with us at the beach, just part time, mind, when she can fit it in. She's told me several times how much she would love to work on the sands in the summer."

"She told me that too. Don't fret, boy, this rug-making is only a phase. Lots of girls worry a bit about committing themselves to a man and a marriage. An intelligent girl like your Eirlys, she's bound to feel trepidation at having to look at your face every morning!" she joked.

Johnny laughed at her teasing, told Moll how much he loved Eirlys and how lucky he was, but he was still unconvinced. How could he love Eirlys and still think about Hannah?

Johnny and Eirlys took the three boys to the pictures that evening and after walking them home and leaving Annie to put them to bed, Eirlys took out some of the diagrams she had drawn. Even with the straight lines that resulted when the "hairpin" method was used, variety could be added with pattern and colours.

"I thought I would use the same pattern and make it in several colours now I have plenty of wool in hand," she said, writing on the pattern the colours she planned.

"Good idea, although most people would chose something dark and practical," Johnny said. "Not that I want a room that's dull and sensible, mind. When are you going to make one for our fireside?"

She picked up a few skeins held together with an elastic band. "That's what I wanted to talk to you about. Do you like these?"

She handed them to him with a canvas on which a design was printed. A design of tree branches, leaves and cherries. The colours were bold, and he nodded agreement.

"Great," he said approvingly.

"Will you help me wind the skeins?" she asked. He held the wool on his hands with arms outstretched and she unwound the skeins and rolled it into a ball. As they worked they talked.

"Have you thought about next summer?" he asked. "I probably won't be here and neither will Taff. My cousin Ronnie will be called up too if our attempt at deferment fails and Granny Moll will be desperate for some help."

"Johnny, I don't want to give up my job," she said, putting down the finished ball of wool and taking up another skein. "I thought you understood. I earn a fair wage and it's right through the year, not just in the summer. We'll need a nice nest-egg for when you come out of the army. With the rug-making and perhaps expanding into other handcrafted items, I'll be building a secure base for us."

"You used to say how much you'd love to work on the sands."

"I did. I still would. It's just that now, with this rug-making idea, I'm distracted from it. I find the idea of having a business of my own, even though it's a lowly one compared with Piper's, great fun. I have to give it a try, Johnny. If it doesn't succeed I won't be as unhappy as I would if I don't try."

"I understand," he smiled, offering his hands for another skein of wool. "I'll help all I can; I promised Granny Moll I'd ask, that's all. Dad has agreed for you to use the spare bedroom as a store room indefinitely. Keep the wool and materials there and also the finished rugs, until you're ready to sell them."

"Thanks, Johnny," she said, hugging him. "It's our future, you know. I want to keep my job at the council offices and if I can start selling rugs too, well, we'll have a good start when you come home. I'll save every penny I can. I know how important the family business is to you and I'm grateful for your understanding, really I am."

They discussed the advantages of a market stall and other ways of displaying the rugs. Johnny suggested using one of the showcases in the seaside rock and sweet shop on the promenade which was run by Granny Moll's unmarried daughter, Auntie Audrey. "It's closed now of course, but later you could use it to show one or two samples, with your name and address on a card."

"Your Granny Moll Piper would never agree to that, specially when I tell her I can't help in the summer."

"Leave Granny Moll to me. She's very fond of me, and very susceptible to flattery! I've called her my gran since I learnt to talk. I can persuade her, I know I can."

When Johnny discussed the idea with his father, Bleddyn offered to go with him to talk to Granny Moll Piper. At first, Moll was doubtful.

"How can you put floor coverings and sweets in the same shop? It doesn't make sense," she complained. But when Bleddyn spoke to her alone and reminded her how worrying it was that Johnny was attracted to Hannah, and how much better it would be for Piper's if he married Eirlys, Moll agreed.

"In fact, there's no reason why she can't put one or two in the window now, while the place is closed," she offered. "People walk on the beach and along the prom even at this time of year," she added and glanced at Bleddyn for his smile of approval. "There are a few sticks of seaside rock in the window we'll have to dispose of, but I think Stanley, Harold and Percival Love might help us with those!"

Johnny met Eirlys from work the following lunchtime. He hadn't slept and yet his mind was clearer than it had been for a long time. He knew he had to commit himself to Eirlys. There were plenty of unhappy marriages because one or the other didn't do just that. Granny Moll was right, once he was married, he would forget he ever felt any doubts.

"I spoke to Granny Moll and she says using the shop to display your work is all right with her," he told her.

"Really?"

"In fact, she suggested putting one or two in the empty window now, as there are often people strolling along the prom when the weather is mild."

They hugged and walked home, buying chips on the way, talking excitedly about their plans. "Because," Johnny told her, "they are our plans, not just yours."

In the days following, they both felt as though they had reached a turning point in their relationship. Johnny faced

245

up to the knowledge that his future did not include Hannah, while Eirlys began to believe that she could marry Johnny and still follow her dream.

Eirlys didn't think she could be happier. She still worked on the rugs in odd moments, completing the cherry design for her and Johnny's future home. Johnny came when he could to help her sort out colours and even added a few geometric designs to her book of patterns.

She loved the Readicut designs but still made many using the method with which she began, the strips of material and the giant "hairpin". These were popular and quick to make.

Bleddyn painted an old chest of drawers for her use, built shelves to store her wool and even sat patiently untangling some of the worse skeins, amid much teasing from his elder son Taff when he and Evelyn called.

Evelyn seemed to accept the forthcoming wedding with a distinct lack of enthusiasm, and when Taff and Johnny asked her to help with the redecoration of the two rooms in Mrs Hibbert's house, she refused.

"If you're getting married in March, Eirlys will have to forget her stupid mats and start making the rooms into a home, won't she? It isn't my place to do her work for her."

Puzzled by her attitude, Johnny and Taff failed to get her to explain.

"I suppose she simply doesn't like Eirlys. We none of us like everybody, do we?" Bleddyn said, unworried by the mild disturbance. "They'll settle down when they know each other better."

–

Eirlys's fears that the decoration of the rooms would use up too much of her time were unfounded. It was Johnny who worked there every moment he could find and his brother, Taff, who helped him. Bleddyn too did a lot of the initial cleaning and it was only a few weeks before the place was smart and looking inviting. They were given a few pieces of furniture to begin with, which they would discard when they could afford new. Bleddyn painted delicate floral designs on some of the dull pieces, much to Johnny's and Eirlys's surprise and delight.

Eirlys took Stanley, Harold and Percival to Mrs Hibbert's one day to show them the place where she intended to live with Johnny. The two rooms were freshly papered and the paintwork gleamed. The floor was covered in linoleum and she explained where the items of furniture they had managed to collect would be placed. There was a kitchen which she would share with Mrs Hibbert, and beyond, a short passage and an outside porch leading to a lavatory. There was no bathroom, but, she explained to the three boys, "Johnny and I will manage well enough in the kitchen with the door locked and we'll go home to bathe once or twice a week."

"We never had no bathroom," Harold told her disparagingly. "Our mum says a bath is a wicked waste o' space."

After showing them the bedroom, stripped of its wallpaper, ready to be transformed, she was conscious of how small the place was and wondered where she would find the space to work. Harold disagreed.

"Two great big rooms all for yourselves? Blimey, we've never had that much room, have we, Stanley?"

"Of course you have," Eirlys said disbelievingly. "You could hardly fit three boys like you, *and* your mother, into less space than this!" Annie had described the tiny room in which the Love family had lived but Eirlys had decided it had been an exaggeration. She thought the boys were exaggerating too.

"One room, we had. Although our mum called it a flat to show off a bit. Stick in a couple of beds and a cupboard and stuff, and there ain't much room to move, is there, our Stanley?"

"Surely there was a kitchen?" she teased. "And what about a bedroom?"

"A kitchen? What for?" Harold asked. "We ate out of the chip shop most nights, except when mum was broke and we just had bread."

"I like chips from our chip shop," Percival said, his whine suggesting serious deprivation.

The boys had never told her much about their home in London, and if she thought about it at all – even though her mother had told her of its lack of comfort and conveniences – Eirlys had imagined they had lived in a block of flats with better facilities than many families in St David's Well. No one could live in a room as small as Annie had described. She was convinced her mother had belittled their situation to increase her affection for the boys who had landed on their doorstep a few months ago.

She wondered what would happen to them when they eventually went back to Teresa. Unless things had changed, they would return to the small room her mother had visited when she took the boys to visit Teresa. It was hardly a flat, Annie had told her, just a large bedroom divided into two sections to provide a bedroom and a living room, with a sink and cooker which didn't work in one corner. There hardly enough room for one, and it was certainly not large enough to accommodate the boys plus all the possessions they had accumulated since they had come to live at St David's Well. Perhaps she hadn't overstated their situation after all.

They were the only evacuees left now. The others had trickled slowly back, having been collected by loving, caring families unable to bear being separated any longer, especially since there had been no bombing in London so far.

In her newly strengthened happiness with Johnny, and the reminder of the poverty from which they had sprung, she felt even more benevolent towards the three boys and after looking at the rooms being prepared for her and Johnny she took them to buy an ice-cream.

She let them choose and they bought a knickerbocker glory but after a few mouthfuls, Percival lowered his head and solemnly declared that, "This ice-cream is boverin' me."

"Eat it up," she told him. "If the war doesn't end soon, there might not be many more."

"Good," he grumbled, chewing painfully slowly on a piece of fruit and making them laugh.

–

Teresa had lost her flat. After failing to pay the rent and causing a disturbance one night when she brought a few rowdy friends back, she had been told to leave. At first she wasn't worried. There were several people who would let her sleep on their couch for a night or two. She managed to keep herself looking smart and picked up men easily enough. Offering money to her friends, insisting they took it, made it harder for them to tell her to go. But when she had spent a few days with everyone willing to help, and seeing the rest turn away, she began to wonder what would happen to her.

Her friend Maureen lived near with her ten-year-old daughter. Her husband was in the forces and for a while she was glad of Teresa's company. Meanwhile, Teresa looked for a flat she could afford, but without success. Then she saw

249

an opportunity to steal the wallet of a man she was drinking with. She helped herself to twenty-four pounds.

She felt sick with excitement as she left him and hurried out of the pub, where she was well known. Foolishly, she hadn't been able to resist taking it out and counting it before she left, and several of the man's friends had seen her. She ran through back alleyways back to Maureen's flat.

When the man returned from the toilet, it was to a chorus of jeers as he announced he had lost twenty-odd pounds. He was soon given the facts and the laughter at his gullibility made his unreliable temper explode.

He ran from the pub and, after listening for a few seconds, heard her tip—tapping footsteps in her high heels and followed her. He caught up with her as she reached Maureen's door and shouted, threatening her with the police. Afraid of getting her friend into trouble by bringing the police to her door, she ran away, kicking off her shoes to run fast and silently, hoping he would be led away from Maureen.

Unable to return, she stayed in a cheap boarding house. Although she went to Maureen's several times in the days that followed her stupid mistake, there was always a man watching the place. She had made an error of judgement, presuming the man would be too embarrassed to complain, unaware of his friends' teasing and the man's hot temper. She shivered as she realised she had robbed a man who wouldn't give up.

If he was not there, waiting for her to return to Maureen's, another man would be standing in the same place. She had to move right away.

But where would she live? Twenty-four pounds was a lot of money but it wouldn't last for ever.

Maureen worked in the pub on the corner and she managed to see her and explain.

"I'm broke and with no place to live I can't see how I'll avoid ending up sleeping under the arches," she sobbed.

"Use Stanley, Harold and Percival," Maureen advised. "Go to the council and tell them you're separated from your sons because you have nowhere to live. They're bound to help you to get a place if there's children involved."

"Bring my clothes to the pub for me to collect, will you?" Teresa pleaded. "I can't afford new."

Maureen tried, but when she walked to work with a loaded suitcase it was taken from her by the man watching her flat and thrown into the canal.

The council were sympathetic when Teresa told them about her husband leaving, especially as she forgot to mention that he had been gone more than five years, soon after telling him she was expecting again. Then they told her they had to see the boys.

"They're on holiday in Wales," she explained. "I didn't have any money to feed them and they had no decent clothes. My husband took everything we had." A few tears here, then she went on, "I have a friend in a small seaside town called St David's Well. She offered to have them for a while, but they'll be back next week and I've got nowhere for them to sleep."

They were adamant. There would be no help unless she could produce the boys.

"This war is bringing a lot of people in for help, and we have to check that we're helping those in real need and not and not cheats," the women explained sympathetically.

With the money left in her purse, Teresa bought herself some clothes to replace those lost to her in Maureen's flat, and went to catch the train for St David's Well. At the station she shrieked and told the crowd that someone had stolen her purse, and several kind people offered to buy her food. She filled her pockets for later and went happily on her way.

–

Eirlys and Johnny were like two people who had recently discovered love. They couldn't bear to be apart. Their kisses were no longer gentle affairs, but passionate and filled with promise of wonderful times to come. Johnny was Eirlys's last thought each night and her first every morning.

If Johnny thought of Hannah at all, it was with the sadness of something beautiful that has passed into memory. He saw her sometimes and took chocolate or sweets for the girls on occasions. Sometimes he went alone, but he didn't go inside. At other times Eirlys was with him, and they stayed while he played with Josie and Marie and she and Hannah talked wedding plans, much of it in muffled, giggling whispers, as Hannah was making Eirlys's wedding dress and Johnny mustn't learn a single detail of it.

If it caused Hannah pain, she determinedly didn't show it.

Bleddyn was still supportive of Eirlys's business plans, thankful that his fears of a romance between Johnny and Hannah had come to nothing. He sold several rugs for her and took orders for more. He also took an interest in her other ideas, for making toys and dolls' clothes and children's clothes with the smaller amounts of the wool they had bought. He encouraged her to think seriously about a shop sometime in the future.

The boys had been promised new clothes for the wedding and Stanley in particular was excited at the prospect.

"Will I be a best man?" Percival wanted to know.

"The best there is," Eirlys laughed. "I couldn't imagine getting married without you three standing near me. I'll need your support, won't I? You are very important to me, all of you."

As she spoke the words she realised how much she meant them. The boys had become such an important part of their lives. With Mam and Dadda still not speaking except when necessary, their presence was especially valuable. The house would have been silent and sad without them. The home revolved around them and their various activities. It was impossible to imagine the house without their filling it with noise and muddle and laughter.

Annie and Morgan took them to the department store and besides buying them each a suit and shirt and shoes, they were given good quality warm coats. Spring was on the way but the weather would be cold for a few months yet, Annie reminded them.

She wanted them to look smart for her daughter's wedding, even if they weren't really her family.

–

It was cold and dark and Annie had put up the blackout curtains and lighted the lamps early. Morgan had carried in extra coal and a few logs and the place looked particularly cheerful when Eirlys came home from work. Johnny was working at the chip shop that evening, and she had planned a lazy few hours writing out wedding invitations and checking wedding lists to make sure nothing was being forgotten.

Annie had made a large fish pie, something that Percival occasionally ate with slightly more enthusiasm that other meals as it required little if any chewing. They were finishing off the food, talking about their various activities throughout the day, when there was a knock at the door – a loud, impatient knock.

"'Ere, come on, let me in before I'm frozen to the doorstep," Teresa complained, and the three boys jumped from the table and ran to greet her, loud in their delight.

She dragged a large suitcase inside, pointed to a collection of assorted bags borrowed from friends and packed with her possessions, and ran to the fire to warm herself, leaving Morgan to carry the luggage and Annie to find her some food.

"I couldn't stay in London any longer," she said by way of explanation.

"Missed us, did yer?" Harold asked.

"More than that, I couldn't go another day without seeing you," she said hugging them all.

After the initial surprise, Annie and Morgan set about finding her a place to stay, insisting that she stayed a day or so, as the boys needed to see her for more than the weekend she had mentioned.

"Sure, are yer? I can easy stay in a boarding 'ouse or something," she said airily as she handed Morgan the last of the bags she carried and settled herself in front of the fire.

She settled in, taking over the small boxroom recently used by Morgan, dumping most of the contents into other rooms to give herself more space. The camp bed was rescued from the bottom of the garden, brought in and put close to the fire to be aired, but this Teresa refused.

"That ain't big enough, for me," she complained. "No, let my boys share. Three to a bed they sleep at 'ome, cosy that is, then you can move the other single in for me."

At once they all set to and did what she asked. No one questioned her: the boys were happy to see their mother and that was enough for Annie, Morgan and Eirlys.

She unpacked her things and spread herself widely. She brought clothes out from her suitcases and hung dresses and skirts around the picture rails and jumpers over the banisters. Shoes and boots were spread along the walls, both upstairs and down, until Morgan offered her several of their cases to use as extra drawers.

"Wonderful. Just what I need," she said, pulling out underwear and dropping it carelessly into the new storage.

"Taken over the damned house she has," Morgan grumbled to Annie and their togetherness against the behaviour of the uninvited guest slowly began to repair their damaged relationship.

Eirlys heard them talking long into the night and was relieved to hear muffled laughter coming through the walls. Smiling, she covered her head with her pillow and settled to dream about being Mrs Johnny Castle.

There was no offer of any money to pay for her keep from Teresa and Annie's hints to that effect were disregarded.

"Another loaf of bread needed?" Annie sighed, when Teresa had been with them four days. "It's certainly more expensive having seven instead of six, isn't it, Morgan?"

"We can't afford any more housekeeping," he said supporting her. "By the time we've paid the bills there isn't enough left for extra." Then, "How long are you staying, Teresa?"

"Oh, I won't go just yet. I can't face saying goodbye to my darlin' boys just yet," Teresa said airily, helping herself to another slice of bread and some cheese.

"No butter on that slice, mind," Annie warned. "That butter has to last us till ration day, and that's Friday."

Making a *moue*, pleading with her eyes, Teresa took a small amount of butter and spread it on a corner of the slice, bit it and threw the rest aside.

A week after she had arrived, Annie and Morgan looked out of the window watching for her to come home from school with the boys. They were already half an hour later than usual. Teresa had gone to meet them, carrying the new winter coats Annie had bought them for Eirlys's wedding. Annie had argued, insisting they didn't need them as they were wearing jumpers and their macs, but Teresa had insisted.

"I like to see Stanley, Harold and my Percival looking smart," she said as though the coats were her gift to them.

When another half an hour had passed and they still hadn't arrived, Morgan suggested she might have taken them to the pictures.

"Typical of her not to bother to tell us," he said.

When Eirlys came in from work, it was six o'clock and Annie was torn between anger at Teresa's thoughtlessness and concern in case something had gone wrong.

"If one of them were hurt, one of the others would have come to tell us," Eirlys reasoned. But she went to see the schoolteacher who lived near and asked if they had been met.

"Yes, their mother met them; waiting outside she was, dressed up and carrying a couple of coats, if I remember."

"Thank you. Sorry I bothered you, but we were worried. They've probably gone to the pictures and forgot to tell us."

"Pictures? That's not likely. They went off in a taxi, and there were several suitcases with them. And more luggage waiting for them at the station I was told. Off for a little holiday with their mother, are they? She didn't say how long they'd be away."

Eirlys left the woman still talking and ran to find Johnny. As the station was on the way to Brook Lane, she ran there first and made enquiries.

"Yes," the ticket office clerk told her. "A young woman did buy tickets for her three boys. Singles they were and she had a return. Such a lot of luggage she had too, and not even a sixpenny tip for the porter."

Eirlys looked stricken with grief when she met Johnny and told him what had happened. Johnny hugged her and said, "They'll write and if things get bad up there, they'll be back."

When they returned to Annie and Morgan, her father told her he had looked into the rooms and discovered that all the boys' best clothes and toys were gone. Further enquires revealed that even the bikes had been sent on as advance luggage.

"So it's true," Eirlys said. "Teresa has taken the boys back to London."

Morgan nodded. "And it doesn't look as if they're coming back."

Ten

With the boys gone and her life lacking the need to keep busy in order to get everything done, Annie was lost. She read and reread the postcards they received, which were written by Stanley and signed by all three boys. They asked about their friends and the donkeys and whether there had been any more snow. Annie wrote back and asked about their new school and whether they had been to the pictures or anywhere else of interest, but her questions were ignored and she had the feeling they did nothing besides exist in the small flat their mother rented. She was even doubtful that they attended school.

She and Morgan went several times to stand and look into the room the boys had shared, as though half expecting them to appear and laugh and tell them it was all a huge joke.

Because of the gap in their lives, they tried to involve themselves in their daughter's wedding plans. Morgan went to see if anything needed doing at the rooms in Mrs Hibbert's house but Johnny and his father and Taff had dealt with the redecoration and everything was in place. He came home after each attempt to help feeling useless.

For Annie it was worse. Since Eirlys was born she had dreamed of the wonderful wedding she would arrange for her. Now, at a time when she needed to have something to fill her days, even that had been taken from her. The organisation of Eirlys and Johnny Castle's wedding had been taken completely out of Annie's hands. Once the wedding guest lists had been shown to Moll she had taken over, giving instructions to Annie and Morgan on their specific tasks and organising everything herself.

Aware of her parents' disappointment, Eirlys began to have qualms about belonging to a family in which Moll was matriarch, and in which everyone so willingly accepted it.

"There's room for thirty guests in the café and if the weather is fine it will be perfect for photographs," Moll announced one evening, having invited Annie and Morgan and Eirlys to discuss what had so far been planned. Evelyn and Taff were there too as well as Marged, Huw and their youngest daughter Beth, who was to be chief bridesmaid. Johnny was helping his father at Piper's fish-and-chip shop.

Eirlys told Beth, "I want to have flowers inside the church and around the porch, as well as on the tables for the reception. But I want you, as bridesmaid, and myself to carry a prayer book and a single rose. I've seen some in silver and white. What do you think?"

"I'd like that," Beth said, her dark eyes shining. "So stylish."

"It will hardly be the event of the year," Evelyn hissed. She made several snide remarks throughout Moll's announcements, most of which she was careful not to let anyone else but Eirlys hear.

Moll was tapping her pencil on her notebook impatiently and said sharply, "Can we get on with this? I have a lot to arrange. I take it that Piper's Café for the reception is all right?"

"How do you feel about using Piper's Café, Mam?" Eirlys asked Annie, hoping she would disagree. She had no real objection to using Piper's Café, in fact it would be a rather charming and unusual choice, high above the sands with wonderful views across the bay, but she felt the need to stop Moll on something, otherwise the wedding would have nothing at all to do with her or Johnny.

"I thought we'd have it in the room above the Oaktree café," Annie said. "They specialise in weddings." She was talked out of that in a few firmly spoken words.

"This is the Piper family and we always have our receptions at Piper's Café." There was no opportunity to argue. Moll had spoken, Annie thought, with irritation rising.

"Eirlys and I will be making the wedding cake," she said, but that idea was quashed too.

"No need, I've already ordered it, Mrs Price. Three tiers and all in white."

"I hope you haven't seen the dress," Eirlys said a little petulantly. "I want that to be a surprise for everyone."

She was shocked to be told even that had been checked by Moll. "I went to see the material to make sure it's the best," Moll said, unaware of the irritation she was causing.

Annie began to wriggle in her seat. Morgan put a hand on her shoulder and told her to stay calm.

"What about the honeymoon, a week in a caravan, is it?" Evelyn smiled, glancing first at Eirlys then at Morgan. Eirlys was startled at her father's reaction. He jumped up and insisted that enough had been settled for one evening and prepared to leave.

The three Prices left the house in Sidney Street and as soon as the door was closed behind them they began to verbalise their frustration.

"It's my wedding. Mine and Johnny's, and it's nothing to do with Granny Moll," Eirlys said, her voice low with simmering anger. "I feel like leaving her to carry on with the arrangements, then running away with Johnny and getting married in a register office!"

"What if we all went to London, so Stanley, Harold and Percival could share it?" Morgan said, and Eirlys spared a moment to remember how much her father was missing the boys.

"What did that Evelyn mean about you having a honeymoon in a caravan?" Annie asked.

"Nothing more than cattiness," Morgan said at once. "I don't know what's got into that girl. You'd think she was jealous of our Eirlys, or something."

"She doesn't consider me a suitable wife for Johnny," Eirlys told them, "but she won't explain why."

"Ask her," Annie said.

"Don't bother," Morgan shrugged.

A few days later, Eirlys and Evelyn came face to face in Woolworths. Eirlys was choosing some ribbons with which to bind a small rug she had made for a baby's room.

"Trimmings for your honeymoon nightie?" Evelyn asked.

Eirlys turned, smiling, prepared to enjoy some mild teasing, but Evelyn's face was stony.

"Why do you dislike me so much?" she asked.

"As if you didn't know!"

"That's the point, I don't know. Tell me, so we can sort it out, please."

"Pretending such innocence," Evelyn sneered.

"Tell me."

"Ask your father," was the swift reply.

Unsettled by the encounter, Eirlys went to see Hannah to see how her wedding dress was progressing.

Hannah was setting in gathers on the frilled layers down each side of the crinoline-style skirt. Bags made of muslin were fixed inside to rest on each hip which, on the day, would be filled with tissue to hold out the sides. Embroidered honeysuckle and Tudor roses trailed down the bodice and the centre panel of the skirt.

As she inserted each neat stitch, Hannah dreamed of wearing it, walking up the aisle to stand beside Johnny. In her head she could hear the organ playing, then the silence before the spoken words of the marriage service, and aloud she said, "I do."

When Eirlys knocked at the door she didn't answer. She went on sewing, a tear in every stitch.

–

Stanley, Harold and Percival were sitting reading old comics and watching the rain through the spotted window of the ground floor flat. Not really a flat, just a room divided into two sections by a pair of curtains.

"Wish we was with Auntie Annie," Percival said quietly.

"What, leave our Ma again?" Stanley said brightly. "You wouldn't want to go away again, not really?"

"I wanted to see Ma, but now I want to see Auntie Annie and Uncle Morgan," Percival said reasonably.

"We haven't even got our bikes," Harold added glumly.

Teresa had sold the three bicycles as soon as they had arrived on the carrier. She dealt with the sale swiftly and didn't think the boys had even seen them, but Stanley had. He guessed what had happened to them but patted Harold on his head and said, "They ain't come yet. That carrier takes 'is time, eh? Tomorrow; perhaps they'll come tomorrow."

Their new coats had disappeared too and several of their games and toys. Teresa had explained the absence of the toys by telling them there was no room, and they had gone to poor little children "who never had a thing to play with". In the sparsely filled room, with nothing but out-of-date comics to look at, that wasn't easy to explain to his brothers, so Stanley didn't try.

Teresa also tore up some of the letters Annie and Morgan wrote. She checked first to make sure there was no postal order inside then threw them into the rubbish bin. When she did find money she kept most of it but bought a few sweets and gave them to the boys as a gift, from herself. Best they didn't grieve too much for Annie and Morgan. She didn't think they would see them again.

They tried to talk to her about their lives with Annie and Morgan and the friends they made but she never had time to listen. She had heard a little about the grand Christmas concert and the fun they'd had in the snow but didn't question them and quickly changed the subject, reminding them how happy she was to have them back where she could look after them properly.

Partly her refusal to listen was fear that they might want to go back, partly it was because she wasn't really interested. What did she care about St David's Well? She loved them and did what she thought was best for them, but she didn't want them to leave again. At least, not till she had the council flat. Then she would manage without them while she built them a proper home.

She went out most evenings, leaving the boys to amuse themselves and put themselves to bed when they were tired.

Coming back home about a week after they had returned, the man whose wallet she had stolen was waiting for her. She panicked and ran away, hoping to put him off the scent. She didn't want her boys harmed or frightened.

It was four in the morning before she felt safe to return. Stanley greeted her at the door.

"Thank heaven's you're back, Ma. Our Harold's got toothache and can't sleep."

Teresa cuddled him after giving him an aspirin and told him it was Annie and Morgan's fault for giving them too many sweets.

"Thank goodness I got you back home when I did, Stanley, or you could have suffered real bad 'ealth," she said.

"Yeah; lucky us, eh," Stanley said as he crawled into the damp bed beside his brothers.

"I'm lucky to have three wonderful sons like you, Stanley. Don't I know it."

When they woke the next morning, she began packing their meagre belongings into bag and said cheerfully, "Come on, stir your stumps, we're movin'!"

–

To fill in some of the empty hours, and escape from the lonely house, Annie went along to the ARP meetings and helped by making tea and supplying a few cakes. She soon became involved in learning some basic first aid, and attended lectures on dealing with incendiary bombs and other devastations which they secretly thought would never happen.

Morgan too became more involved and learned to recognise British and enemy planes by their silhouettes, as well as how to tackle more immediate problems – everything from using a stirrup pump to rescuing people from burning houses.

It was so far from everyday life which, apart from the shortages of food, was going on much the same as always, that it was treated like a game.

Since the death of Irene, Morgan hadn't missed a single shift at the factory and he hadn't been late either. Annie began to hope that their problems were behind them.

"Saving to go and see the boys," he told everyone who teased him about his new-found reliability. "Annie and I want to go up and make sure they're all right."

"The wedding too," Annie reminded him. "We want to do our best for Eirlys – if that Granny Molly Piper will let us," she added with a frown.

"Eirlys and Johnny are happy, and they've found a home a long way from Sidney Street," Morgan said. "They'll be all right. Sure to be."

Annie and Morgan were upset to have a flood of letters from the three boys. Most of them arrived without a postage stamp and they had to pay before receiving them. These had probably been written without Teresa knowing, Annie guessed. There were no complaints, no criticism of their mother, but they were clearly not happy and they were not attending school regularly, their mother waking too late to send them most mornings.

From the postcards they learned that Teresa had a single room in which they all lived. Stanley wrote cheerfully and said nothing about his being unhappy although it was apparent between the lines.

He told them how they missed the walks in the countryside and hoped to see the beach in the summer. Harold wanted to see Mr Gregory and the donkeys. In a P.S. Stanley told them Percival promised he would eat his "taters" if he could come back. These words had been rubbed out but were still readable, and they brought Annie to tears.

"They aren't happy, that much is clear," Morgan said, walking up and down the living room agitatedly.

"You'd be more worried if you'd seen the flat Teresa lived in before," Annie told him.

They were still separated by his betrayal with Irene Castle. Although outwardly relaxed, there were some days when Annie felt the hurt as much as she had in the moment she had been told. Then she would refuse to talk to him or even look at him, unwilling for him to see her pain. Even on the worst days, when they rarely exchanged more than the occasional word, where the boys were concerned they were in complete accord.

"Now she hasn't even got that miserable place," she went on. "Sharing they are, cramped four to a bed into a small room so the council will take pity on them and get them a decent flat."

"They should come back here," Morgan said, not for the first time.

"I know that, and you saying it won't make it happen!" Annie snapped. "I think I should go up there and talk to them, see if I can persuade Teresa it would be better for them."

"Careful, or you'll have her staying here as well, paying no rent and using us as child-minders so she can go out on the tiles!"

"She's stopped all that," Annie said. "She must have. She can't leave the boys alone at night, specially not now, with the blackout making it easier for thieves to break in. I can't bear the thought of them being alone at night." They looked at each other for reassurance. "She wouldn't, would she?"

Morgan thought it was quite likely she would but didn't say so and add to Annie's distress.

"And there's the risk of an air raid, and bombs dropping," she went on. "Just because it hasn't happened yet doesn't mean the danger has gone."

"Another reason for her to let them come home – I mean back here," he quickly amended.

"I think they were beginning to think of this place as home," Annie said softly. "That's probably why Teresa took them away from us."

"I suppose we can't blame her for that. They are her boys after all and she loves them."

"They'd be better off with us, though, wouldn't they?"

"No, Annie, don't torment yourself. With their mother they are and that's got to be the best."

–

Teresa was walking back home after seeing a man she had met the previous evening. The late evening was quiet, just a few cars passing by with their minimal lights, and even fewer pedestrians about. The public houses had closed an hour before and she had spent a while with the man in an empty house she sometimes used.

The figure darted out from the darkness of the passageway at the side of the building like a shadow. Without warning, he grabbed her from behind.

"All right, bitch, I want the money you owe me."

"But I—"

A hand covered her mouth, stifling her protest, then she was pushed and slapped hard across the cheek, turned around and slapped again until she didn't know where she was. The man pulled her handbag from her arm. "If there isn't twenty-five quid in here, you'd better leave it for me tomorrow at the pub. If I don't get it, you're dead, you *and* your kids, Teresa Love." He twisted her and tripped her until she lost balance and fell to the ground. He kicked her several times, then ran off.

She lay there for several seconds, confused and dizzy from the blows and the suddenness of the attack. Then she rose to her feet and hurried to the front door of the house in which she and the boys rented a room of a flat. She felt that vulnerable coldness between her shoulder blades. The darkness closed in around her, isolating her, and the shadows were filled with invisible threats.

Her leg hurt and her head was spinning but she ran as fast as she could, seeking the shelter and safety of the flat. So he had found her again, and was still insisting on getting his money, more than she had stolen in fact; interest, to pay for his humiliation, she guessed. Where could she find that amount? The twenty-four pounds she had stolen from him was long gone.

A lot of the men she was involved with were unable to cope with being bested by anyone, particularly a woman. Little men pretending to be big. Not many were as vicious as this one. Why had she chosen to steal a wallet from him? She had never done that before, she had always played fair with her clients.

Weakness overcame her when she had climbed the first two steps and she longed to collapse, to sit and recover, but he could be still there in the darkness, watching her, ready to come after her again. She clung to the rail at the side of the steps for support and dragged herself to the top, concentrating on staying upright, when all she wanted was to sit down and recover.

She was trembling when she reached the door and had difficulty finding the keyhole. This meant she would have to move again. It wouldn't be easy with the three boys to consider but she had to get away. She fell inside, closed the door behind her and stood for a long time to allow her heart to calm and her breathing to drop to a normal rate.

As she stood there she wondered whether she could leave the boys and go somewhere on her own until the man's anger had died down. Touching her stomach, she was comforted by the tiny bulge of notes she had hidden inside her knickers after her last client had left her in the empty house and she had cleaned herself up. Thank goodness her attacker hadn't known about them.

Her handbag contained less than a pound. Now she would be able to buy those new shoes she had set her heart on, and treat the boys to good meals for a few days. There was no point in trying to pay the man. He didn't want her money, he wanted revenge. He would be watching her, and waiting for the opportunity to hit her again.

Her face hurt and her leg ached where she had fallen awkwardly, and she knew there would be big bruises on her where the toe of his shoe had landed. Bruising was something she didn't like, they could give clients the wrong idea. "And I bet my last pair of stockings are laddered," she muttered to herself, worrying about the trivial to take her thoughts from the serious. It was past eleven thirty, and the flat, which she was sharing with a friend, was in darkness when she moved away from the door and adjusted the blackout curtain. She decided she would have to break her own firm rules; she wouldn't undress or have a thorough wash, in case she disturbed the rest of the household. She had promised her friend she would be home before ten.

Then she heard sobbing. It was quiet – muffled, she guessed, by the blankets across his mouth – but unmistakable.

"Percival?" she whispered, climbing painfully over Harold and Stanley to reach her youngest, squashed against the wall in the single bed.

"I want to go back to Annie an' Morgan," he blubbered.

"Soon, darlin', soon. I promise," Teresa whispered. She wondered how it could be arranged. Perhaps she *could* send the boys back now the housing officer had seen them. It would give her a real chance to save up for something decent if she didn't have the boys to worry about. This time she could really succeed, get them a decent home with proper beds and everything.

She had to get away from this flat, that much was certain. She couldn't risk the man hurting the boys or her friend who had helped her out by lending her a room. If she went far enough perhaps the man wouldn't find her again. If she was lucky with a few quality clients she might even pay him off! Leave his money at the pub he used. That idea was a novelty, being rich enough to pay him back. She might even deduct the money he'd taken from her handbag!

She would let the council housing officer know she'd had to move again, and if it was somewhere worse it wouldn't matter, just for a while, until she got that smart flat. Yes, everything would be settled if she could hand the boys back to Annie and Morgan for a while.

The idea was very tempting and she hugged the little boy and repeated her promise. "I'll write to Mr and Mrs Price tomorrow and ask if we can go back for a little holiday, shall I?"

"I'd rather 'ave a big 'oliday," Percival said sleepily.

"I love you, Percival," Teresa whispered.

Life was hectic for Eirlys, with customers arriving frequently to order one of her custom-made rugs. Some of the requests came as a result of the display Bleddyn and Johnny had set up in the sweet and rock shop on the promenade. Johnny's father was being very supportive of her enterprise.

The machine-made rugs didn't take very long, with her parents helping to cut the strips of material from coats and skirts, and in some cases heavy curtains. The hand-made designs took a lot longer and Annie began to help her make these as well as help with the preparation. So far they had been small hearth rugs and smaller ones for children. She knew she had to find a way of embarking on more adventurous sizes and even different shapes. She had to add variety to what she was offering if she were to expand.

She had spasms of guilt when she realised she was more excited about her burgeoning business than the arrangements for her wedding. She reminded herself that most of it had been taken out of her hands by Granny Moll Piper, and found comfort in that. Yet she knew her lack of enthusiasm was really something far more serious: by her lack of involvement she was letting Johnny down.

On impulse one Saturday she arranged to go shopping with Johnny's cousin Beth.

"We'll look for some special underwear and night-clothes," Eirlys whispered, and they began to giggle like children at the implications.

They caught the train into Cardiff and began looking around the shops, eventually choosing the garments for Eirlys's honeymoon. Clutching their exciting purchases they wandered towards the market stalls, attracted by the buzz of activity now the day was ending and the stall-holders were anxious to sell the last of the perishables. Saturday afternoon was the time for bargains.

They didn't buy meat or fish. With nowhere to store it, their "bargains" would have ended in the dustbin. The fruit and vegetables looked fresh, though, the prices too good to miss, and by the time they reached the railway station they were staggering under the weight of it.

Eirlys and Beth noticed a thin, shabbily dressed man getting on their train but neither commented. The number of sick and exhausted soldiers returning from France made the young man a not uncommon sight. They looked away, embarrassed as he passed them. They felt sympathy but were unable to open a conversation with a stranger.

It was as they alighted at the platform that they saw him again and this time he approached them. It wasn't until he was close that they recognised him.

"Peter?" Beth said. "Peter Gregory? What on earth have you been doing with yourself? Your dad'll have a fit when he sees the state of you."

"Living rough you might say," Peter replied in his polite tone. "I dare say Dad will accept the challenge to fatten me up like one of his Christmas turkeys before I depart once more for – who knows what." He took some of the carrier bags with which they were struggling and they left the platform. To their delight, Mr Gregory was there with the pony and trap and they all piled in.

The conversation was general, Peter asking about their families and congratulating Eirlys on her imminent wedding.

"And you, Bethan?" he asked. "Are you and Freddy Clements still getting engaged on your birthday?"

"Fancy you remembering that!" Beth laughed.

Eirlys looked at Peter's expression as he gazed at Beth and thought it wasn't surprising at all.

–

Peter called for Beth the following day and invited her and Freddy to visit his father.

"There's a chicken cooking in honour of my return and we'd love you to share it."

"Thanks, Peter; I'm sure Freddy will be as pleased as I am."

"What about Eirlys, could she come too? I feel the need for a party. Father's chicken will be the equivalent of the fatted calf. Your cousin Johnny wouldn't refuse a meal I'm sure."

So it was arranged, and six people sat down in the living room of Mr Gregory's cottage that evening and enjoyed a delicious meal cooked in the oven next to the fire.

Peter asked a lot of questions, obviously anxious to hear the local gossip, but Eirlys noticed he rarely answered a question about his own life. Mr Gregory had told them he was unable to discuss his business and they accepted it.

Eirlys also noticed that Peter looked at Beth quite often and there was more than friendship on his mind. She suspected that the "party" was an excuse for him to see her. She wondered if Beth was aware of his interest but, seeing the way she clung to Freddy, she thought not. Interesting though. Attractions weren't always conveniently mutual.

–

Between working at the hardware store and helping his father at the chip shop, Johnny was kept busy, but he went to Mrs Hibbert's house when he had any spare time. He had finished decorating their future home, with the help of his father and

Taff. The furniture was more or less in place, much of it given by family and friends.

Everyone was involved and it was only Evelyn who still treated Eirlys like the enemy. One day, several of her comments melded together and began to puzzle Eirlys rather than irritate her as in the past.

Evelyn's comment about the caravan for her honeymoon had been more than cattiness. She had been looking at her father when she had said it, as though the reference to a caravan meant something to him, and he had left so suddenly after that too. Angry? Upset? Embarrassed? She wasn't sure he had shown any of those emotions now, after so much time had passed. At the time she remembered thinking it was her father's concern for her that had made him leave so suddenly, getting her away from the frustration of Granny Moll's organising and from Evelyn's obvious dislike. Now she wondered if there was something more. She remembered the day she thought she had seen her father walking near where the caravan was parked not far from the old stone barn. Could there be a connection?

The thought drifted into her mind but didn't solidify into something on which she could act. It was curious, that was all. She did nothing about it, because she couldn't think of any way of solving the mystery. She didn't have sufficient facts. The main one was that Evelyn disliked her, and she seemed to dislike her father too.

–

While Peter Gregory was home he managed to see quite a lot of Beth Castle – sometimes with her soon-to-be fiancé, Freddy Clements, who worked in a gent's outfitters in the town, and sometimes on her own.

Wednesday was early closing and the afternoon was when Beth was free from the icy-cold shop selling vegetables. Peter was there when she pulled down the shutters and swept up the debris from the pavement.

"Are you and Freddy doing anything this afternoon?" he asked in his polite way.

"Not really, Peter. Freddy is going into town and I planned to do nothing except get warm," she told him with a demonstrative shiver.

"Come with me and groom the donkeys," he said. "Hardly an exciting invitation but they're very warm and, apart from Charlie, very friendly."

Mr Gregory greeted them and made them a pot of tea then left them to attend to other things. They went to the field in which the stables were situated and talked, using the excuse of grooming the donkeys for being there.

Peter made her laugh, telling her of the people he met and some of the things he had done. She was surprisingly happy. Then, when they were walking back home in the fading light, he stopped to help her over a stile and as her feet touched the ground he held her and kissed her.

"Peter!" she gasped, utterly surprised.

"Sorry, Bethan, but I've been wanting to do that all day."

"But we've never been more than friends," she said, still puzzled.

"Can't a friend kiss a friend?"

"I suppose not, it's just that Freddy and I—"

"Put it down to my long absence and the situation in which I've been working," he smiled. "I promise not to do it again. That is, unless you want me to."

Beth was unsure how to deal with this, but Peter returned to his previous manner and she was soon laughing, and answering him as easily as before. Nevertheless, a part of her felt a guilty wriggle of excitement.

–

Hannah walked into the house after taking her two children to school and nursery one morning, and a shout from her mother made her heart race. What misdemeanour was she accused of now?

"Your father's had an accident," her mother said. "He's in bed and can't be moved. You'll have to miss work this evening and tomorrow morning and help me look after him."

When the facts were explained, and Hannah learned that her father had fallen while riding a bicycle and was badly bruised, she carefully explained that it wasn't really serious enough for her to miss work.

"I'll help when I can, but I can't not go to work and I can't not finish the skirt I've promised Mrs Beynon for next Saturday," she explained. She spoke politely and quietly but the tirade she hoped to avoid came at once. Words like "selfish" and "ungrateful" and plenty more were thrown at her and when Johnny passed in the firm's van an hour later, she was standing in the shadows near the park gates crying.

He parked the van and ran to see what had happened. Hannah's mother saw them on her way back from the chemist.

"Are you all right? Are the girls all right?" Johnny asked, taking her in his arms.

"Don't, Johnny; I'm in enough trouble as it is," she sighed, trying to control her sobs.

She explained what had happened and he led her to the van and insisted she got in. He drove to a place where they could have coffee and cakes, and found them a corner seat where they could talk. Tight-lipped, Mrs Wilcox watched them go.

"We'll have to see if we can't get you a better place to live, Hannah, love. I know you should be grateful to your parents, but they're very misguided in the way they expect you to behave." He was careful not to criticise them, afraid she might turn away from him when he wanted only to help her.

"I can't go away. Where would I go? Living in rooms with strangers could be much worse. At least I know what to expect from Mam and Dad – nothing!" she said bitterly.

He coaxed her to sip the coffee and gradually she calmed down. "I'm going to be strong over this," she told him, forcing a smile that wrenched at his heart. "If I miss work, it's Josie and Marie who will suffer and they are more important than my parents."

When she walked back into the house, her mother said, "There are to be no more men in this house."

Hannah didn't understand quite what she meant until a man called to collect a blouse and skirt she had been altering for his wife, and Hannah was not allowed to give them to him.

When Johnny finished his deliveries and went back to the hardware shop, he was told someone had reported him for using the firm's van to give a lift to a young woman, and he was sacked.

–

Eirlys was very busy. At work there were so many extra arrangements to be made. Men had left without giving anyone a chance to train others to take their place. Eirlys and her assistants dealt with everything, including the deliveries of air raid shelters to those who requested them, arrangements for people unable to erect their shelters without help, and special protection for the elderly and infirm. There were pages and pages of information to distribute to grocers and butchers on dealing with ration-book registration, and dozens of complaints from irate customers who suspected the retailers of being unfair. The variety of her various activities seemed endless, and she loved it.

Permission had to be acquired from owners to enter buildings so that fire-watchers could stand guard, and their equipment had to be distributed. There were payments to be given, and in most cases later cancelled, for housing the evacuees. She and her staff worked many extra hours to deal with the increasing preparations of the country now at war.

When she reached home each evening, Johnny was usually there. He had been kept busy dealing with extra work too, packing and delivering goods which were already slower to restock, as people with sufficient money gathered as much as they could to prepare for the shortages that would surely come.

When he told her he had been sacked for giving Hannah a lift and buying her coffee because she was upset, she showed concern for Hannah. After she had heard the whole story she smiled and said, "Their loss, Johnny. I'm sure it won't take you long to find another job."

When they spent time with Johnny's Uncle Huw and Auntie Marged, Granny Moll, who lived a few doors away, usually appeared and Eirlys dreaded the detailed discussion of her wedding. It was becoming less hers and Johnny's as the days passed. She was relieved when the discussion changed from their wedding to the repainting of Piper's Café ready for the opening in May.

With the six-month summer season taking all the family's time, repairs and redecoration had to be done during the winter months. Much of the painting was done in the weeks running up to opening, but this year they were going to start on the café earlier so it would be looking its best for the wedding at the end of March.

Eirlys sat and thought about what awaited her at the office next day, or the rugs she was working on, and let the conversation drift over her. She knew she should be more involved, more excited, but the truth was, she couldn't rouse enough interest to make a single suggestion. "Partly because Moll always has the last word – and frequently the first as well," she told Annie and Morgan later.

"You are sure about this marriage, are you?" Morgan asked.

Eirlys stared at her father as though the question had never entered her mind. "Sure about it?"

"If you aren't absolutely certain you have to say, love."

"Of course I'm sure."

"You aren't thinking about Ken Ward?"

"Ken and I finished a long time ago."

"And it's really over and done with?" Morgan insisted.

"Over and done with," she echoed. "I'm fond of Ken but I love Johnny like never before."

The conversation disturbed her. It roused in her questions she had pushed aside, tried to ignore. Bringing them out and facing them when she lay in bed that night, she knew she had lied. She wasn't sure about becoming Mrs Johnny Castle. She loved Johnny, wanted nothing more than to be his wife, but she was more and more afraid that she wouldn't be able to cope with his family. The large family, the closeness she had wanted so much, was threatening to destroy her love for him.

She had a brief and foolish impulse to pack a suitcase and go away. It was ironic that less than a year ago she had said goodbye to Ken Ward because she had refused to do just that.

As she drifted into a restless sleep, she heard in her mind the sound of Ken, singing silly songs to the children at the last concert he had given before going back to London and applying to entertain the troops. She saw again the smiling faces of his young audience as they joined in lustily with the choruses. She was smiling with them as she slept.

The following morning there was a letter from Ken, the usual friendly note telling her of the various interviews and auditions and rehearsals that were gradually taking him towards entertaining the troops.

She was, as always, cheered by his letter and she settled to reply. As she wrote, her cheerfulness faded and she began to tell him about their worries for Stanley, Harold and Percival Love in the sad little room in London.

She usually heard within a week or so but this letter had a prompt reply. Ken offered to go and visit the Love family to find out how they all were.

–

With the work on the cafés and stalls looming, and the busy summer season not far off, Bleddyn was busy repapering his house. He felt the need to start a fresh phase of his life now Irene was gone. Starting in the bedroom they had shared, he chose a cheerful pattern and was given one of Eirlys's rugs to complete the transformation.

The living room was next and, unable to stop, he went on to do the hall and stairs, helped by Johnny who, as he frequently did, complained about his lack of height. Only Bleddyn in the Castle family was above average height and it was he who was called on to deal with any job that needed extra reach.

Between them he and Johnny completed the task very quickly. Johnny didn't think the work was needed but understood his father's need for changes.

"Just in time for the wedding," Johnny smiled. "Thanks, Dad."

Although the wedding was not taking place in Brook Lane, Johnny knew a lot of friends would be calling. He also hoped the redecoration was really a sign that his father was recovering from the shock of his mother's death.

One Sunday afternoon, when the sun shone weakly but with a promise of warmth to come, Johnny and Eirlys went over to the beach. There were other couples enjoying the pleasant hint of approaching spring, walking beside the waves, stopping occasionally to collect a shell or a particularly beautiful piece of rock. They recognised some friends but didn't join them, going instead to Piper's Café high above the sand.

They had been asked to measure the shelves so Marged could buy shelf paper to cover them. Johnny used the tape measure and Eirlys jotted down his instructions on a note pad.

They worked busily for a while, then Johnny took a bar of chocolate from his pocket and they sat to enjoy it. Eirlys said very little. He sensed her confusion, and apologised for Granny Moll.

"Sorry about Granny Moll's enthusiasm. She's always been in charge of us all and we just accept it. She's Uncle Huw's mother-in-law, besides being his boss, and he can expect her to make the decisions, but as for Dad, I don't know why he suffers it. He's worked for her since he was about twelve, and he's never known any other way, I suppose."

"She isn't even your gran," Eirlys protested, glad to be able to talk to him honestly about how she felt. "She certainly isn't mine! So why does she insist on arranging our wedding? I feel as though it's nothing to do with you and me, it's a Piper family affair. It's more an initiation ceremony, accepting me into the clan, than you and I starting a life together." She laughed to disguise her frustration and he hugged her, kissed away her frowns.

"Dad called her Granny Moll long before Taff and I were born. She needs to believe we are all one family. And you will be a part of it too. Aren't you happy about that?"

"I love you, Johnny. I want to belong to you — and perhaps one day I might even help on the beach," she added doubtfully.

"You don't have to work on the sands. Mam never did."

"Poor lady. If your father hadn't been so understanding, she would always have felt like an outsider."

"Perhaps that was why she was so unhappy. Taff and I loved the life so much, we should have understood that she didn't and tried harder to help her." He imagined her body lying in the cold, still water of that dock. "God, Eirlys, she must have been so unhappy to do what she did."

"Don't blame yourself or anyone else for her sad and lonely death. She wasn't deprived of happiness. I don't think she looked for it, she didn't think there was any."

"I sometimes think she must have been looking for something better than us. Where did she go on her long walks? Perhaps during her wanderings she found someone else, someone who understood and who made her feel better."

"You don't really think there was someone else?" Eirlys looked suitably horrified.

"I found a note once and it made me wonder. I've never told a soul so keep it to yourself, love. It was on the floor of her bedroom, as though it had fallen out of her drawer with some handkerchieves. It was addressed to 'My Love' and signed 'Your adoring slave'. I threw it away before Dad saw it and I didn't think much about it. But since her death, I have wondered."

"Johnny!" she laughed. "You're crazy if you think that was to your mother from a secret lover! That's definitely schoolgirl stuff! She probably picked it up intending to show you and make you laugh. She would never have looked at another man! Don't even think it."

"Her wedding ring was never found, or her watch. If we find them, we might learn more of what really happened that day. And a pair of wellingtons she used on her walks went missing too."

"She was probably carrying them home, put them down somewhere and forgot to pick them up. They probably ended up on a scarecrow in a farmer's field, or in someone's dustbin. You're letting your imagination go wild, Johnny. 'Adoring slave'! Who would talk like that, for heaven's sake! Don't think badly of her. She's your mam and now she's gone. Think only nice thoughts."

They spent an affectionate hour together in the privacy of Piper's Café, sitting at one of the tables looking down at the beach, the sun spreading its warmth around them. They sat close together, kissing, hugging and promising each other that they would talk over any problems and deal with them before they became large enough to threaten their happiness. That night she tried to remember their conversation. Something was niggling at her memory and she couldn't bring it to mind.

Eirlys felt more positive about her wedding after those hours spent in Piper's Café. She was still very busy both at work and making her rugs, experimenting with wall hangings too after seeing some in a quality home-maker's magazine. When she and Johnny were together they talked easily and about everything. Eirlys knew she would be utterly content as Johnny's wife. She even helped out one evening in Piper's fish-and—chip shop when Bleddyn had a night off.

Unfortunately, that was the evening Taff and Evelyn came in.

"I don't think I want chips tonight," Evelyn said to Taff. Quietly, she added to Eirlys, "Not from your hands I don't."

"What is the matter with you?" Eirlys demanded loudly. "What have I ever done to you for you to treat me as though I'm not fit to look at you?"

Taff and Johnny looked at Evelyn, both waiting for her apology or at least an explanation, but Evelyn simply turned around and left the shop. Johnny went to run after her, but Eirlys stopped him. There was a long queue of customers waiting and enjoying the fun. Johnny smiled at the next customer and asked cheerfully, "What can I get you, Mrs Thomas, the usual cod and chips, is it? And the names and odds offered on the contestants in tonight's fight?" Everyone laughed and the moment was eased.

When the shop was closed, the cleaning done and Johnny was walking her home, Eirlys explained briefly some of the earlier incidents between herself and Evelyn and asked if he knew what had upset his sister-in-law.

He laughed and said, "Whatever it is, it can't be anything for us to worry about. She seems to have a problem accepting

284

that I'm getting married. Perhaps being the only daughter-in-law, being fussed over by Dad, is a role she enjoys. Maybe she hates the thought of having to share his attentions with you, Dad having two of you to spoil and enjoy? He's fond of you, get on well you do, anyone can see that. She might feel put out. I don't know; let's forget it and enjoy the walk home."

It was a shared problem now, she thought with relief, and it drew them closer. The wedding day was something Eirlys began to think about more and more and with greater excitement. For Johnny too, confidence in their forthcoming marriage was stronger. He felt he would be able to visit Hannah and the girls without fear of being tempted by her.

He knocked on her front door one evening, straight from his new job at a greengrocer not far from the one at which Beth worked. A moon was showing through thin cloud and casting a magical beauty over the town.

He had no reason to call, but decided to ask whether the girls would like to go with himself and Eirlys to the last week of the pantomime. He was smiling, certain Eirlys would agree.

The door opened and Hannah stood there, her expression invisible in the poor light. There was no mistaking the voice, though. She had been crying.

"Hannah? What is it? Can I come in?"

"Sorry, Johnny. My mother insists that if I get any men callers I will have to take the children and find somewhere else to live."

"But that's ridiculous."

"I have to agree with her. I have no choice," she said. "I even had to refuse to hand over a child's dress yesterday when the husband of my customer called to collect it."

"Are there any restrictions on coming out for a walk? Josie and Marie aren't in bed yet, are they?"

"No, they haven't had their supper yet. I keep them up a bit later than I should because the evenings are so lonely."

"Get their coats then and we'll walk through the town and peer into shop windows. I used to love that when I was small, didn't you?" He produced an Aero, which he gave to the children. "Who cares if it spoils their supper? It doesn't hurt once in a while," he excused to Hannah, who thanked him then nodded to tell the girls it was all right to eat it.

The moon rose clear of the clouds and lit their way and they walked along the main road, where most of the shops were, stopping whenever something attracted the attention of the little girls. There was a toy shop, and Josie and Marie pressed their noses to the glass, covered the sides of their faces with gloved hands and tried to look at the wonders on offer for those with money. Bicycles and scooters, forts and castles, dolls' prams, houses and everything needed to enjoy them. They discussed what they would buy if they were given a choice and Johnny stood inside the porch with Hannah close to him.

Nothing was said, but their eyes told it all. What he felt for Eirlys was forgotten whenever he was close to Hannah.

In their black woollen stockings and sturdy boots they were well wrapped up, but the girls soon began to shiver and stamp their feet as an icy east wind stole the warmth from them.

"We should be getting back," Hannah said.

"Another five minutes?" he asked huskily.

"Johnny, please don't do this to me." She took her daughters' hands and began to walk away from him, not hurriedly, but slowly, waiting for him to join them after a few paces, talking to Marie and Josie, asking if they had room for supper after the chocolate, which biscuits they wanted with their night-time cocoa. Calm, easy questions, denying the tumult in her heart.

With the girls between them they wandered back, swinging arms and running at times to keep warm. At the gate, Johnny asked whether she would allow Eirlys and himself to take them all to the pantomime. He spoke quietly, afraid of disappointing the girls if their mother said no. He was holding his breath as he waited for her reply.

"No thank you, Johnny. It isn't fair. You and Eirlys have to do things together. I'll take them myself, they won't miss it, I promise."

"Hannah," he pleaded softly, but she told the girls to thank him and slipped inside, lost to him, it seemed, for ever.

He went to see Eirlys later and the confusion of his feelings led him to be extra loving with her.

Any doubts she had felt were long gone. She was marrying Johnny Castle and they were going to be blissfully happy.

She would cope with the strong-minded Granny Moll, and deal with Evelyn's disapproval with Johnny's support and help. They had a home of their own, and the promise of a summer helping out on the beach, but only if and when she wanted to. There was nothing but contentment ahead. Full of emotional well-being, she went in and hugged her parents as she hadn't done since she was a child.

Eleven

Eirlys's euphoria lasted until a week later.

During that week, she and Johnny spent evenings at Mrs Hibbert's, putting the finishing touches to their future home. Eirlys had made curtains and one of her rugs with its design of cherries lay beside the double bed that was already made up with crisp new linen and two Witney blankets.

A chest of drawers and a cupboard in a corner stood empty, waiting for the wedding gifts to come. Many more had been promised than originally expected. Moll had spread the word that one of the Pipers was getting married. She ignored the fact that Johnny was not a Piper but a Castle. As far as she was concerned, Johnny worked on the sands and was therefore family – her family. She had spent some considerable time reminding people of their connection with the Pipers, and contacted the people from whom they bought their supplies during the summer season. By these and other means, she had extended the circle of their acquaintances, making the list of promised presents very impressive.

It was one of those spectacular mornings that sometimes occur during early spring which deceive people into believing that summer is just around the corner. Eirlys was awake early and she knew she would not be able to stay in bed. She went down and found that, early as she was, someone had been up before her. She felt the teapot and found it was warm.

Throwing away the dregs she made a fresh pot and considered taking one up to her parents, then decided against it. Sunday morning was not the time to be roused before you need be.

She drank two cups of tea and ate a few biscuits then, putting on a thick coat and warm scarf and gloves, went for a walk. She had no destination in mind, but when she saw the bright sun giving a rosy glow to the hedges and the graceful birch tree at the end of the road, which looked more perfect than a Christmas tree, she decided to go through the fields. With luck she might see a fox or another wild creature searching for food. There would be catkins or sticky-buds to pick and take home. Her mother loved to see them opening their fresh green leaves.

She walked fast at first to warm herself, swinging her arms, a feeling of well-being lighting her face with a smile. As she reached the lane she slowed her footsteps to gaze in admiration at the trees bordering the road, not quite bursting into leaf but with the blackthorn already decorating the lanes with its white blossom. In the grasses at her feet daisies and dandelions bloomed and celandines showed their golden faces rising from the clumps of heart-shaped leaves. Nature was wearing her ostentatious best as though sharing her joy. She wished she had remembered to bring a camera. The Brownie box camera wouldn't do it justice, but it would have been a memory of today, when she was so very happy.

The field in which the old barn stood was the usual muddy morass. A few weeks ago it had been surfaced with hard ridges, with frozen water shining dully in the dips between them. She stepped carefully across and stood near the entrance for a while, wondering which field the cows were now using. Using the ridges as stepping stones, she made her way across the field until she was in sight of the caravan. Someone was using it. Smoke rose straight up from its chimney in the clear air, and the door stood open.

Curious to know who could live in such a lonely place during the winter, she went to see if there was anyone home. She saw that the door was propped open with a pair of wellingtons. They were very like her father's. She called and stepped closer, then as she had heard nothing she went right up to the door and looked in. A woman's wellingtons were just inside. The thought flashed through her mind that Irene's wellingtons were missing, and her ring and watch had never been found. Perhaps she used this place; Eirlys remembered seeing her nearby once.

Daring to look further inside she saw a man sitting with a coat around him, looking as though he was fast asleep. She hesitated; she could hardly wake him up just to say "good morning". Slowly she tried to back away. Then he opened his eyes and turned to face her.

"Eirlys? What are you doing here?" her father asked.

"Dadda?" she asked with a confused frown. "Can I ask the same question?"

She went inside and saw to her horror that he had been crying. His eyes were bloodshot and tears wet his cheeks. Then she saw that the coat in which he had wrapped himself was not his coat. It was Irene Castle's. She recognised it easily with its brown fur collar.

A letter was near him and as he tried half-heartedly to pick it up, it fluttered to the floor. She stepped forward and was about to give it back but something stayed her hand and she read it.

"Darling M, I will be waiting for you tomorrow at two. Don't be late, I am desperate to see you." It was signed "I".

"Irene?" she gasped. "Were you and Irene Castle seeing each other?" When there was no reply she pleaded, "Dadda. Please tell me it isn't true?"

"It's true. You wouldn't understand." He pulled the coat tighter around him. "Bleddyn gave me her coat, this coat, and told me to cut it up for you to make rugs. I couldn't do that."

"Tell me I'm wrong," she said. "Please, Dadda, tell me I'm wrong."

"You wouldn't understand," he repeated, still not moving or even facing her, curled up hugging himself in Irene's coat.

"Understand? What is there to understand? You were carrying on with another woman and Mam didn't know!" She was trembling with shock and knew that if she didn't allow anger full rein she would howl. Her parents involved in something as sordid as this? It only happened in films, didn't it? Not in real life. She began to shout and scream at him and, as the full realisation came, that she could never marry Johnny after such shame, she began to hit him.

He held her arms and talked soothingly to her, then as anger abated and hopelessness and despair overwhelmed her, he cuddled her as he had when she was a child.

"If we tell no one, there's no harm been done." He deliberately misled her into believing that Annie did not know. If both kept their secret independently, then it would avoid further outbreaks of Annie's recriminations, The arguments, the recriminations, the anger, they would never go away. He didn't think he could cope with any more of it. "Why upset your mother now, when it's all over?" he reasoned.

"How can I marry Johnny after this?" she wailed.

"Not marry Johnny Castle? Why not? He doesn't know, so how can it affect your marriage? So long as we don't tell anyone nothing will change."

"Mam should be told. She has the right to know."

"Why, so you can feel better? Punish me? It won't do anything for your mother except destroy her happiness, and where's the sense in that, eh?" he insisted, continuing with the lie.

"I have to tell someone."

"No, Eirlys, you don't. If Irene hadn't died you might have been justified in telling everyone about us, but now she's gone, and talking about it would only bring more misery. To her family as well as ours," he reminded her.

She didn't wait to walk home with her father, she ran across the slippery, uneven ground and stumbled, still sobbing, into the lane. Several times she skidded on the treacherous surface but she hurried on, unaware. How could they keep it a secret? In a small town like St David's Well someone was certain to have seen them together and although weeks had passed since Irene Castle's death and funeral, that did not mean they were safe from an ill-timed comment that would start the rumours spreading.

Then a thought stopped her hasty retreat and she saw Evelyn's dislike of her very clearly. Evelyn knew. Somehow she had found out and that was the reason for her unpleasantness, her unwillingness to accept her as a suitable wife for Johnny. She knew!

The snide remark about a caravan honeymoon had been directed at her father, not her. The "ask your father" and the conviction that she, Eirlys, knew what had been happening between her father and Johnny's mother. It all fitted together now.

She didn't want to go home, but she had to. She would prepare the vegetables for dinner, and chat to her mother as though nothing had happened. Somehow she had to conceal from her the fact that her life was destroyed. Then, when she had recovered sufficiently, she would have to talk to Johnny, tell him their wedding was cancelled. She would have to tell him, but without explaining why. Only Evelyn would understand, and she would smile in satisfaction and say nothing.

The saddest part of all this was that there was no one in the world with whom she could discuss it, talk to about her feelings, ease away the pain by sharing the whole sordid story. The secret was hers and hers it had to remain.

Somehow she survived the day, using a headache as an excuse to stay in her room for much of the afternoon, and using the same excuse for not eating the meals. All the facts chased round and round in her head until she thought it would burst. She had decisions to make and they had to be made quickly.

When Johnny called, she longed to run downstairs and fall into his arms, tell him everything and beg him to make it all better. She couldn't. She loved him too much for him ever to be told. She persuaded her mother to tell him she was unwell and in bed. How could she see him now? Once she had her tears under control, then she would see him. Then she'd be strong enough to tell him she no longer wanted to marry him.

Darkness fell, ending that most awful of days. Annie came up and fixed the blackout and lit her lamp and still she didn't leave her room. How could she go downstairs and stay in the same room as her father, knowing what she did?

On Monday morning she surprised her boss by offering her resignation.

"If there's a chance of transferring to a similar job elsewhere, I would like to be considered," she told him, "but I have to get away from St David's Well."

Mr Gifford and Mr Johnston questioned her briefly but quickly accepted that it was something she did not want to talk about, for the moment at least. Mr Gifford guessed it was love trouble and thought it wise to do nothing for a while, in case the rift was mended and she changed her mind about leaving.

"Will you please say nothing to the others," she asked as she faced him across his large wooden desk, her fingers twisting, showing her anguish.

"I'll say nothing until you are sure you mean it," he promised kindly. "Problems have a way of sorting themselves out given enough time. If you change your mind and want to stay, then nothing would please me more. You've been an asset to the office from the day you arrived, Miss Price. Hard-working and willing to tackle any task you are given. Whatever you decide, I wish you nothing but the best."

His gentle understanding made tears threaten. She managed to say, "Thank you," before hurrying from his office.

She had to tell Johnny and her honesty wouldn't allow her to write him a note – that would be cowardly – although how she would face him, tell him she wouldn't marry him and at the same time refuse to give an explanation, was something she couldn't imagine. Then there was the other problem of how to tell her parents. She had to move away from St David's Well and start again somewhere far away, yet she didn't have any idea of where to go or how to set about finding accommodation or work. She was daunted by her naivety, her ignorance. She had lived at home with her parents making all the decisions, happy to play a minor role in her own life, and now, at nearly twenty-three, she was trying to move out of that security and cope alone. How could she, without help? Then she thought of Ken Ward.

As Eirlys was dropping a letter addressed to Ken Ward into the post box, the postman was delivering a letter to her from Ken. With the letter from Ken, two letters from the boys were delivered.

Ken had tried to find Teresa and her sons but had failed. No one knew them at the address Eirlys had given him. He promised to try again when he had an opportunity.

The neat, careful writing of Stanley and the ill-formed impatient scribble from Harold were worrying. Annie showed them to Morgan at lunchtime, before he went off to work the two-till-ten shift at the factory. The two letters had been correctly addressed but had borne no postage stamps and Annie had willingly paid the excess amount. "That means Teresa didn't know they were writing," Morgan said unnecessarily. "They didn't want her to be upset at their asking if they can come back."

Stanley was worried about missing school and Harold grieved for his beautiful bike and asked if Morgan could find him another one, adding that he'd paint it himself if Morgan would show him how. The message from Percival was his wish to ride one of Mr Gregory's donkeys on the sands.

"They sound so unhappy," Annie said. "I wish Teresa hadn't taken them away from us. Who knows how long it will be before the bombs start dropping? How can she risk their young lives like this?"

"Most of the other evacuees have gone back too," Morgan reminded her. "I don't suppose you'd want to send your children away to live with strangers, no matter how strong the argument in favour of it, would you?"

"I could write and suggest they come down for a holiday, couldn't I?"

He laughed and said, "Knowing Teresa, I expect we'll have to send them the fare!" He looked at Annie, her face saddened by the words written by the unhappy boys. "Not that we'd mind that," he added soberly.

"Percival says he'll eat his taters, if you let him come back," Stanley had written. This time no attempt had been made to obliterate the sad message.

Harold had promised never to get in another fight, even with the boys at school.

"I think we should buy the train tickets and see if we can arrange for them to travel in care of the guard, if they still do that."

"I could go up," Annie mused.

"Could you cope with the disappointment if Teresa refused to let them come back?"

"We could both go. She might be less inclined to refuse if we turn up on her doorstep."

"No, I think it's best you go on your own. I'll stay here with Eirlys, we can't leave *her* on her own, can we?" he reasoned, unaware of the irony of his protectiveness for his daughter, who was making plans to move right away from their care and protection.

—

Teresa had a new boyfriend and a new job. She had met Ronald when she had moved once more in the hope of shaking off the determined man she had robbed. She wasn't doing right by her boys, she had to do better. Stanley was clever and needed regular school, and the others – well, sitting on their own all the time without even a wireless for company... Remorsefully she admitted to herself they were better off in St David's Well with Annie and Morgan.

She was smart and attractive enough and now that she had made up her mind, she went job-hunting with great determination. She loved her boys and she had to succeed for them as well as herself.

Another visit to the council and the story that her reason for moving had been rats, and she was put on the priority list for accommodation. If things worked out as she hoped, Ronald would move in with her and they'd be a proper family. He would help her manage her money. It had always been a problem. Once she had money in her pocket she was tempted by all sorts of things and was soon broke once again. If only she could save enough to pay the man who was dogging her footsteps.

Ronald wasn't fond of children, he'd told her that, but in her new mood of optimism she felt certain he would succumb to their fascination. Lovely boys they were, anyone would be proud of them.

With this decent job selling clothes on a market stall she'd be home in the evenings to talk to them and play games like they used to, except for when she went out for a drink with Ronald of course. He knew about her past.

"And that's just what it is," he told her. "It's past and gone for ever." By the end of summer they'd be settled. But first, she thought, handling the last few pounds in her pocket, first she needed some new clothes. Her own wouldn't do at all.

Beth was surprised to see Peter Gregory when she opened the shop one morning.

"I've come to apologise," he said.

"No need," she smiled. "What's a kiss between friends?"

"I've had a long, lonely and dangerous time recently and seeing you, so fresh and clean and familiar, I couldn't help it."

"It is dangerous work you do, isn't it, Peter?"

"Things will be easier from now on. I'll be able to get home occasionally and keep in touch. I don't suppose I could ask you a favour, could I, Beth?"

"If I can help… ?" She looked at him expectantly.

"I'd love it if you could write to me. Not regularly, but now and then, just to keep me in touch with things here. So I feel a part of it."

"Of course I will. I'd like that. I've never had a pen-pal before." There was some relief in Beth's reply. After that unexpected kiss, she had wondered what he was going to ask her.

"Thank you. Your pen-pal will be ever grateful. Dad will have my address – I won't know it myself until I get back. He could drop it off at your house, if you think your Freddy won't mind?"

She watched him walk down the road, tall, straight and purposeful. A warm feeling crept over her and she chided herself, reminding herself that Freddy was her love and always had been. Peter's interest was flattering, though, she admitted happily.

Days passed and Eirlys still hadn't found the right moment to tell Johnny or her parents. How many lives had Dadda wrecked by his stupid behaviour? It began with the death of Irene, depriving Johnny and Taff of their mother and Bleddyn of his wife. Her marriage was no longer possible, so both she and Johnny faced a different future to the one they had so happily planned. And Annie: how would she cope if she ever found out, Eirlys wondered, still unaware that her mother knew and was slowly forgiving her father for his weakness. Ken wrote to Eirlys quite often so his letter in reply to hers on Tuesday morning caused no speculation. Neither did the fact that she waited until she was in her room before she opened it. The letter was brief. She had told him only that her father and Johnny's mother had been carrying on and it meant she couldn't marry Johnny Castle. Ken made no comment on this, but stated succinctly that his parents had a spare bedroom which they were willing for her to use until she could get herself something more convenient. He included details of the journey and a diagram of where his parents lived. He also asked her to tell him the time of her arrival and added that, if she would like him to, he would meet her at Paddington. No criticism of her father, no comment on whether her decision was right or wrong, just an offer to help. It was exactly what she needed at that time.

She was working out her two weeks' notice. This wasn't essential – seven days would have been acceptable as she was paid weekly – but she had promised Mr Gifford she would stay until he had found a replacement, which he quickly did.

Three girls came for an interview and one was chosen. Still having said nothing to Johnny or her parents, she worked out the day on which she could leave. Unfortunately she would travel to London on Saturday March thirtieth, the day that was to have been her wedding day. Now, all she had to do was tell Johnny and her parents.

She didn't know how to begin. Johnny and she met one evening intending to go to the pictures, but she persuaded him to walk instead.

"There's something I have to tell you," she told him, her heart racing, painful in her chest.

Johnny smiled at her, her face a pale oval in the darkness. "You sound serious; can't you get the right hat to go with your going-away outfit?" he joked. "That reminds me, I have had a letter confirming our booking at the Sea Crest hotel in Porthcawl."

"Cancel it," she said, her voice little more than a whisper.

"What? For a moment there I thought you said cancel it."

"Cancel the booking, Johnny, I won't be going on our honeymoon. You and I won't be getting married. I'm going away, leaving St David's Well."

"Is this some kind of joke?"

"No joke. Something has happened and it means I can't marry you, ever."

"What is it? There's nothing we can't work out together. Tell me, Eirlys! Let me put things right."

"No chance of that. I'll go to the church tomorrow and I'll send back the gifts and tell the rest of the guests. You can tell your father, and Granny Moll and the rest of your family."

"Tell them what?" he demanded. "You haven't told me anything!"

"I can't marry you. That's all you need to know."

"You don't love me enough, is that it? Pre-wedding nerves, that's all this is. You should have seen our Taff on the days before he and Evelyn—"

"I do love you, Johnny," she interrupted. "I love you more than enough. But something has happened to stop us marrying. It isn't nerves. It isn't anything that can be put right. I can't explain but you must accept that you and I can never marry."

He tried to put an arm around her, comfort her and reassure her, believing that he had been correct in his diagnosis of pre-wedding jitters. She pushed him away and her voice was ragged as she told him to go home and spread the news. "Your Evelyn will be pleased," she sobbed. "She never thought one of the Price family was good enough for you Castles."

"Not good enough? What are you saying? Please, Eirlys, let me—"

His voice carried on the still night air, there was the sound of her hurried footsteps fading, then he was alone, confused and devastatingly hurt. He stood there for what seemed an age, wondering what to do. Should he go after her and persuade her to tell him what was wrong? Or would it be better to go home and wait until the next day, then try to talk to her? It had to be something he could put right. Damn it all, the wedding was only days away!

He needed to talk to someone, but who? If it was sorted out in the next couple of days, he would probably regret telling anyone. His father would worry and Taff wouldn't understand even though he had experienced something similar himself. He was shaking with the shock of it all and he felt as stiff as if he had walked all day. His legs ached and his arms felt as though they had just dropped a heavy load. He was aware of pain around his shoulders and in sudden defeat he dropped onto the kerb at the corner of the street and with his head lowered so his chin was on his chest, he sat, his mind empty of coherent thought.

It was late evening and the girls should have been in bed, but the sky was clear and the stars were out in force. When Josie and Marie insisted they weren't tired enough to sleep, Hannah wrapped them up warmly and took them for a walk around the outskirts of the park, where, if they were lucky, they might hear the chirping, restless sounds of the birds settling for the night. It was something that always fascinated the girls and they stood, arms around each other, in the shadows, as the robin signalled the end of the day and the blackbird gave its mellow settling-down sounds.

"Time to go, the robin is saying," Hannah whispered.

"Can we wait for the owl?" Josie begged and, as they stood there for the promised, "two more minutes", Hannah became aware of the figure sitting not far from where they stood.

"Are you all right?" she asked hesitatingly, not recognising Johnny in the darkness.

"Hannah?" he said in disbelief. "What are you three doing here?" He was overwhelmed with the relief of not being alone, and jumped up and hugged all three in turn. "I have some sweets in my pocket for two good little girls," he said and made a big pretence of searching in every pocket until they were laughing. Then he handed them the bag of coconut mushrooms he had intended to give to Eirlys.

He walked back with them and at the door he hesitated. "Can I come in?" he asked.

"Johnny, you know how my mother feels about men coming to the house."

"All right, I understand."

Hannah had opened the door and the girls had slipped inside, carefully replacing the curtain behind them. "There's something wrong?" she asked softly.

He was aware of her standing so close that he could smell the clean, fresh night air on her cheeks and he longed to reach out and hold her close to him. He tried to bring his thoughts back to Eirlys and could not. "Something wrong? The truth is, Hannah, I don't know."

He hurried away from her. The confusion in his heart had culminated in an almost overwhelming desire to kiss her. He had never been so mixed-up or unhappy in his whole life. He wandered along the empty streets, stopping sometimes to listen to the wireless programmes coming from a house, and, imagining the family groups sitting enjoying them, he felt that his world was in shatters. A surge of almost violent jealousy filled him at the sound of the contented murmur of voices and the occasional laughter. There was no point going home until he had exhausted himself enough to make sleep at least a possibility.

It was three in the morning before he headed for Brook Lane. No sounds from any of the houses now, everyone was tucked up in bed, trouble-free and with nothing to disturb their sleep. The wardens were still on their beat and offered a polite, "Goodnight, sir," as he passed the shop doorway where they hid to enjoy a cigarette. A policeman cycled past, stopping from time to time to check on shop doors to make sure they were firmly locked.

He stood for a while outside the house where Eirlys lived. He looked up at her window, shrouded in darkness, and wondered if she was sleeping soundly, at peace with her decision, or, like him, confused about whether or not they were making a mistake, or rectifying an earlier one.

–

Rumours were already beginning to reach Bleddyn, not about Johnny and Eirlys but about his wife. A woman further up Brook Lane, who seemed to spend a lot of her time standing outside wielding a sweeping-brush and watching what went on, had made several references to Irene's friend, and when he questioned her she smiled and said in a childish voice, "It's not for me to say, Mr Castle. Never speak ill of the dead, isn't that what we say?"

"I don't want you spreading gossip about my wife!" he said sharply. "My sons are upset as it is, losing their mother in that dreadful accident. Please don't make it worse for us all."

"Only saying what others are saying, that's all," she said, sweeping fiercely at a recalcitrant weed on her path. He tried to ignore the woman. Bored she was, always looking for excuses to gossip.

It was when he mentioned her remarks to Taff that he began to wonder.

—

Eirlys told the vicar that the wedding was cancelled and he spent most of her lunch break advising her not to be hasty. She smiled, listened with apparent interest, then repeated her instruction to cancel all the arrangements, promising that she would be in touch to compensate for any inconvenience.

She felt that her mind was floating through a different world. The pavement beneath her feet was there, but the street was no longer the familiar street, the town wasn't the same town, the people passing were strangers unable to see her.

She should have passed the fish-and-chip shop as she left the church and walked back to the office, but she darted down a back lane and avoided it, in case Bleddyn ran out and begged her to change her mind. Johnny would have told his father by now. She mustn't talk to anyone else before she told her parents. They had to be told soon, before they heard the news from someone else.

She tried to think of a convincing story to explain her behaviour to her mother, but failed. Her father didn't need telling, she thought bitterly. He, and only he, knew exactly why she was behaving in this way.

When she had helped her mother to put their evening meal on the table, she tried to build up to her announcement slowly but in the end she simply blurted it out.

"Johnny and I have cancelled the wedding. I can't marry him and I've told him so. The wedding is permanently off. We won't change our minds." As her mother stared at her in disbelief, she went on, "The church arrangements are cancelled, Johnny will tell Granny Moll Piper that the catering won't be needed, and tomorrow I'll start returning all the presents. Will you help me, Mam?" She was amazed at how matter-of-fact she sounded. She might as well have been telling them she'd changed her mind about which film she would see.

Demands for explanations were met with a stony silence. Morgan kept out of it, refusing to comment, fully aware of what had changed their daughter's mind.

–

The following day was Saturday and it was then that Johnny began to spread the news. He told his father, who pleaded with him to go and see Eirlys and put right whatever had gone wrong. Stubbornness, or something else, pride perhaps, made Johnny say angrily, "It's over, Dad. Eirlys has made that quite clear. There's nothing more I can say. And I wouldn't change it now if I could!"

He called to see his brother, Taff, and Evelyn. Evelyn's stilted, "I'm sorry," reminded Johnny about Eirlys's words and the longstanding disagreement between them.

"What did you say to her, Evelyn? This has to be down to you!"

At this Taff became roused in protection of Evelyn. Taff was rarely angry but he turned on Johnny and told him to go.

"How can you blame this on Evelyn? It's Eirlys's decision not to marry you and there's no point in looking for anyone else to blame. It's you she's turning down, nothing we could say would make that decision for her."

When the door slammed behind his distressed brother, Taff turned to Evelyn and demanded an explanation of her dislike of Eirlys. Sitting beside her, she gently told him the truth about his mother and Eirlys's father.

"I hated her because I thought she knew all along," she said sadly when the full story was explained.

Taff wanted to go at once to talk to his father but Evelyn stopped him.

"I don't think he knows and it's best he never finds out. Why add to his unhappiness?"

"It might ease his guilt," Taff said sadly. "He blames himself for not looking after her better."

Anger was Johnny's weapon throughout the day as he went to tell the family what had happened. He told Granny Moll to abandon her plans for the wedding breakfast and found himself going over the same ground as with his father and his brother Taff – "Talk to her, make her change her mind. Put right whatever's wrong." Each time he told someone, they gave the same responses and by midday he could have recited them in chorus with ease.

Several people called to see Eirlys, hoping for an explanation. Even Granny Moll Piper knocked on the door and demanded to know what she should do with the cake she had chosen and paid for. Eirlys refused to come down and speak to her, telling her mother, "She can throw it in the sea for the fish!"

Over the weekend, everyone who needed to be told had been notified. Then Eirlys told her parents her next item of news.

"I'm going away," she said. "I'm going to live in London. My boss has given me a good reference and has given me an introduction to a place looking for someone with my skills."

"What is the matter with you?" Annie demanded tearfully. "First the wedding and now this! Where will you go? Where will you stay? For heaven's sake, Eirlys, what has happened?"

"I'll be staying with Ken Ward and his family until I get a place of my own."

"But why? You've got a home here," Annie wailed.

Her father said little, except to plead with her not to go. He was sitting, his head drooped, a melancholy expression on his face, knowing he was responsible and could do nothing about it.

"It's Ken, isn't it?" Annie suddenly said. "He's the cause of this. Writing letters, unsettling you. He should have left you alone."

"It's nothing to do with Ken," she said.

-

Bleddyn threw down the cloth with which he was wiping up the last of the spilt paint.

"Damn it all," he said aloud, "this wedding cancellation is because of Irene! Eirlys must be worried about her illness, afraid it's something Johnny and their children could inherit. Her suicide in the docks must have terrified her – and understandably, too."

He sat for a while working out how he could help, surrounded by paint pots and brushes and all the paraphernalia of decorating. He had been through the house with Johnny and Taff's help and every room looked different from when Irene was alive. He had needed the cleansing and a fresh start; could Eirlys be in need of the same?

He went firstly to see Mrs Hibbert and paid a month's rent on the rooms Johnny and Eirlys were to have made their home. That gave them time to reconsider.

When Johnny came in, he told him what he had done, but Johnny shook his head.

"Thanks, Dad, that was a kind thought and a good idea, but she's going away; she's got a job in London and for a while at least she'll be staying with Ken Ward's family."

"Is he the trouble?" Bleddyn asked.

"No, he's just a friend."

"Then has she told you why?"

"She won't say, just that we can't ever marry."

"I wondered, well, is she worried about the way your mam died? It's an awful thing to live with."

"How could it be to do with Mam? It's me. She doesn't want to spend the rest of her life with me, that's the only reason. It has to be. Anything else could have been sorted."

–

On what would have been her wedding day, Eirlys was at the station, coldly calm, alone, and waiting for a train to take her

308

to London instead of catching a later train to take her and Johnny on their honeymoon, being cheered on their way by family and friends. It was so unfair. She steeled herself not to cry although inside she felt the aching, barely controlled agony of tears that needed to be shed.

In a corner where the rack to hold bicycles stood, a lone figure watched her board the train. He had to see for himself that she really was leaving. It still seemed impossible for their plans to come to such a sudden and unexplained end.

As the train moved away and disappeared, Johnny stared at the empty rails for a long time. This really was the end. There was no chance of her changing her mind.

-

Annie was devastated by her daughter's departure. The house echoed, the empty rooms mocked her as she wandered around as though the building might have an explanation. First Stanley, Harold and Percival, now Eirlys leaving; not to marry and live a few minutes' walk away, but to disappear into a place they didn't know.

Morgan's thoughts were equally morbid and he knew the only way he could help Annie was to coax her to go to London to see the place where Eirlys was living and to visit the boys. The Ward family had been friends; it wouldn't be unreasonable in the circumstances to ask them to find accommodation for Annie near them, so she could see for herself the place where Eirlys was living. It would help Annie if she were able to picture her daughter in her new surroundings.

Johnny on the other hand, was deliberately and excessively cheerful over the following days. He exaggerated his indifference to combat Taff's sympathy. He did lose his temper once and accuse Evelyn again of being the cause, although he failed to extract from her an explanation. Apart from that brief moment, he whistled and sang as he went about his greengrocery deliveries, making people smile, winking at young girls and old ladies as though life was particularly good.

Besides his unhappiness, Johnny felt embarrassed, a bit foolish. He'd been jilted and he didn't even know why.

The postman's visits were still eagerly awaited by Annie and Morgan, but with greater anxiety now that Eirlys had gone away. She wrote several times during that first week, telling them how interesting the area was and describing some of the places she had visited with Ken's sister Julia.

Like Johnny, she was over-bright, over-cheerful, laughing at everything and nothing, attempting to convince others as well as herself that she was content.

Annie wrote back and asked whether there was time for her to try and find Teresa and the boys. She knew London was big, but it must be possible to get around it on buses and the terrifying Underground trains, she thought.

The need to see that Stanley, Harold and Percival were all right was made doubly urgent after another letter came telling Annie they had moved yet again and were sharing a bed in what had once been a cellar. Stanley also told them that their mother had a new boyfriend called Ronald but that he didn't like Percival very much. Annie knew she had to go as soon as possible. Her greatest fear was that they might move once too often and she would lose touch with them altogether.

"I expect it's a basement flat, you know how Stanley can make a drama out of everything," Morgan said, trying to comfort her.

"I have to go to London, Morgan. I want to see that Eirlys is all right and although she's living in a different area from the boys, I could see them all if I stayed a night or two."

Morgan didn't try to persuade her against going, he encouraged her. He needed a rest from her abuse as well as wanting to know that Eirlys was settled safely. Guilt was a heavy cloak he was unable to remove. Annie had guessed the real reason for her daughter cancelling her wedding and her accusations against Morgan were destroying him. They rarely exchanged a civil word and he had taken to walking around at night rather than stay in the house and listen to her repeated accusations. He had long ago given up retaliation. He allowed her to rain the insults down on him without apparently hearing them. He wondered how much longer he could bear it.

He went to the station with her and kissed her awkwardly for appearances' sake. Then he went back home and for the first time in weeks he slept.

–

The train was full of uniformed young men. Normally Annie would have enjoyed talking to them, but today she had no interest in anyone. Her thoughts were ahead of her, wondering if Eirlys was happy, or ready to come back to St David's Well and face the gossip, and whether she would be able to persuade Teresa to allow the boys to come back to St David's Well until she had found them somewhere decent to live. If there was time, she might suggest going to the housing department with Teresa and finding out exactly what was happening.

–

Teresa had moved again, as the boys had told Annie and Morgan. It was far from comfortable. Any furniture and linen and china she'd had in the past had been lost during her frequent moves. Her attempts at hiding from the man who stalked her demanding his money had been futile anyway. He had found her easily, followed her when she left the public house one night and hit her so she had bruises on her body, making it difficult to work and earn the money to pay him back.

She still worked on the market stall but didn't earn enough for her needs. If only she could pay him back, although she suspected that by this time, the money was not the strongest reason for his persistence. He had been made to look a fool and he told her he wanted to see her come into the place where he and his friends were gathered and hand over the money and make an abject apology. Only then would he leave her alone.

The so-called romance with Ronald had lasted less than a week. He had left without a word but two days later, while she was out and Percival was home alone nursing a head cold, an officer from the housing department came and, finding the place unfit for habitation and the boy on his own, called the welfare authorities.

Two officials were waiting for Teresa when she arrived home at seven, having called in at the pub for a drink on the way. She wasn't a heavy drinker but had hoped to make a date for later on.

The three boys looked frightened, having been warned that they might have to go into a children's home until their mother could get decent accommodation. "We could go and stay with Auntie Annie," Percival said hopefully.

The so-called "flat" was a single room below pavement level, small, dark and damp, and sparsely furnished. After coming in from work and feeding the boys, Teresa habitually left them there while she went out and hung around the pubs looking for likely customers.

Much of what she earned went on herself. Her clothes were smart and quite new. She had to look good, dress expensively, have her hair properly washed and set and, use make-up skilfully unless she wanted to end up with the dregs of humanity. When she met the welfare people, she was aware of the difference in her appearance and theirs and tried to make excuses.

She had to get money, enough to set them up. Her lovely boys deserved more than she'd given them. They'd be better off in a home.

When the boys were asleep she went out to find the man who she called her shadow. He was in the usual pub at his usual table with his cronies around him. She pleaded with him to leave her alone so she could get the boys a decent place to live. "I stole from you," she said. "None of this is their fault."

He hit her as she was laughed out of the place and said, "The money, here, tomorrow, or you're dead." He had no intention of doing more than frighten her, but she believed him. Perhaps she should go to the police? But who would believe her? No one.

–

The boys had not made the address very clear and after reaching the general area. Annie spent several hours searching for them. She was extremely tired. Having found a place to stay and deposited her small suitcase in her room, she hadn't stopped to eat, but had gone straight out to find the boys. Tomorrow she would go and see her daughter, but this evening was for Stanley, Harold and little Percival. She had a few pounds in the back of her purse hoping she would use it to take them back to St David's Well with her. First she had to find them! The traffic was very different from back home, she thought, as two cars skidded around the corner and almost touched one another as they passed. So impatient, and, on the dark streets, very stupid too. She was nearing the address where she thought she would locate the flat when she saw, running along the opposite pavement, a figure she thought she recognised. That funny, tippy-toed run in such ridiculously high heels couldn't be anyone else but Teresa hurrying home after her day in the market.

"Teresa!" she called, relief slowing her weary feet. "It's me, Annie. I've come to see the boys!"

Teresa appeared not to hear her and, still with that silly girlish run, hurried towards the corner. Exasperated, afraid she would lose her and perhaps not be able to find the boys, Annie ran after her, calling her name.

The car that slowly cruised out of a side road was barely visible. But here in London, with more traffic and the hooded traffic signals, the light was slightly brighter than at home. The car's shaded head lights snapped off and the car increased its speed. In the faint glow from other vehicles nearby, she saw quite clearly that the car was heading straight for Teresa. "Teresa!" Annie screamed. "Look out!"

The driver swerved away from Teresa at the very last moment, as he had intended, but couldn't avoid hitting, then running over Annie, who was heading for Teresa in blind panic.

Teresa gave a wail of horror and ran to where Annie's body lay in the dark road. The driver's shocked face was briefly visible as he stared back at what he had done, then he drove off, still without showing his lights. Only Teresa knew who he was.

Cars stopped, people arrived, instructions were shouted, and Teresa lay down beside the still form, unaware of them all, murmuring, "It was meant for me, Annie, it was meant for me." She lay beside her, hugging her, until an ambulance man came and took her away.

She was oblivious of what was said. Questions went unanswered, her brain dulled by the tragedy. Annie dead. And because of her. Stealing that twenty-four pounds had ruined everything and had now caused the death of a friend. How was she going to live with that?

Twelve

Teresa stared down at the peaceful face of Annie as the ambulance men lifted her body on to a stretcher. She knew she was dead. She remained still, her arms wrapped about herself, and silently wept.

In her head she relived the moment: the shouts, the revving engine, the squealing brakes as the car slewed momentarily out of control, then the thump, the awful thump. Unaware of the people approaching, slowly at first, then in a flurry of activity, she hadn't responded to the voices at first, but had sat there on the cold ground nursing Annie, talking to her, telling her it was going to be all right. Then the wailing approach of the ambulance broke into her consciousness. Someone lifted her gently away from Annie's still form and her hands covered her face as the sound of voices invaded her ears. Where had all these people come from? What had they to do with Annie?

Remorse hit her then. What had she done? By that stupid action, stealing the wallet of a man who wouldn't accept his humiliation, she had been chased and attacked and it had ended in not injury to her, but the death of Annie Price. How could she live with this? How could she tell the boys?

The sequence of the events went round and round in her mind, as though next time, the ending would be different.

The next hour was filled with confusion – seeing Annie's body taken away and then questions and more questions, until she told the police that her children were at home, unattended.

"We'll come back with you, and once we know they are safe, we can continue with the interview," she was told.

"Interview?" The word had connotations of guilt. Could they know what had happened, and understand that she was responsible?

"You say she was your friend, a good friend. You must want to help us in every way you can to catch the driver of that car."

"I don't remember anything. It's all a blur, all squealing brakes and the shouting and—"

She sobbed and the policemen accompanied her home and waited, silent and unmoving, until she had recovered. They then continued with their questions.

They were very persuasive and she eventually told them about the wallet, the threats and her convictions for prostitution.

"Just tell us who the man is and we'll do the rest," they told her.

"I'll be made to appear in court. I can't let the boys go through all that."

"Tell us his name, Teri," one of them said, making it clear he knew the name she used when working, and for her prosecutions. "Give us his name, description and the make of car and the number if you know it. There'll be enough evidence on the car to convict him," he coaxed.

Reluctantly, but with the image of Annie lying in the middle of the road to persuade her, she gave them a description, told them where he usually drank and everything else she could remember, to give them a picture of him.

When she fell into bed she was exhausted, but she didn't sleep. The images were too vivid. She lay there in the cramped bed, trying to hug all three boys at once, the need to feel she was protecting them paramount.

As dawn broke on the dark wet morning, she lay for a while longer listening to the rain dripping through the rotten window pane on to the old bedspread placed to catch it, dull and persistent. What should she do? Where should she go? Then the idea flooded her mind like a shaft of warm sunlight on a winter's day; comforting and filling her with a sensation of well-being. St David's Well. She would go and stay in Annie's home, with Morgan Price.

At once she felt more cheerful. With the first move planned she didn't worry about what would happen after that. Knowing her first action was sufficient for the moment.

She woke the boys and said excitedly, "Get dressed, we're going to see Morgan and all your friends in St David's Well. Just wait till summer. We'll see the beach in all its glory, just like Eirlys told you, remember? There'll be roundabouts and donkey rides and sticks of rock and ice-creams and picnics on the sand and more people having fun than you've ever seen!"

–

The news came to Eirlys via the police. There was a loud knock on the door of Ken's parents' house, a brief, whispered conversation, then they came and stood beside her while the constable told her that Annie was dead. She stared at the constable and he had to repeat it as she seemed not to have heard him.

Her first thought, after the initial shock had receded, was that she wanted to see Johnny. She needed him there to help her over this. Instead there was Ken and his family and she was so thankful that she had not decided to stay with strangers in some anonymous bed-sitter as she had originally planned.

"I'll go home with you," Ken said, putting an arm around her. "You aren't in a fit state to travel on your own."

Recovering fast, Eirlys shook her head. Tempting as it was, she knew that at a time like this she could easily give Ken the wrong impression. She loved him dearly, but had no thoughts of a future for them together and she couldn't allow herself to mislead him.

She asked him to let her new boss know what had happened, and then, carrying only a small suitcase, she went by bus to Paddington and commenced the long, sad journey home. She was unaware that on the same train Stanley, Harold and Percival were playing snakes and ladders with Teresa, in between marking their progress on a list of stations in a railway guide given to them by an elderly passenger.

–

Unaware of the tragedy that had taken place, Johnny stood outside Hannah's front door early that morning and knocked. He knocked loudly and stood prepared to push a foot in the door to prevent Hannah from closing it when she recognised him.

It was still dark and rain was falling, cold rain that threatened to turn to snow. As he waited, the first flakes settled on his shoulder, to vanish immediately into the soft navy cloth of his overcoat.

It was late in the season for snow. He remembered Granny Moll calling it "daffy" snow, sudden to cover the ground but staying only a short time. He was unaware of the cold, thinking only of what he would say to Hannah as soon as she opened the door to him.

The door shifted after he had heard the swishing sound of the blackout curtain being pulled across. Then she was there and at once he stepped forward into the hall.

"Johnny, you mustn't come in."

"I have something to say to you and it won't wait," he said, firmly guiding her back into her cramped living room.

"Who is it, Hannah?" a voice called from the back.

Stifling Hannah's reply, Johnny pressed a hand gently over her mouth and called back, "It's me, Johnny Castle, and I have business to discuss with your daughter. Private business, right?" There was anger in his voice but when they went inside the room where the gas light gave its friendly glow there was no anger in his eyes, only love.

"I don't want you to think this is desperation, or love on the rebound, or anything else except this. Hannah, I love you. I want us to be a familiar sight, walking around, doing everything together, as a family. You, me and Josie and Marie, never apart, so everyone knows we love each other."

"Johnny, what about Eirlys and—"

"No one else counts. There's just you and me and the girls. I love them as much as I love you."

"I can't do this, Johnny."

"Why? Don't you love me?"

"There's the age difference for one thing," she protested weakly.

"It hasn't made the smallest difference to how I feel for you so why worry about it?"

"Your father wouldn't be happy about us."

"He isn't marrying you. I am."

320

"How can you want to take us on, when you could find someone young and without all my encumbrances?"

"What encumbrances?"

So far he hadn't touched her and the air around them was fraught with barely controlled emotion. He lifted her chin with a finger and made her look at him.

"Tell me you don't love me and never will, and I'll go away," he said softly. "But before you decide, let me show you how much I love *you*."

For a long moment he stood there, looking at her, staring at her, pleading silently for her to give the answer he so desperately wanted. When he did open his arms and hold her, she couldn't explain the tears except to say that they were tears of happiness like she had never believed in before.

–

The news of Annie's death spread swiftly around the town and people visiting her home with sympathy for Morgan had him almost constantly in tears. He felt hollow but couldn't eat, he was exhausted but couldn't sleep. He just sat and watched the clock going around, drank gallons of tea, and waited for Eirlys to come home.

Mixed with his grief were regrets at how he had made Annie's last weeks so unhappy. Why had he been so stupid and started that affair with Irene Castle? If only Annie hadn't found out, he wailed inwardly. Irene hadn't been a serious threat to his marriage; in spite of his words of love and his promises, she would never have been important enough to persuade him to leave his wife. If only he had ended it sooner, Annie would have died without the distress of knowing.

He heard the latch on the gate click and jumped out of his chair. Through the front window he saw his daughter and for a brief moment wondered how she would behave towards him. Would this dreadful situation ease her return, make them forget the agony of their parting? The words with which he would greet her were on his lips, practised through the long night and day, but he didn't say them. Voices accompanied Eirlys's progress and he stared in disbelief when first Percival, then Harold and then Stanley and Teresa came into sight.

He didn't get to hug Eirlys, or say the words he had planned; instead he was leapt upon by the boys, their faces showing their grief. Yet their relief at being back in St David's Well was soon apparent by the way they wandered around the house reacquainting themselves with it. He was grateful that the moment was eased by their affectionate greetings. Teresa followed her small sons and hugged him as enthusiastically as her sons had done.

Eirlys had decided to ignore her father. How else could she deal with all this? She couldn't pretend to have forgiven him. The death of her mother couldn't wipe out his shameful behaviour towards her. Having someone to blame eased her pain, and added to his.

She had been shocked at his appearance when she walked in, and was glad of the chance to recover while the boys fell on him with such delight. He was pale and his face seemed to have lost its roundness, his eyes were large and deeper in their sockets. It was obvious he hadn't slept since being told of Annie's death last night, and sympathy swelled but receded quickly, as she thought of her mother and remembered how deceived she had been by Morgan.

Leaving Teresa and her sons talking to him, she went into the kitchen and began to prepare a meal for them all. Crosse and Blackwell tinned soups were always a favourite with the boys. With some bread, and with cakes and fruit to follow, it would have to do until she could do some shopping in the morning.

She began to work out where they would all sleep. She unkindly decided that the quickest and simplest arrangement was for her father to give up his room and allow Teresa to use his bed. When she suggested it his look of horror changed her mind for her and she was ashamed. How insensitive she was becoming.

She knew she should talk to him, let him share his grief with her, but she wasn't ready for that, although she knew the moment would come. With complete lack of logic she blamed Morgan for everything, and the pain inside her made her unaware of how unsympathetic she was being, thinking of herself and her own aching misery and not sharing with her father the tragedy of his terrible loss.

—

Teresa made herself at home, spreading her things around the various rooms, demanding various changes in the way the furniture was arranged and accepting Eirlys and Morgan running around after her as her right. While Eirlys and Stanley washed the dishes, Teresa announced that she was taking Morgan for a drink.

"Do 'im good, poor man, it'll make sure he sleeps."

Eirlys wanted to say something but she was too amazed at the woman's suggestion and too offended by her father's swift agreement. She ran upstairs. Teresa's clothes were everywhere, and she pushed them unceremoniously into a corner.

Stanley followed her and said, half apologetically, "'Ard work, ain't she, our ma. She loves clothes and she's pretty, ain't she?"

"Yes, Stanley, she's a very pretty lady, but she'll have to learn that there isn't room for her to spread all her things about. We're seven – I mean six," she corrected sadly, "and there isn't the room."

–

Hannah had persuaded Johnny not to make their love for each other public. They decided that they would wait a few months, and only gradually let it be known that they intended to marry. Johnny had willingly agreed with Hannah's wish, as he did not want people to whisper that he had turned to Hannah in his disappointment over Eirlys.

"It will soon be time for the new season to begin," he told her on the day that Eirlys returned to St David's Well. "I'll be caught up in the last-minute painting and repairing and all the usual stuff that the new season brings, so we won't be able to meet regularly. Then when the season begins you won't see much of me, except when you bring Josie and Marie to the beach, which I hope will he often. The family will soon get used to seeing us together and will soon love you as much as I do."

They had met on the morning Eirlys and the four Loves had arrived, and were taking Josie and Marie to Mr Gregory's smallholding, to see the donkeys. Mr Gregory took them to the barn, which he boastingly called the tack room, and explained about the repainting that would be done on the collars bearing the animals' names before the summer season began.

While Josie and Marie were happily entertained, Hannah asked, "What has happened about the rooms in Mrs Hibbert's house, Johnny?"

"Eirlys told her we won't be using them after all, and no, I don't have any regrets," he smiled. "I don't think Mrs Hibbert has any either; she's had the place cleaned up and decorated for nothing, and Dad paid her four weeks' rent, so she's happy."

He talked about the beach for a while, telling her she must ignore Granny Moll's inevitable pestering and decide for herself whether or not she wanted to help out now and again. "The trouble with Granny Moll Piper is that she loves the sands and can't understand those who don't."

"You love it though, there isn't any persuading needed to get you there, is there?"

"I've worked the beach for so long I can't imagine any other life. When Taff and I were at school, all our holidays were spent on the beach – helping Dad at first, then, as we grew older, we took on one of the regular jobs. In fact I think I learnt arithmetic and lots of other things besides, from the need to give change and to count the takings, and helping Uncle Huw and Auntie Marged with the orders and the like." He laughed, then his face took on a serious expression. "I don't know how much longer I'll be able to enjoy it, though. I'm afraid I might have to accept an enormous change before very long. The call-up of men is increasing to men a lot older than me. Most of my friends have already gone. One has been killed. I have doubts about any chance of deferment, just because we work at Piper's."

"Let's not think about it and be happy while we can, Johnny. I can't bear to think of you going into danger."

Ignoring her reminder of what call-up actually meant, he said cheerfully, "The swingboats and helter-skelter and the stalls and Piper's Café stay open for as long as there's daylight, and I'll be there until everything is locked away for the night. You won't see much of me, but when we do have time to be together, I'll make sure every minute is treated as something precious."

It was as they were walking back across the fields that they learned of the death of Annie Price.

When Hannah recognised the figure of Eirlys walking towards them, she felt a sort of panic that threatened to close her throat so that she couldn't breathe. If Johnny saw her, would he regret telling her goodbye? Would Eirlys reclaim her place in his heart?

Johnny saw her at almost the same time and sensing Hannah's uneasiness, lifted Marie up into his arms and reached out for Josie's hand. Eirlys's first glimpse would see them as a complete group, a family. No words would be needed to explain.

"Hi, Eirlys," he called as they drew nearer. "Couldn't you stay away from us then? London not as exciting as you hoped?" he teased lightly. Then seeing her expression, he asked, "What is it? Is something wrong?"

"It's Mam. She was killed. Hit by a car in London when she went to see Stanley, Harold and Percival."

At once Hannah ran to her and held her. "Oh Eirlys, what a terrible thing to happen. You and your father must be distraught."

Johnny hugged her too, still holding Marie, who insisted she couldn't walk a single step more.

They walked back together, Eirlys explaining that she wasn't going anywhere, just out to get a breath of air and to escape the stream of visitors calling to offer help and sympathy. Johnny set a complaining Marie on her feet and took Hannah's hand in his.

"Your father?" Hannah asked. "Is he coping? Thank goodness you were able to get home so quickly. He must have been so in need of you."

Eirlys couldn't explain her inability to comfort her father, and she didn't reply.

Hannah went on, "My parents have never been very kind to me, they often told me they wish I had been the one to die instead of my brother. But in spite of that, I'd do everything I could if they were in trouble. It's a time for families, isn't it?"

Only then did it occur to Eirlys that Hannah and Johnny were holding hands, and she saw then that the group was more than a few friends out for a walk, but four people joined together in love.

It hurt. Seeing him with Hannah, knowing that he had found with her friend what she had thrown away, she was afraid to stay with them and drink in their happiness. She loved Johnny and her father had ruined her hope of a future with him.

"I have to go," she told them, but instead of running home she went across the fields and stood, looking at the caravan where her father and Johnny's mother had frequently met.

She felt about in the most likely places for a key and found it tucked behind one of the wheels. Going inside she was aware of the cold dankness of the place. Everything was dreary except for the moss which grew at the base of the windows, bright green and alien in that drab place. The windows were wet from winter's melted frost. The ice would have been beautiful, delicately ornamental, with leaves and exotic flowers formed by the tightening of the frozen water into many and varied shapes. If it was beautiful once, all that had gone, and what was left were smells, invasive mildew and cloth already beginning to rot.

She felt an aching and overwhelming sadness as she imagined her father seeking secret and forbidden pleasures in such a place. Mould was creeping across the cushions and there was a smell of decay and neglect. It was a sordid picture, she told herself, but her emotions twisted away from her resentment and anger and hurt and she began to think of her father as a lonely man, weak and foolish but not wicked. Locking the door and putting the key back in its hiding place, she went home. It was time for her to forgive.

They talked long into the night and both felt happier for accepting that they were still important to each other.

"I still want to keep my job in London, Dadda," Eirlys explained. "But I'll come home often and make sure you are all right."

"I'll manage fine," he assured her. "I'm not helpless and there are bound to be those willing to offer a hand. That's the best of living in a small town like St David's Well. There are plenty of friends when you need them. As long as you and I are still friends, that's all that matters to me, love."

The funeral took place in a cemetery which had a light covering of "daffy" snow, making the stark and gloomy place beautiful, if only for a while. Eirlys didn't attend; it was men only at the graveside. She stayed at the house, and, with Teresa doing her best to help, and several neighbours and friends doing what they could, she prepared the food for those who would return with her father.

Most of Johnny's family attended the service and many of them came back to the house. Johnny was there with his father Bleddyn, his brother Taff and Evelyn, but without Hannah, who had no one to look after the children.

In a brief moment between attending to the food and drinks, Johnny came into the kitchen and asked her how she was and what her plans were. It was strange to talk to him as though they were no more than friends. She coped by pretending he was someone she hardly knew, not the man she loved and had planned to marry. Then he spoilt it all by telling her how much he loved Hannah and how it was all for the best, even though he still didn't understand why she had suddenly left him.

"I can't explain, Johnny. Something happened that made it impossible for us to marry. Please don't ask me to tell you what it was."

Then Evelyn came in and, seeing their serious faces, presumed that Eirlys was telling Johnny about his mother and her father.

"So now you know, Johnny. Sordid, mind, hearing this about your own mother, but better that you know."

"Don't, Evelyn!" Eirlys pleaded.

But Evelyn went on, believing she was helping. Her voice was full of sympathy; there was no malice in her expression. She believed that telling Johnny was the best way of dealing with it, and that was what she thought was happening now. "I think Eirlys is very brave and honest to have told you. It couldn't have been easy. But secrets fester and it's always better to deal with things rather than try to hide them, isn't it?" She looked at Eirlys with an affectionate smile. "I'm so glad you faced it, Eirlys. I'm so sorry about the way I've behaved towards you."

In the stunned silence that followed, Eirlys felt tears falling down her cheeks.

"Please, Evelyn, don't say any more," she whispered. "Take no notice, Johnny, Evelyn's mistaken, that's all, it's a mistake." In vain she had tried to stop Evelyn, but by the time the other girl had realised her mistake, she had said too much for Johnny to be able to walk away.

He insisted on hearing the full story and was angry with Morgan and his mother, but, surprisingly, most of all with Eirlys.

"How could you not tell me?" he demanded.

"What would have been the point? I thought the fewer people who knew the less chance of your father finding out."

"That was my reasoning too," Evelyn said. "That was why I hoped you and Eirlys would stop seeing each other. I'm very fond of your dad, Johnny, and I hoped that if you and Eirlys were no longer together, the secret would be safe and he would never know."

"Eirlys should have told me. There shouldn't be any secrets between two people who love each other."

"But you didn't love me, did you, Johnny?" Eirlys asked quietly before walking away.

Evelyn followed her and begged her to listen to her apology.

"Eirlys, I really thought you knew about your father and Johnny's mother. I was so upset for his father, who's such a kind, gentle man, so undeserving of such treachery. I was convinced you must know, you'd been to the caravan, you'd seen Irene wandering about, obviously waiting to meet your father. I hated you for it. I'm sorry. I'm really sorry."

Eirlys looked at her, and, seeing the tear-streaked face, believed her.

"I don't know whether you believe me, Evelyn, but I think I would have acted in the same way," she said as they hugged.

"I'm fond of Bleddyn too. But," she added sadly, "I don't think you and I will ever be sisters-in-law as we once hoped. Johnny didn't deny it when I said he didn't love me, did he?"

–

Johnny hadn't been able to formulate an honest reply. He left the house and walked alone across the fields to think about what he had been told. It all came back: the death of his mother, the doctor explaining her earlier insistence that she was expecting a child and his telling her she was mistaken.

It was almost dark before he returned to the outskirts of the town and he stopped for a while and stared at the looming shadow of the caravan, where, he had been told, his mother had met Morgan Price and made love.

Like Eirlys he searched for a key, convinced that it would have been left somewhere close by. With the aid of a torch which he, like most people, habitually carried, he found it behind the same wheel. He went inside and, like Eirlys, was distressed at the sordid mess that was revealed by the thin beam of the torch.

There was a paraffin stove and, nearby, some matches in a tin which had previously held Oxo cubes. He tried to strike a match, intending to throw it among the bedclothes on the built-in couch, but, damp, they broke apart and he threw them down in disgust.

He was aching with pent-up fury that wouldn't be released. He couldn't bear the thought of people seeing this place and laughing. He tried to push the van off its support but failed at that too. He was sweating with his attempts to destroy the hated thing and all he could do was tie back the door and release the catches on the windows and let the elements do their worst. At the end of the summer there would be nothing left but a mouldering wreck. He'd come back and burn it. Then, as he prepared to leave, he shone the light around the place one last time, and it fell on his mother's coat. It destroyed him as no words had.

It all became real. Until then he had been trying to convince itself it was idle and mistaken gossip. He thought of the number of times she had been seen without a coat, and remembered the time when he had insisted that Eirlys had been wrong when she told him his mother was in the fields dressed only in a thin dress. She had been here, probably walking to meet Morgan Price.

As he walked away, the wind was already gusting in and moving the shabby curtains. The sooner it was a ruin the better. It was a memorial to his mother he didn't need.

He went back to Eirlys's house and when she opened the door, demanded, "You should have told me! I had a right to know why you were walking away from me, didn't I?"

"I hoped you would never find out."

"You didn't mind that everyone knew except Dad and me? That everyone was talking about us and probably laughing?"

"No one knows except Evelyn and she found out long before I did. Like me, she thought there was no value in telling you."

"We would have married if you hadn't discovered their secret, wouldn't we?" he said.

"Yes, and it would have been a mistake. I want more than St David's Well can offer me, and you – you love Hannah, don't you?"

He couldn't deny it.

"I wish you luck, Johnny," she said softly. "And I'm really sorry you had to find out about your mam."

His voice became calm to match hers. "Mam couldn't help it, but she always let us down." He frowned as he thought about his childhood. "When Taff and I were children she never did all the things mothers usually do. That's why Granny Moll and Auntie Marged were always so important to Taff and me."

"She loved you, Johnny. She wanted you and Taff to find the happiness that was denied her."

"Perhaps she did. Perhaps this disaster made us see things more clearly. You and me. She probably prevented us making a great mistake."

"That's a good way of looking at it, Johnny." She kissed him affectionately. "Being the sort of people we are, we'd have stayed together, but you and I would both have had regrets."

"How are you going to find room for all that wool?" he asked with a wry smile. "It looks as though Dad won't get his spare room back for a while."

"As soon as I can find a place I can afford, I'll send for it," she promised. "I haven't forgotten my dream."

"And Ken?"

"Ken is a kind and loving friend and he knows he'll never be anything more." As she spoke the words she had a vision of Ken waiting for her when she returned to London and the thought was far from displeasing.

When Johnny left, she sat and considered her life so far. It was filled with regrets. She had let Ken down and now her love for Johnny hadn't stood the test either. Perhaps she wasn't intended for love and marriage and motherhood, she thought sadly. She was a businesswoman with high ambition. But, she wondered, would that always be enough?

Eirlys didn't intend to stay with her father very long. Unless she left soon she would become caught up in running the home, making arrangements to see friends, and end up staying for ever.

She went to look for him the following day to tell him when she planned to leave. She found him on the allotment that had once been his, talking to the new owner. After telling him her plans, they walked back together with very little left to say.

She stayed to share a midday meal of lumpy mashed potatoes and crisply overdone sausages, prepared, with good intent, by Teresa.

"Not much of a cook, is she?" she whispered conspiratorially, when she found him later, clearing out the shed.

"She tried very hard and I was determined to eat it," he smiled. "Thank goodness for indigestion tablets, eh?"

"When is she going back? I thought I'd leave tomorrow, if that's all right."

"Fine, love. I'll miss you, mind. But I don't want you worrying or thinking of coming back. I'll be fine. You will write often and tell me what you're doing, won't you?"

"And Teresa and the boys?"

"I told them they can stay another day or so. I think Teresa was as affected by your mam's death as any of us, being there an' all. Seeing it happen. The boys are hoping to see something of the beach before they go back to London."

"Be careful you aren't too welcoming, Dadda, or you'll find it hard to tell them to go."

She was delighted when he explained the reason for clearing out the shed. "It's to store your wools and materials, so you can get back to your rug-making as soon as you have a place of your own," he told her.

All anger faded as she hugged him. "Thanks, Dadda. That's exactly what I needed, some help to rebuild my dream."

With the train time chosen for the following afternoon, she spent the hours before she left for the station walking around the town, seeing the familiar and loved places, saying her goodbyes.

She knew where Johnny and Taff and the others would be. With the days getting longer and the sun getting stronger, the thoughts of summer were not far from anyone's thoughts. They would be at the beach, getting everything checked in preparation for the opening of the 1940 summer season. The helter-skelter would be painted and all the safety checks carried out, and the swingboats made ready for their place on the sand. She wondered how she would live through a summer without having the sea so close. She knew she would miss it.

The bus took her to the sands, where several of the cafés were having a face-lift ready for the opening in May. There were quite a few people around, taking advantage of the sunshine. Leaning on the sturdy sea wall, she watched as children ran about and played. Their voices were shrill, and echoed amid the calls of the gulls gliding on the light breeze hoping for a tidbit or two. No summer dresses yet, but the hats and scarves added splashes of cheerful colour; a hint of the wonderful days to come.

As she strolled to the end of the promenade to where a cliff rose up to the path above, she looked at Piper's Café and saw a hand waving. Waving back she walked across the sand to the bottom of the metal steps and climbed up.

Moll opened the door and said, "Come in, girl, and we'll have a nice cup of tea and a Welsh cake. Let's sit in the window and enjoy this bit of sun."

She was disappointed not to find Johnny and Taff and Bleddyn there, but stayed a while, talking to Moll about her plans and listening to Moll telling of her new ideas for the approaching season. Moll said nothing about her cancelled wedding. It had all been said. She hugged the old lady affectionately, then caught the bus back home.

There wasn't time for more than a snack, so she prepared a few sandwiches to eat on the train, collected her suitcase and set off for the station. She hoped to get away without any further goodbyes but as soon as she was on the platform, Johnny came.

There were some rather formal requests to write, keep in touch and look after herself; all the usual clichés that fill the uncomfortable last moments before the train puffs into view. Both were thankful when the sound of the steam engine reached their ears. Johnny stepped back after kissing her affectionately, and Eirlys began patting pockets and looking in her handbag to make sure she had everything to hand. Then she gasped. "My wallet! I've left it home and it has my identity card and my ration book and heaven alone knows what else. Oh, Johnny, I'll have to go back. I'll have to catch a later train!"

They left the suitcase in the porter's room and hurried away, Johnny leaving her at her gate with a final goodbye.

She went in through the back door, careful not to make a sound. The last thing she wanted was another round of goodbyes! The house was silent and she was thankful for that. She wondered vaguely whether her father had taken Teresa and the boys to see the donkeys again, a walk of which they never tired.

She looked around her at the familiar room as she picked up her wallet and stored it safely in her handbag. More untidy than when her mother was there, she thought with a wry smile. Annie had been so fussy. She was sorry to say goodbye to her home, and felt guilty at walking away from her father, leaving him to cope alone.

Should she have stayed a while longer, helped him to get used to being alone? Promising herself she would visit often and make sure he was looking after himself properly, she turned to go. Poor Dadda, he'd find it hard to face the empty days, even though he had put on a brave expression and encouraged her to leave. Again guilt overwhelmed her and her footsteps faltered as she went towards the door.

Then she heard a voice upstairs, a soft chuckle. Teresa, she wondered? Still not making a sound and this time without really understanding why, she went up the stairs on tiptoe.

The door of her room was open and as she peered around the door she gave a wail of anguish. Teresa and her father were naked on the bed.

Slamming the door, and still issuing the wailing, distressed sounds that echoed around her head as though they came from someone else, she ran down the stairs and out of the house.

She ran until her legs threatened to give way and her lungs explode, then she paused and sat on the wall of a garden and stared back the way she had come as though expecting her father to loom into view.

Walking more slowly, she went on and after collecting her case, stood on the platform for the train promised in fifteen minutes. This time the platform was full. Soldiers,

337

airmen and sailors mingled with the civilians who had come to see them off. She remembered the stiffness of her parting from Johnny and wondered if it was the same with most of them. Everything said, couples sharing nothing more than the occasional nervous smile, not willing to go until the last minute, but feeling enormous relief when the signal dropped and the train curved slowly towards them.

Then she heard shouting and pushing their way through the crowd came Stanley, Harold and Percival.

"Eirlys! Eirlys!" Stanley shouted. "Mum says we can stay in St David's Well! Ain't that somethin'? On Monday Uncle Morgan's taking us back to school!"

Uncle Morgan. How different the honorary title sounded since she had witnessed the scene in the bedroom. Before, it had been so innocent, but Annie's death had changed that too. Morgan's resentment about Teresa's casual acceptance of their help had vanished. An uncle to the boys; one of a long line of them, the most recent being Ronald who didn't like Percival.

Strange how helpless some men are when faced with an attractive woman, she mused, her expression hidden as she hugged the three evacuees who had become locals. Specially when they find themselves alone. Solitude would not have been easy for Morgan Price. Why should she expect him to accept it? He couldn't hurt Annie any more.

Johnny had been weak too. He loved Hannah yet, afraid to face the doubts and criticism, he would have married her, Eirlys. She wondered if she would find a man who was strong, or whether a strong-minded man would bring less happiness than men like her father. An equal partnership sounded wonderful, but was it that easy to find?

She didn't have time to ponder the question, the train was hissing to a stop, and she had to find a seat. Amid the shouting of last goodbyes, and the scramble for seats, she heard her name called and, looking at the fence alongside the platform, saw Johnny and Hannah and the children. She blew kisses and smiled to show them she was happy for them, hoping her tears wouldn't show. Then a couple came and stood beside them; Teresa and her father, solemn-faced and ill at ease. A feeling of love for her father flowed over her. He was her Dadda and she couldn't pretend not to love him. Not even for the sake of her mother's memory.

Who was she to criticise? How could she accuse her father of callous indifference to her mother's death? She had made it clear that she wouldn't change her plans and stay home and look after him, hadn't she? She wasn't in the position to act as judge and jury, or to understand her father's need to be flattered and loved.

She forced a smile and waved a hand to them before stepping into the carriage.

A shrill whistle sounded, the guard waved his flag and slowly the giant pulled its load out of the station, and her journey towards a new life began.

Ironic, she thought, as the boys waved her off. It's only a few months ago that they were arriving and what a lot has happened since then.

If Teresa and Dadda stayed together it would at least be a happy ending for the boys. Annie would have been pleased about that.

–

Ken was waiting when the train puffed importantly into Paddington. He had waited while three trains arrived and departed, knowing she would eventually turn up and would be glad of a familiar face.

Paddington was crowded and among the uniforms she saw couples dressed smartly, some with confetti on their shoulders and in their hat-brims. Everyone was in such a hurry to marry. This damned war was to blame; everyone wanting to grab what they could just in case… The sentence was never completed, it was too frightening to contemplate.

She was in no hurry and walked along the platform allowing others to pass her. When she reached the barrier and held her ticket for the inspector, she saw him. He was smiling widely and obviously glad she was back. Ken, reliable, nonjudgemental, and very dear.

He had a car parked close by and when they were on their way he asked casually, "Did you see Johnny?"

"Yes. He and Hannah will marry, I think."

"And are you all right about that?"

"Yes, I am. But it doesn't say much for me as a person, does it? I left you, then Johnny. My love is very short-lived."

"Or stronger than you realise," he said enigmatically as he helped her out and kissed her lightly before following her into his family's home. "Maybe your dream of marrying Johnny, and being a part of the Castles on the sand," he joked lightly, "were short-lived because you were wrong to leave me."

One day, when her jangled thoughts settled, she might take his suggestion seriously; just for now, she wanted nothing more than to find a niche for herself and find out who she really was.

"Wait till summer," she smiled.